THE CURSED

AND THE

BROKEN

CHLOE HODGE

About the book:

A story of succumbing to wicked desires, death, and the temptations of a deliciously dangerous love. *The Cursed and the Broken* is a steamy, enemies-to-lovers dark fantasy romance perfect for fans of Jennifer L. Armentrout and Kerri Maniscalco.

Please note: This series contains explicit content which may be triggering for some. This book will include explicit romance, mature language, violence, reference to drug use, and emotional manipulation. This book is intended for readers 18+. This is book one in a series.

The Cursed and the Broken
Copyright © 2022 by Chloe Szentpeteri
First edition: April 2022

Paperback ISBN: 978-0-6453849-1-8
Hardcover ISBN: 978-0-6453849-2-5
E-book ISBN: 978-0-6453849-3-2

Special thanks and acknowledgement to:
Editor; Aidan Curtis,
Cover artist; Cover Dungeon Rabbit
Formatter; Imagine Ink Designs

Find me at: www.chloehodge.com
Instagram: @chloeschapters
TikTok: @chloehodgeauthor
Facebook: Chloe Hodge Author

Also by Chloe Hodge

Guardians of the Grove

Vengeance Blooms

Retribution Dies

Fury Burns

For Grandad.

With love and family, we are rich with happiness.

BEFORE

Death always knocked on our doors on the Day of the Cursed. The doorknob would curl, the wooden slats would rattle, and the scraping of his claws would sound as he circled our homes, hungry for the souls of the innocent.

In the end, it was always blood that saved us. We would smear it across the threshold, along with murmured whispers of protection. Spells to hide us from his sight, to seal us from his sense of smell. For he could scent the blood of witches.

Our blood.

I flinched as the wind shrieked outside, the howling force sending tree branches shivering against windows and the thatched roof above. Our livestock bleated their protest too, the faint tinkle of their collared bells jangling from the barn by our home.

A bang ruptured the night and Eszter screamed, clutching my arm so tight her knuckles turned white. Burying her head in my

1

shoulder, I swept my fingers over her curly hair, smoothing out the knots, trying to ease the trembling of my bones.

"Be still, girls," Mama said sharply from her perch by the fire, sewing needle and cloth clenched between her deft fingers. Eszter lifted her head, and Mama's brown eyes swept over us, softening upon seeing her fear.

She beckoned with a crooked finger, and we scooted to her feet, Eszter nestling into her skirts. "Do you remember why Death comes for our coven on the *Elátkozottak Napja?*"

How could we forget? Mama would tell the same story on the same day every year. *The Day of the Cursed.* She had drilled it into our brains since we were children, and even though I was eighteen, it was a tradition she held. My mother respected our history and insisted knowledge, before our magic, was the first power we should turn to.

Hugging my knees to my chest, I stared into the crackling fire, yearning for the warmth to seep into my veins. But my blood ran cold as winter frost tonight—nothing would alter that. It was the same for all the witches in my coven, and it was all because of *her.* Sylvie Morici, otherwise referred to as the Dark Queen.

"The first boszorkányok were cruel," Eszter recited dutifully. She was four years younger than me, still eager to please Mama and innocent in the ways of witches. "They abused their power and channelled into demonic arts."

Mama frowned, her lips twisting with disdain. "Not at first, child. Witches were peaceful beings upon the dawn, eager to help

 2

and heal those in need. But over time, the humans grew distrusting of their gifts, enraged by fear and greed. They commandeered witch hunts, oppressing and murdering those who had only ever helped them. That's when the Dark Queen stepped in, twisting our lore, corrupting our spiritual beliefs into cultlike factions of dark magic. The witches hexed freely, destroyed crops, livestock, families."

She shook her head, her curly brown hair bouncing with the movement. "Witches became wicked, and their wretched ways brought us only ruination. It was the most powerful of the first witches, Sylvie Morici, that tethered our world to the hell realm. Her spells called upon Death ... and he answered."

Eszter's wide brown eyes blinked at me before gazing up at our mother, who tenderly laid a hand on my sister's cheek and shook her head. "She tried to bend him to her will, steal his power to destroy all in her path, and, furious with her boldness, he cursed us forevermore, vowing to take the lives of any witches without protection. For a long time, many witches fell to his thrall, taken in their prime, either on the run from humans or on the move to resettle in safe havens. Eventually, the covens came together to lay the foundations which would prevent this threat from taking more of our kind. Thus, we must ask penance and prepare ourselves on the *Elátkozottak Napja*."

Bumps broke out over my flesh as I imagined the reaper himself tilling witches like wheat fields, scythe in hand and hood covering his skeletal face. Of course, no one really knew what

3

Death looked like, and those who did were dead or weren't long for our world.

Unfortunately, the spell wasn't a complete failsafe. Somehow, witches still succumbed to his call despite our spells and precautions. Those whose power had awakened upon their eighteenth birthday, whose magic thrummed deeper and sung sweet harmonies to spirits both evil and benign. Witches like me.

As if reading my thoughts, Mama pursed her plump lips and pottered to the stone hearth to boil some tea, scowling at the boarded window as if her rankled mood would repel foul spirits. The blustery night only rattled the shutters harder and I, too, glared at the window.

A dark shadow swept past the cracks, and my stomach plummeted in fear. Mama turned to us both, a finger raised to her white lips, a fear in her eyes I'd never seen before. Perhaps the threat was higher now that I was of age, for she was a lion among lambs, and she did not scare easy.

Eszter made to dart to her, but I grabbed her bony shoulders tight and pulled her to my chest, clutching my sister in protective arms.

"Don't move," I whispered in her ear, my breath pluming against her cheek. A foggy draft spilled into the room from under the front door, a coldness pooling before our feet known only to the dead. Eszter whimpered, and I clamped a hand to her lips, stifling the sound of life. Hoping Death would continue his hunt elsewhere.

The door was locked but not barred. He could touch the threshold, but he couldn't enter—not without becoming trapped in the pentagram drawn one step inside the home. I drew ours with chalk provided by the Barna family, who owned the most wheat fields in our village. Never had I been more thankful for shrewd old Marta.

Three thumps sounded on the wood, then the gouging of claws swept down the grain. We all held our breath, not uttering a sound as Death lingered at the threshold but, sure enough, the cold abated and the darkness lightened just a little, signalling his passing.

We were safe. Well, those of us in the main house.

The terrified bleats and whinnies of our sheep and horse sounded from the barn nearby, and my heart filled with dismay. My gaze darted to Mama, the words tumbling from my mouth. "I thought he was only interested in the souls of witches."

Her silence spoke volumes, even if confusion distorted her features.

My breath caught in my throat as I clutched Eszter and closed my eyes, as if shutting out the world would prevent such terrible things from happening. Those poor animals. And it wasn't just their lives at stake, it was ours, too. Our livelihood.

I snapped my eyes open again, but Mama only shook her head firmly, knowing my impulsiveness, the look in my steely gaze. I wilted against Eszter, the curve of her back pressed against

 5

my chest, her form trembling against my grip. She was crying. Not for us, but for the animals. Her heart was as tender as they come.

Which is why I should have known better. She wriggled from my clutches and made for the door on agile feet. She was a skinny slip of a thing, and I cursed the lack of a bruising grip that might otherwise have detained her. Rising from my perch on the floor, I stumbled after her, my socks slipping on the cold stone as my hand snatched at her dressing gown.

Too late. She ran out the door and into the unforgiving night. Mama shrieked, moving faster than I'd ever seen her. But I was quicker.

I wasted no time in snatching a knife from the kitchen bench. If I could catch my little rabbit of a sister before she found herself trapped in the hunter's claws, all might be well.

"Kitarni, no," my mother yelled as I slipped past her and shoved out the door, but there was no time to consider. With a flick of my wrist I summoned an invisible wall, blocking her exit. She slammed into it, pounding her fists against the forcefield, terror in her eyes.

"I'm sorry, Mama," I whispered, guilt ripping at my heart as she clawed at the barrier like a wild animal. She would be safe inside, hidden behind her wards where no harm could come to her.

I had always been impulsive, perhaps rash, but for Eszter? She was my world. There was nothing I wouldn't do for the girl. Even ... even face Death.

I prayed Mama wouldn't lose two daughters this night.

Gods save her, I thought as I bolted down the gravelly path towards the barn looming in the distance. The night was dark, the moon hidden behind clouds gathering ominously above. Frost licked up my veins, seeping into my skin, but the adrenaline coursing through my body set fire to my blood, burning my limbs to pump one foot after the other.

Branches snagged on my gown as I pushed myself, running against every warning in my body that demanded I turn around and seek the comfort and safety of my home.

My breath huffed out before me. No. I would not fail her.

Eszter's scream pierced through the shrieking winds, causing a flock of birds nearby to escape to the sky and my heart to pound like war drums before battle. I would fight if it came to it. No matter that I hadn't a clue how to wield a blade—especially against a being that was neither living nor dead, but something *other*.

I slowed to a crawl as I approached the barn doors swinging violently before me. No sound now came from inside, not from the animals, nor from my sister. I peered around the door, feeling frost creeping up the hand that clung to the wood. Pain throbbed as it spiralled towards the tendons, but I held fast, needing something to ground me to reality at what my eyes beheld.

Death stood facing my sister as she trembled before our animals, her arms outstretched, gown ripped, and innocent face streaked with tears. What chance did a fourteen-year-old girl have against the harbinger of doom himself?

My sister's eyes in that moment were those of pigs before the slaughter. A sixth sense of what awaited, knowing not what happens in the steps before, but what awaits at the end. It was enough to spur me into action. He took one step towards her, or perhaps glided—I couldn't tell beneath his shrouded from—and reached out a skeletal hand.

"Don't you dare lay a single finger on her," I said firmly, the undertones of fear quavering my voice.

Death turned painfully slowly, and when he looked upon me, I saw nothing beneath that hood. No face, just emptiness, like a black hole that sucked you in and suffocated all oxygen and warmth from the air.

He merely cocked his head, a predator weighing up his prey, but when his attention moved away from Eszter, I allowed a small sense of calm to bolster my resolve. There would be no running past Death, for even a featherlight touch was enough to end one's life. Even witches, for all their power, were but flecks of dust for him to flick away with skeletal fingers.

We Bárány women weren't without cunning, but as our family name suggested, we were shepherds, and I refused to leave my flock.

At the back of the barn was a hatch in the wall a few feet high, not so generous as to allow someone of my size through, but enough for Eszter's tiny frame to slide under. I shifted the knife to my left hand, twitched my right ever so slightly towards Eszter's only chance of escape. She was an observant girl—if not ruled by

 8

her emotions—and she nodded just once as she edged toward the hatch.

Death had eyes only for me, not that I could see any. I wondered if beneath that hood there would be naught but hollows. "What *are* you?" he asked in a raspy voice.

My skin prickled with revulsion at that unearthly tone. Swallowing the rising bile, I scoffed. "Can you not identify a witch when you see one? You've been killing us for years, after all."

"Your power speaks volumes to me, girl, but I smell something else in the air. You reek of its stench." Death seemed to look right through me then, as if studying my very core, and whatever he found, it seemed most intriguing to him.

I wasn't sure if I should breathe in relief or run for my life. Death's interest was not high on my priority list. The whole encounter was so odd, I couldn't help myself. "Why have you not claimed my soul yet?" I said brazenly. "Lost your touch?"

I must be losing my mind. Mama would have died three times over if she'd heard me. Probably would have come back to haunt me, too. I might be rash, but I'm not stupid. Eszter would soon be out of the hatch and back home to safety. I needed to keep Death preoccupied a little longer.

A world-weary sigh echoed in the barn, the hideous sound scraping against the threads of my sanity. "Do you think me a fool?" he hissed, causing the animals to tremble at the sound. "I know your precious sister escapes as we speak. But I did not come for the lamb."

9

My skin prickled at those words, and fear filled the cup of my stomach until it overflowed from every pore. I lifted the knife with a shaking hand, but one flick of his wrists and the blade whooshed through the air to thud into the barn hanger.

He stalked towards me, foggy plumes stretching out before him as he stopped inches from my face. My instincts screamed at me to run, to fight, to do *something*, but I stood frozen, rooted to the floor. His breath puffed over my cheeks, the rank odour smelling of spoiled meat and mouldy fruit.

I raised my chin, refusing to be defeated in this moment. My sister was safe. That was all that mattered. Biting my lip to keep from quivering, I stared into the hollow where his face should be. Defiant to the last, even if I wanted to throw up from fear or melt into a puddle of terror.

"I'm not here to end you Kitarni Bárány."

Wilting in relief, I glanced at him curiously. "Then what—"

"Fate has much more in store for you, and I wouldn't cross her path. She holds quite the grudge. I should know, she was to be my bride once." His voice carried a hint of longing, and Death studied his bony fingers, cocking a head as he, presumably, regarded me once more.

I blinked. Death, one of the four horsemen, is stood before me, pining over a long-lost love who wants gods only know what. This couldn't get any stranger. Taking a deep breath, I narrowed my eyes as the weight of what he said hit home. Fate? I hadn't realised there was a spiritual entity threading the course of our lives.

Lifting my chin, I took a cautious step back from the entity before me. "If you're not purging any souls tonight, why are you here?"

"You've been lied to, Kitarni. Your life is but a prison forged from deceit. Just ask the banya of the forest."

"Baba Yana?" I shook my head, my brows pinching together. "The old witch has always kept our village safe. Why would she lie to us? She is our protector, the wisest and most powerful of us all."

"And why do you think that is?" Death asked, his voice laced with dark amusement.

Confusion swept through me.

For centuries the banya had protected this village—hidden us from men and the warmongering of invading civilisations. Even our Romanian neighbours would find themselves magically turned around from the woods if they entered our territory. Such was the banya's power. Her loving protection.

"None of that matters now, Kitarni. Your thread is tethered to future events. Your actions change the course of the future. For good or ill. You, a witch who is not what she seems, hold more power in your hands than you know."

I stiffened at his words and my head pounded with an influx of information. What did he mean? I pressed my fingers to my temples, rubbing them insistently, as if I might erase the last five minutes. Then I noticed Death advancing, one hand outstretched ominously, the claws reaching for me.

"What are you doing?" I asked breathlessly. "You said you wouldn't harm me."

Death laughed. "I said I wouldn't kill you tonight. You are marked, Kitarni. And you are anything but safe."

PART ONE
THE BLOOD OF SHEEP

ONE

"Hanna has been missing for five days now," Eszter gossiped behind a petite hand. Her brown eyes sparkled, as did the silky strands of gold in her hair as the sun beamed through the window. That mischievous look was in her eyes again, which was an undeniably bad sign. Somehow it always ended in a misbegotten adventure, inevitably resulting in the reprimands of a fierce Nora Bárány.

Naturally, being the eldest sister, I took the brunt of Mama's wrath. Eszter, with her cherub-like face and her charming personality, got away with everything. Everyone in the village loved her, even if she was the envy of all the girls her age.

We were physically alike, with the same curly brown hair, bow-shaped lips and straight nose. Our skin was olive, glowing in the prime of our youth, and our figures were slim—mine perhaps more muscled than Eszter's, for I was both hunter and shepherd for my flock. But Eszter was naturally charming and courteous, skilled at finer arts and crafts that were more of a nightmare for me. Her beauty and poise were classical, graceful.

I seemed to rub people the wrong way. Beautiful? Yes, I could admit that. But the elders said I was too spirited, too stubborn. A little rough around the edges, not prim and proper like Eszter. It didn't bother me.

At least, that's what I told myself.

Truth was, I had always been different to my kith. We were a small village of around one hundred witches and, of the magic coursing through our veins, mine had always been different. *Dangerous.*

The other girls my age shied from it. From me. Where most witches' magic in our village harnessed the earth, mine was fire and brimstone. I had always hated it—being different, being an outcast. I couldn't grow or tend crops, vegetation, and flowers, and I was useless at mixing herbs or poultices and often botched simple spells that aided our day-to-day duties.

Instead, I had been gifted strength. Power that could hurt, maybe even kill. And it was useless in a peaceful place such as this. My affinity for fire made me a friendless, forgotten outcast.

Thus, I had always preferred my company to that of others ... or at least of my witch kin. Power was an obsession amongst the girls my age. I stayed clear of the popular circles. Trying to engage with them only painted a target on my back.

Hanna was the worst of them. We had been friends once. Long ago when we were children. Before power became purpose

and becoming a lady meant acting the part. And oh, did she throw me away when she grew into her grace and status. Stepped on our friendship with her fine boots and ground her heel until there was naught left but dust and days forgotten.

No, people did not agree with me. Animals, however, were fine friends to keep, and we had many. I was shepherd of our flock, and one thing I was good at was tending to them, giving them the best life I could.

"Aren't you worried about where she's gone? She was your best friend once," Eszter pushed, dragging me from my thoughts.

I took a bite of my palacsinta and groaned as an explosion of flavours filled my mouth. The syrupy sweetness of the crepes rolled with fruits and nuts never failed to lift my spirits. Mama often said my sweet tooth would be my downfall. She wasn't wrong.

Swallowing the delicious morsel, I raised a brow at my sister, who was jiggling impatiently in her seat. I rolled my eyes. "Hanna was always prone to recklessness; she's probably been sneaking off with a táltos. I wager she'll be back any day now."

Eszter slumped in her chair, pouting her rosy lips. "Hanna has all the fun. Why can't a boy whisk me away from this village and take me on an adventure?"

I smirked at her as I put my feet up on the chair. "Eszter, your idea of an adventure is raiding the seamstress's store for new dresses. Your turn will come. The spring festival will have many suitors lining up for your hand, I'm sure."

She brightened at the mention of our annual celebration. It was the most joyous event of the year for our coven, when the táltosok came to court the maidens of our village. Every so often, the banya would honour a family by selecting an apprentice to study under her. It was the highest blessing a witch could receive, and our coven was nervously awaiting the day the banya would choose again.

I had my doubts about the banya. I kept my faith in the gods, but why should I blindly place my trust in a witch who didn't deign to bless us with her presence? No, I had no interest in being picked. My sights were set on the world beyond our borders and, naturally, Eszter was focused on boys and status. At seventeen, she was of age to be wooed by eligible men, which was alarming. Her beauty and innocence would have her snatched up in an instant.

The táltosok, like witches, were powerful non-humans living in the woods, right near the Romanian border. Much like shamans, their power was spiritual, forming a connection between the living and the dead. The strongest could re-animate the dead. It gave me shivers just thinking about it.

Still, the men from that village were fathers, sons, brothers ... and though we lived separately from them, they were essential. Unlike human families, ours were unconventional in that we parted ways. The girls would return to their mothers' covens to learn how to weave their magic, and the boys would train with táltosok to harness their gifts.

I'd always wondered why anyone thought it was a good idea

to break families apart—why it had to be this way at all, but it wasn't worth the trouble of finding myself in the council's crosshairs. The chief elder was *not* someone to trifle with.

My father had passed away years ago, and it still irked me how he had been so close yet so far. A figurehead, little more than myth. After Mama fell pregnant with Eszter, our little family had returned to our coven. They never married, he never visited, and Mama never spoke of him. It was only when news came of his ill health that she took me to see him one last time.

My last memory of him haunts me still. Skin and bones covering a deflated stomach. Barely a vessel to hold his heart and soul intact. It had scared me how emaciated he was in his sickness, and yet, there had been kindness in his eyes. Hazel, like mine. He had patted his bed with a frail hand until I sat before him, and he had looked upon my face. I was six then.

He had taken my hands in his own and whispered words in another language. Ancient. Powerful. The hair on my prickled skin had raised and my blood had seemed to swell with hunger. A devouring of power. Only I didn't know what that power meant. What I could do with it once I realised what a gift he had given me.

And what a curse.

I had been too young to understand the depth of his gift back then. It's not like he had time to explain the magic's use, and we never had a deeper bond. My lack of attachment to my father was not unlike the other witches' feelings towards their fathers and

 19

brothers.

To live to every womanly whim; such was the way in our village. To cavort with others was a primal instinct, if nothing else, to preserve our line without sacrificing independence and authority. Adult witches took human lovers from time to time, but the unfortunate souls would soon find themselves in the woods without a clue how they got there.

The elders didn't mind, so long as we remained safe. Secret.

Of course, their laws didn't include teens running off to roll among the tree trunks with táltos boys. We weren't human, but the elders enforced many of their traditions, and keeping our maidenhood safe before marriage or childbearing was high on that list.

Arranged marriages were rare, but not unheard of. These days, witches and táltosok usually bonded to produce heirs or to strengthen a house's blood. Táltosok would come to court witches on the spring festival and bonds formed thereafter.

Not all witches followed such rules.

Including me. My virtue had been lost to a stableboy in the town over. I'd hidden myself in one of the trade wagons headed to the markets and had explored in *every* sense of the word. Mama had given me an earful about it, but it was one of the best days I'd ever had. I think, deep down, she knew what I'd done, but she had never asked about it and I hadn't offered.

More importantly, she had never stopped me from going again. Or, at least, I'd grown smarter about how I planned my

 20

trips. Mama was usually none the wiser.

Being hidden in plain sight amongst the humans always filled me with a sense of exhilaration—filled me with wonderment and joy. In our small village, I'd always felt trapped and alone. But out there the world was full of possibilities. And more, there was comfort in the arms of another. Comfort I never found among my own people, bar the embraces of my family.

I know Hanna also sought such comfort—snuck out at night to meet with lovers in the woods. Eszter had learned Hanna was promised to another and, if she was to be wed soon, her dalliance would not impress the groom. Nor her mother.

It was so like Hanna to run off and leave everyone worrying. She was a beautiful, well-dressed bully. A conceited creature who valued power, beauty and status, and she used those tools as weapons to prey on those who didn't conform to her society's standards.

I snorted. Her vanity was so far up her ass, she could wear it as a hat.

Despite my animosity towards her, a niggling feeling deep within my gut told me there was more to her absence. Five days? A long time to be left in the woods, especially during winter. There were many creatures within the surrounding forests that wouldn't take kindly to her lingering and, worse still, there were those that preyed on witches and the weak-minded.

Hanna was the latter. I wouldn't miss her, but she hadn't always been horrid. We'd even been friends once upon a time, and Hanna's mother had always been good to me. She didn't deserve the worry and I *suppose* Hanna didn't deserve to be eaten by wolves ... or worse. Lidércek, tündérek, and changelings—*incubi and faeries*—were mischievous and self-serving. There were many good ones, of course, but come across evil and evil will devour flesh and soul.

Regardless of my feelings towards her, I felt compelled to protect my coven, to keep other witches safe.

"So you *are* worried," Eszter said with a pointed look at my hands absentmindedly bunching up my skirts.

I rolled my shoulders casually. I wouldn't let her see how concerned I really was, but Hanna wasn't the first girl to go missing. Ever since my eighteenth birthday, witches had disappeared. None had returned.

I *might* have spied on several of the elders' council meetings to gauge their thoughts on this. Safe to say, they were equally concerned.

I chewed my lip. Hanna and I were not friends. She had burned that relationship long ago, but a small part of me still held on to happy memories. I might despise what she'd become, but I didn't want to see her hurt.

"I still think Hanna is reckless, but if she's injured or worse ..." I sighed. "We'd better look for her."

Eszter grinned with wolfish delight and I rolled my eyes before my smile spread. Yes, Eszter always started our mischievous adventures, but I spurred them to action. I couldn't help myself.

The woods called to me. Sitting still for too long was not in my blood.

"We'll go first thing in the morning after chores. Mama will have our necks if we don't get our work finished."

"I'll have more than that if you're going to sit around eating me out of house and home," Mama said with a playful smile as she swept into the room, a basket full of spools in bright pops of colour in the crook of her arm. She rounded the table and gave us each a kiss on the forehead. "And how was your day, girls?"

"Robi ate all the chicken feed today," I said as I popped more palacsinta into my mouth. "The ladies were less than impressed."

Mama scowled. "The devil sent that rooster himself, I'm sure of it. It's a wonder he gets any attention from the hens at all."

Eszter laughed. "Robi is a softie at heart."

"Tell that to my ears when he crows well before the dawn," Mama grumbled as she set to work preparing dinner. "Eszter, darling, can you help me?"

My dutiful sister braided her long, voluminous hair efficiently and grabbed an apron from the hook on the wall. She gave our mother the side-eye as she began chopping tomatoes. "Another girl has gone missing," Eszter said carefully.

Mama froze, her hands halting over an onion. "Who? How long?" Her voice was quiet, strained. Tension rippled from her in waves and I shifted in my seat.

"Hanna, the herbalist's daughter. She's been missing for five days now. Her mother thinks she left in the middle of the night,"

23

I offered quietly.

"And her sister said Hanna's cloak, travelling boots and blade were still in her closet," Eszter piped in.

I shot her a sharp look. "You didn't mention that earlier." That information changed things. No one in their right mind would venture out willingly in the middle of winter without layers or protection—not without a death wish.

Eszter's eyes widened. "I thought you said"—she blushed as she glanced at Mama—"I thought you said she was going to the woods to ... you know."

Frowning, I looked at my family. "Hanna is the fourth girl to vanish within the last three years. It happened again. Another girl has disappeared, never to return."

"You don't know that she won't come back."

I set my jaw. "Mama, we should go look for her."

My mother shook her head fervently. "Kitarni, I won't have you running off and putting your sister in danger. There are things in those woods that are better left alone. The banya will search for her."

"We don't even know where she lives," I snapped. "For all we know, the banya has forsaken us."

Perhaps that was a stretch, but only a select few had ever been in her presence and, ever since Death visited me three years ago, I hadn't been able to forget what he'd said about her. He'd implied that she'd *lied* to us.

Many stories were told of her, but she was an enigma to me,

24

little more than folklore to keep witches in line and remind us of a higher power. Someone who *supposedly* kept us safe.

Even when she picked an apprentice, the banya came and went like smoke. Gossipers said she came veiled, her face hidden. Some stories said the gods favoured her and her form would blind any who looked upon her divinity. Others said they had defiled her face. Such was the price of her magic.

I didn't know what to believe, but the witches loved and respected her, worshipping her like a god. Although I yearned to be recognised, for my power to prove worthy of something, it never sat well with me how little we knew of our so-called protector.

"Kitarni Bárány," my mother said sharply. "You will not utter such blasphemy in this house. She is as close to godliness as a witch can get. If that poor girl is within her domain, the banya will know and return her to us."

I scoffed. Would she though? None of the banya's apprentices had ever come back, and all the girls who'd gone missing remained lost. Whatever the banya did to occupy her time, it seemed a few wayward witches weren't enough to concern her.

My cheeks warmed and I jumped out of my seat in anger. "We are witches, Mama. We can use our power to find her, to bring her home. What if I went missing? Or Eszter?"

The blood drained from Mama's face, and her knuckles whitened as she clenched her apron. "I will not lose either of you.

25

Ever since that night. Ever since ..."

I knew what she wouldn't say. The night Death came for us—for me—it changed everything. Mama had grown stiflingly protective, to the point of devout with her protection spells and the charms she would make us wear. She had coddled Eszter especially, keeping her under a close watch.

My sister was capable, but she was naïve and trusting. Combine that with her beauty and personable nature, Mama barely let her out of her sights. Eszter tolerated it for now, but there would come a day when her wings would spread and she would leave the nest.

I never told Mama what had really happened that night. The exchange between Death and me. Something told me she wouldn't have believed me if I did. She'd say I'd been under a spell or lost in an illusion.

But there were some things that were undeniable.

Three jagged lines down my back from where Death had marked me. The scar. *The promise.*

He never said what my future would entail, only hinting at a life shrouded in lies.

Something told me that had more to do with the girls going missing than I yet knew.

TWO

There was silence at the kitchen table. Only the sounds of spoons scraping against bowls broke the quiet. I peeked at Mama from beneath my lashes. The food had brought colour back to her face, steadiness to her hands. I couldn't stay mad at her. She'd made chicken paprikash. My favourite.

I devoured it, drinking down the juices and inhaling the aroma of paprika. It was a frostbitten night, but the fire was crackling and my belly was full of the warmth only Mama's cooking could provide. It would do for now. Poor chicken; Robi would not be pleased.

Which made me wonder. Mama usually only made this dish on special occasions. We kept most of our farm animals until old age took them, opting instead to eat venison or small birds—if eating meat at all. Our village wasn't exactly wealthy. As peasants, we had no estates or castles to speak of, though our magic was richer than any gift that money could buy.

I narrowed my eyes as I set my spoon down. "Thank you for the lovely meal. It's rare we are lucky enough to eat dishes such as this," I said, eyeing my mother, searching for a hint of what she was up to.

"We have been fortunate this year," Mama said matter-of-factly. "Earth magic runs strong in our young witches' veins. This year's harvest was bountiful and the vegetables plentiful."

A pang of jealousy surged through me. Mama didn't say it to hurt me, but it reminded me of my magic's uselessness, that my contribution to our livelihood was small. My sister squeezed my hand, as if she sensed where my thoughts had gone. I offered her a small smile, grateful for her kindness. My family loved me dearly and I knew Mama had never judged me ill.

She said it was a gift, but I knew better of my curse.

I was her daughter and that had always been enough for her. "You are special, little cub," I remember her telling me after I'd come home sobbing my heart out. My new dress had been torn, my face and hair splattered in mud after a group of girls had bullied me. Laughed at me.

Mama had only knelt before me, lifted my chin with steady hands and peered into my eyes, her own gaze blazing with a mother's need to protect their child. "Being different is not a sin, nor does it make you lesser than others. Straighten your shoulders, lift that chin. Your magic will remake our world one day, Kitarni. Never forget it."

And I hadn't. I held on to that kernel of wisdom,

28

remembering it when the days grew dark or my world grew lonely. I would repeat it to myself while I wandered the woods in solace. While the other ladies laughed over their teacups or needles, or helped mothers do family business, I dared to dream of a bigger world, played with blades, read books about epic quests and burning romances.

It had been enough for a time. But I wanted more. To see the world for myself and write my story. The village grew smaller by the day, those dreams a little blurrier.

Still, I smiled at my mother. At the little things in life.

"With Eszter's help," she continued, "our embroidery has been an enormous success with the nearby human towns. The women can't get enough of her perfect stitching and patterns."

Eszter beamed with pride. "If we're fortunate to find quality materials the next time witches go to market for trade, imagine the money we could bring in, Mama!"

Nudging her feet under the table, I crooned, "I'm sure the men will line up too, just to speak to such a beautiful maiden."

She shoved me in the arm, a pink flush gracing her face, but she glanced at Mama slyly, waiting. Mama said nothing to that, of course. Eszter had been begging to join the groups who regularly frequented the markets, but Nora Bárány was having none of it. *"It's too dangerous,"* she would say. *"Men will see your beauty and fall in love, and the women will say you've put them under a spell."*

I rolled my eyes at the thought. Humans would give any reason to blame us for their misfortunes. Bad weather? Low yielding crops? A spot on a pretty girl's nose? Witches!

Eszter slumped, disappointed by the pointed silence, but Mama was smiling ... a little too widely for my taste. "Girls, I have some good news to share."

Rarely did I agree with that statement. I clenched my fists in my skirts as she pulled an envelope from the folds of her homespun dress. It bore the seal of a black wolf atop crossed blades—the symbol of the Wolfblood Clan settled on the other side of the woods.

My sister practically bounced out of her seat in excitement, her rosy cheeks glowing in the firelight, the reflection catching in her brown eyes. I might have smiled too were it not for wariness raising its hackles. Nausea roiled in my stomach and I bit my lip in anticipation.

Inch by painful inch, Mama sliced the envelope open, plucking a crisp letter smelling of the beechwood trees out. And she read, one horrifying line at a time:

Dearest Nora,

We send our warmest wishes during winter and hope this letter finds you well. As the spring equinox approaches, it is my fondest desire to see our families united. My son will soon take his place as lord of Mistvellen, and your daughter, by his side. The wolf awaits an heir.

I eagerly await your reply.

Best,

Lord Farkas Sándor.

 30

"Arranged marriage? What the hell were you thinking?" My nostrils flared and my seat shot back with a clatter as I erupted from the table.

Mama remained calm, but she flashed me a stern look. "Mind yourself, Kitarni, you will calm down so we can discuss this rationally."

I wasn't having any of it. "How could you do that to Eszter? She should have the freedom to choose her own suitor, to live her life before being tethered. Why marry her off, anyway? We're witches. We don't DO marriage."

My sister was slack-jawed and trembling from her perch at the table, but she still looked dainty as ever—calm, even. I paced back and forth before the fireplace, earning a lazy side-eye from our hound, Laszlo. He was the true ruler of the house, as his name suggested, and the pampered vizsla was curled up on Mama's favourite chair, watching our row unfold.

"Kitarni, sit down," Mama ordered, and a rumble loud as thunder cracked through the room, causing the fire to snuff out and the mugs, hanging herbs, and various embroidered artworks to wiggle on their hooks.

I forced myself to breathe, lest my power get the best of me. I'd always struggled to control it when emotions were high, and now it threatened to overwhelm me. Eszter's hand graced my arm, and she turned me slowly to look at her, sweeping my hair out of my face. "It's okay," she whispered. "It's all right."

 31

She must have been using her magic, for I felt soothing warmth trickling through my veins, gently stroking the pressure points in my head and calming the pumping of my heart. The smell of copper filled my nostrils and a rosy mist wreathed around her palm as the magic seeped into me.

In less than a minute, I felt serene and I nodded slowly as she ushered me back to my seat.

My mother's lips thinned as she took me in. "Are you quite done with your tantrum?"

I nodded again, too weary to argue.

She took a deep breath, glancing between her daughters before settling on me. The look in her eyes had my stomach jolting again.

"Good. Because it's not Eszter that's getting married, Kitarni. It's you."

THREE

Marriage. I was being forced to marry someone I had never met. The idea was so absurd, I had stayed awake most of the night, tossing and turning until, finally, I'd fallen into a fitful sleep. Dreams had plagued me, of girls going missing in the woods, of dark shapes, rivers of blood and bodies of witches piling high.

My eyes were crusty come morning. Robi crowed on schedule—which was around an hour before dawn. Stupid bird. At least he was consistent, and today I welcomed the early start.

I felt like the living dead as the rosy hues of dawn splintered through my window. My bones were stiff and my head ached with every movement. If I was to remain with my coven, to give my family the best future possible, I had to marry this stranger. For whatever reason, Mama and this Farkas fellow wished to unite our families. But why? I stuffed my face into my pillow. Trying to make sense of it all was only making my head pound harder.

Apparently, my groom-to-be was the son of the táltos leader—the wealthiest and most powerful family in their clan. I snorted. Well, if they expected a dowry, they wouldn't get one. Our humble cottage was larger than most, but it had little in the way of luxury and I hardly expected the men there would know what to do with doilies or flowered tablecloths.

I wondered, why me instead of Eszter? She was more beautiful, meeker and milder, and less likely to cause trouble. Everyone loved her. Not to mention she was younger.

At twenty-one, I was well past that. While most men in the human world traded their daughters as child brides, witches and táltosok preferred to wait until the witch came into their prime—usually after her eighteenth birthday when her power blossomed.

But, given a witch rarely tied herself to anyone, I supposed I was the exception to the rule. Some of our coven preferred the company of other witches, or just weren't interested in sex or procreation at all. We were all different here and our freedom of choice suited us just fine.

Sometimes, if a witch fell in love with a táltos, they gave up their coven or clan altogether and eloped elsewhere.

So why? Why marry me off at all? Mama had never seemed bothered by money, power, or influence. Granted, this marriage would mean my family would be set for life—and ensuring a future for Eszter would be the *only* reason I'd consider it—but Mama was an elder of our council, a respected witch in the community.

There was something she wasn't telling me, and I was damn

well going to find out. But not today. I had other answers to hunt—a different quarry.

I crawled out of bed, almost yelping as I stripped off my bed clothes and quickly dressed in attire fit for hunting. The cold floor bit my toes as I padded around my room and I strained my ears for any sounds of Mama waking, but the house remained quiet. In the floor-length mirror, I glimpsed the scars on my back.

Three dark, jagged streaks swept down my spine. Ugly, crude things that pulsed, refracting the light. An unnatural magic slept beneath my skin. Death would come for me one day or, *worse*, his ex-girlfriend would. I sighed, rubbing my temples as I looked at my reflection. My hazel eyes were dull, the black circles under my eyes a testament to lack of sleep. My olive skin was pale, causing the freckles across my nose to stand out. Even my dark brown hair was a mess of knotted coils this morning. I thrust it into a tight braid, shoved my feet into fur-lined boots, then slung a wool wrap over my shoulders.

Time to go.

Creeping silently along the stone floors of the cottage, I snatched some bread, a few apples and some aged cheese, stuffing them into my satchel. Then, carefully, I plucked out the few blades we kept stored in a chest and donned them, strapping one around my leg for quick access. I couldn't shoot a bow and arrow for the life of me, but under the tutelage of my teacher, Erika, I'd practiced throwing daggers for a while now. I always hit my mark.

Peeping my head into Eszter's room, I smiled at her sleeping

 35

form. Buried beneath her covers, she lay spread-eagled and drooling, her hair covering most of her face. It satisfied a small part of me to see she wasn't *always* so ladylike.

It was better that she hadn't awoken, for I had no plans to bring her with me despite this trek being her idea. Regardless of what Mama had said, I was going into the woods and I *would* find Hanna. I tried to ignore the voice in my head that prompted, *dead or alive?*

Mama was right on one account. It was unsafe for Eszter—for anyone who didn't know their way among the roots and streams of the *Sötét Erdő*. The bowels of that forest never saw the sun, the trees there were so thick that blackness reined and supernatural things dwelled. The *Dark Wood* seemed a fitting name. Most would find that frightening and steer clear. Which, of course, is why I loved it.

If you knew where to look, one could find small glades dotted with wildflowers and ponds near the trees bordering the thickest part of the wood. Magical places that sang to my soul. Water faeries often frequented the small lakes, and while some faeries were mischievous, evil things, most weren't worrisome at all. I'd even grown friendly with a few.

Unfortunately, my path was unlikely to lead to any pockets of paradise today. If Hanna was with the táltos clan, Farkas, by duty, would have escorted her home. I highly doubted she would have run away without a coin to her name or more clothes on her back. She was in one of the more popular circles of the girls my age here and her mother made good coin from her apothecary. Why leave?

Hanna must be in the woods.

I slung the satchel over my shoulder and stepped outside into the brisk morning, Laszlo bounding past me on the way out. I gave him a scratch behind the ears, and he dutifully trotted to the barn to await me.

The myriad of flowers in Mama's garden had long since wilted and the green shoots of various plants curled inwards on themselves, but it was still a pretty sight. I'd always thought of Mama's magic as a reflection of her true self—nurturing, pure, and wholesome. When she wasn't cooking feasts fit to feed the town, or stitching with perfect precision, she was in her garden. Weaving her fingers with delicate care, encouraging seeds to take root, nourishing vegetables to grow or planting flowers of the most stunning colours. Mama was a woman of the earth.

Eszter's gifts lay in the same vein of power. But mine ... I frowned as I glanced at the frostbitten garden before me. My magic had always been aggressive. *"Fiery, like your spirit,"* Mama would say. I rarely used my true power—the one that awakened when I felt cornered, angry, or scared. The one that was wild, dark, *dangerous*.

I'd never seen another witch who shared power like mine. It was part of the reason they steered clear of me, part of why I'd become a pariah of sorts. They were afraid of it, afraid of *me*. Especially after gossip had escalated about Death's visit to our home upon the hill. News in small towns spread like wildfires.

37

Such nosy creatures, witches.

I rolled my neck and looked down the valley, forcing foreboding thoughts from my mind. As our village sat nestled along the edge of the forest, nature blessed us with wheat fields and rolling hills in the north and west and forestry to the south and east, which then sprawled into the state of Transylvania.

Frost clung like glass baubles to the blossomless trees surrounding our yard and rose-filtered light glowed as it crested the hills. Powdery snow dusted the landscape, glistening in the light of the rising sun. The village was still sleeping, tranquil and undisturbed. Our home was on a slight rise, so we had the best vantage point in town. It overlooked the quaint cottages below, their walls sprawling with ivy, the pebbled paths lined with candles, petals, and strung-up herbs meant to guard their homes or bring luck and fortune to those who passed by.

It was a small village, but it was home. I turned to the barn next to the cottage, trotting down the yard towards the bright yellow doors. Eszter and I had painted it together last year, as per her request. She loved colour, and given her sunny disposition, it seemed fitting even if the barn was my domain. Mama charged me with the livestock and animals and they were my loves in life. All but one, at least.

"There's a good boy, Laszlo," I praised our hound as I entered the shelter. The sheep were impatiently jostling to be out and I laughed as I stroked their woolly hides. Laszlo herded them towards the pastures and I turned to face my nemesis.

 38

His name was Sami and he hated my guts. An evil glint flashed in the goat's eyes and he bleated in warning, pawing at the straw and readying to charge. It was the same dance every day. As soon as the latch on his stall clicked open, it was war.

I scowled as I crept towards him, hands raised placatingly. "Sami, you're going to play nice today, right?"

The goat glared at me and only lowered his horns in answer. I sighed. Time for a little magic. More of a trick, really, as all witches could wield their power, bending reality to aid them in minor tasks. Mama would kill me if she saw me using it for such a trivial thing, but if there was one thing that scared me, it was this demonic horned hell spawn in the barn.

I twisted my wrist through the air and the lock on his pen slid free. Sami charged, horns lowered and ready to headbutt me to next Sunday. Taking a breath, I lifted my arms, raising an invisible wall of steel around me to block the goat's advances. The slightest smell of copper climbed my nostrils and a faint mist of red fluttered like dust motes before me. All magic left a colour imprint after being summoned and each one was unique to the user. It unnerved me that mine was red. Not the bright red of apples or the rusty hue of paprika, but the ruby red of blood.

Sami rammed right into the blockade, causing the opaque wall to shimmer and ripple. I grinned at my foe, cocking my head at his repeated attempts. Eventually, Sami tired of the game and trotted off to the pasture for the day.

Eszter was the only one he showed genuine affection for. She loved him dearly, which is the only reason Mama hadn't cooked his grumpy hide for our dinner. We had found him wandering our fields when he was just a kid with absolutely no idea where he'd come from. Mama's soft heart had melted when Eszter claimed him as her own. The rest was history.

"Good morning, Arló," I greeted our horse, raising a hand to stroke his sleek muzzle. He nibbled on my fingers instead, and I laughed. "It's nice to see you too."

He was magnificent. Black and glossy like a raven's feathers, with dark eyes that seemed to see and know all. Arló was gentle, intelligent, and his characteristics spoke volumes about his sassy nature.

As I measured his morning oats into a bucket, Arló reached his neck over the stall, nosing at my satchel and flipping it open until he found his prize. Snatching an apple from the pack, he scoffed it down quicker than I could blink.

Crossing my arms, I raised a brow. "Really?" His response was to bare his teeth in a comical display. I rolled my eyes even as I grinned. "Well, I hope you're happy. There goes my lunch."

As I peeked out the barn doors at the rising sun, the muffled sounds of villagers emerging from homes carried on a light breeze. I was dawdling and, if I didn't hurry, Mama would lecture me to death.

Arló devoured the oats like it was his last day on Earth. There would be no leisurely picking at grass today but, like me, he seemed to enjoy meandering through the woods. The safe and

sunny areas, at least. I hoped he wouldn't begrudge me for trekking deeper, for I highly doubted we'd find Hanna so close to home.

After opening his stall door, I led him outside before closing the barn doors and mounting. Laszlo bounded back over, keen for today's adventure. Eszter would have to tend to the ladies and his lordship, Robi. The chickens were such lazy creatures, they were probably pleased to have a sleep in.

The woods beckoned, the trees on the border swaying in the breeze, their branches bowing, as if calling me closer. Dappled sunlight trickled through the canopy, casting a warm glow over the foliage at their roots. From here, the woods appeared peaceful, dreamy. But I knew better. Deep within, where the sunlight failed to shine, were wicked, ancient things. They wouldn't welcome us, being more likely to drink from our veins or feast on our flesh.

I gulped, suddenly unsure if I had the courage to step into their domain. But if I didn't, who would? Witches weren't heartless, but there was an unspoken law in our village. A witch who wanders is a witch forgotten. Anyone who enters the Sötét Erdő does so at their peril and damned be the consequences.

It's why no one would search for Hanna and why no one had looked far and wide for the others who'd disappeared. Once you left the coven, you were on your own. Funny that everyone assumed those girls did so on purpose. What if someone took them against their will? Kidnapped them?

Mama might have believed Baba Yana would step in, but she never had before, why should she start now?

Laszlo huffed as he gazed up at me with golden brown eyes and Arló snorted, rolling his own. I looked at my impatient companions with pursed lips.

"You're right. There's nothing to be afraid of. We'll be quick and quiet and out in no time. What could go wrong?"

FOUR

We'd been travelling for a few hours, meandering slowly through the forest. The beechwood trees were evenly spaced, allowing Arló plenty of room to walk. Snow crunched beneath his hooves as he stepped carefully over frosty roots. The sun still dappled the forest floor and the occasional animal or bird passed by, seeking cover when sensing our presence.

Laszlo patrolled around tree trunks, snuffling at every scent, tongue lolling and eyes alive with happiness. His big ears flapped comically as he trotted around. I snorted. At least one of us was having fun.

There had been no sign of Hanna—not a single boot print or disruption to the foliage. I sighed, rubbing a gloved hand over my neck. I had expected this. Deep down, I knew I'd find her in the place none dared to travel. Deep in the Sötét Erdő.

Winter had many creatures snuggled up in burrows and

 43

sleeping away the cold, so we were reasonably safe. For now. The weather had a bite to it, but with spring approaching, the days were more temperate, growing longer and warmer. Soon the woods would teem with activity and birdsong and spring would bring forth new life.

But not at the heart. There, it was quiet and cold. Dead, some witches said. Which couldn't be true if the banya lived there. Who would live in such a place? I had never really thought about it—why she lived in solace. No one questioned her choices. No one questioned anything about her, even when it meant sending daughters off on mysterious apprenticeships.

I felt stupid but, despite my reservations about this so-called saint, I wanted to win, if only to see what she was made of. To see why the elders heralded her as godlike in her power.

A scuffle in the brush had my heart pounding. Laszlo bared his teeth but, upon closer inspection, his nose soon bumped into a deer, the poor thing frozen with fright.

No, I realised as I hopped off Arló and bent down. Not fright. *Pain.* Its rear leg was broken. The deer was shivering, either from shock caused by the injury, or from the cold. The wound was dribbling blood, revealing large teeth marks—a bite and strength one might expect from the jaws of a wolf.

The deer had escaped their clutches, but if the wolves didn't come back to claim their kill, starvation or other carnivores would.

I gritted my teeth. The wound was fresh, which meant the

predator could still be in the area. But wolves hunted in packs and at dusk. Judging by the arc of the sun, it was around noon. What would prompt a change in hunting patterns?

A howl ruptured the stillness and I froze, bumps prickling over my skin as the eerie call echoed through my bones. First one, then another, and another. Arló pranced nervously, and Laszlo darted before him, ears pointed, hackles raised.

I looked deep into the deer's brown eyes as every bone in my body told me to run. I should leave—it wasn't my place to interfere with nature, nor my duty to tend to its wounds. But I was a caregiver of animals. A shepherd. And I couldn't bear the thought of this creature being torn to pieces.

Lifting my hands to the deer's leg, I closed my eyes, letting the world dissipate until only my magic and I remained. Well, my father's magic, once upon a time.

I blocked out all thoughts, furrowing my brow. The energy speared through my hands and into the wound. My eyes snapped open and I gasped as golden light flashed—a nod to my father's gift. The deer scrambled away before the light had fully dissipated.

Pain fired through my ankle and it felt as though someone had taken a sledgehammer to the bone. I grimaced as I peered at my leg. Not broken, thank the gods, but it was safe to say sprints were out of the question.

After several attempts at channelling the magic and suffering the consequences, I'd learned to take a blade to my flesh in anticipation. Bloodletting was payment enough for the power and it was better than losing my mobility. I'd tried hiding it from Mama, but she almost always spotted the bandages and scabs. She never lectured me about it, but I knew she hated this magic. What it cost me.

The power frightened her. After seeing the price I had to pay, she'd likened it to dark magic and necromancy. We'd had the conversation several times and I'd always argue, "How could a healing magic be evil?" but she would purse her lips, remaining firm.

What she didn't know couldn't hurt her. I'd helped many of our livestock from suffering critical injuries, prevented the spread of disease, even stopped them from dying by foolish missteps before.

An eerie whine swept through the trees, closer this time. The hairs on my neck stood up, and my heart thumped erratically in my chest. Laszlo rushed to my side, whimpering as he sniffed my wound and licked the deer's blood from my fingers.

"Shit."

I hadn't spilled my own blood for fear it would bring the wolves right to me, but it seemed they'd followed the animal's scent and had realised there was bigger prey on offer. I almost howled myself, frustrated with the turn of events and cursing myself for a fool.

"Arló," I began, but another onslaught of howls had the horse bolting through the trees. I blinked at his majestic form retreating. "Really?!"

The sounds of shuffling foliage and twigs cracking forced me to move, rising to my feet with a grunt. I unsheathed the blade at my thigh, dashing through the woods. My ankle blazed with every step, sharp pain slicing up my limb.

Branches snagged at my hair and clothes, gnarled roots crisscrossing in a maze-like tripwire at my feet. I couldn't outrun them. Not like this. "Should have left the deer," I said between breaths.

Laszlo whined beside me in agreement.

I made the mistake of looking over my shoulder, and then I spotted them. Six black wolves, their jaws wide and fangs bared, their eyes sharp and cunning. Blood dribbled from their maws, and terror struck my heart as I turned, ready to—

I collided with something tall and hard, tumbling to the ground and almost slicing myself. It made an 'oomph' sound as they, too, stumbled. Sweeping my hair from my face, I glanced at my attacker and stared into dark brown eyes.

"You're a táltos," I breathed.

"How observant of you," he drawled, stepping before me, sword raised and shoulders squared. "Get behind me and stay out of my way."

I could only sit there dumbly, blinking back my surprise and staring at his towering form. My jaw set as my cheeks reddened. Who did this arrogant bastard think he was?

Laszlo whimpered, nudging my face and bringing me back to my senses before he whirled on the approaching wolves.

47

Pain spiralled up my limb as I limped to my feet, one hand brandishing the blade, the other stretched before me, readying my power.

I shouldn't use magic after the toll of healing. It always left me weak and nauseated—and that was when I pulled from my blood, rather than taking on the afflicted one's injury.

The pack prowled back and forth, snapping as they assessed us. Their eyes glinted a strange silvery blue. "What's wrong with them?"

My companion said nothing, and I glanced at his eyes to find them studying their movements, judging their patterns. Finally, he shoved me behind him again with a muscled bicep and I yelped as I almost rolled the injured ankle.

The wolves struck, the biggest launching a deadly bite towards the man's jugular. A flash of silver so fast it was almost blinding swept down and embedded in the wolf's fur. Blood spattered in a crimson arc.

Laszlo collided with another wolf mid-air, their bodies thudding as they hit the ground and rolled in a flurry of fur and teeth. Panic climbed my throat as my dog attacked relentlessly, sinking teeth into flesh and kicking with his powerful legs. But he was so small compared to the wolf and he barked in pain as the primal creature sank its teeth into his neck and tossed him aside.

He slammed against a tree and did not rise again.

Fear turned to rage, instilling courage in my bones. I tossed my blade in the air, catching the tip between my fingertips and, with a steadying exhale, I threw the dagger at the wolf's heart. It hit home and the creature was dead before it hit the ground, tongue lolling as the breath left its lungs.

The stranger's eyes flashed with surprise—and was that a hint of admiration? More wolves approached from the direction he had travelled from and my heart sank as they surrounded us. We found ourselves back-to-back, and I could feel every shift of his muscles as he pressed into my spine.

"I don't suppose you have any more blades to repeat that, do you?" His voice was calm, measured, and I wondered if his heart betrayed the fear that mine raced with.

I gritted my teeth. "Actually, I find myself a little shorthanded at the moment."

His laugh rumbled through my back. How could he find *anything* about this amusing?

"I was hoping you'd say that."

The world dimmed as shadows uncoiled from the ground, an unnatural stillness settling over the woods. Wisps of black smoke seemed to hiss from the dead wolves' bodies, which twitched erratically. The limbs jerked before unfolding stiffly, then the eyes blinked—black as voids.

He was animating the dead. Using *necromancy*. The power was ... it was unholy. To see dead things walk again, to control an otherwise powerless thing. It seemed wrong. And yet, we had no other options, and he was a táltos after all. Spirit magic ran in their blood.

I supposed it didn't matter if it went against all religious constructs, anyway. The Christian churches vehemently spurned witches—hunted them even—and humans didn't even know táltosok existed. Why look to men when a woman wears the weight of all injustices?

The wolves faced off, snarling at each other. They pounced and the man's sword flashed as more blood coated the dappled forest floor. He grunted as fangs sank into his bicep, the blood dripping down his arm in scarlet waves.

Even with the aid of the undead, they outnumbered us. I couldn't hide behind him forever, couldn't run. My vision spotted as nausea roiled through me and I swallowed the urge to vomit.

A wolf lunged for me and I scrabbled back in alarm, my spine slamming into a tree trunk. Time seemed to tick slowly, giving me an eyeful of a maw filled with daggers and glowing eyes fuelled by bloodlust.

A hum buzzed deep inside me and the power that reared its ugly head when I felt threatened, scared, or angry unleashed. My fingers curled as I raised both arms before me and I screamed into the maelstrom of black and misty red that exploded from my fingertips, engulfing the pack before me.

They disintegrated into a mess of blood, bones, and fur. All that remained standing was a very shocked looking táltos. Vaguely, I saw a flicker of hunger in his eyes as he looked at me.

My vision dimmed, my head swimming and weightless and I closed my eyes, sinking into an abyss.

 50

FIVE

Muffled sounds reached my ears as I stirred to consciousness. My head pounded, and I didn't dare open my eyes just yet.

"Can you hear me?"

My brain struggled to make sense of the sound, to block out the pain surging through my body. A fogginess clouded my mind and my ankle barked with hot flares, setting my veins on fire.

"Can you hear me?" the words repeated. A man's voice.

I opened my eyes and groaned as reality came crashing back in. He was gazing at me and I noticed a gold ring in his pupils that I hadn't seen before. Beautiful.

I blinked several times after realising I was staring and grew painfully aware that my head was in his lap, his calloused hands gently holding my face. A blush stained my cheeks and he smirked, as if he knew what I was thinking.

"Are they—are they all gone?" I asked as I sat up slowly, half

51

wanting to stay in his arms, but keenly aware of the intimate position I lay in.

He swept a hand through his dark brown hair and a ray of sunlight caught his strands, highlighting reddish hues amid the brown. Gods, he was irritatingly handsome. I blinked again as his face morphed into one of wicked humour. Did I say that out loud? What's *wrong* with me?

His crooked grin sent me into a panic and I found my gaze lingering on the dimple that formed with that smile. Just one on his right cheek. I pushed to my feet as he stared at me, those dark eyes penetrating deep beneath my skin. It felt like he could see all of me, knew all my secrets.

"My, but you are interesting."

The way he said that made me feel like a lamb about to be devoured and I scowled. What annoyed me even more is that my skin tingled where his gaze dragged over me. Averting my eyes, I glanced around the forest floor and flinched at the sight. Blood pooled everywhere, congealing on frosted leaves and logs. Scattered bones glowed eerily in the filtered sunlight, clumps of black fur and strips of skin still clinging to them.

I had done this. I had decimated the pack in seconds. My hands still trembled with the aftermath of using so much magic. I had always known something dark slumbered inside me—had seen flickers of that misty red power when I'd been frightened or angry before, but this ...

The power was more violent than I ever could have expected.

Was there something wrong with me? My brows pinched together, lips wobbling as I struggled to understand what that was—what *I* was. I lifted my hands before me, failing to suppress the shivers wracking my palms. A lump formed in my throat as I realised the destruction I could have wrought on countless occasions. If I'd ever set this power free on Hanna and the other bullies who so often tormented me ... I didn't want to imagine it. I looked at the carnage around us, my gaze lingering on the matted clumps of hair and glistening pools of blood.

Fuck.

My stomach churned, and I stumbled, but the stranger caught me in two capable hands. I peeked up at his face, shoving my thoughts deep down and taking a calming breath. "Who are you? Why were the wolves chasing you?"

"I believe they were chasing you," he said with a raised brow. "If you'd been watching where you were going, I might have avoided this mess."

His tone was irritable, as if I my being injured was an inconvenience and he glared at me from his towering height.

"You're blaming me?" I spluttered, shoving him away. "If you weren't the size of a small house, I'd have slipped right past you."

His eyes narrowed and whatever temporary alliance we'd shared while fighting seemed to shrivel to a blackened crisp. "Go back to your spinning and needles, witch. The forest is no place for little girls."

My hackles rose at his blatant disrespect. *Little girl?!* I just

saved us and he has the nerve to tell *me* to leave?

"You arrogant, pig-headed brute," I said, enunciating each word with a hard poke to his chest. "If it weren't for Laszlo and I—"

The words trailed off as renewed panic flooded my veins, shortening my breath and sending a wave of dizziness through me. My head was still so foggy, but I hated myself for forgetting my dog even for a moment.

I whirled, spotting his crumpled form cradled in a tree's roots. "Laszlo!" Running to his side, I checked he was breathing and wilted in relief to see his chest rising and falling. Blood crusted the scruff of his neck, but he was alive and that's all I needed.

"Your fierce protector will be fine," the man said, his voice slightly softer. "He'll be a little disoriented, and in some pain when he wakes, but the bite wasn't severe. With a few spells, I'm sure your villagers can attend to him once you get home."

I stroked Laszlo's head as tears filled my eyes. Guilt speared through my stomach. He looked so fragile in my arms, so small. I shouldn't have interfered with the deer. "My horse bolted when the wolves approached. I won't be able to carry him with my injury. I need to heal him *now*."

At that, he cocked his head, interest burning in those strange eyes. The kind that drew you in but left you wondering what lay beneath. He was intimidating and alluring all at once, even if he had all the charisma of a stone.

"You can heal on top of, well, this?" He gestured at the

54

ghastly scene before us, his eyes darkening. "Such power. You would make a fine prize on the arm of any táltos."

Shit. I'd said too much. It was rare for witches to be adept in over one vein of magic. I didn't want to reveal my father's gift—I didn't know this man or what he might do with such knowledge. My village already treated me poorly. If they knew my gifts were even stranger, who knew what they'd do?

And that word he'd used. *Prize?* I glared at him, my lips twisting. "I am *no one's* to claim. My power is mine to do as I see fit, so you can shove that charming sentiment right up your entitled ass."

His gaze dipped to my mouth, and my chest constricted at his smirk. "So spirited."

His phrasing had me jolt with surprise. *Spirit?* I almost snorted. The elders said it was one of many things that made me a poor match for marriage. The words sent a happy little hum through my bones. Even so, the man was insufferably cocky. Clearly no stranger to cavorting with women.

I narrowed my eyes. "You never answered my question. What were you doing before the wolves attacked?"

"Hunting," he said with a lazy shrug.

I glanced at his attire, trying not to linger on the tight black breaches and black tunic hugging his torso and muscled arms. He wore a hooded red cloak beneath his gear, and a spaulder shaped in a snarling wolf's head clung to his shoulder—the emblem of the Wolfblood Clan. A pin with an insignia of a skeletal hand afore

 55

burning flames clasped to his chest, and I wondered what that symbolised.

His clothes were of fine make, but he didn't have any gear to corroborate his story. I raised a brow. "Hunting without a bow and arrow? Did you plan on snapping the animals' necks with your big, brutish hands?" I said sarcastically.

His eyes glimmered dangerously and I didn't miss the streak of anger that flashed over his face. "You ask a lot of questions, witch. I'd be careful if I were you, or that pretty little mouth will land you in trouble."

My stomach jolted with self-preservation, but I laughed, brushing off his threat with a coy smile. "It wouldn't be the first time."

The man surveyed me for a few quiet moments, his gaze dropping to my mouth before meeting my eyes again. I stared him down with my hands on my hips, not wanting to be the first to back away.

At last, his lips curved with the slightest smirk. "I can only imagine the company a hellcat like you would keep. Hopefully, far away from me." He looked at me dismissively, an almost bored expression plastered over his face. "Go home."

I couldn't leave yet. There'd be no way Mama would let me out of her sight after today's events, and it was clear the villagers had no interest in sending a scout party. *A witch who wanders is a witch forgotten.*

If Hanna still lived, the winter nights or more of those

strange wolves would soon take her.

I studied the stranger. He stared back blankly, arms crossed over his chest. And, fine, if he didn't want to share, I could deal with that. But a witch was in danger. Our communities had always been friendly, and táltosok were honour-bound to assist a witch in need. Besides, any decent man worth his salt would help.

He turned his back to leave and I bit my lip. I needed help. My damned pride would just have to suffer the consequences. "Wait! I'm searching for someone in the woods. A witch. She's been missing for several days."

His shoulders stiffened and he turned his head ever so slightly towards me. I didn't miss the strange look that crossed his face again—the way his brown eyes deepened, the flash of gold. He knew about Hanna's disappearance, or at least that a witch was missing. Well, this was an interesting turn of events. Had the elders sent a message to the Wolfblood Clan?

He turned fully and my traitorous eyes scanned every inch of his back and perhaps a little lower. Those pants wore him like a glove.

"It's too late to venture farther into the woods now. Wouldn't want you to fall into a ditch or be ripped apart by wolves," he said, his tone dripping sarcasm. "Come back tomorrow once a healer tends to you and your dog, and perhaps once the horse is found?"

His voice held a sharp edge I didn't care for, but my cheeks heated with embarrassment. *Damn you, Arló.*

Huffing my irritation, I gently laid Laszlo's head on a bed of leaves and stalked towards my dagger, wiping the bloodied blade on my leggings. Screw the táltos. I would do this with or without him. Drawing the dagger over my palm, I winced at the cold bite of steel on my skin. Blood dribbled down the blade and I wiped it on my slacks before sheathing it.

I sensed the man's eyes on me, that dark gaze burning holes in my face and hands as they hovered over Laszlo's wound.

Eyes closed, I concentrated my magic, willing my life force to impart energy, to give strength to my dog. I knew the stranger would see the swirling mist of gold funnelling into the bites on Laszlo's neck, his flesh knitting together before turning a healthy pink. I had never shown this power to anyone beyond my family.

To do so now was reckless—foolish—and perhaps the rebel in me wanted to break the rules, to see the look on the man's face as he saw my magic. How powerful I could be.

When I opened my eyes and saw a hungry glimmer in his own, a thrill shivered down my spine, and I smirked. Mission accomplished.

"Well, Freckles, aren't you full of surprises?" he said as he prowled toward me, stopping to scratch Laszlo behind the ears. The dog only yawned lazily, as if awakening from a dream.

"Freckles?" I snorted. The muscles in his arm rippled as he tore a strip off his tunic and took my hand in his. His touch was surprisingly gentle given his hostility towards me. I narrowed my eyes as I watched him work, trying to ignore the callouses on his palms as they grazed my skin.

I sucked in a breath as he leaned mere inches from my face. He was close enough to kiss and my stomach jolted at the unfamiliar sensation firing through my lower belly. I wanted to reach out and trace the stubble on his jaw, but I let my hand flop like a limp noodle. This was *not* okay. I didn't have time to be flirting with a dark and broody táltos. Especially one as entitled as him ... Even if his ass was impeccable or his jaw was sharp enough to—

"All done," he announced after tying the bandage. Amusement rippled over his features when I snatched my hand back, but his face turned sombre, his brown eyes darkening as he stared at me. "Those wolves were sick. Tainted by a magic not meant for wild things. This is your last chance, witch. I won't be there to watch your back and, if you die in there, I shan't lose a wink of sleep over it."

Gods, I'd never wanted to punch someone in the face so much. That ought to knock him down a peg. "If I'm such an inconvenience, why bother helping me at all?"

"You're bleeding all over the forest," he said matter-of-factly. "You may as well paint a sign on your back that says, 'eat me', and I don't want to deal with more wolves in a blood frenzy while I'm around."

I snatched my hand back. *Of course* he was only thinking of himself. "How very chivalrous of you," I sneered. "I'd take the wolves' company over yours any day. You give me the impression you're just as likely to sink a blade between my shoulders as you are to support them," I hissed. "Besides, I've been into the Sötét Erdő before, and I am not afraid."

His eyes raked over my skin, settling on the bloodied bandage. "You should be."

I bristled at his tone, the underlying current of danger that seemed to drape over his shoulders. "I am perfectly capable of protecting myself and I am *not* going home without Hanna."

He froze, almost preternaturally still for a split second at the mention of her name. His muscles relaxed just as quickly, but the crack in that beautiful facade was enough. Dread sluiced through my stomach.

"You know her, don't you?"

His silence was deafening, only irritating me further. Worse, his brown eyes landed anywhere but my face. Suspicion, warm and syrupy, slid through my blood. "Did you hurt her?"

A coldness entered his expression, his full mouth hardening. "If you're looking for someone to blame, witch, look to your own kind."

My hackles rose, and I glowered at him. "I'm surprised you can walk straight with balls as big as yours. Maybe I should have let the wolves rip you to shreds, táltos. Aren't they your spirit animals, after all? Next time, find a leash if you can't tame them. Perhaps we can find you a matching collar."

A muscle pulsed in his neck. "Those beasts were wild," he said. "We train our wolves from pups. Now, if you're done wasting my time, I have anywhere to be but here."

"Prick," I said under my breath.

For a moment, I could have sworn his shadow deepened. My feet stepped back before my mind could catch up, self-preservation kicking in.

"Your friend is gone," he said flatly. "The forest has her now."

I stared at his retreating form incredulously, panic rising in my throat. "What do you mean the forest has her?" I shouted. "You're just going to drop that and disappear?"

He looked over his shoulder with a crooked grin. "You said so yourself, Freckles. You can protect yourself. I so hope that's true; it would be a shame for a body like yours to be wasted."

Squeezing my eyes shut in frustration, I ignored the anger surging through my veins and took deep, soothing breaths. His words echoed ominously in my head. He had spoken of the woods like a living thing. A creature who craved blood and preyed on the living.

When I opened my eyes, the stranger had disappeared. Deathly silence blanketed the trees as I stared at the space he'd occupied previously. It occurred to me I hadn't even asked his name. But one thing was for sure.

He knew Hanna, and I was going to find out how.

SIX

It was impossible to tell time from deep within the woods. The tree canopies squeezed so tightly together the light of day could not pierce through the blanket of green. I shivered, wrapping my arms around my body, biting my lip as I wandered through the undergrowth. It was approaching mid-afternoon, if my calculations were correct, which meant time was running out. I would not, *could not*, be here when the sun went down. If this place posed a danger during the day, night-time was another story.

Mama said demonic creatures roamed the Sötét Erdő in the darkest hours. Only the most desperate of animals would dare venture out at dusk. Even the incubi returned to their caves and the water faeries to their fabled homes beneath glistening pools. One did not make deals with the devil and to cross his servants' paths only ended in suffering.

Attempting to ward off the unwanted chill of both winter

 62

and wickedness, I summoned a ball of light to guide me, the golden globe humming faintly as it floated above one hand.

Laszlo crept along beside me, his tail between his legs and ears alert as we trekked deeper into the heart. I wished he wasn't with me. His presence was a comfort, but after earlier events, I couldn't bear the thought of him getting hurt again.

"At least the wolves won't bother us, right boy?" I whispered, stroking a hand along his sleek back. He didn't deign to answer and my voice seemed to carry unnaturally loudly over the forest floor. Gnarled roots twisted before my feet and the bark cladding tree trunks seemed to be stripped from many of the surrounding trees. It was normal for deer to chew on it or stags to sharpen their horns, but the teeth marks and claws striping their trunks suggested a much larger animal was the cause.

The air was stifling, the atmosphere filled with a hazy smog that dulled the senses and stole the energy from my limbs. Something was wrong. The woods were never this ominous, even with all the wickedly horrid creatures that patrolled its depths. The dagger on my leg was a comforting weight, and I found my fingers latching onto the hilt, keenly aware of the deadly steel.

My thoughts drifted to Eszter. She'd be so upset at me, but I knew my sister—she'd cover for me for as long as possible, which should get me to dinner time at least. We always ate together, and Mama would be suspicious if I was late, then hysterical once she realised where I had gone.

I sighed. Tonight would not be fun.

63

Mama's wrath was the least of my worries. Something squelched beneath my boot, and I halted, crouching to discern the source. It was wet—viscous and black as tar. The smell of rot climbed my nose and I stifled a gag as I studied the pool of ... whatever it was. The trail only continued and I cautiously followed the path, eyes darting around me as I noted the same substance clinging to curled up leaves. Everything it touched was blackened and dead.

Laszlo whined and I dropped lower, instantly drawing my dagger and winking out the light. Darkness overcame us and I strained my ears for any sound, hearing nothing. Laszlo whimpered again, this time bolting ahead through the trees.

"Not you too," I groaned, running after him. "Laszlo," I hissed, but my words fell on deaf ears. I scrambled through the foliage blindly, hoping against hell that we didn't have more creatures to fight.

He skidded to a stop and I almost slipped in a large pool of slick liquid when hands grabbed me from behind and hurled me backwards. Panicking, I struggled against muscled arms, far too strong for me to escape. A hand clapped over my mouth, silencing my cries.

"Quiet," a familiar voice hissed into the shell of my ear. "We're being watched."

Ceasing my flailing, I looked around the clearing we'd come to, noting strange silvery-blue eyes now gleaming from the darkness. The reflection of the fire from the stranger's discarded

 64

torch rippled in their eyes. What was happening to the creatures in this place?

I suppressed a shudder, leaning against the warm, hard chest behind me just a little. We stood for several quiet moments when whatever watched us from the shadows slowly slunk back into darkness.

We waited a little longer before the táltos released me. "I told you to go home. The woods aren't safe." His eyes blazed with anger, as if he wasn't used to someone disobeying him.

I rolled my eyes. "Oh, sure, but the big, brutish táltos can strut around like he owns the place. I told you, I wasn't leaving without Hanna. Why are you here? Did you develop a shred of decency while I was gone?"

"Naughty witch," he replied drily, ignoring my questions. A flicker of amusement swam in his eyes. "You followed me here, didn't you?"

Indignation overrode my senses, and I whirled on him. "It amazes me how self-absorbed you are. I'm surprised your head isn't dragging on the ground with how full of shit it is."

He scowled, but I could have sworn his eyes glimmered with amusement for a split second. At least the bastard had a sense of humour, even if he was still lying to my face. But I could play along if it meant I might find some answers.

He sighed, the mirth leaving his face, his muscles growing taut as his gaze swept behind me. "I found Hanna, but she's ..."

His sentence trailed off, but he sounded ... regretful, almost.

65

Not quite sad, but sympathetic at the very least. My heart skipped a beat as his words sunk in, salty to swallow and heavy as stones in my stomach. I made to turn, but he clasped me firmly by the shoulders. "Don't look. This isn't something you can unsee."

An icy shiver spider-walked down my spine, those words sending my heart thumping to an erratic, discordant drum. But I had to see her. I shifted slowly on the spot and his fingers eased, letting me slip away. I missed the warmth as soon as his hands left my shoulders and I hated that I hadn't listened a second later.

Hanna's body lay sprawled over the forest floor—what remained of it. Her once golden skin was pallid, her flesh mottled and eyes wide with terror and shock. Animals had preyed upon her body, and bites and missing meat riddled her crumpled form. But it was the hollowness that made my stomach revolt, forcing me to swallow rising bile.

The body was deflated, as if someone had sucked her dry of blood and bone. The killer had cut her heart from her body—the precision matched by that of a small, serrated blade. I noticed raven feathers and black candles circling her body, along with the faint aroma of ash and smoke in the air. And, above it all, remained the waft of rot and ruin.

I gagged as the stench seemed to settle in my throat. My palms were cold and clammy and I wiped them on my pants. This was the work of someone with magic. A ritual. *A monstrosity.*

"Fuck." The breath whooshed out of me as I stumbled away from the fallen witch. I hadn't expected to find Hanna in good health or even alive, but this was so much worse than I could have ever imagined. I stared at her eyes, realising the once blue irises were now glazed and milky.

My troubles with Hanna seemed so far away now. So miniscule in the grand scheme of things. When had we ever started fighting? Would we have ever found a way to be friends again?

I could torment myself by asking these questions for an eternity, perhaps even punish myself for not being there for her when she needed me, but it didn't matter now. She was dead, and her soul was in the gods' hands.

Laszlo nudged my fingers, startling me from my daze. I looked to the táltos, only just remembering his presence. "Do you"—I swallowed—"do you have any idea who would do such a thing? You knew Hanna, don't deny it. Who would want to hurt her like this?"

He shook his head, lips set in a grim line as his hand clutched at something around his neck, hidden beneath his tunic. I was sure it hadn't been there when I had been with him earlier. "Magic can make monsters out of all of us."

It was such a cryptic answer, laced with an undercurrent of emotion. But as he looked at Hanna's body, I couldn't help but notice it was clinical. Detached.

He certainly wasn't sobbing over her death. Whatever connection they'd shared had obviously meant little to him and I wasn't sure how to feel about that. My skin prickled. Could he be the killer?

My hand itched to clasp my blade, but I suppressed the fear. Better to tread carefully until I knew more.

Clearing my throat, I studied Hanna's body, trying and failing to smooth my face into a mask and ease my raging emotions. "I've never seen anything like this before. Whoever did this can't be a witch. Not an earth witch, anyway. This is dark, forbidden magic. The kind our elders don't teach us, let alone speak of."

"This wood, the creatures," he said slowly, "I told you there is a sickness spreading, taking root and corrupting the forest. Even the wolves in our village grow restless." He shook his head, eyes glued to Hanna's lifeless form.

Though I'd never seen one, Mama had told me stories of the lupus—the black wolves of the Wolfblood Clan. They were giant, with golden eyes, fangs sharp as knives and paws as big as clubs. Their ancestors descended from the árnyalat bloodline, an ancient order of protectors who defended the old gods.

Unfortunately, Mama knew little of the old gods. Over the years, the historical texts were lost to us as humans warred over country and title. They forced witches and táltosok alike into hiding. Paganism was a dying religion and our tethers to the old world were crumbling to dust.

Invaders had infiltrated the Kingdom of Hungary so many times over the years it had been hard to keep track of, as were the religions of those who sought to conquer us. We caught snippets

 68

from the nearby human village, but it mattered little. Their religions were their own for, in the eyes of men, witches were ungodly creatures who deserved to burn at the stake.

Best we stay cautious, hidden behind our shrouded walls. It was said the banya was responsible for erecting magical wards to keep our village safe and our powers secret.

Still, I had always questioned what god would condone such a thing—condemning others for being different. For being *wrong* in the eyes of the many. Our Mother God, Istenanya, had always blessed us with her love, and Isten, the father of all gods, watched over us fondly. Witches were not unholy or inherently evil, but I suppose I could say the same for humans.

I knew one thing, though. For the lupus to have survived this long and to have remained loyal to those chosen by the gods, that was a miracle. Supernatural beings were a dying breed and we had lost many to the ravages of time and a changing world. I refused to believe witches would do the same.

Swallowing, I glanced at the táltos beside me. "We need to leave this place before dusk falls. Better not to tempt the things that come out after dark."

"First good idea you've had all day," he grumbled.

I ignored his snide remark. "The witches will want to bury her. We can't just leave her here."

His brows scrunched deep in thought as he gazed at Hanna's remains. His eyes darted to mine, a frown already marring his striking features. "I don't have a horse, and it seems you're not

69

qualified to handle yours. We can't take her."

My own lips twisted and I balled my hands into fists. "So, you want to just leave her here? You are such an asshole."

Amusement tilted the corner of his lips at my remark. "I've been called worse."

I sighed, feeling exhausted from the ordeal and the shock of, well, everything. He was right. We had no means of carrying her home and, even if we did, Hanna's mother would be distraught if she looked at the body.

Still, if it were my daughter, I would want to know what had happened to her. I would want to *see*.

"Okay," I breathed, scrunching my eyes shut. "She has a family heirloom—a necklace passed down by her mother. That will lend some truth to my story and ease her mother's pain."

As I stepped towards Hanna's body, the man's calloused palm hauled me back, his hand slipping into my own. He was warm and steadying and I looked into his dark brown eyes, the ring of gold almost glowing in the darkened light. He smelled of leather and wood and his gaze was intense, almost intimate, as his other hand reached for the necklace at his chest.

A round sapphire lay at the centre of a gilded cage, its delicate filigree claws twisting out from the edges to spiral up a silver chain. It was beautiful ... and it was Hanna's. Eyes wide, I let go of his other hand to clasp it in my palms, turning the jewel. It was so dark it appeared almost midnight in the growing dark.

"Where did you get this?" I whispered. It was her most prized possession, one she bragged about to the other girls.

"She gave it to me."

Alarm bells rang, and I recoiled, resting a hand against the blade strapped to my thigh. "*You're lying.* I knew Hanna well. She never took that necklace off. Never. Why would she give something so precious to you?"

His eyes flashed as a sinister smile crept over his lips. "Perhaps you didn't know her as well as you thought."

I didn't know why, but those words sent a pang of sadness through me. Maybe because he wasn't far off the mark. "I did," I whispered. "Once upon a time."

He crossed his arms and a mocking grin spread over his face. "Poor witch. Risking your life for someone who wanted nothing to do with you."

Tears threatened to burn my eyes, but I blinked them back, refusing to let this monster rile me. I drew my blade, showing him I meant business. "I grow tired of your company, táltos. Tell me the truth. How did you know her?"

He ran a hand through his hair. "We were seeing each other. We'd come to the woods every so often to ... get to know each other better. Not that it's any of your business."

I narrowed my eyes. "So you were fucking. I'm not surprised. Everyone knew Hanna was ..." I drifted off, not wanting to insult her memory, nor the man before me. His tongue might have loosened, but he could still be a murderer.

"I'm aware she had other lovers," he said simply. "We made

71

no promises to each other."

Perhaps not, but Hanna had with another. Could a jealous bridegroom be the killer? It still didn't explain the ritual and use of dark magic. Such things were well out of táltosok' area of expertise, and witches too.

"When was the last time you saw her?" I bit out.

He waved a hand lazily. "We were supposed to meet this morning. When she didn't show, I feared the worst."

"Is that so." I frowned, raising my blade a little higher. "For her lover, you don't seem choked up about this."

He shrugged. "Hanna was many things, but our interest in each other was strictly sexual."

"You're disgusting," I spat. "And you're a fool. Girls don't give priceless treasures for a romp in the woods. This necklace was a promise. You meant more to her than sex."

His eyes softened for the briefest moment as he glanced down at her body, but when he looked at me again, his face was a careful mask. "I guess now we'll never know."

Anger roiled in my stomach, blazing beneath my skin as I looked at him. Did he have no compassion? He was treating this whole situation like an inconvenience.

What was his game? I sensed there was more to his story—and perhaps his feelings, too. First, the questionable affair, and then finding him by Hanna's body with a precious heirloom in hand? No. It was too fucking strange for my liking.

"You're lying," I said slowly, backing up with my weapon held high. "If you expect me to believe your little story, you're even stupider than you look."

A muscle throbbed in his cheek as he took a step forward, his face a mask of carefully contained anger. Only his eyes glimmered dangerously, and I had the sudden sensation to flee before I was caught within his snare. "Careful how you speak to me, witch," he snarled, taking another step towards me. "If I really did kill Hanna, what makes you think I wouldn't hesitate to dispose of you too?"

Fear sluiced through me as he began to circle me slowly, but I didn't take my eyes off him for a single second. I spat at his feet. "Go to hell."

A cruel smile carved his lips. "Make me."

I lunged without hesitation, tossing my blade through the air so it spun in a silver blur towards his head. He moved his shoulder back smoothly, causing the blade to sail past harmlessly so it sank into a tree trunk with a dull thud.

His smug grin widened in victory and he rolled his neck, adjusting his tunic smoothly.

My cheeks heated and the breath shuddered from my lungs. I *never* missed. He was fast—too fast—and I barely had time to slide my next dagger free before he slammed me against a tree. My back barked with pain as he twisted my wrist, causing the blade to fall uselessly to the ground.

I choked back a cry as he pinned my arms above my head and squeezed my wrists. He looked at me with disdain, as if I was beneath him in every way. "What a pathetic effort. I expected better, even from a witch."

"Let me go," I hissed, squirming against his hold as I stared at him, willing every ounce of fury into my gaze. I couldn't summon my magic without freedom of movement, and he knew it.

He laughed mockingly, releasing me and cocking his head. "Stupid girl. Do you honestly think a táltos is capable of the magic required to perform this spell? Look around you. We harness spiritual energy, not blood spells. And if you still don't believe me, look at Hanna's body. It's been there for at least a couple days."

My eyes drifted to Hanna once again and, begrudgingly, I realised he was right. Her body was too bloated for the murder to be recent. The signs of rot—not to mention the stench and the parts mauled by animals—were too far along to ignore. And to my knowledge, táltosok could not harness magic of this magnitude.

He was a warrior, of that I had no doubt, but this ritual went beyond the skills of any soldier, or indeed any magic I'd ever seen or heard of. Unless he had help from others, this wasn't the work of a táltos.

I let my guard down just a little but kept my distance. "Even if you're telling the truth, I still don't trust you. You may not have killed her, but you were the reason she was in the woods in the first place. A good man—an honourable man—wouldn't lure another man's bride out here. "

 74

He sneered. "I couldn't give two shits what you think of me or my arrangement with Hanna, but I didn't do this. I might not have cared for Hanna in the way that she wanted, but I would never have hurt her. She didn't deserve this."

I stared at him for a long minute. His eyes shone but he didn't shift under my gaze. In fact, he seemed entirely unphased by my scrutiny. Nothing about his expression suggested he was lying.

Sighing, I scrubbed my eyes. Exhaustion dragged at my bones, and all I wanted was to wash the blood off and curl up in my bed. Seeing Hanna like that was not something I'd easily forget. The táltos was right. Hanna didn't deserve this fate—no one did.

"I'm going home," I said suddenly, storming towards my dagger and yanking it from the tree trunk. I returned it to my belt along with the one on the ground. "I need to see my family."

"Wait." His hand snaked out, grasping my wrist. I growled a warning, but he went on undeterred. "You should know, there are rumours of other girls' bodies being found in similar fashions. This isn't the first ritual to take place."

"What?" I took a shuddering breath, the hostility towards him blinking out as shock surged through my bones. "Why hasn't your leader conferred with the elders?"

He blinked before schooling his features into indifference. "I was under the impression he had. Whoever is doing this is targeting witches. Stay *away* from the woods unless you want to

end up like Hanna."

A tremor rolled through me. The other girls weren't just missing, they were dead. I knew deep in my bones it was the truth. But why would someone want to harm the witches in my coven? And if Farkas—the Wolfblood leader—had told the council about these rumours, why hadn't the elders informed the villagers?

I thought of Death's warning. Of the lies circling my life. But how deep did they go? And why was this insufferable man warning me? It was clear he didn't like me much.

I rubbed one wrist and then the other, sweeping my thumb over the bone. The feeling was mutual.

Feeling defeated from the day and utterly done with this man, I glared at him, raising my blade in earnest. I didn't trust him, and I certainly didn't want to be around him anymore. In fact, I'd be happy if I never saw him again.

"Get out of these woods," I said in a low voice. "You're in my territory now, and if I see you near a witch again, I won't hesitate to drive this blade through your heart."

SEVEN

"Kitarni Alexandra Bárány, where have you been!?"

My mother's voice bellowed from the front door of our cottage, and I winced at her posture; hands ground into her hips, eyes glaring murderously as I skulked up the path towards her. Using my full name ... she meant business.

It was well past dusk now, which meant whatever lies Eszter had told in my stead, Mama would have long since ironed out.

Eszter peeked out from behind my mother's frazzled hair, but one glance from Mama had her shrinking back into the home. Bolstering my defences, I stepped before her, head bowed, and shoulders slumped as I awaited punishment.

"You look like hell," she said, perusing my filthy tunic, my bandaged hand and the wild hair. Who knows what filth covered my face? I hoped there was no blood or ash.

"I'm okay, just a few bumps and bruises, nothing serious. Arló is missing, though. He bolted in the woods and—"

"That skittish horse of yours returned hours ago, looking like he'd seen the devil himself. How do you think that made me feel, hmm? Seeing him riderless and terrified. I had all kinds of ill thoughts running through my mind! I was just about to march into the woods myself."

Gods, I hadn't even considered what drastic actions she might resort to had I arrived any later. "I'm so sorry Mama." My heart felt empty, my head heavy with the image of Hanna sprawled out over the forest floor.

Mama looked long and hard into my eyes and apparently found what she was looking for because she nodded sharply, just once. We stood and stared at each other after that, and I waited for the hammer to fall.

To my surprise, Mama burst into tears, hauling me into her arms and clutching at my tunic as if it were my last day on Earth. "Good gods, girl, you scared me half to death. Don't do that to me again. Please." She huffed between sobs. "Please."

Hearing her so distraught sent guilt spearing through my stomach. I had never been the perfect daughter, was always in trouble, but this was different. Despite the shock of the day, I wouldn't change what I'd done, but I regretted causing my mother such stress.

I nestled into her hair, which smelled faintly of lavender. Mama's hugs felt like home. Her skin felt like a little hearth where it pressed against me. I hadn't realised how cold I was. From shock or the weather, who knew?

Finding Hanna had been horrifying and, even more so, the implications behind it. I knew, despite my reservations and the bizarre circumstances, that my strange companion had been telling the truth today. Not the whole truth, perhaps, but I believed he hadn't been the one to murder Hanna. What motive did he have? He clearly hadn't cared much for her, so he had no reason to have been jealous over a bridegroom or vengeful that she was marrying another. And the power used was beyond that asshole's skillset.

Someone who could practice with dark magic was doing this to witches in our village, and this knowledge? It was armour. A way to prevent it from happening again.

That's if the elders listened to me. The táltos said Farkas had told them of the rumours, which meant he'd either been lying, or the elders were keeping secrets. But that couldn't be right. Mama was an elder and she'd never keep this from Eszter and me. Not if it compromised our safety.

But ... tomorrow. I would tackle confronting the council tomorrow. For now, I had a mother to console and a sister to confide in. And dinner. Bad news was not as hard to swallow if paired with a hot meal.

"Mama, I'm okay," I said. My eyes welled with emotion, betraying the lie. Today had been long and fleeting all at once, and I still had to break the news to my family—to Hanna's mother. My heart sank. The thought of that made me want to crumple into a ball and burrow under my covers. How did you tell someone the light of their life was gone? How could I tell her there was no body to lay to rest? No soul to honour and guide to the afterlife?

There hadn't been enough left of Hanna to bring home, even if Arló hadn't bolted.

Sorrow climbed my chest until I sobbed, too, nestling into my mother's shoulder as she gently cooed and stroked my hair. Skinny arms soon wrapped around my middle as Eszter joined us and the world disappeared as I melted into our bubble. I was so thankful to have such a loving family. I was lucky to be alive.

Others weren't, and it was that realisation which hit me deep in the stomach. I pulled away from my family's embrace, searching my mother's eyes. She smiled weakly, fear dulling the light of her brown eyes. Somehow, she knew Hanna was dead. I was sure of it.

"Come inside, girls, let's get some food in your bellies," she said. With a glance towards the stables, she shot me a stern look. "Your horse was tended, as well as the other animals, thanks to your sister. There was much complaining about it too, I'll have you know. And I swear by the gods, Kitarni, if you drag her into your schemes again, I'll—"

"I'm sorry, Mama," I cut in, shoulders sagging. "I didn't mean to make you worry, and I would never lie to you, but this was different. Someone needed our help and I ... I just ..."

She laid a hand on my shoulder. "I know. You're a Bárány. We don't know when to quit."

 80

I snorted at the truth in that statement. She was right. All three of us were stubborn creatures, and when we set ourselves a goal or made up our minds about something, we would stop at nothing to see it done.

"Especially when it's at the cost of others," she added. "You are fierce and brave, Kitarni, and it's one of the things I love most about you." She kissed my forehead and smiled tenderly. "I'm still locking you in this house, though. Don't even think about sneaking off again."

Chuckling, I stepped over the threshold as she trotted to the kitchen. "I figured you'd say that."

"Good. Your chores are doubled too. That ought to keep you from getting into trouble."

From her perch at the dinner table, Eszter gave me a pointed look that said *I doubt it*. I agreed. Her eyes burned the back of my skull as I pottered around the kitchen and I knew she would grill me for answers once our mother had gone to bed. But, for now, all I could think of was food, and the steady rhythm of chopping and stirring helped calm the tension roiling in my stomach. We were having goulash tonight and my stomach grumbled eagerly as the pot bubbled away and the scent of stew climbed my nose.

I realised again how lucky we were. We weren't nobles, nor did many in our coven have much wealth to speak of, but our life was bountiful in many other ways.

With the magic flowing through our veins, the witches grew vegetables, fruit, wheat, herbs—all in abundant supply. The

witches knew how to spin a bargain, peddling our wares at competitive prices at market. The elders forbade witches from using magic to coerce the humans, but they did anyway. Perhaps a spell or two to make jewellery shinier, fabrics softer, or steel of better make.

Our hunters were skilled, perhaps with a little magic guiding their arrows, and we were fortunate to eat meat more than most peasants could afford. Even in winter, ample stores kept us well fed. Our bellies were full, our hearths were warm, and our beds kept us cosy at night. There was wonder in our days, for witches had the world at their disposal. Powers children would dream of or read about in stories, and gifts humans would see as devilry and destruction.

Our home didn't have the finery of nobles—expensive dresses, jewels, furniture and the like, but that's not to say our wares weren't worthy of new homes in their base forms. Our coven was a diverse one in terms of professions. Jewellers, seamstresses, bakers, blacksmiths and herbalists. The witches even made the furniture in our homes from their earth magic, carving beds, chairs, tables and the like out of tree trunks. We all had a part to play in keeping our community fed, comfortable, and happy.

Happy. My family certainly seemed to be, but could I say the same?

"Kitarni, would you set the table please?" Mama said, pulling me from my thoughts.

I set the crockery down on our wooden table, smiling at the hand-painted flowers in reds, yellows and blues adorning the white bowls. Mama's and Eszter's were perfect, of course, whereas my lines were less precise, more like wobbly splotches. Still, they were happy and bright, something that represented our little family. Usually.

Chewing on my lip, I served the meal, ladling out the goulash and slicing crusty bread that Gisella, the village baker, made fresh every morning. She was one of my favourite witches in town, always red-cheeked and smiling, flour or icing always dusting her frocks. As a child, Gisella would always gift me treats when I raced through her bakery. Nothing had changed.

We ate in silence, the sounds of spoons scraping bowls clanging through the tension. I devoured the stew, even helping myself to seconds, mopping every morsel up with my bread until the white of my bowl was squeaky clean. I slurped at my water noisily, the warmth in my belly pulling my eyelids down. But the night was still young, and I couldn't bear the sidelong glances from my family any longer.

Mama knew it, too.

"Kitarni." Her tone was soft, but firm as she stared at me, her voice commanding the room. "She's gone, isn't she?"

My body stilled. They would have known the truth when I came back alone. But hearing her say it ... it seemed so abrupt. So real. Swallowing, I nodded my head slowly. "I found her deep in the Sötét Erdő. By the look of her body, she'd been dead a few

 83

days."

Mama inhaled a sharp breath and my sister merely stared at me in shock, her eyes wide as saucers. Silence swallowed my statement as they chewed over the knowledge and I prayed no one would ask me what had become of her. How she had died.

"What happened?" Eszter asked, her voice barely audible. I glanced at her, not wanting my little sister to hear the truth. But I couldn't shield her, not from this. The more the village knew about this monstrosity, the better equipped we'd all be to deal with it. Eszter would be safer knowing—even if Mama kept her locked up in this cottage for all eternity after hearing of it.

Steeling my spine, I looked at Mama. "Hanna didn't die from the cold or even the creatures of the forest. Someone murdered her."

Eszter gasped, her dainty hand flying to her mouth. Mama's eyes only hardened and, in that moment, I didn't recognise the woman before me. Her lips tightened, her eyes burning with the fierce resolve of a soldier. No, a queen.

"How?"

That simple word brooked no room for argument or sparing any details. "Her body lay within a ritual circle, black candles and feathers strewn about the forest floor. Whoever it was, they didn't expect anyone else to be venturing so deep into the woods."

I kept the appearance of the mysterious táltos to myself. His connection to Hanna—while bizarre—explained why Hanna had left the village without supplies for a long trip. But something didn't sit right and, until I had more evidence, I wasn't ready to point fingers. My lips pursed as I thought of the táltos. It hadn't gone so well the first time.

"What state was the corpse in?" Mama said, her lips tightening into a thin line.

I blinked. *The corpse.* My mother's shift in behaviour sent warning bells ringing through me. This was not the face of shock, but a different mask. One that recognised the calling cards of this. Narrowing my eyes, I shifted in my seat. "They drained her body of blood. And her heart ..." I glanced at Eszter, but my mother was too focused on my recount to pay her any heed.

"They ripped her heart from her chest," Mama finished for me. I gaped at her, and Eszter's rosy cheeks blanched. My sister clutched at her skirts, fingers white-knuckled with her iron grip. Mama sighed. "Eszter, darling, please fetch some wine? And three goblets."

My sister cocked her head. "Three?"

Mama nodded grimly, massaging a hand to her temple as she squeezed her eyes shut. Another world-weary sigh escaped her and I had the urge to cradle her in my arms. My mother, so proud and sure, looked frail in the light of the flickering fire. Lines settled around her eyes and in the gentle curves of her bone structure, making her look older than her years.

My mother was a beautiful woman. Her long brown hair was glossy, her smile radiant and her brown eyes clear, but the years had been hard for her. She would never admit it, but I think she

85

missed Papa sometimes. Despite the strange rules separating the witches and táltosok from forming a united community, I think my mother had loved him in her own way.

Idleness begets loneliness, and for that reason she constantly kept busy, constantly moving and providing for our family and the village.

She leaned in, whispering for my ears alone as Eszter pottered about, collecting the wine and some treats, clanging and clinking as she went. Even I didn't have the stomach for dessert right now, but I expected it was habit guiding her hands more than anything.

"I had hoped I'd never need to speak of this with you girls, but this isn't the first time I've heard of such a ritual taking place."

The táltos had spoken the truth. If Mama recognised the signs, others would too. Perhaps it would help us discover who was behind the murders. "I figured as much. Who would do such a thing, Mama? What kind of spell even exists in our realm of magic?"

She shook her head. "That ritual is an abomination. An abhorred magic only practiced by dark witches. It's forbidden, and the texts containing such spells were supposedly burned long ago. I'm sure it doesn't surprise you to learn it was the Dark Queen who first created this spell."

"What does it do?"

Her lips twisted. "Originally, she created the spell for

executions—to make the victim's death excruciating and lengthy. Ironically, the same spell was used just once after most of her cult paid for their crimes. Once covens began electing elders to run the individual factions, they finally captured Sylvie and put her to trial. With the long list of abhorrent crimes she committed, they executed her at the stake. The witches cast her own spell on her, drawing out the pain. A point well made, and a warning served to all would-be practitioners of dark magic who attended her death, which included every witch in the Kingdom of Hungary we hold records for."

I mulled over all she had told me, feeling my stomach flip as images of bloodied and bruised men and women flashed before my eyes. Their deaths would have been horrible, inhumane. How anyone could have such a darkness inside them ... I shuddered. What had made Sylvie become so twisted? The angry beast inside me roared at her crimes.

Eszter set a tray filled with wine, goblets, and szaloncukor—little chocolates filled with hazelnuts or caramel—down on the table with a clunk, startling me from my spiral of darkening thoughts. I eyed the chocolates with a raised brow. Despite the morbid mood, she winked, flashing me a knowing smile. The little devil must have been hoarding them, knowing I would have long since eaten the delectable morsels.

Unlike me, Eszter had the willpower to say no to temptation. It was, in part, thanks to her that I wasn't the size of a house. Still, I marvelled that she'd kept them since Szenteste, the Holy

Evening before Christmas. I smiled weakly, appreciating the gesture. She always sought to lift my spirits, even in the face of such dire news.

Eszter paused before sliding into her seat, one finger curling her long, golden-brown hair. "You said *originally*. Was the spell adapted?"

I should have known she would listen in this whole time. Her banging about had been a little too suspicious. She caught my frown and flicked her hair like a prized mare. Mama poured us half glasses and filled her own goblet—right to the very rim.

She took long draughts and finished it quickly, and my sister glanced at me with a raised brow, a smirk curving her lips. Hysterical laughter bubbled in my throat and I took a sip from my cup, the wine sloshing the odd emotion down my belly. There was nothing remotely funny about this situation. For Mama to have offered Eszter a tipple at all spoke volumes to her distress.

"The council elders held true to their threat. They spent years trying to find the Dark Queen's followers, sending a network of spies across the country to glean information on occults and their leaders. Unfortunately, Sylvie's stain had spread too far, too deep, and no matter how clean the cloth, such blots refuse to budge."

My lips twisted in disgust. "Her magic makes its mark even still?"

Mama nodded. "Don't underestimate the power of persuasion. Sylvie's magic lay not just in her talent as a witch, but

88

in her persona. She was manipulative, controlling, and she warped her followers' minds until they believed in her cause. Bled for it."

"Cut the head off the snake ..."

"And three more take its place," Mama said. "Her work continued even after her death, just like she planned. Over time, her followers adapted the teachings, morphing old spells into new. I'll bet they've been searching for ways to bring her back from places none should follow."

"They tried to bring her back from the dead?" Eszter asked, her cheeks filled with colour since sipping on wine. Gone was the doll-faced girl in this moment and instead a woman sat beside me, her beauty still etched into every line of her body. But she sat rigid, alert, her eyes bright with calculation. A wolf in sheep's clothing if I ever saw. I wondered, then, what kind of warrior lay within, if ever circumstance should call.

Mama scoffed. "Tried and failed, as far as we know. The power required to raise one from the dead remains unknown to witches for now. The combined councils erased records of spells created from that lunatic. But who knows what those fanatics might do? I am certain many would give their lives for hers if they could, and that ill thought still finds me in the dark hours of night. With girls disappearing over the last few years and what you've told me about Hanna, I can't help but think the worst."

"You think they're connected?" I stated, tilting my head. "The ritual performed on Hanna is a part of their occultism, isn't

89

it?"

"The way you described Hanna's body makes me believe they are draining girls of, not only their lifeblood, but their power. A transfer of their energies to another party. The question is ... to whom?"

It was a question none of us had an answer for, but if Mama was right, there may be more than one culprit to find. The Dark Queen's followers sounded devout, unfaltering, so could it be they were hunting for a way to return their mistress?

If so, the deaths weren't personal at all, but merely a means to an end. I just hoped we could snuff them out before anyone else fell to their dark magic. There was more to this mystery, and now it seemed our lives depended on solving it.

As I lay in bed later that night, Laszlo sprawled across my feet, not even his warmth could stave off the chills that haunted me.

EIGHT

I replayed yesterday's events in quiet moments—and there were many—given Mama had demanded I stay indoors. Despite our shared truths last night, she'd still threatened me to stay home. As an elder, my mother would bear the weight of responsibility at the council meeting today. The others would respect her words, even if they might not believe their merit. Not if they came from *my* mouth.

Breathing deep, I paused my stirring to lick the wooden spoon in contemplation, the sticky sweetness of the *bejgli* clinging to my tongue. Even poppy seeds and walnuts doused in sugar couldn't lift my spirits today.

Perhaps the elders were right to dislike me. *Well, mostly just one.* But as chieftain, her decisions held the most sway. Caitlin thought my stubbornness caused trouble, as did my disregard for etiquette and feminine propriety.

I snorted. What a load of crap. If I hadn't searched for

 91

Hanna, who would have? Would the elders have formed a scouting party? Would they have lifted a finger to help Anna get her daughter back?

My heart sank as I thought of Hanna's mother. She was a timid woman. Reserved, but always helpful. She had a good heart and had healed many a witch when sickness struck our village. Anna owned the town's apothecary, running operations behind the scenes while her daughter tended to customers. Everyone had liked Hanna, lapping up her charm like cats do warm milk.

The apothecary would be a lot quieter now. The whole town would.

I pushed the sombre thoughts from my mind, watching Eszter weaving magic through the window instead. Her delicate fingers twisted and curled as she focused her attention on a gigantic pumpkin. It was her pride and joy, and she'd kept a careful watch over it during the winter months.

The fat gourd was as big as Laszlo, and I wondered how big it could grow before it might burst. My sister smiled as she lifted her hands, the tell-tale blush of her magic wafting around her like clouds of perfume.

The pumpkin had been neglected for a few days, but with a wave of her magic the dull skin returned to a vibrant orange, and its leaves flourished and curled. The fruit was even fatter when she finished.

I smiled. Once, that feat alone would have tired Eszter out, but now she was moving onto other vegetables, restoring those with signs of rot, encouraging others with wilted leaves. What a miracle, earth magic was. It suited my sister so well; she practically glowed when using her magic.

My mixture bubbled and I focused my attention back to stirring. I couldn't stand to drown in my woes and, even more than that, I hated every ugly, jealous thought I had when it came to earth magic.

Why couldn't I share in that gift? Why did the gods mock me so?

"Stress baking?" My sister's voice nearly had me shedding my skin as I flinched in fright. She laid a hand on my arm, soil still clinging to her nails. Her eyes crinkled in worry. "Hey. Are you okay?"

"Yes? No? I don't know." I sighed, setting the spoon and bowl down and heading for the hearth. "Yesterday was intense, Eszter. Seeing Hanna like that? It's not something I'll soon forget."

My sister grimaced as she sat on the floor beside me, her brown eyes peering into the crackling fire. "I'm sorry for what you went through, Kit. That must have been hard to deal with by yourself."

I avoided her inquisitive stare as I toyed with the fabric of my cream sweater. Eszter had made it for me the Christmas before last and it felt all the cuddlier for it.

"Kitarni." She drew out my name. "You were alone, right?"
"Wellllll ..."
"You're kidding." Indignation flared in her eyes. "You left

93

me behind and took someone else?"

"Actually, no. I might have met someone else. A man."

Her expression sped from excitement to wariness and, finally, to gobsmacked. "A human?"

I laughed. "Not quite."

Her eyes widened with interest. "You met a táltos?" she whispered in a conspiring tone, as if someone might be spying.

I looked around to confirm no one was indeed listening. "Met a táltos, almost died fighting a pack of wolves, conjured a new power." I shrugged. "Nothing unusual."

"But you met a táltos!?"

"I tell you I almost die and that's what you focus on?"

Eszter waved her hands. "Yes, yes, we'll get to the other stuff later. Now tell me, what was he like?"

"My gods, you're like a hound on the scent. I'm not sure we should let you off your leash for the spring festival after all," I teased.

She swatted me playfully and I laughed, momentarily forgetting the horrors I had seen. But there was something—or rather, someone—who my mind kept darting back to. Only ... "I never got his name."

"Is it because he was so devilishly handsome, he took your breath away?"

"Don't be absurd," I scoffed. "He *was* stupidly handsome, but he was *infuriating* and I don't trust him one bit. Anyway, we didn't have time for introductions. A pack of wolves attacked us

 94

and everything spiralled into chaos so quickly. The wolves, Eszti, there was something wrong with them. The forest corrupted them somehow."

Eszter bit her lip. "Do you think the Dark Queen's cult lives in the Sötét Erdő? Maybe their magic is spreading through the woods, affecting the animals there."

A shiver raked long claws down my spine. "If so, that's way too close for comfort. We weren't even in the darkest part of the woods when the wolves attacked us."

She frowned. "How strange."

I snorted. "It's fucking bizarre is what it is."

"What was the táltos doing there in the first place?" Eszter asked, wrapping her arms around her knees as she peered into the fire.

A good question. One I still wasn't sure I had the whole truth of. "He and Hanna were lovers. Said they'd planned to meet in the morning, but when I first mentioned her, it was like I'd backed him into a corner. Instead of being honest, he just bailed on me, then showed up at the exact spot I found Hanna's body. It's all very ..."

"Suspicious? Kit, for all you know, he might have been the murderer."

I shook my head absentmindedly. "I thought the same at first, but not anymore. He was telling some truth and, even if he wasn't, the magic used for that ritual was beyond that of any táltos. Mama said only witches could wield dark magic like that.

Hanna's body was drained when I found her, and animals had ..."
I swallowed, unable to form the words, but the look on Eszter's
face showed she understood.

"That's disgusting."

I blew out a long breath. "Yes, it was."

We sat silently, each condemned to our thoughts. The earth
had quaked beneath our feet, splitting open to reveal hidden
truths and even uglier consequences. Our quiet village was under
threat.

It was time to do something about it.

Jumping to my feet, I held out a hand for my sister, pulling
her gracefully to her feet. Perhaps she saw the fierce resolve in my
eyes, for she grinned mischievously. "Where are we headed then?"

I flashed her a devious smile. "The one place we can cause
the most trouble. Where else?"

The temple winked at us from a distance, the tall spires reaching
heavenward. Its gilded flowers latticed on the window arches
glinted in the afternoon sun. Creeping ivy lined high stone walls
and the grand mahogany doors were carved with the Turul—one
bird of prey on each door, guarding the councillors and
worshippers inside.

We made our way down the hill, past the outer homes and
through the square surrounded by stores. The temple sat at the

other end of our town, nestled amongst the trees that fanned around it.

It was one of the more beautiful buildings in the village, but it was the garden where the true charm lay. Tulips in glorious shades of every colour of the rainbow bloomed in neat rows lining the path winding up to the great doors, and a wisteria tree arched over a small pond at the rear. We used its flowers to weave onto maypoles for the spring festival, and soon the village would be vibrant with lavenders and white bellflowers.

I sighed, shoulders slumping under the weight of despair as we walked. The spring festival was my favourite time of the year. A time when witches forgot or forgave any animosity and disputes, and all came together to embrace our womanhood. To lift each other up and celebrate ourselves as goddesses. *As witches.*

We would feast for days on end, drink until our cups overflowed with magic, dance and dance until our legs gave out.

The time of year meant new beginnings, new adventure and, for many, new love. Girls dressed in pretty frocks and put ribbons in their hair, their cheeks flushed with youth and happiness. Men came to court budding beauties and women watched their daughters win the hands of eligible bachelors—matches made for power, if not marriage.

Gifts exchanged weren't gold, but that of glory—of power to pass down the line and keep our magic strong. It mattered little that our village was but a grain of sand in a much bigger world. Power was power. Magic was might.

 97

And, of course, there was the banya. Like a shadow, she descended on the homes of the chosen, where she would whisk away a new apprentice every other year, never showing her face or revealing her cards. At least, that was the rumour.

Baba Yana was a perfect stranger idolised and honoured by all. The witches tittered she was overdue to pick a new star apprentice, and I wondered if she would come this year. With Hanna's death, I felt compelled to keep Eszter close by my side. What if she was picked?

"Someone's coming," Eszter hissed, dragging me from my thoughts and into a prickly bush beneath a window at the back of the temple.

"*Ow*," I grumbled, swiping a stinging cut trickling fresh blood.

She winced, but we tightened our lips at the sound of approaching footfalls. I looked up through the maze of leaves, spotting a stern nose, a hard slash for a mouth and narrowed grey eyes glaring out the window. Caitlin Vargo. Chief elder and my worst enemy.

The woman despised me—intolerable crone. She was the oldest in our village—far too ancient to suffer my innumerable crimes against her withered old heart. These being stubbornness and brashness unbecoming of a maiden, a disregard for rules and common courtesies, and having an opinion on anything.

Right. Because that was going to change. Truly, I think she hated me because I had let Sami loose once when she came to call

98

on Mama. A girl must draw the line somewhere and that day she'd been awful to my mother.

I'd never seen her withered bones move quicker. Her panicked shouts still made me chuckle to this day. I had pleaded innocence, of course, but she knew. Battle lines were drawn that day.

"If the cultists have returned, we must assume the worst," a low voice carried out the window. "They may have discovered how to revive the Dark Queen."

My ears pricked at the mention of the Dark Queen. *Sylvie Morici.* Eszter and I looked between each other, and hope blossomed in my chest. *Did the elders believe me?*

"We cannot jump to conclusions," Caitlin snapped, turning to storm towards the speaker. "That girl has a knack for causing trouble. It wouldn't surprise me if she made the whole thing up."

I sighed. *Apparently not.* I shuffled closer to the window, ignoring the barb of branches and the old wretch's words. We raised our heads, peeking over the edge of the windowsill.

Mama's voice broke the awkward silence that followed. "*That girl* was the only one brave enough to look for Hanna. My daughter may follow the call of the wilds, but do not mistake her wanderer's heart for one filled with treachery. There is no reason for her to lie and no way for her to have known about the cultists. Our history and those despicable spells are under lock and key. Only this council and Lord Sándor have access."

Eszter frowned and I knew we were thinking the same thing.

99

Those despicable spells could only be what Mama had referred to as Sylvie's records. But she'd said they no longer existed.

Mama had never lied to us before. Never. It frightened me she should start now, when things would surely worsen.

"It would be unwise to ignore this information, Caitlin," Erika said.

My muscles relaxed slightly upon hearing her voice. Erika was my magic tutor, who also taught me how to throw blades. Albeit secretly, lest Caitlin discover another reason to despise me. She was a practical, no-nonsense woman, who kept her heart guarded behind high walls. But I'd been whittling her down ever so slowly and her honesty was one thing I liked most about her. I could have kissed her now, for hers was a voice of reason I was most happy to hear.

"As your commander," she continued, "I advise we listen to Nora. Even if nothing comes of this news, we need to prepare for the worst. It is my duty to protect this village and, if the cultists' numbers are increasing, they may launch an attack. It wasn't so long ago Mistvellen experienced a similar assault."

"I remember," Mama said, her eyes glimmering. "Many died that day. Lord Sándor's wife among them."

Erika sighed. "We will not suffer the same fate. Winter is nearly over, and longer days and warmer temperatures may encourage the snakes to leave their nest. I'd rather be as lively as possible for the upcoming festival."

Caitlin sighed a rattling breath. "What do you propose?"

"Guards placed around the village perimeter, double posted during the spring equinox. We cannot risk more girls being taken."

"Hanna was a fool to leave the safety of the village," Caitlin muttered. "A lamb led to slaughter." For once it wasn't admonition in her tone, but pity. She paused, and a long-suffering sigh followed after. "A fool, but a good girl. One who minded her elders and kept to her duties. She was not the type to go venturing in dark places. So what lured her out?"

"Not *what*," Mama said, her head cocked in thought. "*Who*. Gods forgive me for speaking ill of the dead, but Hanna was no maiden. Girls gossip, Caitlin, and I'm sure you've heard the rumours."

Caitlin's lips twisted as if sucking on a lemon. "Unfortunately, yes." She smoothed her hands over her skirts before steepling her fingers. "May the Gods guide her path and protect the children of our flock."

Her steel eyes darted to a beautiful woman in her late thirties, with blonde hair cut in a sharp bob. Her blue eyes sparkled like sapphires, but there was a hardness to them I'd rarely seen. I'd always thought her a strange creature, like a spider, weaving her webs and collecting information like insects. I preferred to keep my distance. Beneath Iren's subtle curves and careful countenance was something unforgiving. I knew nothing about her, save that she acted as an emissary and gathered intelligence for the elders. That's all Mama had said despite my prying, but I had the feeling the knowledge she gathered were things kings killed for and soldiers died to protect.

As chieftain of the elder council, I wondered how much Caitlin knew about Iren. Or whether the high elder pulled more strings than I yet knew. Perhaps the weight of those duties led to the harsh decline of her sagging muscles and weary bones.

Iren glanced at the chieftain with a stony expression. "I will contact the network leaders and alert them to what's happened. See if similar attacks have taken place around Transylvania. I can even contact some witches in Wallachia, though I doubt they'd care about what's happening here."

"And the banya?" my mother asked, her voice casual, body relaxed. I saw the tension behind her eyes, though. The slight curl of her fist. "What of the witch of the woods? Surely she would know cultists sweep the floors of her domain."

"You presume much for your station, Nora," Caitlin said venomously. "The banya will contact us if she deems it necessary. It is not our place to question her rule."

Mama's lips pursed. "The council governs our village, not Baba Yana. I will not bow to stories and subterfuge. Should she wish to work with us, I welcome the fact, but a proud witch does not allow vermin to scurry through her house unchecked. We must find these rats, lest our village becomes the cheese from which they gnaw."

"You blaspheme. Ever the wolf in sheep's clothing, playing at our faith. If you don't believe in her might, you're welcome to

crawl back to Mistvellen." Caitlin sneered. "I suspect it's not so lovely without Adrian."

Eszter gripped my arm, her nails digging into my skin. I didn't notice the pain, concentrating wholly on that horrible woman's choice of words. Why the hostility towards my father? And was Caitlin suggesting Mama could live there without him?

But that couldn't be right. Witches and táltosok lived separately. The coven demanded it.

Our coven, I realised. But maybe not all of them. Things might be different beyond our small village. Perhaps Mistvellen was different. I'd always thought it strange Mama had left my father. She never spoke of him, but I knew she'd loved him dearly. Had Caitlin interfered in their relationship?

My mother's eyes burned with fury, and I recognised the rage lining her face, her muscles twitching with barely contained anger. The Bárány family were known for our tempers.

"Gods spare me," Erika muttered before Mama lost it. "The enemy is out there in the woods, not among us."

Mama took a breath, brown eyes shimmering from the glow of the brazier set in the hall's centre. "Yes, you're right, of course. Speak to your contacts, Iren. I will confer with Lord Sándor. We will need the aid of the Wolfblood Clan if the cultists are gathering. Should these extremists wish to purge our witches of their magic, they will find themselves a fight."

I stared at my mother in awe, wondering who this warrior woman was before me. I followed the motion of her hand moving

to her hip, and my eyes widened at the sword sheathed at her waist. The pommel bore the insignia of the Wolfblood Clan and a generous ruby worked into the gold hilt. A wolf indeed. The sword itself seemed to be of fine make, though I wouldn't know for sure unless wielding it.

Whatever relationship my mother and father shared with Lord Sándor, it was a generous one.

Despite the drab brown skirt she wore and the worn shawl about her shoulders, I might have mistaken her for a noblewoman with the sword at her hip and the raised chin. A woman of fine stock.

Had she ever been to battle? Where did the sword come from, and why did she wear the táltos insignia? Mama had never married Father, had never taken his name, but she never spoke of him either. And Caitlin's words ...

There was more to this story. So much more.

The voices of the elders faded as I turned, sinking into the bush. My heart pounded like a war drum, the breath rattling from my lips.

We were Bárány women. Strong and stubborn and proud.

But we didn't keep secrets or lie to each other, right?

Never.

NINE

The village was a tapestry of colour, woven from mother nature and the careful fingers of my witch kith. The last snow had long since fallen and the days grew longer, bright with the sun's golden rays. Our garden had burst to life with renewed vigour, petals unfurling and vines curling free from their coils.

The apricot-coloured tulips were my favourite. Orange was a peaceful colour, vibrant and happy. It allowed no room for darker thoughts, unlike its red brethren planted farther along the gate.

Frowning, I gazed at the picturesque scene before me, studying witches who smiled and tittered as they walked arm-in-arm, new ribbons in their hands. Others weaved flowers through the maypoles or hung fabrics from rooftops and street signs so that they fluttered in the breeze.

Happiness. And ignorance.

This was the season of new. Only, this year, my every step

 105

carried the fear of the unknown. For fanatics to come blazing through our homes or for more girls to go missing. Weeks had passed with no sightings, nor the slightest hiccup from the usual plodding pace of our quiet town. Fear paddled in the pit of my stomach, churning the waters of my well every day as I waited for a sign. For an attack.

Life for all but a miserable few remained as normal as ever. The elders hadn't told the witches about the cultists, keeping Hanna's murder silent. Mama, after arguing at length with Caitlin about it, had all but told the crone to go shove her lies where the sun doesn't shine, refusing to be the bearer of deception. She had said Hanna's mother deserved to know the truth. It seemed Caitlin had no qualms feeding the woman lies instead.

I sighed, shaking my head. Since finding Hanna, I'd been under strict orders not to leave the village, or to do anything untoward—to do anything at all if Caitlin had her way. It was ridiculous, but maybe a little warranted. Naturally, the woods called, as did my need for answers and, in idle moments, my thoughts strayed to the táltos with his damnable dimple and that devilish smile.

Why was he on my mind at all? He was a secretive asshole and I was quite comfortable with never seeing him again. I certainly shouldn't be wasting my time dreaming about those pants on that impeccable ass of his.

I sighed. Still, thinking about him was better than the

alternative—I still couldn't get past the lies my mother had told. I groaned, trying to force those thoughts from my mind. But unlike most things my mother served me, this was hard to swallow. Too hard to ignore. If I didn't find answers soon, my head would explode.

Nudging a pebble with my boot, I set off down the path, leaning into the waning sunlight as it kissed the horizon. Spying on the elders a few weeks ago had made me paranoid and jumpy. The thought of fending off fanatics had me on edge so, naturally, I had asked Erika to up my training and teach me the way of the sword.

She hadn't asked why. I hadn't offered.

And as much as I wanted to interrogate her for more information regarding the cultists, I let sleeping dogs lie. In return, she kept quiet, training me in the early hours or just before dusk, before or after magic tutelage, history, and letters. We practiced in a clearing within the woods, after she made me swear to come alone and keep my mouth shut, of course.

Donning my hood, I glanced around one last time before entering the woodland border. The treeline beckoned with waving fingers, their branches shifting in the late afternoon breeze, green buds sprouting and blossoms bursting.

Their shadows swallowed me whole as I winded through roots and trunks, eyes scanning the forest floor, ears alert. The cultists may be watching, gauging our activities from afar and that helplessness had my stomach churning again. When had I become so afraid?

A twig snapped somewhere ahead and I stilled, spine rigid. Both hands gripped the twin daggers on my thighs. My heart thumped beneath my bones, so loud I feared it would sing the song of my doom. Not a single animal disturbed the stillness, nor could I spy any threats.

My breath caught as a figure swept out from behind the tree before me, their blade swiping through the air. Sucking in a breath, I bent backwards, the sword sweeping through the space my head had been just seconds before.

Instinct kicked in, my body firing with adrenaline. Grunting, I swept my leg out, hoping to catch the perpetrator off guard. But they were too quick, vaulting backwards before charging again. My daggers nestled into my flesh, my fingers wrapping lightly around the hilts.

I had a split second to make a quick decision. Try to deflect and allow them within my guard, or throw the blades and risk losing any protection? I chose the latter. Breathing deep, I steadied myself before firing both blades in quick succession.

My opponent's sword swatted them like flies without losing momentum, the blades clanging uselessly to the ground. Shrinking back, I altered course, heading for the tree behind me. My attacker seemed to know my path before even I did, stretching out their boot to clamp my own to the ground. I faltered, stumbling as they repeated the action on my other foot.

When their blade met the naked flesh beneath my collar, I

froze, hands rising in supplication. My attacker tutted as they lowered their sword and pushed me from their chest.

"Sloppy," Erika grinned as I turned. "Don't let your thoughts consume you, Kitarni. Your body betrays every emotion, and a quick study is soon a dead one."

I glared daggers at my tutor, but even they missed their mark. Sighing, I raked a hand through my braid, straightening my spine as I looked at the canopies surrounding us. "Hardly a fair fight," I scoffed. "I'm armed with toothpicks while your blade is sharp as a teenage princeling's prick."

Erika inclined her head, the sun splintering through the trees to form a halo effect on her dark skin. "Charming."

I curtsied with a dramatic flourish. "Thank you."

Erika unsheathed the spare sword at her waist, throwing the blunt blade without a care. The sword could barely scratch an itch, let alone skewer someone, but oh, how it still bruised. My ribs were black and blue from her endless prodding.

"Ready your blade, girl. Show me what you've learnt." Bracing myself, I altered my stance, holding my sword against my chest and charging. "No," she said, batting my blade down. "By the Blessed Lady's tits, do you want to impale yourself before the fight even begins?"

Erika thwacked me in my gut for good measure and I doubled over, wheezing as the breath left me. She flicked her long braids over her back, her brown eyes glittering with amusement in the waning sun.

And so began the dance. We moved to that rhythm for a long, painful hour, Erika barking at me for every misstep, her blade punishing my flesh for every unguarded movement or slow manoeuvre. When we finished, I collapsed on the mossy ground, legs unfolding beneath me, sweat pouring down my face and back in rivulets.

She tossed a waterskin to me and I drank greedily, flopping on my back when I'd had my fill. Erika joined me after a moment, stretching her long legs out beside me. The evening air was brisk on my heated body and I welcomed its cooling kiss. Swivelling onto my side, I glanced at Erika's gleaming dark skin, the secrets hidden beneath her lips and eyes.

She was a stunning woman. Impossibly beautiful bone structure, full lips and cunning eyes—eyes that had seen the best and worst of the world. She came from lands far south of the Kingdom of Hungary, sold off to a lord like chattel and, like a humble daughter, she had accepted her fate. But she had not stayed silent for long. I knew only that her husband had been an abusive, terrible man. A dead one, now. And whatever Erika had endured at his hands, her skin was thicker for it, her steel will unyielding.

I admired her strength.

Her family were nomads, so I suspected she would never see them again, feel the comfort of a hug or a softly spoken word. I hadn't asked if that was good or bad in her books. Erika didn't dwell on her past, only looked to the future. Pragmatic as ever and wise to the ways of the world. The witches respected her, even if she was a little hard to befriend. I think she preferred the quiet and, honestly, her no nonsense manner and strong opinions kept most people in line and on their toes.

And though she was a hard woman, Erika was never unjust. She treated me as an equal, listened to my views. That's all I'd ever wanted, really. Mutual understanding. I'd never been one to pry, but after her generosity in training me, after the silent questions never asked, I felt compelled to know her better, to hear her story, so I started with something easy.

"Why did you first come to our village, Erika?"

Her eyes widened slightly, and I thought she wouldn't answer at first, but after a time her lips curled in sadness, her face morphing into the look of someone lost in painful memories.

"I could tell you the story of my life, but I'm afraid we'd be up until morn, speaking of things best left forgotten. I suppose I simply sought a new beginning. My heart yearned to belong, but after the many messy, bloody years, I had yet to find a home. A sanctuary." She sighed, eyes glazing as she shook her head. "No place is ever truly safe, it would seem."

I didn't need to ask to know she meant the cultists. We weren't safe, not by a long shot. "After you left his lordship's manor, how did you come to be in our village?"

A soft smile curved her cheek, a genuine fondness tugging the corner of her lips. "It was Anna's kin who showed me redemption. Elena was my lady's maid, my confidante. She stayed

111

by my side through it all, even after—"

She faltered then, brown eyes hardening to stone, jaw clenching. Erika's chest heaved with the strain of that memory. Of the moment she killed her late husband, I presumed. I could only imagine why she'd snapped. And the dark part of me thrilled at knowing the world was free of one less tyrant. Another abusive man in power. The kind where crimes lay concealed in shadows and money could seal even the most wagging of tongues.

"When his lordship departed this world," Erika continued, "Elena helped me cover my tracks and, at the end of it all, she urged me to come here. To a sanctuary where I would never have a hand laid on me again, never have to hide who I truly am. A place I could call home."

Her eyes were wet with unshed tears, and I smiled, clasping her hand in support. "Our home is all the brighter to have you in it. I hope those ghosts have long since left."

"They haunt me still on sleepless nights, but the weight is easier to bear with Elena by my side. Her warmth staves off the chill of dead men walking."

My brows shot up my temple. Erika and Elena were a couple? My heart softened like a fluffy blanket. It seemed so obvious I could only chuckle. "I must be blind to have not realised sooner. I'm happy for you both, and I'm glad you found each other."

She smiled again and this time it was full of genuine warmth. "You are a special one, Kitarni. Your veins sing with power, your heart beats to its own drum."

Erika always had a way with words. Pride swelled in my chest, but the disapproval of my peers washed over me, snapping that momentary comfort. Caitlin's upturned nose, the jeers and jaunts of my fellow witches, my mother's pitying eyes every time I returned home after yet another humiliation. A stain that spread to my family name.

"Maybe being different isn't a good thing," I sighed. "No one knows the rhythm, no one understands me. The elders, even the girls my age, they see me as strange. A problem child who needs to be collared and my leash pulled when my actions offend others."

My tutor sat up, pulling me with her. She tilted my chin gently, looked into my eyes without judgement. "People push away what they don't understand, accepting the norm—the safety in the familiar. In this witch, human, any other supernatural creature, we are all the same. You push boundaries and sing unsung truths, Kitarni. Only the brave bear the weight of purpose. Only the brave don their sword and armour, battling for a better world."

I thought about my future then, wondering what awaited and whether my boundaries might lie within this forest forever. Or, perhaps, if the wide world beyond would take me lovingly in her arms. Where I could stand firm in my beliefs, where I could wander at will.

If we survived. If my future *husband* didn't keep me caged and bound by law. Unmarried witches had freedom of choice at least,

but I would have no such luxury. Bitterness coated my tongue and sorrow welled within, swelling to fill every crevice, every hollow of my being.

"And what is the weight of *my* purpose, Erika?"

She tilted her head, her long brunette braids falling over her shoulder. "Only Fate can tell you that, little warrior."

Wrinkling my nose, I snorted in distaste. "Oh, I'm counting on it."

Foliage rustled and the sound of leaves crunching underfoot had us both stiffening. I straightened, straining my ears and holding my breath as I glanced at Erika. "Did you hear that?" The woods were dark now, the trees looming high above, their long nails raking at the air.

Slowly rising, we drew our steel blades—Erika with her short sword gripped tightly in hand—my throwing knives splayed and ready to throw in succession. Twigs snapped in multiple directions. "An ambush," Erika mouthed. "Make ready."

I nodded resolutely, altering my stance, waiting. The hairs on my arms raised and my mouth dried as a bloodcurdling scream pierced the air, following a hooded woman sprinting into view. Her billowing black robes made her look like a wraith borne on a phantom wind and, behind her, more followed, daggers and clubs raised in palms carved with an inverted pentagram.

Others circled, trapping us within a sea of black. They moved with predatory slowness, faces hidden beneath their shrouds. My traitorous heart pounded as fear sluiced through my veins.

Cultists. Come to claim more girls? Or perhaps to spill the blood of those who shirked their order.

Sparing a glance to Erika, I took courage in her calm. Her face was almost serene, eyes bright and jaw set. She rolled her neck, squaring her shoulders as she held her blade aloft in careful fingers, the wiry muscles in her slender arms flexing as she stared down our attackers.

"We need spill no blood today. Leave now or face the truth of my blade."

The cultists only laughed and I suppressed a shiver at their dry tones, the strange, garbled sounds. In answer, they raised their weapons, the steel shining in the moonlight.

The fear writhing through me turned to panic and I willed my hands to remain steady, smoothing my face into a blank mask. The air rattled from my lungs in shuddering gasps and I forced myself to breathe. I had never fought another witch with magic before. Not like this. And I knew the cultists would take no prisoners today. It was my life—my very essence—they would drain, else I slicked the forest floor with their blood.

Could I kill another? My teeth gritted together, eyes burning with determination as the answer came in barely a blink. To save my sister and mother from these fanatics? I set my jaw, nudging the beast within me. *Yes.* I would do anything. Magic thrummed through my bones, setting my blood on fire, humming as if in answer to my question. That dark power in me uncoiled, awakening from slumber. *Fight,* it seemed to whisper. *Destroy them all.*

The allure of my magic called to me, a slick and oily power burning through my veins, and for a moment I forgot the world. A part of me ached to set it free and harness that power. *I wanted to let it loose.* To see the destruction it could wreak and to see the cultists burn like those wolves had. A small smile curved my lips.

"Kitarni."

I blinked several times, finding myself planted firmly in reality again. What had just happened? Erika's eyes crinkled as she looked at me.

"Focus," she barked.

I shuddered, shaking my head to clear it. Disgust curdled in my belly as I realised how close I was to losing myself. I shoved that dark power deeper, ignoring the low hum inside me as I gripped my blade tighter. Summoning a fireball in my free palm, I offered a grim smile to the cultists. Let them see the conviction in my eyes, the readiness of my body.

The first moved so fast I barely had time to dodge the blade in their hands and, sidestepping, I wheeled, slamming my elbow into the back of their head. They crumpled to the floor and I moved to my next target, sending a blade whistling through the air to sink into the soft flesh of their belly.

Erika whirled with grace, her sword flashing as it arced down on one cultist's spine before slashing the exposed ribs of another. Muted cries rang out as blood misted over the clearing. Orange lit up the night as I threw fireballs to scatter the group, vaulting out

116

of the way as a club swished past my head. I sent another dagger hurtling through the air to implant into the cultist's chest.

They toppled to the ground, clutching at the hilt embedded in their breast. Adrenaline fuelled my blood, my nerves tingling with the thrill of a fight. Later, I'd question that feeling, shiver at the power snapping hungrily at its leash. But now, my instincts silenced all things, the need to survive blanketing all else.

A sharp pain sliced through my leg, a thin scrape sending warmth trickling down my thigh as the cool air sighed upon naked flesh. Grimacing, I turned to the cultist and, as the moonlight glanced off their features, horror squeezed my heart.

Eyes as black as a bottomless sea glittered from a pale face, the colour blanched from the papery skin. He'd sewn his lips shut. Botched needlework piercing through infected flesh of swollen red and oozing yellow. Vomit climbed my throat as I stared, momentarily rooted by shock.

"Kitarni," Erika roared, shaking me from my daze. I wasted no time twisting out of the way as a screaming woman—presumably the leader—fell upon me. We rolled in a tumble of limbs, her spittle flying on my face, her arms strong as we grappled. She was a small woman, but her strength was unyielding as she pinned me to the ground and straddled me.

Her elbow jammed into my throat and stars flashed before my eyes as my lungs expanded, my airways blocked and head pounding with exertion. She raised a rusty looking blade, the steel stained by blood but still deadly sharp. And, putting all her

weight into the motion, she stabbed the blade towards my face. I barely blocked her attempt, my arms wobbling as I wrapped my hands around hers, the blade falling like a hammer ever closer to my eye. And all the while she screeched, her ungodly wails raising the hair on my arms. Wild, berserk, and *so strong.* I was fading out of consciousness and I heard another voice yelling at me to fight. Far away, as if in a dream, yet commanding enough to heed. With one last surge of strength, I jerked one fist out, slamming it into the woman's throat.

She reared back, choking, and my own throat opened again, coughs spluttering from my lips. Her dark eyes widened as I plucked the last dagger from my belt and plunged it into her heart, angled just under the ribs. Blood dribbled from her lips, and right before the last sigh left her mouth, she smiled, voicing three words that turned my blood to ice.

"She will rise."

I sat there staring at her limp body, the blood pooling from her fatal wound. Chaos unfurled behind me, Erika gliding over the clearing with finesse, her sword a blur of steel. Black-robed bodies dotted the clearing, and blood ... so much scarlet on green blades of grass.

All I could think about was the blood on my hands, the death I'd wrought today. My fingers shook as I breathed deep, smelling copper in the air, tasting metal on my tongue. Moans sounded around me. The gargles and cries of the dying soon silenced once Erika drove her blade home for the last time.

 118

Only one remained. A thin man buried in drapes of sable threads, eyes of the same inky hue, lips pulled back in a sneer. He struggled beneath Erika's unwavering grip, thrashing like a madman as she tied his hands with a strip of torn cloth. The sight of him churned my stomach, disgust settling like a stone in the pit of my soul.

"If you don't sit still, I'll slit your throat and throw you to the wolves," Erika growled, shoving him to his knees. She spared me a glance, eyes crinkling with worry as they lingered on my wound. "Are you okay?"

Adrenaline still coursed through me, numbing the pain, but as I looked at the crimson staining my brown leggings black, I grimaced at the fresh wave firing up my thigh. "I'll be fine." I jerked my head at our captive. "What's to become of him?"

A guttural sound came from his throat, but she merely kicked him in the sniffer, crunching cartilage and bone. Blood streamed from his broken nose. "That depends on whether or not this filthy bloodborne is going to share."

At my puzzled frown, she gestured at the man's robes, the star painted on his palm. "It's what we call the cultists devoted to Sylvie. We no longer recognise them as witches or warlocks. They turned their backs on our faith long ago, dishonouring our magic and birth right. Our purity."

Rising from my position, I towered over the man as he leered at me, his gaze lingering a little too long. Shoving the hood back from his head, I studied him closely. Long black hair hung limply

to his shoulders, making his pale skin seem even ghostlier in contrast. Upon closer inspection, I noticed the dilation of his pupils, the sweat beading his temple and the blood thumping impossibly fast in his veins.

"They've taken some kind of potion," I informed Erika, chewing on my lip. "It might explain their strength and speed, but gods only know what kind of drug could heighten such things."

Erika's face blanched. "I think I might. There's a fungus deep within the Sötét Erdő that thrives in darkness. It's said to give users a rush—to amplify their senses. When combined with blood, they can distil it into a potion that enhances one's strength, their speed, their agility. It's called bloodmorphia."

"Distilled with—with blood?"

She nodded gravely. "A practice invented by the bitch queen herself."

I shivered. "You're saying these leeches are drinking us, too? Sucking us dry like fucking vampires? Witch's tits, that's insane." I glanced at the man before me, toeing him with my boot. "Is there anything you maniacs don't do?"

He said nothing and somehow the silence was more unnerving. Anger boiled inside me, bubbling to the fore. That dark power rose within, almost stifling in its need to be free, but I clamped down on that feeling, lest I lose myself ... and our only lead.

"Speak, wretch," Erika hissed, slapping the man hard across the face. "Why are you taking girls from our village? Where is the

cult hiding?" His silence was deafening in the stillness and I watched, holding my breath as my tutor leaned in, her blade pressed to his gut. Anger blazed in her brown eyes, her lips set in fury. Hers was the face of a warrior now. An executioner who knew no mercy. "Tell me where you're hiding. What spells you're using to drain our girls."

A muffled moan escaped his lips as she drew him close, her blade sliding home. Still, he said nothing. I might have admired his determination had so much not been at stake, but nausea filled me instead, my head still faint from air loss earlier.

Blood gushed from his wound as Erika pulled her sword loose and he doubled over in pain, head bowed before her. Erika's nostrils flared in irritation, her fingers tightening on the sword hilt. And to my surprise, the bastard started laughing. A mocking, cruel sound that seemed muffled. *Wrong.*

Pulling one of my daggers from a cultist's chest, I stalked back to the man and glowered down at him, reaching in with my blade. Hesitating, I glanced at Erika, who nodded once. She positioned her sword over the man's privates. "Move an inch, and your Dark Queen will find herself a eunuch in her army."

That earned a reproachful glare, but the man stayed still as I parted his lips with the flat of my blade. He clamped his teeth shut. "Open your damn mouth," I barked and, with a broad grin, he slowly opened his jaw.

I flinched at the open cavity before me. He was tongueless, nothing but blood and pink gums riddled with veins. The man

only laughed with that strange sound, not a laugh at all, but a strangled cry of victory.

We were right where we started. Nothing to go on, no information to glean, only the knowledge the cultists were growing bolder and our village was very unsafe. I paced away from the fanatic before me, raking fingernails through my hair and pulling until it hurt. "What now?" I asked helplessly.

Erika lunged, cleaving her blade through the air so fast I could barely blink before the cultist's head toppled from his body, silencing that mocking tone forever. She wiped her blade clean on her tunic, sheathing the sword before turning to me. "There could be others circling the village. We need to get back and inform the patrols. I'll report to the elders."

I grabbed my daggers from their fleshy cages before looking her square in the eyes. "And me?"

She sighed. "Go home, Kitarni. Rest, hug your loved ones. Pray these fanatics do not bother us again tonight."

I gave her a weak smile. "Mama might put up more of a fight than this lot. She'll be furious upon seeing me in this state."

Erika stalked towards me, placing a warm and sturdy hand on my shoulder. "The time for punishments and stern words is over. Her cub became a wolf, a girl no longer. You've shed blood now, Kitarni. It won't be the last time."

We hurried home and I mulled over her words, knowing the truth in them. We were four feet in shite. The time for silence was over. The cultists had made their move, which meant the head of the snake was rearing, venom spreading fast.

As we parted ways on the village boundary and Erika threw me a quick wave before dashing off to her duties, I could think only of the words that cultist had said before I killed her. The conviction in them would stay with me. A haunted lullaby to sing me to sleep.

She will rise.

TEN

Lavender, rose, and bluebell ribbons whispered in the light breeze, streaming down from trees dotting the village. Flowers in lemons and reds and whites curled around maypoles, and petals crunched under bare feet as women danced.

Eszter grabbed my hand with glee, giggling as she pulled me along the path, winding under arches and around girls as they laughed and made merry. Earth witches weaved their magic, sprouting new life in green vines and smiling flowers.

It felt surreal to be here after last night. Life and love and unhindered happiness—the very things those cultists sought to steal from us. I'd barely slept a wink, instead curling up on my bed, shivering not from cold, but shock, and the realisation I'd killed someone, no matter that it was self-defence. I could still see the blood on my hands now, despite having scrubbed them red, raw, and squeaky clean.

I'd almost let the monster inside me loose and I could still feel the pull of my darker power. It was like a low ache in my chest—like an itch I couldn't scratch—begging to be released. I wondered what I'd become if I gave in to it. Would I lose myself to its pull? Would it change me at my core, take me on the path that the Dark Queen went down?

My skin prickled at the thought and I shuddered as a cold draft wrapped its hands around my shoulders. The thought of becoming anything like Sylvie *terrified* me and the mere idea of it sent spiders crawling down my skin and my heart galloping.

Am I being paranoid? Would it be so bad to try to harness that power? If I did, I might be able to use it to protect my people. Use it for something good.

I gritted my teeth. More questions I didn't have answers to.

Surprisingly, Mama had said nothing when I'd told her what happened with the cultists last night. She had only sat quietly after ushering me into a warm bath, soaping the gore from my hair, the blood on my skin and under my nails. Erika had been right. She didn't berate me for disobeying her rules, didn't scream or shout. Instead, she seemed resigned, sorrowful.

Did she judge me?

Last night changed me. I had killed. I would never be her little girl again. And perhaps that was a good thing. Too long had I suffered the ills of others, the reprimand of my elders, the gossiping of my peers. I was a warrior. Last night had proved my gifts were not to be squandered or laughed at and I had to believe I could use them for the greater good. *Yes.* My magic was

protection. Power.

My lips lifted at that. Caitlin begged me to be a sheep, but I was a wolf, and I would howl loud and proud.

Eszter nudged me from my thoughts, her brown curls gleaming with gold beneath the sun streaming down on us. She was so beautiful. Lips painted red, a flower crown in her hair, white dress flowing to reveal slender legs and bare feet.

Mama dressed me similarly. I wore a fitted bodice of white, sage coloured thread weaving intricate patterns lining the seams and tying the corset at my back. Mama had washed my hair with lavender-scented water last night and curled my hair until it damn well obeyed. She had finished with crushed rose petals, painting them upon my lips and adding a gentle blush to my cheeks. Kohl lined my eyes and, when I'd looked upon my reflection in the mirror, I hadn't recognised the girl looking back.

A pleasing reflection. Even if my muscles held a tightness, my eyes were a little darker than usual. And though a sadness still glimmered in Mama's eyes when she gazed upon her work, there was pride there, too, as she looked upon me this morn. She had leaned in close, placing a kiss upon my brow. "Do you know what today brings, my child?"

I had nodded slowly before raising my chin high. "I am to meet my suitor. Today shall mark the first step towards our marriage."

Mama had smiled then. "I'm proud of you, Kitarni. I know this isn't what you want, nor what you would have chosen for

126

your future, but this matrimony will bind our peoples together. You honour your father by continuing his legacy with a táltos."

I had stayed silent then, let her preen over my appearance as I'd mulled over my future. Marriage.

Arranged.

Fucking.

Marriage.

To someone I'd never met. Someone who might be as awful as Erika's now deceased bag of bones. Perhaps I'd do him in the same, I'd thought with amusement. But that had quickly fizzled, curdling deeper in my gut as the memories of last night once again flashed before my eyes.

Shaking myself of dark thoughts, I let Eszter drag me towards the dance and I could do naught but smile as she tapped her feet and clapped to the music, revellers around us lost to the sound of freedom. Golden balls of light twinkled around us, conjured by witches to suspend us in a cloud of golden dust. My worries fell away as the rhythm found my feet, climbing up my bones, my soul clinging to the joy of that pagan beat. These could well be my last days as a free woman.

So I allowed myself permission to enjoy. *To live*. And we danced. Me, wild and free, Eszter, graceful as a dove as she twirled and twirled until we were dizzy and laughing, hearts in our throats and fingers clasped in each other's.

When my temple beaded with sweat and I could bear the endless whirls no more, I stumbled off the grassy knoll to fetch a drink. Witches raided the inn and wine flowed freely today, everyone's cup filled. After a quick glance to ensure no one was watching, I sculled the contents of my cup and I wandered.

The day was still young, the weather sun-kissed but crisp. The smell of poached fruit climbed my nose, accompanied by the sweet scent of sugars and pastries. Treats lined stalls dotted through the town square and I busied myself with one of each, stuffing my face with sticky fingers.

Despite the merriment, I found myself atop the hill overlooking the town. I'd always welcomed the quiet, found peace in nature's gifts. But today, surveying the groups of girls laughing and dancing, the comradery on their faces, I'd never felt so alone. Were it not for the guards patrolling our village in droves, I might have ventured into the woods in search of the fae. Creatures who accepted me as I am. Who welcomed individuality and all kinds of magic.

"Not one for the crowds, I see."

I nearly shed my skin at the sound of a deep voice, one I recognised immediately. A thrill coursed through me as I turned and there he was. Brown eyes encircled in gold, dark hair that glimmered red in the sunlight, his face and jawline a sensual tapestry of sharp planes. My eyes lingered on his mouth as he smiled, a predatory gaze as he sized me up. "Hello, Freckles."

He dressed finely today—a white shirt beneath a black doublet, a silver brooch embellished with the symbol of the táltos clan clasping a fine grey cloak about his shoulders. Silver wrist

128

guards encircled his arms and a silver spaulder hugged one shoulder. But it was his blades that captured my attention.

Twin long swords were sheathed at his back, the steel covered in scripture too small for me to see from afar. The hilts held snarling wolves—a testament to his clan. Either the táltos had a highly talented blacksmith, or this weapon was a nod to a great man and perhaps an even greater house.

Who was he? Handsome, mysterious and rich too, apparently. The gear covering his exceptional body was expensive and certainly not something I'd have expected from a táltos. Were they not peasants like us? Did they have dealings with the world of men?

I scowled, remembering that the man beneath that perfect facade was a selfish, rude, arrogant asshole who I was perfectly content to go on hating. "I warned you not to come here again. Do you *want* to get stabbed?"

We still hadn't exchanged names, but there was something thrilling about playing with fire. The man was mysterious and—despite my better judgement—wildly intriguing. Besides, names formed attachments, and I didn't care to know him any better. I didn't have the luxury of growing close to anyone, not when a doomed marriage awaited.

He looked me up and down and my body burned beneath the weight of his gaze, but I refused to give him the satisfaction of hiding. He looked away dismissively. "If the last time I saw you is anything to go by, you wouldn't last a second in a real swordfight."

I rolled my eyes and huffed, turning my attention back to the town below. "I know you're trying to get a rise from me, but that would require me caring about what you think. Besides," I said with a smirk. "I wouldn't want you to get any scratches on those perfectly polished swords."

He chuckled darkly as he inched closer to me, his body warm, the scent of leather, earth and musk filling my senses. He smelt like a man, not like the boys I'd dallied with in the past.

I stepped away from him, annoyed I'd thought about him long enough to notice and unwilling to be cornered once again.

"Why do you stray from the festival?" he asked.

It was probably the most agreeable tone I'd ever heard from him—filled with curiosity more than anything—so I supposed it wouldn't hurt to divulge. Lifting my chin, I met his eyes unabashedly. "People don't agree with me. Never have."

He smiled knowingly, eyes glinting in the sun. "Because they know your power. And they fear it," he stated with a tilted head.

I blinked, the only sign I'd show of my surprise. He caught it all the same, that smile shifting into something devilish, a dimple carving through the stubble on his cheek. "I ... I'm not sure they're afraid of me. More that they misunderstand me. My magic is complicated. I don't share the earth trait like my sisters here."

"No," he said, his gaze burning into my own. "Your magic is much stronger." His face was blank as he said it, like that fact didn't bother him in the slightest. I expected a snide remark to follow, but my breath caught in my throat as he leaned over me, taking my chin in one calloused hand.

His touch sent waves of awareness tickling over my skin and his eyes enraptured my own. "No *proper* lady would enter the Sötét Erdő, brandish her blades, cutting through flesh like biting winds to bone. What you did to those wolves would impress the Wind Mother herself. Of course, you couldn't best me in a fight." He shot me a sly grin, creeping a little closer. "Aren't you going to apologise for accusing me of murder? The fact I'm still standing here must mean you've realised I was telling the truth."

I did feel a *little* guilty about jumping to conclusions, but it wasn't as if he'd acted like a saint. No, he'd gone all savage on me and pinned me to a tree instead.

I summoned fire, threading it through my fingers as I cocked my head. Apologise to that asshole? "I'd sooner burn at the stake," I replied sweetly. "If you like, I can arrange one for you too. The flames don't care if you're a táltos or a witch. We're all just blood and bone in the end."

His expression darkened as he gazed at my fire. Oh, how easy it was to push his gilded little buttons. I had to bite down on my laugh, but the victory smile fell from my face as my mind drifted to Hanna.

Visions of her body assailed me. The rot, the caved-in chest and milky eyes. And I didn't dare forget the fact her heart had been carved out like a bloody stuck pig. I hadn't forgotten about her, but I hadn't mourned her loss either. Still ... Guilt speared through me as I glanced at the stranger. He'd been her lover, for

131

gods' sakes, and here I was playing whatever game this was between us.

I didn't know why he'd sought me out, but I hadn't exactly told him to leave yet either. He was an asshole, but he was attractive as all hell. As much as I tried to deny it, my body came alive around him.

Even when we'd fought in the woods, my body had thrilled at his touch—at the danger—and that was wrong in so many ways.

I closed my fist and the magic extinguished. My mind turned to the dark power within, to the cultists I'd killed. I supposed there were many things wrong about me. My sanity was ripping apart and my power, my heritage? It was at the centre of it.

"I wish I was like the Wind Mother," I whispered in response to his earlier comment. "With her power, I could destroy the cultists, blow this mess away. The witches here aren't prepared for a fight."

The man moved a little closer, his warmth heating my skin. "We received a missive from Lady Bárány. Dark days lie ahead for the witches, but the clan will answer your call. The soldiers will fight for the coven—to preserve the alliance between our peoples."

Thank the gods, the táltos was a handy news source, if nothing else.

I breathed a sigh of relief, allowing my muscles to relax ever so slightly, but the shadow of yesterday still clouded my thoughts. "They attacked last night. Ambushed Erika and I in the woods." My voice sounded small to my ears. Weak.

"Hadúr's blade."

A bitter laugh escaped my lips. "The god of war doesn't care for our troubles."

His face darkened as he looked me up and down. "Were you hurt?"

I smirked. "You almost sound like you care."

A low rumble that sounded suspiciously like a growl rumbled from his chest. "Answer the question."

I rolled my eyes. "It's nothing I can't handle." Though, truth be told, my wound barked like a bitch in heat, throbbing angrily beneath the bandage on my thigh. The drink had dulled it some, but even with a dagger strapped to my other thigh, I felt vulnerable.

That devil's grin stretched upon his face as he approached, like a cat pouncing on his prey. "You lie." And, lifting my dress slowly up my leg, he perused the bandage, speckled with fresh blood and seeping into my frock.

"Well fuck," I sighed. "This is my finest dress." He ignored me, sweeping a steady hand up my thigh, so high I felt tingles where I had absolutely no right to. I should stop him. The immodesty of it, *the boldness* of his actions. Had anyone seen, it would ruin my reputation.

I snorted internally.

Of course, that would require having something to lose, and my reputation had already been burned and swept forgotten under a rug. "I'm flattered, táltos, but etiquette demands you

133

court a lady before looking beneath her skirts."

He grinned up at me, teeth flashing, and my heart might well have skipped a beat at that expression. A genuine smile. The táltos *does* have a heart.

I looked back towards the festival below. After his inspection, his fingers curled even higher up my leg, sending pinpricks over my skin. It took every effort to slap his hand away and paste a bored expression on my face.

"Your bandage needs changing, milady."

I snorted. "Oh, please, spare me the courtly dribble. You'll need it elsewhere."

He raised a perfect brow in answer.

"Caitlin Vargo," I explained. "She's the chief elder of our council and if she catches you cavorting with any ladies, she'll split your sack two ways from Sunday."

"You've quite the dirty mouth on you, Kitarni Bárány."

My eyes widened. "How do you know my name?"

"I know many things." He grinned, those stupidly perfect dimples curving on both cheeks as he turned to walk away. "Get that dressing looked at. Unless you'd like me to do it for you? I'm quite good with my hands."

My cheeks blazed again at the insinuation. Preposterous. A trap if I'd ever seen one.

My traitorous body thrilled at the idea. "Keep your dirty paws off. I can do it myself."

His eyes flashed once more before he stalked away. "As you

wish. See you at the festival."

Sighing in frustration, I watched him go with hands on my hips, sparing a glance at that impeccable ass clad in black leathers. I'd changed my mind. I needed to know who this damnable rooster was, if only so I could knock him on his ass. "*Who* are you?"

A dark chuckle was all that answered me.

ELEVEN

"By the gods," I groaned, leaning against Eszter. "I don't know how your feet aren't flayed to ribbons. You've been dancing all day."

My sister laughed as she curtsied before me. "You should try it, Kit. Do you even remember the concept of *fun?*"

I scowled. "Forgive me for not crying for joy about tonight. I can hardly dance with a partner of my choosing seeing as I'm to be married soon. Mama is to introduce us to Lord Sándor shortly, and I suspect he will be displeased if he's met with spoiled goods."

She rolled her eyes. "A simple dance is hardly a romp among the sheets."

"Well, colour me impressed! My little sister grows bolder as the hours grow later. If Caitlin heard that potty mouth of yours, she'd send you to a nunnery swifter than a priest getting his bells tolled."

It was Eszter's turn to purse her painted lips. "She's busy

cosying up to the Wolfblood leaders. We're safe from her dragon's breath for now. Come, dance with me, before—"

She stopped herself, but I knew the words she wouldn't say. "Before I'm carted off to become someone else's property?" I snapped.

Eszter's shoulders drooped, her eyes glimmering with unshed tears. "What will I do without you?"

Softening, I placed a hand over her own. "You will carry on, dear flower. Who knows, you might have a match of your own soon. A new adventure to embark on. I've seen you dance the night away with all those eligible bachelors, their jaws have been dragging on the floor, along with some drool, I think."

Her face brightened again. "My dance card *has* been full. Thank the gods. An older gent keeps trying his luck and I haven't had the heart to tell him to keep his sweaty paws off." She spared a glance at a rotund balding man, his scalp so shiny I wondered if it would reflect other surfaces. Catching her gaze, he smiled and bowed, and Eszter quickly looked away. "Please, Kitarni, I'm too young to die."

"So dramatic." I rolled my eyes. "But it would appear your next suitor will do quite nicely."

A young man a little older than me bowed before he approached and I nodded with approval. His eyes were the amber of smooth honey, gentle and kind. Full lips complemented a straight nose and his royal blue jacket, leggings and hose clad his dark skin like a glove. His countenance was most pleasing to look

137

at and he seemed … honest. A person's eyes reveal much, and his were truthful—daring, even.

They sparkled as he looked upon us both, dipping his cap before replacing it in a rakish tilt upon his dark locks. "Milady. May I have the honour of this dance?" he asked Eszter, and I had every notion she used all her willpower to avoid squealing.

"Go," I whispered, nudging her gently. "Have fun."

They disappeared into the crowd, arms looped around each other, swept away on the silken wings of butterflies and soft promises. My heart swelled with happiness for her. She was young, beautiful, overflowing with innocence.

These past weeks had been confusing for the Bárány house. I hadn't wanted Eszter to feel the sharp sting of sorrow, nor to feel the cold clutch of fear. But the cultists were only beginning their dark work. And I knew their rot would spread, corrupting our serene waters with misery and death.

This festival was a boon for her, to enjoy life's simple pleasures, to simply forget for a while. Táltosok flocked to her all day, bowing and scraping like beggars at a feast. As though she might bear them to her bosom like Istenanya herself.

Erika slunk through the crowd, sitting beside me with a world-weary sigh. She wore simple brown leggings and a vest over a white shirt, blades bound by leather to hips and legs. Her braided hair was coiled like a crown atop her head, eyes lined with kohl and sprinkled with dusted gold.

"Trouble?" I asked upon seeing her crinkled face.

138

"No sign of the cultists. But I think I'd rather take them on than deal with ... this." She gestured at the revellers partying, a frown marring her features.

I chuckled, patting her leg in understanding. "Trust me, the feeling is mutual. But they deserve this. Only the gods know how far the fall shall be. Their bubble is about to burst, their world about to be pulled at the seams."

"I'm still pissed Caitlin is keeping it all a secret," Erika growled. "The cultists might be licking their wounds today, but last night was a polite knock on the door. When they cross the threshold, they'll burn the house down."

My lips curled with distaste. "Keeping secrets will only add oil to their torches. Caitlin is a fool if she thinks they will not return in large numbers. What chance do we have when we're short an army?"

"Are we?" Her gaze slipped to a man who could be none other than Lord Farkas Sándor, leader of the Wolfblood Clan and, one day, my father-in-law.

He commanded attention. He had silvered hair, imposing dark brown eyes, and a jagged scar slicing from cheek to brow. The strong jaw and eyes were striking and strangely familiar, and he was tall and broad. Grizzly in appearance, though handsome still. A wolf, just like his namesake.

A stone lodged in my throat. "So an alliance will be forged."

She nodded once. "Our ties are ages old, and it all began with Sylvie. That treacherous bitch unknowingly brought coven

139

and clan together during the dark age. We were fledgelings then, our witches, the coven still in its teething stages as the elders sought to free witches before they burnt upon the pyres of men. But in joining with the táltosok, we were able to hunt down the cultists and capture Sylvie before she was put down. It was our alliance that allowed us to push the fanatics into hiding and found this haven."

Sipping my wine, I let that information slide down my throat, tasting the rich earthy tones of a smooth red. My mind wandered to what Sir Fucking Mysterious had said earlier today. *"Our soldiers will fight for you,"* he'd vowed.

"What makes you think the táltosok will join us once again?" I asked. "Why risk their men if the cultists are only targeting witches?"

"We don't know that for sure," Erika replied with a shrug. "My guess is Lord Sándor seeks vengeance for the death of his wife. He never confirmed if the cultists were behind the attack on Mistvellen, but I'd bet every coin in our coffers that they were. Even so, I have every confidence they'll fight for us. Because we have you."

I burst out laughing. "I didn't take you for a fool, Erika. I might be worth a pretty penny to my family—to secure them a comfortable life—but I'm worth less than the shit the king spits out every morning."

Erika studied me then, her gaze long and hard. And finally, she shook her head, pity filling the depths of her brown eyes.

 140

"My dear girl, you really don't know, do you?"

Frowning, I returned her fervent stare. "Know what?"

She sighed again, longwinded and tired. "You are special. You swim against a storm of ignorance, but you'll know the truth of it soon enough."

I blinked. "Wh—what are you talking about?"

But she was already gone, stalking into the throng of dancers. The music pounded my skull like a drum, her message repeating in my mind.

Just another question left unanswered.

Another puzzle to be pieced.

TWELVE

Mama had arranged formal introductions with Farkas and his brood to take place in the impressive gothic temple. We would meet beneath the gods in their house of worship, each of them looking down from stained glass windows. Isten, the Golden Father, ruler of the Middle World, and Istenanya, Blessed One, goddess of the moon, fertility and childbirth.

Their sons followed around the high walls. First, Napkirály, King of the Sun and rider of his beloved silver-haired horse. Second, Szélkirály, King of the Wind, charged with the winds, rain, and storms. And last, Hadúr, the god of war, also known as the blacksmith god, brilliantly imposing in his copper armour.

Ours was a world divided into three—the Upper, Middle, and Lower realm. The Upper World belonged to the gods, the sun, moon, and stars. Humans and various supernatural creatures like myself populated the Middle World, and below? None but the dead and the undying ventured there.

The brothers and sisters of the Holy Roman Empire would quake in their skirts and habits if they ever saw our pagan halls. Right before they set fire to the walls and burned all witches within it. Such was our blasphemy. The so-called devil's blood in our veins.

I studied the red carpet running the length of the hall as we walked, the oiled pews in their rigid rows. There weren't many. We thanked the gods with sacrifices and offerings, and most preferred to send gifts along rivers. Others left them within the woods as far as they dared tread—which was to say, not far at all.

Our coven was a superstitious lot. Fancy that.

We walked on silent feet, padding to an adjacent hall where the council took their meetings. And there he stood. The grizzled wolf himself—though, interestingly, his son was nowhere to be found.

Mama curtsied before him, graceful and elegant. She had dressed for the occasion, brown hair coiled into a coronet, a ruby dress of crushed velvet adorning her slim body. I didn't miss the pin with a wolf head on her breast. A sign of respect and loyalty. I also didn't miss the lingering look Farkas spared her.

She was a catch, sure and true.

"May I present Lord Farkas Sándor, chieftain of the Wolfblood Clan, baron of the realm."

Stone-faced, I filed that morsel away. *Baron of the realm?* Mama had never mentioned my suitor came from such good stock. His land must be extensive and he was powerful indeed if

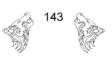

he had bannermen at his call.

The arrangement of marriage had likely been made years ago—perhaps even approved by my father. It suddenly made more sense. Lord Sándor's position in office afforded him power, wealth, the ears of the people. I'd be more than comfortable and, of course, Mama and Eszter would be cared for too.

But she had to know that, aside from my family's wellbeing, these were not things I cared for. Things I didn't need to be happy. A house, however gilded, was still a cage.

Eyes downturned, Eszter and I curtsied before his lordship. My sister executed hers like she was born to it, yet I stumbled, the wound in my thigh burning with the movement. The grizzled wolf caught me, his cutting gaze like knives upon my flesh.

His eyes raked over my features and I couldn't tell if he was valuing my worth as a woman or the sum of my person. I said nothing, but I knew my own eyes burned in challenge. In defiance. He only grunted as I stepped away and the good Nora Bárány quickly carried on with introductions.

"My firstborn, Kitarni," she said swiftly, placing steady hands on my shoulders. "And my youngest, Eszter. You honour us by journeying today, my lord, especially given circumstances of late. Please, take a seat."

Farkas nodded, swirling a goblet in his hand. "The days deepen with the shadow of dark magic, but rest assured, Nora, the táltosok will stand by your side in hour of need. But let's not talk of such matters. Today we pledge unity between our families and,

beneath the gods, family is above all things, sacred."

Mama dipped her head demurely. "On that, I can agree wholeheartedly." Her sharp gaze scanned the room. "Pray tell, where are your sons?"

Eszter and I shared a glance. So there was more than one sprat. A den of pups, then.

"They will be along shortly. I wished to speak with Kitarni first."

The wolf lord beckoned to a man standing silent and watchful behind him. Broad of chest, with long raven hair and dark eyes. I'd guess he was Farkas's second in command, judging by the black leathers, the steely gaze of a soldier.

The táltos listened intently as his lordship whispered in his ear, then departed with a polite nod to us women. Farkas took a long sip of his wine, eyes narrowed in thought. "Do you know why your mother and I arranged this courtship, Kitarni?"

"I've been asking myself why since Mama told me," I snapped.

"Kitarni," Mama hissed in warning.

"It's all right. I imagine this news must have come as quite a shock. But I want you to know, you will have your every freedom. This marriage does not bind you in any way beyond the oath of matrimony to my son. You will be respected, treated as an equal, protected as one of our own."

I took a breath, keeping my rising anger in check. "And if I refuse?"

Silence filled the chamber. "You don't want to do that." His voice was quiet, but it rang like a belfry all the same.

"And why not?" The words dripped from my tongue.

Farkas looked to my mother, his dark eyes searching. Questioning.

She wilted like a flower bitten by frost and, after a long minute, she nodded, her face stricken. Her eyes met my own, pleading, as if I might cast her aside like unlucky dice on a gambler's table.

"Kitarni," she started slowly, "your magic comes from a long line of powerful witches *and* táltosok. Your ancestors were among the first to find their power, long ago when the Middle World was a realm of supernatural beings and humankind were but bairns in a kingdom of magic. We believe you are the only living daughter left in a long lineage and, thus, you are blessed with gifts—the last of that line."

I nodded, chewing over her words. Whilst my magic scared me, it was a small relief to know its origin. If I could understand it, I might master it. But something else stood out like a beggar at feast. "What do you mean I'm the last? Why didn't it pass to you and Eszter?"

Mama swallowed, and the dread on her face, the colour draining from her skin ... I felt a million insects crawl over my skin, knowing her next words might change my world forever.

"Eszter and I cannot harness your power, my love, because it is not in our bloodline."

I shrank back as if slapped and the agony of her words rattled in my skull, shock numbing my body as I sank into frigid waters.

 146

A darkness pulled me deeper, no matter how hard I might paddle for the shore. I couldn't breathe, couldn't think. Eszter held my hand with a vicelike grip, but I felt nothing beneath that crushing squeeze.

Slowly, my gaze lifted to my ...

I didn't know what she was—*who* she really was. Her brown eyes filled with tears. I used to think they looked like mine, but it wasn't her blood running through my veins, her features on my face.

"Who?" I said quietly, one word heavy as sledgehammers in the stillness.

No one answered.

"By all the fucking gods, who is my mother?" I roared, slamming my palms upon the table as I rose.

Mama flinched and Farkas's hand strayed to his sword pommel. Aghast, I sat down quietly, only then noticing the bloodred misting around my palms, my silhouette darkening. They were afraid of me, I realised. Threatened by the dark monster within.

Taking a breath, I willed the magic to slow, the blazing anger dulling to a gentle simmer. The threads of my sanity began to fray as I waited. Tears filled my eyes, and Mama's—Nora's—spilled salty drops upon her cheeks.

She took a deep breath. "You are descended from the Dark Queen herself. Sylvie Morici."

The breath punched out of my gut, the fire filling my blood

now turning to ice, chilling me to the bone. My ancestor was a heretic. A fucking bloodletting fanatic. My fingers shook, and my stomach roiled, threatening to empty over the council table.

"And my mother?" I asked quietly.

Nora lifted her chin. "I am still your mother, Kitarni. I have always loved you as my own."

I snarled. "My *real* mother."

Another tear rolled down her cheek as her shoulders curved inwards. "We don't know. You were just a babe when I found you, red-cheeked and squalling in a bundle of furs near our home."

"And Papa?"

She stiffened, smoothing her skirts and avoiding my eyes. "His blood runs in your veins. He refused to speak of her, but you were conceived while he and I ..." She swallowed. "I think your father ended things with her because of me. Whoever it was, I think she wanted me to find you, so you could be raised in a coven with your own kind."

With a sigh, I shook my head. "I have been marked by Death. I am a slave to Fate. If what you say is true, the blood of the Dark Queen runs through my veins. Who do you think the cultists will come for next? Whose power will they drain once they have claimed me for their own?"

"They might not know about you, Kitarni. And even if they did, the gods will watch over you. We all will."

I barked a bitter laugh.

"The gods cannot protect me now. No one can."

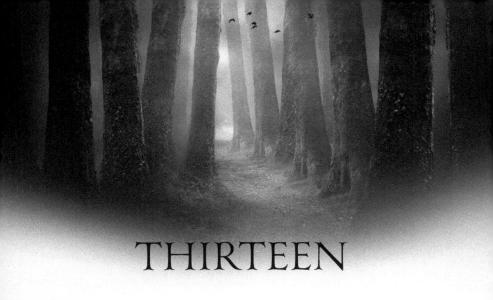

THIRTEEN

Tears streamed down my face as I turned my back on that chamber and the people within it. I ran blindly, tearing past lovers in darkened corners, skirting the square filled with drunken revellers.

My feet pounded the cobblestones of the town square, the flower crown upon my head falling to pieces as the petals unravelled one by one. My leg blazed with pain and I welcomed it, the harsh bite of agony as I stumbled away from partygoers. The music and the laughter of witches and táltosok alike.

My people. And yet not.

The slice to my thigh opened again, bleeding through my bandage and staining the white of my dress. It seemed fitting, in a way. I was far from pure. A killer in sheep's clothing. A dark and dangerous thing.

I welcomed the pain, feeling the burn as it rippled up my body, adding to the hurt in my heart. The dark creature—that child of chaos—it roared inside me. As if my newfound awareness of my ancestry gave it licence to unleash its talons and roam free.

It took everything ... everything I had to force it back into the cage. To quell my wrath, the rising need to hurt something or someone. Choking on my sobs, I ran as fast as my feet could take me, blindly trying to outrun my pain.

Before I knew it, I had crossed the treeline, finding myself surrounded by stalwart trees. Silent and steadfast. Their trunks blanketed the music in the distance and I slowed to a walk, eventually finding myself in the clearing.

Was it just yesterday I had been here, blades flashing and blood spilling? The earth was stained with scarlet, the only sign of a brawl now that the bodies had been taken away and burned. We always burned our dead and blessed them for their journey to the beyond, to the land of milk and honey the gods watched over. The cultists would have had no such service or ceremony. Erika must have seen to it last night.

May they rot in hell.

I should have been appalled, should have turned away from this place, now tainted with darkness. But instead I felt numb. Empty. Flopping to the ground, I lay on my back, staring up at the sea of stars above. It was a cloudless night and those jewels sparkled upon black velvet.

Boots sounded on the forest floor, loud and deliberate, and I knew who it was without looking. "Do I need to put a fucking bell on you?" I snapped.

He chuckled softly, stepping into the moonlight but, upon seeing my tear-streaked face, he halted, his eyes flashing with an emotion I couldn't place. "Rough night?"

I sighed, feeling too emotionally spent to battle with him right now. "You have no idea."

Leaning against a nearby tree, he surveyed me at length. "I might have an inkling."

Groaning, I twisted to my side, noting his gaze dance over my bare legs. I could have sworn his eyes flashed gold. Hungry. "Does the whole village know, then?"

"About your heritage? No. But your mother is looking for you. And his lordship."

Rising, I stepped towards the táltos, cocking my head. "And you came to collect like a loyal little messenger?"

His grin was devilish. "I come here of my own volition. I heard them talking, saw you sprint through the town like a hellhound. I wanted to see if you were all right."

Frowning, I took a step closer to him. "As if you give a shit. Will your master give his loyal dog a bone if you deliver me to him?"

He smirked, but he said nothing. I wanted him to bait me, to send my blood boiling so I'd have an excuse to start a war. He only raised his brow, as if he could tell what I was thinking.

I sighed, levelling him with a stony stare. "I just found out I'm descended from a psychopath, I'm most likely going to be hunted by cultists, and I'm also supposed to meet my betrothed tonight. So, yeah, I'm fucking overjoyed."

"There goes that dirty mouth again," he purred.

I growled, raking my hands through my hair before storming over and prodding a finger at his muscly chest. "Don't you have anything better to do? Why are you stalking me?"

"Believe it or not, little hellcat, but I don't find much pleasure in tormenting people. Well," he amended, "not when they're already down. It takes the fun out of it." He smiled slyly, but it didn't reach his eyes.

My skin heated, the power inside me building. Misty red began to swirl around my fists, and I opened my mouth to shoot a string of curses at him, but he went on, undeterred.

"I know what it is to feel lonely. To feel trapped, caged by the will of others, never free to make choices of your own. But it could be different for you, Freckles. You could run away now, elude your prison before the chains bind you and the cultists come to destroy all you hold dear."

His honesty made the magic fizzle from my fingers. I gaped at him in surprise, staring into his dark eyes, searching for the trap. I found nothing untoward in the seriousness of his posture.

"What are you saying? You want me to forget my duty? Steal off in the night like a coward?" I scoffed. "I will not abandon my family, and I certainly will not leave my kith to fight the threat of these cultists on their own."

His brow creased. "I'm not suggesting you run away. I'm saying I want you to make your own choices. While you still can."

152

Why was he being nice to me? It was unnerving and I almost wished he'd say something snarky so I could snap back. Him seeing me like this, it made me feel vulnerable. Weak. Like any moment he could ensnare me while my guard was down.

I searched his brown eyes, emotions flashing one by one in those orbs. A fierceness colliding with fear and, deeper still, *want*. My blood warmed at that expression, something hot and heavy jolting through my core.

I saw myself reflected in the golden rings—wild eyes, tearstained cheeks. My skin tingled at his nearness and, damn it, I did want to do something for myself. Something wild and reckless and utterly *stupid*.

And before I knew what I was doing, my lips crashed into his own, bruising in my need. If he was surprised, he didn't show it. His arms wrapped around me, his lips answering my kiss with equal fervour.

He pressed me to his chest and swept his tongue across my lip before I opened for him. Our tongues searched each other's, hungry for more and I fell into that bliss. His touch was fire to my skin, his kiss hot and heavy and all-consuming. I had kissed boys before but this? He devoured me, claiming my lips for his own and I answered with angry, passionate kisses. I drowned my rage, my sorrow, in this moment. My body sparked with desire, my core clenching as waves of pleasure swept downwards, erasing the thought of anything but this. Anything but us.

He groaned as I bit his lip and fisted my hand in his hair,

tugging his head back. Not a lover's gentle touch, but that of a woman who burned with anger.

One of his hands stroked my spine, the other curling round to my breast, his palm sliding between my bare skin and the dress. I gasped at the feel of his calloused hand and, even as my breasts begged for his touch, he didn't dare tread any further.

I might have lost myself in that moment. Rage still coursing through me, desire tearing through my blood. I was a careless, foolish creature, allowing the heat of my emotions to cloud my judgement.

Sensing my hesitation, he pulled back, tucking a stand of hair behind my ear as he gazed upon my face.

"I can't do this," I breathed, shoving him away. Already I missed his warmth around me, my body still pulsing with desire.

He tilted my chin up, commanding my attention. "You can do whatever you please, Freckles. Don't let anyone tell you different."

I snorted with frustration. "I can't do this"—I gestured between us—"whatever this is. I'm promised to another. If anyone saw us, my reputation would be ruined, my family's name dishonoured. The marriage would be annulled."

His teeth scraped my earlobe before he placed burning hot kisses down my neck, thumbs scraping my decolletage. I sucked in a breath, trying in vain not to sink into his touch. Never had I unravelled so quickly. His touch was sin, his kiss treacherous.

"Actually," he purred, still kissing my neckline. "You've done

nothing wrong, save for being unchaperoned with your intended." He looked down his nose at me. "If that's something you're afraid of your little elders seeing."

I blinked, his words dousing the pleasure vibrating through my body. A cold gust of air seemed to slam into my stomach. My mouth dried out and I licked my lips, staring at him incredulously.

"What did you say?" My voice was sharp as knives, low and dangerous. A feline smile curved his face as he let go, leaning once more against a tree. I ran a hand through my hair, pacing back and forth. "Is this a joke?"

"Actually ..."

My punch silenced him, pummelling into his rock-hard stomach before his stupid mouth could spout anything further. Instead of shock I found a wide grin on his face, a new kind of intrigue twinkling in his dark eyes. Was this all some joke to him? I felt played, toyed with like a cat's dinner. He wasn't concerned for me. He was damned well playing his own game.

"You," I snarled. "You knew who I was this whole time? Why didn't you tell me? You lied."

"Technically," he said with a raised finger, "I simply omitted the truth. I wanted to get to know you without the shadow of this marriage impacting your behaviour. And I must say, I'm intrigued by what I've seen so far."

"You can shove your technicalities up your ass. I hope you choke on them." Anger roiled through me, the dark magic I

inherited rising to my skin once again, the misty red now pluming around my body like a cape. He had the audacity to grin even further, not just one, but two dimples winking at me in encouragement. He was enjoying this, I realised. The insolent bastard.

"I know you're angry," he said, as if to a cornered animal. I couldn't blame him, I suppose. I was ready to tear his head off. "But even you can't deny I wouldn't have seen the real you had we not met before tonight's meeting."

"Perhaps not," I said grudgingly. "But it doesn't excuse your behaviour, past and present. You should have told me when we first met in the woods, not to mention you were fooling around with another girl, who is now dead." A wave of guilt roiled through me, followed by a sharp stab of jealousy, which angered me even more. Stupid, traitorous body. My nostrils flared as I looked at his spiteful, idiotic smirk. "I *still* don't know your name!"

"Say please," he crooned.

I wanted to rip that fucking grin off his face. Instead I crossed my arms, glaring daggers at that stupidly handsome smile.

He chuckled. "I suppose I owe you that much. Dante Sándor, son of Farkas Sándor and heir to the Wolfblood Clan." He bowed low, perusing me with far too keen an eye than he had a right to.

"Well, Dante," I said coolly, stepping so close my lips were but an inch from his own. I felt his eyes dip hungrily, his mouth parting on a breath. I turned, pressing myself against his pants,

 156

guiding his hands to my breasts. His arousal met my ass and I smirked, having achieved my goal. "I hope you're not looking forward to an amorous marriage, because I'm going to make your life a living hell."

I stalked away, leaving my husband-to-be alone under the starlit sky. Before I was out of reach, I heard his whisper on the breeze.

"I can't wait."

FOURTEEN

I sat cross-legged on my bed, Laszlo's head in my lap as I went over the night's events. He looked so peaceful as I stroked his velvet ears. Utterly oblivious to my problems. What I wouldn't do to feel such calm right now.

"What am I going to do, Laszlo?" I sighed, leaning back against my pillows. He cracked one eye open in answer, blinking lazily at me before dozing off again, soft, muffled snores sounding rhythmically.

In the space of a month my world had spiralled into a nightmare. Our haven was under threat of attack, our witches vulnerable to cultists wanting to spill their blood—or consume it. Tonight was ... it was too much. My mother had lied to me. Keeping me in the dark about my true heritage and power. She was one of two people in my small world I had always been able to rely on and trust.

Betrayal *hurt*. Twisting like a knife in my heart, bruising my

 158

shoulders as reality hit hard and fast. I had never felt so alone, never felt sorrow so keenly. Tears filled my eyes again as I considered how my upbringing had been shrouded in lies. My very existence birthed from monstrosity.

A shiver rolled down my spine. My ancestral line dated back to Sylvie Morici. The Dark Queen of destruction and terror. A heretic who blasphemed the gifts from our gods, who corrupted pure magic, turning it dark and devilish.

My mother was a cultist. Revulsion coiled in my stomach at the thought, but even knowing what she was, I still felt the sting of abandonment. She hadn't wanted me, leaving me as a baby for Nora to find instead. Why? Was it a way to protect me from the cultists or the act of carelessness? I sighed as I combed through my wet tangles. Even a fanatic had discarded me. It was no wonder I wasn't good enough for anyone in this town. Indifference seemed to run in my blood.

My thoughts turned to Dante. I was still furious about his lies but, frustratingly, I couldn't stop thinking about that kiss. Passionate and devouring. Was I imagining the fervent way he'd returned it? Why was I imagining it at all!? *We hate him, Kitarni,* I reminded myself. Sighing, I pressed my knuckles to my eyes. The thought of him filled me with confusion and annoyance. A good kisser he may be, but he was still an insolent ass.

I had kissed many boys over the years. On my escapades to the human markets—even when I was younger and táltos boys were still with their mothers before they journeyed to the clan to start their new life.

Such was the way of things. The way of our people. It had never really bothered me before, but with the táltosok visiting our village and the way witches lit up around them, it made me wonder.

Why rip families apart? Why not unite as one community instead of separating witch from táltos? It was something I'd have to learn more about. With more knowledge, perhaps I could abolish some of these archaic constructs. Do some good in my position as lady of the Wolfblood Clan.

A gentle knock on the door revealed my sister, hanging on the threshold as if afraid of what might happen should she enter. Another pang of sorrow fired through me. Did she hesitate because of where I had come from, or who I was?

"You look like a mare ready to bolt," I said softly. "I won't bite."

She padded in, lips still painted, flowers still coiled around her head. The young girl I remembered was set aside today. A beautiful woman stood before me, far too stern for my liking. Patting the bed, I watched her sink into the mattress, one hand drifting over Laszlo's sleek fur as she looked at me.

We said nothing for a time, staring at each other as if locked in a spell. When it seemed clear she hadn't the words to break the silence, I sighed, taking her hand in my own. "Eszter, everything Mama told us tonight ... it doesn't change our relationship. You are still my sister. My sunshine."

160

Her eyes welled with unshed tears and she bounced into my arms, nearly crushing Laszlo in the process. "I'm sorry, Kitarni," she sobbed. "I'm sorry for everything."

"Shh," I crooned, stroking her head. "None of this is your fault. You were left in the dark as much as I was."

"I can't imagine how sad you must be right now," she said, her voice muffled from where she pressed against my chest.

I leaned back, looking at her big brown eyes as they lifted. "Sad? I'm not sad, Eszter. I'm furious. Mama lied to us both. *About everything.* All those years she watched me struggle to find my place in this village. Every damned day I would come home in tears from the bullying of others. From feeling useless. She could have prepared me. Might have taught me what to expect from my magic."

My sister shifted in my arms. "Perhaps she has been lying to herself, too."

"What do you mean?" My brows scrunched together, wondering how my sister could possibly be casting a line for our mother.

"I mean," she said slowly, "perhaps she has been shielding herself from this knowledge all our lives. She loves you with her whole heart. You are not her blood, but you are more her daughter than your birth mother could ever claim. Maybe forgetting that was easier than facing it. Maybe she was trying to protect you from the pain of the truth. Once these things are said, they can't be taken back."

I sagged under the weight of that confession. Perhaps my sister's statement was wise, but it didn't make it right. It didn't make it fair or just that she kept this hidden. The truth hurts, but I'd rather face that fire a thousand times than live in darkness.

"Is she still at the festival?" I asked quietly.

Eszter nodded.

"Was she angry I missed the formal introductions?"

"Mama was too upset to be angry with you. She went to commune with the gods in the temple. His lordship retired not long after. I've no ken where your betrothed was."

An image of lips crashing together, wandering hands and arching bodies flashed before me. Anger flared once again, red and raw as I thought of Dante. "I do."

Eszter's eyes widened. "You met him?"

"Oh, yes," I replied, teeth gritted. "You recall the stranger I met in the woods? Well ... it seems our handsome táltos was the bloody heir to the Wolfblood Clan himself. Kept it quiet this whole time."

"My gods," she breathed. "But this is good news, right? You've formed a connection already, without the overbearing eyes of a chaperone. And you *did* admit he was attractive. I'm curious to see him for myself."

I threw daggers her way. "Attraction does not mean he's a good match. He lied to me, Eszter. I can't help but wonder why. Is our marriage just a game to him, or is he hiding something deeper?" I huffed, shaking my head. One thing had stuck with me

162

after my little tryst with Dante. My mind kept returning to it, and the more those words went through my head, the more ominous they seemed. "He suggested I run away. In his exact words, to 'elude your prison before the chains bind you, and despair comes to destroy all you hold dear'."

Eszter tilted her head, brown eyes searching. "What on earth is that supposed to mean?"

My eyes narrowed. "I don't know. But I sure as hell am going to find out."

PART TWO
THE BLOOD OF MONSTERS

FIFTEEN

Tea was the only thing getting me through breakfast. The warmth seeping through my mug grounded me, keeping my anger in check. Mama had arranged a soirée in our home, putting on quite the spread for our guests, of which both were currently staring at me.

Farkas was stone-faced while he observed my movements, scrutinising with a hawk's eye until I began to feel every motion would unravel all my secrets. I almost snorted. They had all been laid bare last night ... I hoped. If Mama was holding back any other important details, I might just burn the house down.

It took every effort to avoid the lingering gaze of Dante. I felt his eyes burning holes in my head, and I knew if I looked I'd find a smirk plastered to his chiselled face. Thoughts of stabbing my fork into his hands flashed through my mind, granting me some respite.

Those thoughts quickly turned to what else he might do with

his hands, which only irritated me further. Cutting into my eggs viciously, I shoved a forkful into my mouth, focusing on the yolk and crispy bacon.

No one broke the silence and I could stand it no longer.

"Why do you want me to marry your son, Farkas?" My words were frost-licked. Cold.

"Kitarni," Mama admonished with wide eyes. "You will speak to his lordship respectfully."

Farkas waved his hand. "We don't care for titles in the Wolfblood Clan. We are all each other's equal, bound by the same laws, the same magic running through our veins. Let the girl speak her questions. I will answer truthfully."

"You may call the girl by her name," I growled. I smoothed my skirts, cocking my head and looking into brown eyes so dark they were almost black. Waiting.

"Forgive me." He nodded his head before scratching his beard. "Your bloodline bears strong magic—the likes of which your kith do not have. As you are the last of your line as far as we know, we would like to see it ... continued."

The implication was all too clear and I curled my fingers into fists. "So I'm to spread my legs and give you an heir, is that it?"

A strangled protest came from Mama's throat and out of the corner of my eye I saw Eszter struggling to swallow a laugh. I only raised a brow and lifted my chin, refusing to back down.

Farkas blinked, the first sign of surprise I'd yet seen from the man. "We are not animals, Kitarni. We do not take what isn't

offered. By agreeing to this marriage, we hope to continue both your bloodline and mine, but naught shall come of this without your consent. You will be courted as is proper and it is both Nora's and my fondest hope you will both come to care for each other in time. Dante is my firstborn son. Beyond my bloodline, I should also like to see him happy."

I almost laughed. If only the good lord knew just how familiar his son and I already were. "Where *is* your second-born? I've yet to meet him."

"I believe your sister and Lukasz are well acquainted," Dante said with a wink at Eszter. "They spent most of last night together, after all."

Mama's eyes narrowed on my sister, and Eszter blushed. "We were just dancing," she squeaked.

Amused, I crunched into my bacon, pleased for the distraction. Lukasz must be the handsome young man who'd saved her from the sweaty paws of that elder gentleman last night. He'd seemed charming and well dressed, and now I understood why. But he must also be—

"Lukasz is my half-brother," Dante explained. "A result of a few happy nights in Transylvania." He glanced at Farkas, whose scowl intimidated even me. Dante only grinned. "He's on patrol, but he seemed in quite a good mood this morning. Kept talking about a girl he met last night."

Eszter shrank into her chair, but I could see the twitch of her lips, the barely contained smile threatening to bloom. I smiled, happy for my sister. Excitement danced in her eyes—the innocence of a hopeful girl with dreams of a happily ever after.

"Where is his mother now?"

My humour faded quickly as I noted the sadness flickering in Farkas's eyes, so fast I almost missed it.

"She passed when your father did. Struck by the same sickness that plagued our town."

A glance at Dante revealed he was less apt at hiding his emotions. His eyes were shadowed with grief, his jaw set, shoulders bowed ever so slightly. I wondered who this woman had been to him. Had she become a parental figure? Another mother he had lost? The sorrow in his eyes, it came from a deep, dark place. Another thread to untangle.

"Maria and I were friends," Mama said softly, sharing a smile with Farkas. To my surprise, his own lips curved. "We all were. She was a skilled healer and one of the bravest women I knew. She accompanied the soldiers during wartime."

"Your father was one of my closest friends," Farkas added. "Adrian was one of my finest fighters, an honourable man to the last. I miss his guidance even now."

I cocked my head. "He was a soldier?"

He nodded. "We fought together many times during the invasion under Subutai and Batu Khan. The Mongolians may have conquered the Kingdom of Hungary, but we weren't about to let them ravage our countryside and neighbouring villages. Had they occupied the towns nearby, there was a good chance

 169

they might have moved past our wards, discovered both our clan and your coven."

I leaned forward in my seat, intrigued by this newfound information. "What caused the Mongols to retreat?"

It was Dante who supplied an answer. "Mother Nature. During their advance through the western kingdom, the rivers froze solid, allowing them passage to conquer cities in the following months." He shrugged. "We aren't entirely certain why they left, given our armies were dwarfed against their hundreds of thousands of troops, but I'd put it down to flooding. As the frosts thawed, the grasslands turned to marsh. Without solid ground, their mounts struggled in the terrain, and they lost access to adequate food supplies."

"After all that they just abandoned the cause?"

Dante flashed a wolfish grin. "Mother giveth, she taketh away."

It was odd to think a country at war was saved by something so small as a change in weather. I wondered then if the gods had been watching. But which ones? Many Hungarians had forgone our pagan ways, putting their faith in Him. The one who lived in the heavens. They called Him the "one true god".

I turned to my mother, who looked lost in memory, conjuring up visions of days long gone. She wrung her hands together, an anxious trait my sister shared too. Mama looked worse for wear today. Dark shadows lined her eyes and her skin was pale. Her usually impeccable hair was all too happy to escape its braid. A sign of her guilt. And her worry.

My heart softened. It, too, thawed like those icy rivers once upon a time. Perhaps the floods would make way for a tentative peace. I still hadn't forgiven her—I likely would need a long while before I could move past my emotions, but Eszter was right.

Nora was still my mother. I loved her fiercely.

"You never told me Papa was a soldier," I said to her softly.

She shook her head, brown eyes refocusing on mine. "He never spoke of those days. I think the war took its toll on his mind, so he preferred to leave old stones unturned. I only hope he found peace beyond the grave."

"I wish I had known him," Eszter sighed. "I can't remember what he looked like or the sound of his voice."

My hand found hers, squeezing gently. I wondered again why it was that the coven and clan did not live as one. Why separate loved ones? Why split families at all? Had it not been for Papa's illness, would we have ever truly known him? I didn't think so. Mama seemed to love him in her own way, but a part of me thought perhaps she'd never truly allowed herself to, knowing her place was among her coven, and his among his clan.

Perhaps, if I were to accept this marriage, I might establish new rules for generations to come. A choice for families without fear or exile or abandonment. But first ...

First there were bigger fish to fry.

My gaze travelled back to the Wolfblood lord. "Last night you made your allegiances to our coven clear—that you'd fight for us

and protect our flock. Does your word still hold?"

"There is nothing more sacred than a man's truth," Farkas replied flatly.

I nodded, chewing over my thoughts. If a war was brewing between Sylvie's followers and our peoples, we would need all the manpower we could get. Magic alone wouldn't be enough to staunch the flow of cultists. Fighting in the woods had proven as much. If they were drinking these blood potions, attacking with berserk strength, we would need blades to fend off the beasts.

Especially given my kith had no experience with weaponry, nor had the power required to turn their magic into something monstrous.

But I do, I realised. For the first time in my life, I and I alone had the power needed to keep our village alive. My magic was murderous, the dark creature within writhing to be freed. A blessing in disguise, come to rise and bare its teeth.

This was purpose. A chance to prove myself, to untether my wild heart from its leash.

"If you pledge your men to our cause and bolster our defences as soon as you're able," I said slowly, "I will allow Dante to court me. If *both* of us find it agreeable, only then will I accept this marriage proposal. We are not human, your lordship, we do not conform to all human traditions and, as such, I believe it's within my power to bend the rules. It is my right to have a say in my future."

Approval gleaned in Farkas's eyes. "You are a bold one. Most

172

women wouldn't dare tread above their station."

I lifted my chin before shifting my gaze to Dante. "I am a witch. There is no place I will not tread."

The gold in his eyes glinted. So dangerous. Something dark lay beneath the surface. Was it because of me? Because he dreaded a future by my side? No. Dante didn't strike me as someone who begrudged his duties, who would shy away from responsibility.

I didn't know what frustrated me more; that I couldn't penetrate his wards, or that a small part of me wanted to, if only to see that smug smile and haughty countenance wiped from his face.

Were I not so furious at his antics I might have forgotten myself then, but I remained poised, maintaining a queenly air of authority. If I was to become the lady of his house, I might as well start acting like one.

"Just so," Farkas chuckled. He was silent for a few moments. "In a show of good faith you will live at our estate. It will be a chance for you to familiarise yourself with your new home, and you will be safe under the careful watch of my guards."

Dante's brows knitted together. Apparently, this was the first he was hearing of Farkas's plans. "Is that really necessary?" he said dryly.

I had the impression he wasn't all too happy with this update but, frankly, I couldn't care less whether he liked it or not.

"Are you mad?" I blurted. "My family is at risk, and you want me to leave? You know the witches here aren't fit to protect

themselves. Our guards are few, those truly handy with a blade even fewer. I'm sure I don't have to point out that our good witches are blessed with earth magic—not exactly fighting spirit."

"Don't dismiss our power, Kitarni," my mother said softly. "Magic can be wielded in many ways. The gods saw to that."

"You *will* relocate to my home in exchange for our numbers," Farkas said darkly. His tone brooked little room for argument. Well, for the meek and mild perhaps, and I was anything but that.

Inwardly, I seethed. Leaving my family in a time of crisis rattled me to my core. Especially Eszter. Who would look out for her? Who would lend a comforting shoulder? I certainly couldn't imagine any táltosok doing so, nor did I want any of them stepping a foot in our door.

She was a child no longer, but I would always look out for my little sister. Half-blood or not, she meant more to me than anything in the world. For her, I would sacrifice my happiness, my future. In turn, she would *gain* a future. A bright one, if Farkas paid his dues and looked after them. She would have enough money to buy all the finest materials in the world so she could sew to her heart's content and maybe even set up her own business.

Had there ever really been a choice? I sighed. "Fine. Under the condition you will include me in war talks. I want to know all your offensive and defensive strategies. If the cultists are coming for my people—for me—I will be included in our plan of attack."

Farkas raised a brow. "War is no place for women."

My skin heated as I placed my palms on the table, breathing

deeply to keep calm. I let him see the determination in my eyes. "If I am to live among wolves, then the world shall know my claws."

"If I were you, Father, I would heed her words," Dante remarked. "She is no lamb. I mentioned a pack of wolves attacked us in the woods. Well, Kitarni took down the lot of them."

I folded my arms, surprised and perhaps a little guarded to hear such praise. He said the words so simply, without a hint of animosity or embarrassment. My stomach did a little flip of gratitude, but Dante was a predator. It wouldn't do to forget that. To forget he wasn't without other games to play.

Farkas's eyes lit up. "Interesting. Your magic, I assume?"

Nodding, I straightened my spine, recalling the image of those wolves turning to dust. Only remnants of flesh had remained, still clinging to the bones. As if everything else simply scattered like ash on the winds.

I had felt the gentle nudges of that magic since, but nothing close to the primal instinct that had summoned my power that day. It thrived on anger and despair. If I felt cornered, threatened, the magic would surge to my palms, red and raging. If I lost control ...

I didn't want to think about the consequences.

In the woods, I'd felt desperate. Wounded, scraping for a chance to survive. And the magic—Sylvie's magic—had simply exploded.

There a second and gone the next, just like my enemies. It

frightened me still. More so now I knew whose veins it had once surged through. The thought of that power was no longer freeing. Instead, I felt like it tied me to Sylvie and every treacherous and foul thing she had ever done.

If my magic derived from a monster, could I tame the beast inside? Or would it bite and claw and rip the throats of anyone who cornered it?

I didn't know. And that scared me more than anything.

I dreamed that night. Feverish, I tossed and turned as images flashed one after another. A blackened forest, the leering faces of dead cultists, the ashes of those wolves. And blood. So much red spilled in crimson waves, pooling before my feet. When I looked down at my hands, scarlet stained my palms—every inch of my skin until I was bathed in it.

I begged for it to stop, for those images to go away, but still they flooded my senses until my mind began to fray and my bones began to break from the pain of it all. I was crumbling, my body deflating as if all the world feasted on my flesh. My own blood being sucked from its veins.

And right before the nightmare would come to an end, I would kneel before Death's outstretched hand, his black robes billowing, nothing but a void where a face should be.

"She calls for you," he would say. "She comes to claim her

debt."

I knew, even in my nightmare state, that he could only be referring to Fate. Every time I tried to speak, to question their intentions, the dream would fade, the clock would reset, and then it would start all over again.

One hateful, horrid sequence after another.

SIXTEEN

O f all the places I could go, I found myself bound for the temple the following morning. While the sun still slept and the crisp cold of pre-dawn crept up my toes, I shuffled down the stone floor, past the barn and out into darkness.

I wasn't sure what spurred my feet. Perhaps it was the memory of claws still clutching at my shoulders, or the endless waves of blood breaking against me again and again. My thoughts kept returning to Death's words—a warning, or a threat.

"She calls for you," he'd said. *"She comes to claim her debt."*

A flash of pain speared down my back and I hissed in discomfort. My scars burned as if confirming those words. Dread sluiced through my stomach, tying my innards into knots. Fate was coming for me. The Weaver, the Seer, Death's scorned mistress.

But what did she want? I wracked my brain, searching for

178

answers that wouldn't come. Since Death came to our door three years ago, we'd not been disturbed again. If it weren't for the ugly scars streaking down my back, I might have been foolish enough to forget that night.

Unfortunately for me, such musings were passing dreams and nothing more. Fate *was* coming, and I had a feeling that, whatever she would ask of me, the price would be steep.

I trawled through everything I'd learned in the last week. I was a cursed daughter. The last witch—or so my mother and Farkas believed—of a broken bloodline. Sylvie herself had once dared to claim Death's gifts as her own. Perhaps Fate was involved too?

Maybe she planned to make me pay for such a slight. Or maybe she sought to use my gifts to destroy the remaining scourge of cultists. Wipe them from the face of the earth for good.

I sighed. Until Fate blessed me with an unpleasant visit, I doubted I'd find out. But I would be stupid to ignore my dreams. The message within.

Lost in my thoughts, I strode through the square. Many witches and táltosok had continued the festivities for a second day. There were several witches who'd never made it back to bed— some still stumbling around the square, mead wobbling precariously in clumsy fingers. Others had face planted in cobblestones or the prickly fingers of bushes.

As ours was a small town, the innkeeper could afford to house only the most important of guests: Farkas, Dante, a small

contingent of their personal guards, followed by bannermen and nobles within their village. The remaining Wolfblood clansmen had sought refuge in the arms of witches or in makeshift tents they'd erected upon arrival.

The perimeter bordering the treeline twinkled with the odd lantern as I passed, likely belonging to the unfortunate souls who'd been tasked with patrol overnight. Thankfully, the cultists hadn't returned since Erika and my rendezvous with them, but I knew they were watching. The hairs on my neck stood to attention at the thought, goosebumps rising on my skin.

I snatched a forgotten goblet from the ground and took a swig. Honeyed mead dripped down my throat, washing away the bitter taste of fear. I'd have to be careful not to reveal my power, which meant fighting with fire or the old-fashioned way. Patting the dagger sheathed at my thigh, I smiled grimly. The gods know steel works just as well as magic.

Mama and Farkas had spent most of yesterday in talks with the council and Dante had joined patrols to assess the security of our village for himself. I snorted. Just as well. His face was just as good as any punching bag and I didn't care to be around him right now.

He'd known everything about me and hadn't said a word—would have realised who I was the moment my magic exploded in the forest. I didn't know why it annoyed me so much. We weren't friends or lovers. It's not as though he owed me anything.

But he was one of few people I could be myself around. Hell,

I'd thrown daggers, punches and insults his way and he hadn't batted an eye. He didn't judge me, and it meant more than I had dared to admit. But despite all that—even the accusations I'd thrown his way—he'd said nothing.

I sculled the remains of the goblet, tossing the cup on the ground. What would telling me have changed?

Absolutely nothing, I realised. Whether it was from his mouth or my mother's, the truth would still have stung as sharply. I snorted. Didn't stop him from kissing me in the woods, though, did it? I wondered if I'd still have kissed him had I known the truth.

I sighed, shaking my head as I slipped through the temple doors. It didn't matter. The most important thing now was to ensure my family's survival. To protect the ones I loved. And even if this village had brought me misery and loneliness, there had always been light here, too. Love.

The temple was silent. Ghostly. I knelt before the gods as the sun streamed through the stained-glass windows, painting my world in fractured colours of reds, pinks, purples. Istenanya's arms stretched before me, and the light catching on her eyes made it seem as though she watched my every movement.

I bent my head in reverence, closing my eyes in prayer. "Why is this happening, Mother?" I asked her. "What would you have me do?"

Only silence answered. Deafening and cold. My exposed skin chilled as the room seemed to plummet in temperature and, even

with my eyes shut, the darkness deepened behind my lids. Fathomless.

A shriek blasted the doors open as wind hurtled through the chamber and, snapping my eyes open, I saw him.

Death.

He looked exactly as I remembered. Black robes billowing around him, skeletal hands, a hood covering a black void where his face should be. "She won't answer, Kitarni," he purred. "The mother cannot intervene; her gaze is set beyond the seven-pointed-star."

I glared at the black chasm with all the strength I could muster. "I suppose I don't need to ask why you've come. I received your message loud and clear."

He picked at a piece of lint upon his robes, bone fingers smoothing out the velvet shadow of the fabric. "I thought the dreams were a nice touch. I can't very well visit you in person, what with the scores of charms your mother has erected around your house."

"Almighty Death can't even conquer a few simple charms?"

Death chuckled and it was a raspy, awful thing that sent shivers down my spine. "It would be impolite to enter uninvited."

I was holding a conversation with a well-mannered murderer with a fondness for mistresses of doom. Could my life be any weirder? Scoffing, I rose from my position, daring to take a few steps toward him. "Didn't stop you the first time."

He waved his hand dismissively. "Semantics. Would you have

opened the door if I knocked?"

I crossed my arms in answer.

"Didn't think so. Now, she will come for you two nights from now. But be warned, child, should you ignore her call there will be consequences."

My skin prickled. "I don't respond to threats," I replied haughtily. "Why don't you tell your mistress to do her own dirty work instead of calling in her lackey?"

The room grew colder as Death swept towards me. My blood pumped sluggishly, my heart slowing as he approached. A single finger swept down my cheek, cold as ice. The moment he touched me, I sagged under the weight of his power. Any warmth fled my skin and I curled inwards. He was draining me of energy.

His breath plumed on my face, smelling musty, like a bouquet of decayed flowers mixed with dirt and rotting flesh. The scent brought back memories of Hanna's body, and it took all my willpower not to choke on it, to paw my throat for fresh air. His hood lowered inches from my face, and the void where his own should have been ...

Terror sliced through me, sharp as knives as I beheld an eternity of despair within that void. It sucked me in, dragging me to a vortex of pain and emptiness. I clawed at his fingers now, lungs closing off, blood slowing, slowing, slowing.

Death held me lazily in one hand, my limp body dangling from long, thin fingers. "I like you, Kitarni, but don't mistake me as a benevolent being. Messenger I may be, but that is my mark

 183

you bear on your back. I am the ruler of the Under World, not Fate. Cross me, and you'll see just how much power I hold over you."

He dumped me unceremoniously on the ground, leaving me to gasp and dry-retch shamefully under the gaze of our pagan gods. Slowly, warmth returned to my bones and my heart, though racing in my chest, resumed its steady pulsing.

"Well then," Death said cheerfully, as if nothing had happened. "You will meet her loveliness in the woods two nights hence."

I sighed, searching for a way out of this. "I will be en route to Mistvellen tomorrow, accompanied by a contingent of guards from the Wolfblood clan. How am I to escape their watch?"

"You needn't worry about arranging a distraction or a petty excuse. Your men will be pre-occupied. Understood?"

Anger coursed through me at being treated as such, but I didn't dare let a spark of red come to my fingers. I had toed the line—no, stepped well over it with my foolishness—so it was just as well Death was in a good mood today. Sighing, I steepled my fingers to my chin.

I was a small piece to play in a bigger game.

Fine then. I would obey for now and, hopefully, I would have answers soon enough. Gritting my teeth, I forced the word from my lips. "Yes."

Death nodded, his robes fanning behind him as he turned to walk away. "Always a pleasure, Miss Bárány."

"Wait," I croaked. He halted, his form preternaturally still. Yet another reminder he was not of this earth, not *mortal.* Sifting through the onslaught of questions, my useless brain could manage only one stupid word. "Why?"

He sighed, long and world-weary and, if it wasn't for nearly dying seconds ago, I might have almost mistaken him for a human. Almost. "You witches," he mocked, his voice laced with wonder. "It is always the same. Why me? Why now? Why, why, why. I suppose I'm not surprised. Gods, in all their arrogance, created you, so it's no wonder their wicked ways rubbed off on the children of their making."

"Please." I hated myself for begging, for grovelling at his feet, but I needed reason now—something to make sense of this nightmare. If I didn't get that, I'd crumble. Piece by piece, until there was nothing left.

His next words were soft, but they were anything but gentle. "Let me make this clear, witch. You were not chosen or pre-ordained to change the course of the future. You are the unhappy accident of an addict consumed by bloodlust, blinded by her drug. She was a plague upon the earth. A weak, sick woman whose greatest achievement was baring a babe with the power of a witch long lost to this kingdom. Whose veins sang with the gifts known only to those of her bloodline."

My eyes narrowed. "Sylvie."

Death nodded. "Your mother recognised the signs. The wisest decision she ever made was fleeing their clutches, whisking

185

you away to someone who might protect you from their greedy gaze. Someone who would shield you until the time came for you to embrace your power."

Swallowing, I clutched at my skirts with white knuckles. "Is she ... is she alive still?"

A pause. "She died fleeing the cultists. The forest claimed her shortly after."

Silence filled the temple as I let everything sink in. Surprisingly, a part of me hurt to know she really was gone. Mama and Farkas were right. If my birth mother had been the only living descendant of Sylvie, I was the last of my line. That made my life even more dangerous. I was the last living witch with Sylvie's power and it was then I knew—gods dammit, I knew—I was the cultists' one hope for salvation.

My mind drifted to the fanatic cultist in the woods. *"She will rise."* The girl had seemed so sure of it. Their purpose was suddenly all too clear. Why they had been taking girls from our village, bleeding them dry over ritualistic sacrifices. They were experimenting, searching for the girl with blessed blood. *Her* blood.

They weren't just draining girls for the fun of it. They were hunting.

I was the missing piece of their puzzle. The last ingredient to ensure their ritual was successful in resurrecting the Dark Queen. We couldn't let that happen. If the cultists captured me, Sylvie would rise again, and gods only know what chaos she would wreak upon our lands. Upon the world.

"You see now, child, what awaits you should the cultists claim you. You are a symbol of hope for the occult. A gateway to ruin."

"I will not let that monster return," I swore.

Death laughed. "A sentiment shared, my dear. Unfortunately, I cannot intervene in Middle World affairs. A shame. I should have liked to torture that wretched witch. Remind her what it means to cross a greater power. I might have forged armour from her ribcage, made a throne from her bones."

"You sound genuinely depressed," I said drily.

"Verily. Alas, 'tis the gods who have all the fun and then there's me. Just a noble horseman, come to collect the dead. I rather like your spirit, girl. For your sake, I hope you keep it some years longer."

He dipped in a mock bow before gliding from the room, leaving me alone. Somehow, I preferred the company of Death to the hum of my thoughts. The temple felt cavernous now, looming.

Death told me the gods were no longer watching, no longer listening to prayers. At least, not from me. The mother, the father, they didn't care about my troubles.

And if there was one thing I knew for sure now, it was that my magic wasn't a gift.

It was a curse.

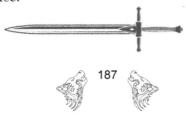

Since the festival, Eszter had been called on several times by interested táltosok. I grinned as she bounced around our living room, glowing with happiness and pride. She danced with Laszlo, who allowed her to whisk him around the room on two unsteady paws.

Snorting, I shook my head at the amusing sight, trying to commit this moment to memory. I was leaving tomorrow and everything familiar, comforting, safe, would stay while duty swept me from these doors.

A part of me was excited about the adventure, but the other half trembled at the thought of the unknown. Mama and Eszter would be protected, but could the táltosok protect them from themselves? The women in our family were stubborn creatures and I wouldn't put it past my mother to do something bravely stupid should the cultists attack while I'm gone.

The thoughts haunted me all morning, even as I pasted on a smile for my sister. She deserved to be happy and I wouldn't let my worries ruin her excitement.

"Can you believe it?" she sighed blissfully as she twirled her skirts. "Nine suitors this morning alone. Nine!"

Her dress was lavender today, cinched daringly with a white corset dressed in beautiful flowers in the traditional Magyar style. With her ringlets and rosy cheeks, she was a vision. It was no wonder the men clamoured for her attention. We'd been receiving gifts all day—jewellery, flowers, silks.

Eszter loved pretty things and adored being doted on—always

had. Women in our day were rarely afforded the luxury of love with marriage, so, when suitors of good stock came calling, she set her standards high. The most charming, the wealthiest, and by the gods' graces, the most handsome of her suitors.

Her dreams lay in comfort and status. Romance was an afterthought.

I scoffed. Sometimes I forgot how different we were. "Half of them were balding, overweight, or ready to keel over. They're old enough to be your grandfather, for gods' sakes. You can't seriously be considering a future with those withered old co—"

"Kitarni," she gasped. "We can't afford to be picky. Either I stay in this village forever, with little in the way of prospects, or I find myself on the arm of a wealthy, respected nobleman."

"Please tell me the wealthiest of all wasn't our sweaty friend who sought a dance with you all night. What's his name? Earl Rikard Boros."

She winced. "He was quite sweet. A real—err—gentleman."

"Ah-huh. And when it comes time for him to put those sweaty paws on you?" She opened her mouth, but I waved a hand. "No, don't answer. We aren't entertaining the notion. I'll not leave your virtue in the hands of ... that. I saw the way his eyes wandered. You cannot marry that man. I forbid it."

Eszter wilted in relief. "I wouldn't have said yes ..."

"What about your embroidery? You're talented, Eszter. I've seen the designs you've hidden. Rather poorly, I might add. They're incredible. You could open your own store like you

189

wanted."

She pursed her lips and sighed. "Do you really think so?"

I didn't miss the longing in her eyes. Tugging her skirts so she tumbled onto the couch beside me, I took her hands in my own. "Yes," I replied firmly. "I really do. And then you wouldn't need to marry any of those old fools."

"Well ..." she dragged out the word as she contemplated. "My talents would be wasted were I to stay locked behind high walls all day."

"Exactly. Besides, if you decide to marry, it should be to someone young and handsome. Someone who will show you the world, bring joy and love to your life." I paused, my tone turning devious. "You know, I saw you dancing with some handsome young men at the festival. Perhaps a little green, but still from good stock."

"Oh, yes," she sighed dreamily. "I could have danced all night."

"You *did* dance all night. A few too many times with a deliciously handsome young man with dark skin. Impeccable manners, charming, well-dressed? A jawline that could cut glass and an arse that wore the heck out of those pants? I think a certain someone mentioned the man's name was Lukasz. Any of this sound familiar?"

"I ..." Her cheeks flushed as she looked away, smoothing her skirts.

Grinning, I sidled up next to her, poking her in the ribs.

"Gods. You like him, don't you?"

"He was quite charming. But he hasn't called on me." She slumped into my lap. "I really thought we'd connected but—"

"Did you kiss him?"

She blinked at me. "No. What—"

"Men enjoy the chase as much as the victory. Let the other suitors try to win your favour. Go for walks in public, have a picnic, spend as much time as possible being wooed in front of Lukasz. When he sees you lapping up the attentions of other men, he'll come running."

"How can you be so sure?"

Winking, I patted her hand. "Call it womanly intuition. When he asks for your hand, don't say yes, either. String him along. Make him work for it. Dante said his brother will be staying to oversee the village's defences, but I suspect he has another reason."

"You really are devious," she replied with a smile. Then quieter, she added, "I'm going to miss you."

"Find yourself a táltos and you won't have to."

I'd meant it as a joke, but my words resonated and her eyes widened, a gleam in her eye that hadn't been there before. "I hadn't even thought of that."

Smoothing out her curls, I placed a gentle kiss on her brow before pulling away. "It was a joke, sister. Let's just make the most of today. We'll stay up late, tell stories, gossip about your suitors and eat sweets. And when I'm gone? I'll write, we'll visit each

other. It won't be so bad, I promise."

"If we even make it through the spring," she muttered bitterly.

"Don't say that. We're going to get through this. With the wolves on our side, the village will have extra protection and you and Mama shall be safe."

"Will you?"

I blinked. It was a simple question, but the answer was anything but. I would be protected by Farkas, by Dante, but was it enough? We had no idea just how many delusional cultists were gathering in the woods and the time would come when my powers were outed. I just knew it.

Tucking a strand of hair behind her ear, I smiled. "Of course. We'll figure out a plan of attack and, when the time comes, we'll be ready."

Eszter frowned, her brown eyes flashing in irritation. "We can't just sit around and wait for the hammer to fall, Kit. We should be looking for them, sending scouts into the woods to find their base. Even with the men guarding our walls, it won't be enough to stop an attack. We need answers."

Defeated, I leaned into the couch, wishing the plush fabric would swallow me up. She was right. We needed time to assemble our forces, to prepare for *any* threat. I doubted the cultists would attack before their master was resurrected, but who knows? They were fanatics. Blind to reason, lost to a darker power.

They were desperate, and desperation made people

dangerous.

"You're right," I whispered. "I'll speak to Dante about it."

Eszter raised a brow.

"Fine. Caitlin too."

She stared at me as I made for the door. "Wait."

I turned, batting my lashes innocently. "Yes?"

"You've got that look on your face, Kitarni. One that promises pain."

"Oh, sweet sister," I said with a grin. "You have your battles. I have mine."

SEVENTEEN

It didn't take long to find him. Dante leaned against the barn door, posture relaxed but eyes alert as he scanned the trees bordering my house. Always ready, should danger call. When his eyes snapped to mine, his gaze stripped me bare. I felt naked under the weight.

"Hunting again?"

His lips curved in a smile. "Guarding the prey, more like."

I rolled my eyes, stalking past him, refusing to drown in his gaze any longer. "Walk with me."

He chuckled. "So bossy." A pause, and then in a deeper tone, "I like it."

No. I would not entertain him. *You're mad at him, foolish girl.* It didn't help that my body enjoyed his husky voice, the connotations behind everything this blasted man did. Lifting my chin higher, I swished my hips as I stormed ahead. "I hope you're ready for a real predator, then. There's someone I need to talk to and I think you should be present when I do."

I risked a peek out of the corner of my eye, and the bastard was grinning. "You want to talk to the chieftain," he said matter-of-factly.

"And that amuses you. Why?" I huffed.

"You've got bad blood, you said so yourself." His eyes flashed. "I'm just surprised you'd allow her to walk all over you, is all. The girl I met in the woods wouldn't take any shit from a crone."

"I—what," I spluttered. "I do not allow anything of the sort. She's a hateful woman, but I can fight my own battles, thank you very much."

"Ah, so that's why you bring the bodyguard." His voice was laced with amusement, which only served to annoy me even further. Of course he'd turn this around and make it seem like I couldn't fight my own battles. "Do you want me to disarm her with my good looks or should we charge in, swords drawn?"

"I brought you," I hissed, "because the matter concerns you and your people. Now, kindly shut up and move."

"Hold it," he said, tugging my elbow so I whirled around. "I want to make a deal."

I scoffed, shrugging out of his grip. "And what could you possibly have to offer that I'd be interested in?"

His eyes glimmered in amusement. "Aside from the fact that you stare at my ass when you think I'm not looking?" I opened my mouth in indignation, but he pressed his fingers to my lips and continued. "It would be in both of our interests to find some common ground. I'm merely asking for a truce. If we are forced to marry, we can at least work together, fighting for the same cause."

His offer caught me off guard, but I batted his fingers from my mouth and glared at him as I considered. A truce seemed harmless enough. The energy I spent hating him would be better spent on other things, and if he wasn't baiting me all the time, perhaps it would make time spent in his company more bearable.

Not to mention our marriage.

"Fine," I huffed. "But this doesn't change how I feel about you. You're still a prick."

He flashed me a winning smile in answer and, simmering, I pushed open the temple doors with a bang, sweeping into the council chamber. As expected, Caitlin was seated at the head of the table, conferring with the other councillors.

"My lord, it's an honour," she said with a curtsy, the others mimicking her movements. She eyed me off, not bothering to hide her disdain. "Kitarni, what a ... surprise."

Unpleasant for me, too, bitch. I nodded to the others—including my wary mother—before smiling sweetly at Caitlin. "So lovely to see you all. I request a word, if I may, to discuss the village's plans of attack."

Caitlin's own smile was sickly sweet, but her words dripped venom. "You may not. The village's affairs are ruled strictly by council members only. I'm afraid that doesn't include you, even

196

with family present. Though, that's not quite true, is it? What with your real mother being a bloodmorphia addict and a cultist."

My blood heated, cheeks flushing with shame. Low, even for her, though not unexpected. My mother rose indignantly, but a pointed look from me had her sitting back down. There was no point dragging this out. My pride could take the hit.

I narrowed my eyes, pinning them sharply on Caitlin. "Blood doesn't make a family, Caitlin, bonds do. But my, such an unpleasant discussion, and in front of our esteemed guest, no less." I tsked before pasting a smile on my face. "Did you hear the news? Dante and I are to be wed. Isn't that wonderful? Not only will I be the lady of Mistvellen, but I'll be privy to all missives that pass through, as well as overseeing the welfare of my people. That includes the witches here, Caitlin. It's my duty to protect them, after all."

A vein ticked in her forehead and, somehow, her white skin paled even further. "Being the lady of the Wolfblood Clan does not grant you the right to rule our people," she seethed. "Once you leave, you forfeit your right to our customs and care."

Pouting, I twirled a strand of hair around my finger. "That's no way to speak to someone higher than your station, is it, Dante?"

His lips twitched, and I wondered if he'd play along with my little game. "Certainly not. You should apologise, Ms Vargo. The proper address is 'my lady', as I'm sure you know. You would do well to remember it."

I had to suppress my grin. It was nice not to be on the receiving end of his haughtiness for a change. Of course she knew. Caitlin curtseyed low, her jaw dangerously set. "My apologies, my lord, it will not happen again."

Dante smiled with full teeth, a dimple curling his cheek. I thought that might be the most dangerous look I'd yet seen from him. "To the lady, Caitlin. Apologise to my lady."

My lady. My stomach thrilled at the game we were playing. He'd humiliated her—twice. Leapt to my aid without a second thought. I didn't know what he was getting out of this, but frankly, I didn't care.

As I watched him out of the corner of my eye, I sensed his enjoyment and something else, too. *Anger*. It rippled from him in waves and I swore the faintest flicker of black smoke curled from his frame. The same misty black I'd seen from him in the forest.

I couldn't be certain, but I think Caitlin noted it too. "Of—of course," she stammered, curtseying again, this time directing her attention to me. "My humblest apologies, my lady." When she rose, the look in her eyes promised murder.

Silence filled the room, so deafening you'd hear a pin drop. No one, *no one* pointed out the obvious. I wasn't yet married, meaning my threats were just that. Until I married Dante, my words carried little weight, and Caitlin knew it. Still, I had her attention and, if she was smart, she'd keep her thin lips firmly shut lest she be on the receiving end of Dante's wrath. Given a simple sentence had ruffled her entirely, I suspected his words were just as sharp a weapon in his arsenal.

Dante approached the end of the table and I took that as my cue to sit to his right, but to my surprise, he took that for himself, leaving the head empty. Blinking, I glanced at the faces of the room. Caitlin glared at me from the opposite end. Mama gaped and Erika just grinned devilishly. Iren was absent, likely visiting the Transylvanian coven over the border and alerting them to our plight.

Sliding into my seat, I placed my palms flat on the table, taking a breath. Dante had given me the reins, and that small act was an olive branch. Not an apology for his brutish behaviour thus far, but close enough. The gesture would not be wasted.

"Now that the festivities are over, it's time to prepare our defences and assemble our forces should the cultists decide to attack. As it stands, an invasion would topple us entirely. Earthen magic can only go so far, and most of the witches here are without combative experience. Even with Wolfblood soldiers bolstering our forces, we are weak. Vulnerable."

"What do you propose, Kitarni?" Erika asked, straightening her shoulders. As she commanded the meagre fighters we had, she was tasked with all things offensive.

"We can't sit around, waiting for vipers to strike. I propose we send scouting parties through the woods—to the nearby towns to gather intel. Iren has her connections, yes, but we need to know numbers, need to see what the cultists are planning."

Mama studied me as she tapped a fingernail on her lips. "It's

199

dangerous. Doing so would risk lives. Is that a weight you're willing to bear, Kitarni?"

Straightening, I set my jaw stubbornly. "If we don't do this, more lives might be lost than saved. Besides, I'll be leading the hunt."

"What?" My mother shot from her seat, spearing me with her gaze. "Absolutely not, that's out of the question."

"I have to do this, Mother. Witches are dying, and it's only going to get worse. With more information, we might stand a chance of saving our people and prevent the deaths of more innocent girls."

"I'll go with you." Dante's voice was smooth as silk.

Surprised, I glanced at him, noting his assessing gaze, the dark depths of his brown eyes. I don't know what he saw in me but, somehow, the challenge in his eyes made me feel stronger.

"We'll take a small group of Wolfblood soldiers, of course," he continued. "Rest assured, Lady Bárány, I will let no harm come to your daughter."

"Swear it," she said, her words rushing in a strangled tone.

Caitlin and Erika sucked in a breath and my heart jumped in my chest. She had overstepped. But I counted the seconds, waiting to hear Dante's words.

Slowly, almost languidly, he rose from his seat, strolling around the table until he stood before my mother. Someone gasped as he bent the knee, his expression perhaps the sincerest I'd ever seen it. "I swear on my life, I will die before I allow any

200

harm to befall your daughter. From now until the stars take me, I swear it."

I choked back a laugh. 'Before I allow it'. *Arrogant bastard.* A pleasant warmth spread in my belly all the same. And a warning bell. I couldn't let my guard down around him. So far, he'd yet to prove he did anything that didn't meet his own agendas.

Mama looked him hard in the eye before her eyes slid to mine. They were resigned, sad, but I saw a spark in them too. A kernel of something I hadn't seen before. After an age, she nodded once.

"And what of our village?" Caitlin intervened impatiently, shattering the moment. "We were promised protection."

"Which you shall have," Dante said quietly as he rose. His voice brooked no room for argument as he appraised her from his towering height. That stare; he could level mountains with the slice of his eyes. "My father left this morning to make arrangements for our peoples and, tomorrow, Kitarni and I will leave for my home. My brother, Lukasz, shall remain with a contingent of guards to continue patrolling." His gaze darted to Erika. "They are at your disposal."

She dipped her head regally, her long braids tinkling as the gold beads threaded through her hair swished together. "We are grateful for your assistance."

I breathed a sigh of relief. "So, it's decided then. Once we know more about these fanatics, we'll plan our next moves. In the meantime," I said with a crooked grin to Erika, "I think these

witches need whipping into shape."

She winked, dark eyes lined with kohl flashing mischievously. "My thoughts exactly. I will post a notice for volunteers." She glanced at Caitlin pointedly. "Our sisters need to know what's coming, and I have no doubt once word is out about the cultists, our lovely ladies will exchange needle and thread for swords and bows in no time."

"Temporarily," Caitlin grumbled.

"Oh, I don't know, Caitlin, you might find a little melee will do you good," I said sweetly. "Course, at your age it might be too hard on your bones. Perhaps it'd be best if you cheered the girls on instead." Before she could utter a word, I rose from my chair, making sure to drown out her protests as I scraped the legs along the floor. "Well, duty calls. A lady never sleeps, you know."

With a dismissive sweep of my skirts I left the temple with a lighter heart and a smile on my face. Knowing Caitlin wanted to rip it off only made my grin wider.

"What made you decide to play along?" I asked Dante warily as we strolled through the gardens. Sunlight dappled the grass through the canopy above, gilding the petals of flowers. Wisteria creeped in lavender and blues, winding over archways of wrought metal. White and pink roses bloomed from either side of us, their thorns shiny and glinting.

There wasn't a cloud in the sky and the weather was warm. Pausing, I closed my eyes, basking in a patch of sunlight, embracing its kiss upon my brow. Tomorrow we'd be entering the woods, passing through the Sötét Erdő to get to Mistvellen. There would be no sun, no warmth where we were headed.

I cracked an eyelid to find him staring at me curiously and his eyes darkened as he answered my question. "I've met people like Caitlin before. Obnoxious, power hungry. Leaders like her are dangerous because they have the ears of the people. I saw it in her eyes. She fears for her position and of losing the witches' devotion. She fears *you*."

I scoffed, shaking my head at the idea. I was hardly a threat to her station. She could keep her council; I didn't want it. Dante watched me impassively, but I had the sense he was still simmering over Caitlin's behaviour. Could it have anything to do with the way she spoke to *me* specifically?

No. That would mean he'd have to care, which he clearly didn't. I pinned him under my stare. "Are we going to talk about the other surprise you dropped in there?"

"What surprise?" Dante replied innocently.

His dark hair tumbled over his forehead, the reddish hues gleaming as the light hit his crown. His olive skin shone like burnished gold and, as he moved his arms, I noted every muscle twitch, every vein.

He gave me a crooked smile and I realised I might have stared a little too long. Drawing my gaze back to his own, I frowned.

"Don't play coy. You just swore an oath to my mother. Why would you offer that? You don't know me. You don't owe me anything. This marriage of ours? It's nothing more than a farce."

His answering grin was devious. "Such wicked words from a lady. You're to be my wife. Whether we like it or not, I am honour-bound to protect you. You're stuck with me, Freckles. Might as well get used to it."

"Go to hell," I snapped, tiring of his games. I didn't understand him at all. And I hated it. What did he want from me? Friendship? Sex? Something to amuse him until he found his next conquest?

"Perhaps someday, but I think I'm having too much fun to leave you just yet. I know you felt something when we kissed. Admit it, your body wants me, even if your mind does not. I wouldn't blame you," he purred.

Temper flaring, my dagger was drawn in less than a blink as I shoved him against a tree. I angled my blade to his throat, eyes fixed on his own as I reached up on tiptoes. "There is nothing between us," I hissed. "*Nothing.* What happened in the woods was a momentary distraction. It will *not* happen again."

His arms swept around my waist, pulling me closer and my breath hitched as he drew my face to his own. Our lips were an inch apart and I felt his warmth, his hunger as he brushed his lip ever so softly against my own. Not a kiss, but a gentle teasing. "Keep telling yourself those lies, Freckles. We'll see who's the first to fall."

Nostrils flaring, I pressed the tip of my blade down harder, drawing a single drop of scarlet.

"Ah, ah," he tsked, waving a finger. "Truce, remember?"

I snarled in frustration. Somehow, our little arrangement made my anger at him rise even further. I lowered the blade just a little. "You are going to regret the day you were born, Dante Sándor."

The mirth faded from his smile, a flicker of something else I couldn't place flashing in his eyes. "Oh, darling, I passed that long ago."

The sincerity in that statement stole the anger from my bones. Withdrawing, I studied his face, but his mask was back on, eyes dancing once again.

Sighing, I stormed off towards my home.

I was leaving everything I knew and loved for this man.

And I was already regretting it.

EIGHTEEN

Taking a deep breath, I took in the view from the hillside by my house, scanning the thatched roofs of the village below—the temple's spire, the gardens and the town square. Dawn painted a pretty picture of my home. Rose-gold kissed the cobblestones of paths and buildings. Flowers and greenery bloomed as they draped over windows and signs or crept the walls of homes.

Our town wasn't grand, but it was magical in its own way. Quaint. There were few I'd miss, apart from my family and Erika, and a part of me hoped to find new friendships. And perhaps acceptance in some place new.

I'd never fit here, always at odds with the other girls, always different.

Maybe in Mistvellen that would all change. Maybe I might just like my new life. Blowing air from my nose, I turned my sights to the rolling wheat fields by my home and, adjacent, the grassy pastures where our animals roamed free.

A new shepherd would need to tend the flock and I prayed whoever took my place would give the animals the love and care they deserved. I strolled through the field, brushing my palms over the fuzzy stalks. With winter behind us, the witches would soon begin preparations for the sowing season, gathering oats, beans, peas, barley, and so on.

The earth was rich where we lived and, with a little magic, we rarely had a poor harvest. But there was no longer a 'we' anymore, I thought bitterly. I was not a part of the equation and, truthfully, I never really was.

Something glinted in the rising sun and I squinted to see Dante and his guards plodding up the path on their mounts, armour and swords equipped.

It was time.

Lifting my chin, I took a deep breath and turned my back on all that was. Mama and Eszter were waiting for me by the barn and my heart broke to see their faces. Eszter was sobbing already, her cheeks tear-stained and flushed.

We made eye contact and she burst into fresh tears, diving into my arms. I patted her head gently, hushing her. I'd stayed true to my promise yesterday. We'd stayed up most of the night sharing stories and gossip and eating our fill in sweets. Me teasing her about her suitors, her begging for juicy details about Dante.

I put on a brave face, promising to visit, to write, to see her soon, and she nodded. Neither of us said a word about the

cultists. We didn't need to. She knew what I'd chosen to do and she respected it, even if it frightened her. That's one thing I loved about my sister. She'd never judged me for my choices. For being *me*.

My heart shattered as I kissed Eszter's head and gave her the fiercest bear hug I could muster. When she laughed and protested, I turned to my mother, and that's when my courage fled.

Her eyes said everything words could not. *I love you. I'll always love you. And ... I'm sorry.* A tear trickled down my cheek and I held her close, snuggling into her warmth, her smell, her comfort.

At last she pulled away, sniffing, lifting her chin high. She gripped my arms in her fingertips. Mama had never been one for sentiments, but as her brown eyes blazed with emotion—pride and love and fear all at once—she nodded, just once.

A blessing and a goodbye.

I couldn't help myself. I threw myself into her arms one last time, needing some of her courage, her bravery. She softened beneath me, almost wilting, but I wouldn't let her. And just as I pulled away, I whispered in her ear, "I will save the witches. I will keep Eszter safe."

Her voice caught as she whispered back, "I know you will. Now go, child, and don't look back."

My gaze shifted to Lukasz, who was standing a little off to the side. I smiled at him and he tipped his hat, shooting me a disarming smile. But his amber eyes hardened resolutely. "I will watch over your family," he said, placing a hand over his heart. "You have my word."

His gaze flicked briefly to my sister and I nodded, satisfied that he spoke honestly. He exchanged a few words with Dante, followed by a quick embrace, and then my betrothed boosted me onto Arló.

Squaring my shoulders, I set my jaw, blinking the emotion from my eyes. I would not let them see my tears. I'd have no use of them where we were going.

As we set off into the trees, I didn't look back.

The group was silent as our horses trekked through the undergrowth. The day was cool, a chill settling over my skin. Maybe that had more to do with our journey through the Sötét Erdő than anything else. These woods were once my sanctuary, my escape. But now, trepidation crawled down my spine like spiders.

I wrapped my cloak tighter around me, thankful for its warmth. It was a dove grey velvet with gorgeous silk ties and a draping hood, the silver trim embroidered with sweeping vines and florals. Mama's parting gift. It was well made and far too expensive for what we could afford, but I sensed it had been with her for some time. Perhaps she'd always planned to pass it on.

Her perfume wafted every time the breeze shifted, bringing fresh tears to my eyes. I scratched Arló behind the ears as he

walked, Laszlo bounding along beside us. Mama and Eszter had insisted I take them, to keep me company among strangers. We couldn't afford a dowry, but Arló was a handsome stallion from good stock. *A little too skittish*, I thought with mild irritation, recalling him running for dear life and leaving me stranded. We'd work on that.

As for Laszlo, he was a little lordling, but he was fiercely protective of me and, as much as it begrudged me to admit, he *did* seem fond of Dante.

The subject of my ire nudged his horse toward mine, casting me a tentative glance. "You okay, Freckles?" His tone was mocking, certainly anything other than genuine.

I glared at his insistent use of that nickname. "Fine," I snapped. "Just eager to reach Mistvellen. I feel like the woods are watching."

His brown eyes scanned the trees. "There are many creatures who dwell within the dark."

I raised a brow. "I know the outer reaches of these woods like the back of my hands. Nothing has ever attacked me this close to the village."

He cocked his head, studying me. "Yet. The cultists' influence over these lands has changed things. You recall the wolves when we first met?"

"How could I forget?" I replied drily, recalling their berserk behaviour, the feral brightness of their eyes. I'd never seen any creature act like that before.

210

"When we found Hanna, did you notice the foliage seemed sick?"

"Corrupted," I agreed, remembering the sticky black that oozed over leaves and sticks. "Do you think their dark magic is destroying the forest?"

Dante frowned, his lips pressing thin. "We can only assume the worst. Something tells me the wolves were just the beginning. If their dark magic is messing with the balance of nature, it could be more creatures in this forest have been affected."

My stomach jolted. There were worse things than wolves in there. Much, much worse. I prayed we didn't meet any. My thoughts turned to the gentler beings of the forest. "The faeries," I said with a start. "What if they're at risk?"

Dante's lips quirked ever so slightly at my outbreak. "Friends of yours?"

"A couple," I admitted, thinking fondly of Jazmin and Lili. The sisters were the most beautiful creatures I'd ever seen. Jazmin had sable skin, tight ringlets and a face to rival a goddess, and Lili's skin was pale, her white hair flowing in gentle waves. Both had skin tattooed with florals, the ink like silver veins snaking across their flesh. Both were the closest thing to friends I'd ever had.

A small smile curved my lips as I thought of the last time I saw them. We'd spent a summer's day lounging in a rock pool, sharing stories about our peoples and laughing together. Jazmin had taught me how to weave fishing nets made from grasses, and

 211

Lili had showed off with her water magic, creating animals out of water and sending them skipping around the pool. Time spent in their company was always magical, always fun.

It had been a simple day, but one I deeply cherished. The sisters always found a way to make me feel on top of the world. They treated me with respect and kindness and unending warmth. It reminded me that I wasn't alone. That being different wasn't always a bad thing.

The thought of something happening to them—to their homes—was terrifying.

"Faeries are powerful creatures," Dante replied, pulling me from my thoughts. "Their magic is bound to the forest itself. Should danger come, their power will protect them."

I relaxed a little in my saddle, curiosity getting the better of me. "How do you know all this?"

He grinned, his gaze sliding lazily over me. His palm stretched out to my thigh, squeezing gently, causing my spine to stiffen. "Dangerous creatures have always interested me."

I had the distinct feeling that included me. Batting his hand away and shooting him daggers, I shook my hair from my face. "Dangerous creatures shouldn't intrigue you, Dante. If you had any sense, you'd stay well away." I gazed at the leaves littering the ground as we wound our way around trees, all too aware we were doing the exact opposite.

"Now where would the fun be in that?" His lips caught the shell of my ear as he whispered and I nearly fell off my saddle. His

arms snaked out and caught me.

"Prick," I hissed under my breath.

He only laughed, urging his horse to the front of our party. I watched as he talked with his guards. Not with the snobbish air of a lord commanding officers, but as a comrade—an equal. They looked at him with respect that was earned by deed and not by title. Impressive. I wondered if this easiness would encompass all Mistvellen. If so, perhaps there was hope after all.

I rode alone for a while, not really seeing or hearing as we progressed through the forest. My mind was too caught up in a tangle of thoughts, and my heart deflated in my chest with each step away from my home.

I didn't even notice when Dante rode back, another rider in tow. They flanked either side of me until I was boxed in and finally I looked up, a frown marring my face.

"I'd like to introduce you to a friend of mine. This is András, my second in command. He's a bastard, but a necessary one. Don't pay him much mind."

On my left was a fair-skinned young man with cropped blond hair and green eyes. He was *very* pleasing to the eye with a heartbreaker smile and a body a sculptor would swoon over. If he wasn't careful, Dante would have a run for his money. Before I could apologise for his royal ass's behaviour, the man beat me to it.

"It's true, my lady," he said with a sparkling smile. "I'm a bastard born and bred, but no less charming, I promise. It is an

 213

honour." He took my gloved hand and kissed it gently.

I smiled sweetly in return before glancing at Dante. "The lesser of two evils, I'm sure. I don't know how you put up with him, András. His head is so far up his ass, I don't know how you can carry him all the time. You deserve a medal, or at least a raise."

András laughed. "Oh, I like her," he said to Dante before turning back to me, leaning close and whispering in a conspiring tone. "I think you and I are going to be great friends."

For the first time since we'd left home, I genuinely smiled, already sensing this one was trouble. Delight rang through me at Dante's narrowed eyes. Was that jealousy? Wriggling in my saddle, I leaned in even closer. "If I'm to put up with him, I'll need one."

Dante scowled. "Don't trust a word out of his mouth."

I patted his arm. "Don't pout, my lord. It's unbecoming."

With that I took András's reins and slowed our horses, leaving Dante looking less than pleased on his stallion.

Since saying goodbye to the sun, I'd felt on edge, skin crawling and stomach curdling with nerves. Creatures had skittered in the undergrowth, tracking our progress, but not once were we approached. I'd been thankful for that, at least.

Dante had been alert all day, as had the guards flanking us. Both András and himself had drifted close by, their hands settled on the pommels of their swords, eyes always watching the foliage.

We'd seen no sign of the corruption; the skin of the trees were marked only with the scars of time and the weariness of a life lived without sunshine. The canopies high above would feel its kiss, of course, but down here where dangerous things stalked our steps, we were without a guiding light.

I'd never ventured so far into the sprawling undergrowth. Here, I'd lost all perception of time and place. The woods were so dark, the party had lit torches to light the way. Many times I thought we'd surely lose our way, and yet the faintest glimmer of magic ensnared my senses. The scent of it lingered like incense, climbing up my nose.

Witch magic. Old magic. I'd been wondering for some time how the táltosok picked their way through the woods without a path to follow, but I realised they did have a marker—a magical one. Closing my eyes, I reached out to the tender thread of magic, twitching my fingers gently to test its friendliness.

The spool unravelled cheerfully, perhaps sensing a fellow witch. When I opened my eyes, a faint dusting of gold twined through the foliage, its glitter beckoning as if to say, "You can trust me. Here I am."

András's green eyes sparkled as he fixed me with a cocky smile. "Took you long enough."

I smirked and rolled my eyes. "Excuse me for thinking you lot hadn't the skill to conjure a wayfinder spell."

"You wound me," he said with a hand over his heart. "But

you're not wrong. A táltos doesn't have the ability for such tricks. Our shamanistic ways appeal to the spirits of the dead and to aid in healing practices. We can harness these spirits to do our bidding, not unlike necromancy, but we always send those souls back to the Under World. In return for our trespass, we serve with healing magic. There must always be a balance to nature. The World Tree demands it."

Witches and táltosok were among the few who still believed in the World Tree. As the Roman Empire converged upon the Kingdom of Hungary and their churches began to sprout over our earth, our beliefs were quickly dying. Christianity was the new religion and our gods were scorned as our houses of worship were toppled, one by one.

But I still believed. Magic was too great a gift to be ignored, and such gifts were given by none other than the gods themselves.

Chewing on my lip, I whispered, "If the cultists continue to upset the balance, what do you suppose will happen?"

András ran a hand through his hair, grimacing. "Pray that does not happen."

"And if it does?" I prodded.

"Then we'd best hope the gods are on our side, because the world as we know it will quickly fall to ruin, and the realms will collapse."

I latched a hand onto his arm, my gloved fingers digging in. "Wait. Collapse? Are you suggesting the cultists have the power to bring down the gates?"

216

He shook his head, brown hair bouncing as he looked at me pointedly. "Not the cultists."

I stared at him, dumbfounded. "Sylvie." The name tasted like ash on my tongue. Fitting, considering András was suggesting her resurrection may as well be a sign painted in bold red letters with "the end is nigh" written across it.

His lips curled in distaste at her name. "You know, our peoples despised each other once upon a time. The only good thing to come from that wretched creature was an alliance with the táltosok and witches."

Startled, I jolted in my seat. "Our people were at war?"

András chuckled. "We hated one another. Vehemently. The boszorkányok and the táltosok were antagonistic, battling for power and territory. It was a bloody age—one we moved past when Sylvie came and shit all over our feud. It was then our ancestors decided to work together. Of course, the friendship was tentative at best, which is why we chose to live apart in separate colonies."

"My gods. That's why the council still clings to such archaic constructs?"

András shrugged. "Old habits, I guess. Dante is trying to change that. When he takes the mantle from his father, I expect many things will change."

I looked at my husband-to-be with newfound interest, trying not to stare too long at his handsome face lest he catch me and gloat about it. "When we get out of this mess, András, I'll hold

you to it."

"If we get out of this mess, my lady, I'll write the damn reforms myself."

I nodded, thinking of my people's history—of Sylvie's abuse of our magic. She'd led witches to ruin, twisted their beliefs until the roads ran red with the death of innocents and the lifeblood of their own kith.

All this and more, she threatened once again.

NINETEEN

The cabin was a dilapidated sprawl of rotting wooden slats and musty thatching. It leaned so precariously I wondered what was keeping it upright. Turning to Dante, I folded my arms, frowning.

"Absolutely not. I'm not sleeping in there."

"Would you rather sleep outside?" Dante asked, gesturing at the ominous tangle of foliage. I spied a few yellow sets of eyes blinking at me from the bushes and shivered. He pounced at my discomfort. "If you're cold, I'm sure there are a few bodies that would happily keep you warm."

Yanking the door open, I huffed over my shoulder, "You're such an *ass!*"

His chuckle followed me into the room, where I abruptly stopped in my tracks. I might have stepped foot into a faery tale cottage. The room was cosy and in perfect condition. A fireplace beckoned from the other side of the room, a couch and two wingback chairs in red velvet brocade settled around it. A small kitchen sat tucked in the corner to prepare quick meals for the weary traveller.

A shaggy white rug lined the wooden floor and, in the adjoining room, a four-poster bed lined with plush pillows and coverlets of creams and golds.

The fittings in this cabin hinted at comfort, with just the right amount of opulence. It was perfect except for one small detail.

There was only one bed.

Dante caught my gaze after staring at the bed chamber and my cheeks flushed. His lips curved in a slow smile, somehow knowing where my thoughts had gone. Making a show of surveying the room, I risked a peek at him, pleased to find his eyes lingering on my attire.

I wore black leather pants today, fitted scandalously tight over my thighs and ass. Beneath my cloak, I wore a plain, simple shirt beneath a brown corset. The cloak covered much, but a small part of me was pleased to note his gaze dropped to the exposed hint of collarbone, the slight dip where my shirt crept open.

"You've enchanted the cabin with a cloaking spell," I remarked at last, turning slowly to stare at him. "Giving it the appearance of a ramshackle building to the unknowing eye. Honestly, I'm surprised there's enough room in your brain for such cleverness, given how much your arrogance takes up."

"Not just a handsome face," he purred.

"No, you're exceptional at annoying me as well," I grumbled, heading towards the fireplace. I flicked my fingers lazily at the hearth, sending flames crackling to life before taking a seat on the couch. "I'm not sure how this cabin will fit the two of us with that pride of yours. Perhaps you should camp with the guards outside."

He slid into the wingback chair beside me, legs dangling carelessly over the side, one hand propping his chin up. The reflection of the fire glittered in his dark eyes, causing the gold ring to gleam dangerously. "Not a chance. You're not leaving my sight while we're in the woods."

"So bossy," I said with a smirk. If I was being honest, I liked that about him. He was so sure of himself. So confident. I feigned indifference as I studied the room. "So, what would you like to do while we wait out the night?"

His lips quirked ever so slightly and I found my gaze drawn to them. "Many, many things."

My stomach flipped at those words—the husky tone in which he said them. A small part of me entertained the road they could lead towards. Would it be so bad to let him court me? It was just another game, wasn't it? And he did so like his games. We were to be married after all. Perhaps we could at least find some middle ground.

If I let him. If I let down my walls.

Dante padded to the kitchen while I toed off my boots,

sighing in relief as I massaged the balls of my feet. The fire crackled before me and I flinched as a log snapped in the biting embers. She would call on me tonight. Fate would dig her nails deep. I only hoped what she wanted from me was in both our interests.

A warm hand curled over my shoulder, startling me from my thoughts. Dante set a platter of food down on the round table in front of us and my stomach grumbled at the sight of bread, cheeses, grapes and ... chocolates?

I raised a brow. "Nora?"

"I asked your mother what your favourite foods are." He popped a chocolate into his mouth and I couldn't help but stare as it sank between his lips. "She told me you have quite the sweet tooth."

"You ... you brought these for me?" It was the first genuine gesture he'd shown that wasn't centred around himself. A small act, but right now it felt monumental. Warmth bloomed in my chest at the gesture, but I didn't thank him. I wouldn't give him the satisfaction.

The chocolates sat nestled in one of Mama's wooden boxes and I stroked a finger on the bright yellow lid fondly. Dante said nothing as he watched me devour the food. "Whumf?" I said, mouth full and cheeks reddening.

He shook his head, quietly amused. "You're exactly what I'd expected."

That caught me by surprise. "If by that you mean you're

looking for a loner with a penchant for profanity and a problem with obedience, then yeah, I'm your girl."

"Bullshit," he said flatly. "Bull. Shit. You want to know what I think?"

"Not really," I mumbled.

"You're so used to people walking over you and treating you like trash that your perception of yourself has changed to fit their mould. You are an intelligent, beautiful young woman who knows what she wants. And, more importantly, you're brave. Brave for standing up to dated ideals and close-minded individuals. I don't see anything wrong with that."

Tears pricked my eyes and I hid my face shamefully. My cheeks blazed from the truth of those words. The hand of oppression I'd been dealt because I didn't fit society's moulds.

"Not just a handsome face," I whispered.

His fingers found my chin, tilting my head ever so gently. "Don't hide from me, Kitarni. You never have to hide from anyone again."

I stared into his eyes, lost in the sincerity of his words, and damnit, my betraying heart fluttered at the use of my real name from his lips. Blinking, I leaned into his touch slightly, just enough to let him know I was thankful. That I was grasping the line of trust he'd thrown me.

"When you learned we were to marry," I asked him slowly, "what were your first thoughts?"

He leaned back, steepling his fingers under his chin, silent as

 223

he pondered my question. I felt the absence of his touch keenly, but his every movement was graceful fluidity and I couldn't help but stare, mesmerised. His shirt strained against the hard muscle of his arms, every wrinkle in the fabric stretching taut. At last, those dark eyes met mine and for once they were humourless, thoughtful.

"Honestly? I was angry. I knew the day would come when my life would be bartered for the betterment of my house. I suppose knowing and acting are two entirely different things, though. For one, I would have liked to court my bride under less harrowing circumstances."

"Really? You've given me the impression you quite like anything dangerous and deadly," I teased.

He grinned crookedly and that damned dimple winked into existence. "I love to play."

Rolling my eyes, I prodded him with my toe. "You're a little damaged, you know that?"

Dante cocked his head, assessing me with a predator's gaze. "Aren't we all?"

My skin prickled under the studious sweep of his eyes, my core thrilling at the look he was giving me. Hungry. *Devouring.* Images of him crushing me against him and using that mouth in sinful ways flashed through me. "I—I think I should go to bed," I choked out.

I didn't want to go, not really. Falling asleep would bring me closer to seeing *her.* But the way he was looking at me, it stirred

something deep inside, something I couldn't allow to consume me.

And Dante made me feel bold. Daring. Like I could do anything in the world, including falling into his arms, becoming someone I wasn't sure I was ready to be. I liked this game we were playing. Perhaps I liked dangerous and deadly too, and Dante was certainly both of those. Maybe *I* was damaged for being drawn to that darkness.

"We should both get some rest," he agreed, rising beside me. When he headed to the bedroom, I narrowed my eyes, storming behind.

"What are you doing?" I demanded, hands planted on my hips.

He peeled his shirt over his head and I swallowed as the muscles on his stomach rippled with the movement. The inky scrawls of a howling wolf snarled from his chest and a sword surrounded by flowers angled towards his pants. I stared at the ink, then followed the sword down towards his pants. Istenanya's tits, he might have been a bronzed god himself.

When his shirt was removed, he lay it slowly over a settee in the corner of the room.

Turning, he smiled, and I had the feeling of being trapped in what now felt like too small a room. "Undressing for bed," he drawled, taking a step toward me. "Need some help?"

"Absolutely not," I snapped. "And you're not sleeping in here."

Dante took a step toward me. Another. "Oh, come now, the couch in the lounge is far too short for me."

"Then sleep on the rug by the fire," I huffed, my breath coming shorter as he advanced another step.

"And leave you unguarded for the night? Not a chance."

Bastard. He was thoroughly enjoying my discomfort. The second dimple appeared as he flashed me a saccharine smile. I cursed the god who invented such a thing. They made me want to melt into a puddle of goo.

"Fine," I said begrudgingly. "You can sleep in here."

"What a relief," he replied smoothly. "I'm sure the floor won't be too uncomfortable for you."

"Wh—what?" I spluttered, fuming. The audacity! "You can't be serious."

He took one final step, bridging the gap between us until I was forced to bump into the wall. He placed one hand on either side of my head, the golden rings in his eyes glinting with amusement. "Well, unless you want to sleep in the bed with me. Course, I can't rely on you to keep your hands to yourself. They might wander in the night ..."

Furious, I pushed off the wall and onto his chest, glaring up at him. "You arrogant son of a ..." I took a deep breath and hissed, "I would *never* stoop to your level of depravity." We stayed that way for one heated moment. My core thrummed with need and I felt his own excitement press against me.

His hand strayed to my thigh, sliding higher, higher, until he

cupped the apex of my thighs. I gasped, every part of me alight with that touch.

All it would take was another kiss. A moment of weakness to fall into his arms.

"What's the matter, Freckles?" he breathed onto my neck, twisting a stray curl and tucking it behind my ear. "Afraid you'll like what I can give you?" His hand trailed up the waistband of my pants and he traced the sensitive skin there, making me shiver in delight.

I groaned, his lips a breath away from mine. I squeezed my thighs together, trying to alleviate the building tension. I wanted him so bad I ached with desire.

Nostrils flaring, I couldn't help arching my spine into his touch. What's wrong with me? "You can't give me what I need," I whispered back.

"But I can give you what you want." His lips grazed my neck and I had to stifle a gasp. His touch was fire, burning my skin, blazing down my body to places that had no right to be pounding so painfully. So deliciously.

I held him at arm's length, slapping a palm to his bare chest. "If we do this, it's just sex," I said a little breathlessly.

He lifted his head, staring at me dangerously. "Just sex," he purred. "And we can go back to hating each other in the morning."

Dante leaned closer and, so help me, I closed the gap between us, crashing my lips against his own. He pinned me to

the wall, grinding against me as I weaved my fingers through his hair and sighed against his lips.

My hand travelled down his stomach, feeling each ridge beneath my fingertips until I traced the vee above his pants. He stiffened beneath my touch, his cock riding higher. I was charting dangerous territory, but gods help me, I craved his touch so badly.

His fingers dipped lower down my pants and I knew he could feel how wet I was. As if he could read my mind, he pressed one finger against my nerves and lifted it to his lips, tasting me.

My gaze darted to the bed and I swallowed. This wasn't like the times I'd been with other boys. A man stood before me and I had every confidence he knew just what to do with those hands. With his cock.

I was way out of my league. My insecurities swept in—my fear of abandonment and betrayal sucking the breath from my lungs and splashing water on my heated skin.

A frustrated sound ripped from my chest. "I can't do this."

I shoved him out of the way, storming to the corner of the room and gulping down a few breaths. I needed air, needed space, or I might just buckle under the pressure. He was right. I did *want*. My body thrummed with it, the memory of his touch still sending waves to my core. Why was I so afraid of letting go? He was going to be my *husband* and, regardless of whether we liked each other, I may as well try to enjoy the parts of him that *didn't* talk back or bait me.

His eyes burned holes in my back, but he didn't pry or try to

persuade me. He simply gave me the space I needed, let me think in peace. Gods, I was such a fool.

As I removed the corset with painstaking difficulty, I suddenly realised why I was holding back. Like a punch to the stomach, the air rushed from my lungs, releasing the tension inside. No one, *no one* bar my family and Erika knew who I really was. I'd tried once, to open up to others, to share a piece of myself with my kith. I'd done so with Hanna, and once she tired of me and found better things, she'd ripped my dignity to shreds and played on my fears.

It pained me to admit, but I was scared. Terrified of letting someone in, only to be hurt once again. Even if it was just sex, even if it was only physical. I told myself those lies, but did I really hate him at all? Even a little?

I sighed.

If I let down my walls for Dante and he hurt me, would I crumble past the point of coming back? Could I rebuild my foundation? I didn't think so. Not with a war looming, the cultists out for blood and Fate coming to claim me for her own undoubtedly terrible schemes.

Better to be distant. To keep him at arm's length, even if that put a strain on our relationship—our marriage.

When I shucked off my pants, ready to dash into bed before Dante got a good look at the exposed skin my shirt didn't hide, I turned only to find him curled up in bed. Snoring. My heart sank with disappointment. Of course he didn't care what I was going through. He had given me no indication he would give two shits in the morning.

Besides, I had been the one to call it off. Still, a part of me hoped maybe he'd change my mind. It wouldn't have taken much to convince me.

Who falls asleep that quickly anyway? Now that's a magic power I could use. Sighing, I thought about sleeping on the floor, but to hell with him. I slid under the covers, still aching with the need to release some tension.

Shuffling, I considered sliding a hand down my underwear, but before I could summon the courage, his giant arm wrapped around me and pulled me towards him.

I squeaked, feeling myself practically lifted into his embrace. He was pleasantly warm and his scent of leather and musk washed over me like a gentle kiss. I nestled in, his muscled bicep like a comfortable blanket to weigh me down.

Right before I nodded off, I shuffled my ass into his crotch, smiling to myself. I hoped he had good dreams over what he was missing tonight.

If he was going to tread dangerous waters like *cuddling*, I could too. Spiteful of me? Maybe.

But two could play this game.

TWENTY

I heard the call even in my dreams. A strange beating of drums, pulsing in tune with the rapid thumping of my heart. Snapping my eyes open, it took a few seconds for my vision to adjust. The room was pitch black and, for a moment, my heart raced from the unfamiliar.

Dante's arm flexed against my stomach and I relaxed, smiling softly as his weight pressed against my back, his arm curled protectively around me. He must have shifted over in his sleep. It felt so natural. I wanted nothing more than to lay there, swaddled in his warmth, lulled to a sense of safety by the steady rise and fall of his chest against my back.

His heart pumped solidly. *Thump. Thump. Thump.* Then the drums of Fate's siren song picked up their frenzy, the sound drowning out my momentary peace. She was waiting. I knew only I could hear the sound. She wouldn't want an audience, after all. No chaperones for me.

 231

Easing my way out of Dante's arms, I slid quietly from the bed, putting on my pants and making my way to the lounge to don my boots and cloak. Hastily braiding my hair, I took a deep breath, then ventured out into the night.

I had the sense I'd only been asleep a few hours, but without the moon or stars to map the sky above, I couldn't be sure. The guards slept in a small huddle a few paces from the cabin, most of them snoring softly, all of them lying close to the fire crackling at the centre. I supposed it was the only source of comfort they had, though perhaps not the wisest. Still, the guards on watch needed light to see by if they had any chance of protecting us against threats.

We all knew there were creatures in this place who moved with careful claws and could see us in the pitch black, even if we couldn't see them. Taking a leaf out of their book, I crept on silent feet past the group of sleeping men, tiptoeing behind the guard on watch.

I thought I'd made it, too, until a hand snaked out, gripping my boot heel. Jumping, I turned to see András's face peering up at me, sleepy dust crusting his eyes. "Where are you going?" he demanded sternly.

Suppressing my irritation, I offered him a sheepish smile. *Nothing to see here, just a girl about to meet a mistress of hell.* "I need to relieve myself. I'll only be just outside the light."

Frowning, he darted up from his rucksack, immediately on alert. "I'll accompany you."

"András," I sighed, feeling my annoyance rising. "Unless you want to hold my hand while I piss I—"

A low keening drowned out my words, sending shivers shooting up my neck. The sound was accompanied by another, and another, until it seemed we were surrounded by the low drone of something supernatural.

The guards roused from their sleep, eyes widening as they rose, unsheathing swords and bows and arrows. "Cultists?" one mouthed, but I shook my head.

András was by my side in an instant, green eyes focused, stance lowered and sword ready. "Do you know how to fight, Kitarni?" he asked in a low voice.

Sliding the dagger from the holster at my thigh, I smiled grimly, conjuring a floating ball of fire in my other palm. "I know a thing or two."

Nodding, he grabbed my elbow, tugging me closer as we stood with our backs together, weapons raised. My fire blazed brighter and, from its flicker, I saw a glimpse of hooves. Two fawn legs that morphed into the soft flesh of a woman. The hooves were crusted in a black substance and I swore under my breath.

"Lidércek," I hissed to András. *Succubi.* Sexual creatures who roamed the province, taking humans as their lovers. Many of the more wicked lidércek fed on the human's blood, sometimes taking on the form of dead wives or husbands. The worst were said to prey on the lonely and drown their victim in nightmares until they wasted away.

They were seldom aggressive, usually seeking amorous pleasure in the arms of lovers, but given the forest's afflictions—the mark of corruption visible on their hooves—I was inclined to believe they were looking for more than a lustful romp among tree trunks.

The first lidérc approached slowly and I sucked in a breath as she stepped into the light. She was one of the most beautiful creatures I'd ever seen. Long black hair flowed over her shoulders, covering a bare torso and a body of sleek curves. She had bow lips and a bone structure so rigid it might well have been carved, but somehow, the sharpness added to her allure. Her eyes, though, they were black as voids, utterly engulfed by the sickness of the woods.

No, these creatures were anything but friendly.

My skin puckered as she spoke, but her words were foreign, said with a honeyed tongue as they slipped into the guards' ears. "What is she saying?" I asked András, but when I turned, his face was blank, eyes dreamy as he gazed upon her.

The others stepped closer to our circle and they, too, whispered sweet nothings to the men. Tugging at András's sleeve, elbowing him in the ribs, even slapping him across the cheek did nothing to break his trance.

Sighing, I stepped around him to face the lidérc. She hissed as I approached, razor-sharp talons unfurling as her nails lengthened into daggers.

Smirking, I raised my dagger, calling the darkness inside me

234

to the surface. Red misted around us, shrouding me in a cloud of magic, the sharp copper tang climbing my nostrils. Through the fog, her eyes narrowed into slits and she stepped back, fangs bared, clawed hands raised aggressively.

"Not today, bitch."

I unleashed my power, sending a tunnel of fire barrelling to her stomach. Her screams reverberated through me, causing my blood to frost over as the discordant tone rang through the forest. Dread filled the cup of my stomach as the others hissed in rage, their attention turning to me.

András stumbled into my back, finally freed from whatever sex-filled fantasies the lidérc had inflicted him with. Death by sex wouldn't have been so bad a way to go, but I gritted my teeth as my enemy approached. Not tonight.

The other men snapped from their stupor, swords now raised and their stances ready. The creatures advanced and the dance began.

I dodged a swipe of deadly claws, spinning on my feet to kick her legs out from beneath her. She tumbled to her back, only to arch her spine and kick off from the ground—right into my stomach.

The air whooshed from my lungs, nausea roiling as I doubled over, winded. I'd be lucky if my ribs were all intact and there'd be a nasty bruise from that hoofmark tomorrow—if there was a tomorrow.

Snarling, I refocused on the lidérc, sending a blast of fire

hurtling toward her head. Gracefully, she bent a shoulder backwards, allowing the flames to hurdle past harmlessly. She grinned, fangs cutting a sneer, black pools glittering with malice.

Beside me, András grunted as he kept his enemy at bay, shredding her piece by piece with precise slices. Blood splattered around us in arcs of black and red, converging in glittering puddles upon the leaf-strewn ground.

A guard fell, his screams piercing the clearing as a lidérc slammed all ten talons deep into his chest, twisting those blades, piercing his organs. Blood bubbled from his lips and the last breath hushed from his body a moment later.

Rage coursed through me and I turned my attention back to my own foe. Baring my teeth, I swivelled my blade so the tip shifted between my fingers. Breathing deep, I let it fly, needing only a second to take aim. It flipped through the air, sinking home into her heart.

She was dead before she hit the ground, black eyes unseeing as her body crumpled.

Sighing in relief, I looked to the guards. It was chaos. Shouts echoed as they battled, claws soaked in scarlet, blades blackened with the ooze of blood. Two of our men were down, but the odds tipped in our favour.

Through the throng, I saw Dante, his movements elegant, his swordsmanship precise. The shouts and rings of steel must have roused him from sleep and his hair was still swept in messy waves, his doublet left forgotten. Not that he needed it. Dante moved as

 236

if born for battle. Sleek and swift, a deadly assassin wrought from muscle and the nectar of the gods.

His eyes locked on mine as he moved and the breath left my lungs. Seeing him like this had my heart surging in my chest, fearful of seeing him hurt. My power swelled, fingers curling into claws. It took all my willpower not to unleash the dark magic, to watch them all *burn*. But I couldn't risk hurting him or any of the others. I dropped my left hand to my side, suppressing the emotions roiling through me.

I shouldn't have worried. In the next sweep he decapitated a lidérc, immediately moving on to his next victim.

Drums pounded against my skull again as Fate demanded my attention. Right. Growling in frustration, I turned on my feet, ducking into the darkness and away from the battle still raging behind me.

Someone called my name and, vaguely, I noted the worry in that tone—*the fear.*

But Fate was calling, and one did not make the mistress of destiny wait.

Picking my way through the undergrowth, I cursed the dark and gods forsaken place. Without my fire I would be blind, but even the crackling flames of my fireball did little to light the way. The darkness swallowed me and the branches clawed at my hair, tangling within the knots.

Sighing, I stumbled on, the drums pounding harder and harder until I feared my head might split open. Pain exploded behind my eyes and I swallowed the rising sickness in my throat. When the sounds of steel and shouting faded, I at last stepped into another clearing.

The grey trunks of dead trees encircled me and even the grass beneath my feet was blackened. The whole place was lifeless. The hairs on my neck rose as I approached a pool in the middle of the clearing, its depths sending no reflection back at me.

Curious, I bent over, studying the ripples of its surface. Black smoke erupted and, yelping, I jumped backwards, raising my fireball higher in defence. I'd left my dagger in the dead lidérc, leaving only a small handful of knives at my belt.

Something appeared behind the smoke and I craned my neck, trying to spy the source. I needn't have bothered. My instincts screamed to turn and run and my blood went cold, the familiar prickling of the supernatural crawling over my skin.

The smoke dissipated and, at last, I saw her.

Slender ankles and legs standing on the body of water. An hourglass figure wreathed in black satin, the cut of the dress leaving little to the imagination as it clung to her curves and revealed much of her glowing flesh.

Her light skin was golden, her lips painted red and piercing blue eyes lined with kohl. Golden hair in an angled slice framed her face and smoke clung to her body like a second skin.

Her lips cut a sharp grin as she gazed upon me, stepping over the water's surface to stop mere inches from my face. "Darling," she purred. "I've waited so long to meet you. My, you are beautiful."

She glided around me, lifting a hand to clench my hair, to sniff my neck, to run a bejewelled finger clad in gold and black gems along the exposed flesh of my throat and the dip between my decolletage. With a sharp press she extracted a perfect gem of my blood, lifting it to her lips and curling a tongue around it.

I said nothing, did nothing as she did so. My body recoiled from her, every cell inside me protesting her presence. Death was an ass, but at least he had manners and wit. He had little business with the living, only collecting that which is already dead. But Fate ...

I'd never been so terrified of anything in my life. Her aura screamed nightmares and ruin, the end of all things. Power oozed from her in pulsating waves. Every careful sweep of her eyes sent invisible spiders skittering across my skin. But I would not let her see my terror, would not shiver or shrink before her.

Could she kill me if she desired? Was she allowed to intervene in middling affairs? As the weaver of time, I supposed not, otherwise she wouldn't need me in the first place.

She closed her eyes, relishing the taste of me upon her tongue, *moaning*. It sickened me to my core.

"You, my dear, taste delicious. The power running through your veins, well, I haven't felt that since ..." Fate drifted off, lips

pursed in thought. Still I said nothing, waiting for a question, a command, anything that would get me away from her as soon as possible.

When I could stand it no longer, the words burst from behind gritted teeth. "What do you want?"

Her lips twisted in a cruel sneer. "*Everything.*" A tremor racked through my body. "You are a child born of blood magic. It runs through your veins, filling you with purpose. You've felt its call, yes? The song of violence?"

Begrudgingly, I nodded. I'd felt it keenly. The need to hurt someone. To destroy. It worsened when anger struck hard and fast and lately I was *always* angry. I'd almost loosed it upon the lidércek, but I didn't understand my limits yet, didn't know if such power could be tamed so as not to hurt others in the crossfire.

Fate's eyes were sapphires. Hard and cold and empty of warmth. "I have need of that power."

I blinked, a slow sneer spreading over my face. She stared at my lips hungrily, but I didn't flinch at that depthless gaze. "You would beg a mortal's strength? Why should I help you?"

Her nostrils flared, eyes flashing dangerously. "If you don't, your precious family will perish, the woods will die, and the rot will spread into the hearts of every man, woman and child across this earth. Do you wish for the end of all things, girl? For that is the card I offer should you defy me. From the blood of witches, a new world will dawn."

The colour fled my cheeks as my face drained of blood. "You would allow the world to burn out of spite?"

She smiled sweetly, a slash of red in the dark. "I allow nothing. Demons may not interfere in mortal affairs—not unless a bargain is struck. Even if I wanted to, I would be powerless against Sylvie and her cult."

That name slipped like silk from her tongue. A silvered slip of truth from the snake's mouth. Lifting my chin and looking her square in the eye, I whispered, "Sylvie is dead."

"Not for long."

My knees felt weak, my bones wobbling beneath me but, to my surprise, Fate took no pleasure in her delivery. Her lip curled as she waved a dismissive hand. "The cultists will succeed in resurrecting her and their forces shall scourge this land. This thread be sewn, thy fate unaltered."

The Dark Queen threatened to destroy everything I held dear. Everything good in this world. Blinking, I stared at her, curling my fingers into fists. A hate so blindingly bright flared to the surface and sudden realisation filled me. I *hated* Sylvie Morici, this ghost of the past. Hated her so vehemently it fused my bones with iron strength until rage consumed me.

All I saw was red. My vision swam with it and the dark creature inside me roared, clawing to the surface, scratching to be free. Blood-red misted from me in violent waves, snaking around every branch, sizzling over every surface in proximity. It poured from me until it consumed everything within a ten-foot radius.

When the last of my frustration turned to a simmer, the red mist coiling back inside me, I saw the destruction. The decimated trees. Nothing but blackened husks remained—if anything at all. My power had just erased most of them from existence.

Fate stepped into my vision and the bitch was smiling. Smiling as if this was one big game and she was the game master.

"What do I need to do?" I asked, determination now filling the void my anger had left in its wake.

She placed a hand on my arm and the lifelessness I felt—the sheer coldness—grounded me. Brought me back to reality and purpose.

"It's quite simple," she said, casually picking at a thread on her dress. "There's only one way to rid ourselves of the Dark Queen and that's bringing her back to Earth. Right now, she's rotting in a dungeon under the watchful eye of hell's caretaker. She died as all mortals do, so I may not gift her with my"—she caressed my arm with that sharp claw—"favour. But if the cultists resurrect her using magic, she's anyone's game. She will not be a witch when she comes back, but an imitation of her old self. No less powerful, mind, but not strictly mortal either."

"So if she's a supernatural entity, all bets are off," I said, following her logic. But one thing kept niggling at me. "Why? Why go to all this effort to destroy Sylvie? I'm guessing it's not from the goodness of your heart."

She laughed, a cold, humourless thing. "Only an idiot would believe I cared for the wellbeing of you pitiful creatures. No. Sylvie

took something from me before she died. I want it back."

I raised a brow, but she simply swished her skirts, striding towards the pond. The light from my fireball seemed to sink into her dress, consumed by the darkness within. Honestly, I couldn't believe something so evil was embodied in perfection's form.

Narrowing my eyes, I glared at her back. "And you want me to search for it," I drawled. What item?"

She turned, pursing her lips. "A crown. A very powerful artefact. That's all you need to know."

I sighed. Of course she wouldn't tell me more. "Why do you need my help? Once she's resurrected, can't you take it for yourself?"

She laughed again and this time the sound seemed to spear smoky tendrils into my heart. "Oh, poor girl, you really do not know what lies ahead, do you?" She cocked a head, her gaze piercing my very soul. A sliver of pity flashed in her eyes. "In order to defeat the Dark Queen, you must deal the final blow. It's all in the blood, you see. But there's something I should mention before I go."

My stomach flipped, anxiety forming in painful knots. I couldn't bring myself to ask and trepidation demanded I leave this place before my world could be shattered. But Fate, that damnable demon, waited with a sly smile until at last I nodded just once, resigning myself to whatever horrors awaited.

"Blessed be the blood overflowing from their cups. And when her heart dost cease to flutter, the dead will rise, rise

another."

Nostrils flaring, my temper poured out. "I don't speak in riddles. What are you saying?"

"You have the power to raise the dead, Kitarni. But such power demands sacrifice. You must pass through the veil, journey through the Under World to return to this plane." She smiled, her eyes glittering with cold humour. "*If* you can make it back."

Fate disappeared in a flash of smoke, her voice echoing in her wake. My head pounded, ears ringing with the tolling bells of doom. There was no mistaking the message. It suddenly made sense why Fate needed me so deeply. It always circled back to one thing. Blood.

"Oh gods," I whispered, falling to my knees.

No, no, no. But there was no denying the outcome. Fate had said so herself—the threads were fixed. The weaving of the future could not be changed. To save my home and indeed, the world beyond, I would have to die.

There was no other way to put it.

I was utterly and royally fucked.

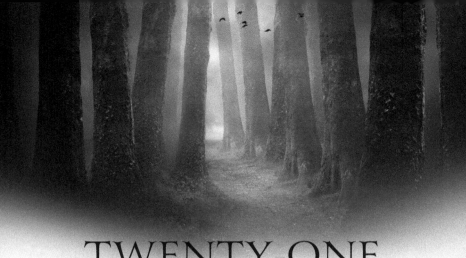

TWENTY-ONE

"Kitarni!"

Strong arms encircled me as I slumped into Dante's embrace, too tired, too dazed to recall how I'd found my way back to the cabin. A small part of me registered the concern in his tone, but I was too exhausted to care. My stomach was hollow, my heart stuck in my throat.

I'd tripped over several gnarled roots and stumbled into prickly bushes on the way back, scraping my hands until the skin was raw and angry. Leaves and twigs littered my hair, caught in the curled strands, and my face was caked with dirt and tears. I could only imagine what I looked like.

Hating myself for nestling into the warmth of his chest—for letting my guard down—I squeezed my eyes shut, shoving my despair deep down in my chest.

He couldn't know. He'd only do something foolish to prevent it. I didn't know what we shared. Whether it was simply lust, a mutual need for release and freedom, or perhaps the promise of something more. I couldn't deny he sparked something inside me. Despite his insufferable nature, he made me feel alive. I enjoyed the easiness of his company, however irritating he could be, and he was a man who challenged me. I could see myself on his arm one day, if not happily in love, then as an equal to rule with at least.

But not now. Fate had other plans and allowing him to get close would only risk pain for us both. *He doesn't care about you anyway*, a small voice reminded me.

"Where have you been?" He tucked a strand of hair behind my ear, his hand lingering on my cheek as he brushed a knuckle over my skin. My body tingled at the touch and, as I peered at his dark brown eyes, the gold flashing in the dark, my breath caught in my throat.

Fear filled those windows. And rage. Not from the fight itself, but fear for me and anger for the lives lost. But why? My throat bobbed as I pulled out of his arms. "I ... I was dealing with more lidércek out of the clearing. There were others lurking in the shadows."

Liar.

He nodded, running a hand through his dark locks. He hesitated for a moment, gripping my chin lightly as if needing to touch me, to confirm I was safe. "I thought we'd lost you." His voice was too soft.

My heart cracked just a little at those words, at the concern lacing his tone. Where was the selfish, arrogant táltos I'd first met in the woods? But I said nothing, instead following the direction of his eyes as they swept over the clearing. The warmth left my body as I scanned the carnage. Blood congealed in sticky pools of black beneath a pile of twisted limbs, hooves and horns.

There must have been at least ten lidérc. The signs of corruption climbed their fingers and ankles, consuming their pupils and creating black voids. The sight chilled me to my core. Their beautiful faces were frozen in death, mouths open in silent screams or stretched back in sneers.

It was odd to see them all together. They usually hunted in solitude, tending to their many desires in privacy.

The woods were driving everyone mad. No, not the woods. The cultists.

My anger resurfaced, devouring the emptiness in my gut, the helplessness. Was this all there was now? Death and destruction for what remained of the road ahead? I balled my hands into fists as I looked upon the fallen. Fate said I had to die, but she also said I was the only one capable of defeating Sylvie.

I watched as the táltosok set fire to the bodies, as András tended to the injured with steady hands and a smile that had no business in this place. And my rage mounted, nipping at my bones, snarling at my heels, ready to devour me.

Without a word, I stormed for the cabin before anyone could see me break, slamming the door behind me.

247

Tears streamed down my face, hot and heavy. I slid down the wall of the lounge, the tears seemingly endless as the pain burned me from the inside out.

The door clicked shut behind Dante as he strode in after me. I felt his gaze searing my skin, the weight of his stare digging deep.

"What's wrong?"

It sounded more like a command than a question. I set my jaw firmly, still too overwhelmed to talk and unsure what to say anyway. I couldn't tell him the truth. A lie was hardly better.

Kneeling, he reached out a hand, but I recoiled, curling my nails in the wooden floor. "I don't want to talk about it."

"Kitarni, I'm here for you. You can tell me anything."

"Leave me alone," I seethed, pulling my knees to my chest and burying my face in the cradle of my arms.

He paused, but still he stayed by my side. "I know this isn't easy, but we'll get through this. We'll be in Mistvellen tomorrow, where you'll be safe."

"Safe?" I lifted my head to glare at him, my eyes blazing with cold fire. I laughed bitterly. "No one is safe anymore, Dante. People are dying, innocents are being corrupted by this godsforsaken place. Two of your men are dead!"

Dante stiffened as he rose. "And you think *I'm* to blame?" His eyes flashed dangerously, his voice dipping.

Standing, I stalked closer, my blood boiling. "They died fighting for you while you were safe and sound, tucked away in bed. You were too late."

I regretted the words as soon as they left my mouth. It wasn't fair to blame him, to use him as a punching bag. No, this was Fate's fault. I'd felt her call before the fighting had even started and Death had said she'd have a distraction. Was this all her doing?

Dante blinked, the muscles in his neck quivering in anger. His gaze was thunderous, dangerous. He took a step back, opened his mouth, closed it again, as if thinking better.

He looked at me then with a strange expression in his eyes. Something like sadness or pity and for a moment I wondered if I'd shattered whatever peace we'd started to build.

"I know you're lying about what happened in the woods," he said coolly, crossing his arms. "And fine, I won't push, but if your secrets place us in danger, you will answer to me, witch."

Red misted at my fists, swirling up my arms like serpents. The power coiled around my body, ready to strike with merely a thought. I couldn't be around him now. He had a way of getting under my skin and my rage was doing that well enough on its own, begging to be unleashed.

"Get out," I said quietly.

He stood his ground, refusing to move an inch. "You want someone to blame for your problems? Look outside." He lifted his arm, jabbing a pointed finger at the world beyond these four walls. "Your enemies are out there, waiting to pounce at the first sign of weakness. I know you're angry at your bloodline, your

power, your duty, but we're in this together. Don't push away the only lifeline you've got."

Nostrils flaring, I took two steps towards his chest, peering up into his stupidly handsome face. Everything he said was true and I hated it. Hated what Fate required of me, hated that I couldn't let Dante in, hated that he knew I was so alone in this life.

Hated, hated, hated.

And so I said the words I knew would win this fight. "Why would I want to be on the arm of someone so weak? Someone who can't save his men from a mere handful of enemies? Perhaps you should focus your efforts where they're needed, Dante. They're certainly not wanted here."

I turned away, not wanting to see the expression cross his face, but I could only imagine the hurt I might find in his eyes. I'd been cruel and such unkindness found a way to burrow into the cracks of the soul. I knew he'd already be punishing himself for tonight, cursing himself for not being fast enough, strong enough, wise enough, to save those men.

It wasn't his fault. All had been silent. All had been well. Even the most watchful of guards couldn't have avoided a lidérc's snare.

Dante's footsteps sounded, the door clicking ever so softly behind him as he entered the night. I blinked back the tears threatening to spill over my cheeks. I'd said I'd make his world hell.

It seemed I was fulfilling that promise, only it didn't feel as good as I'd thought.

Reality was so much worse.

TWENTY-TWO

I was sitting in the armchair, book in hand and Laszlo at my feet, warming my toes while he stretched by the fire when Dante returned. Dante must have kept him locked inside earlier. The poor thing must have been terrified.

The lazy dog looked up, staring at Dante momentarily before dropping like a deadweight to the floor.

He really was a useless guard dog.

Dante had been gone for what felt like hours, but it was little more than one. I'd cried for a while before picking my sorry ass up and pacing the chamber. Slowly, my anger had dissipated, but still the power lingered, scratching at the surface. It was better I'd sent Dante away. I had been so close to slipping—dangerously volatile. He wouldn't have let me out of his sight had I left the cabin, so hurting him ...

I'd had no choice.

After wearing tracks into the floor, fretting over my

 251

behaviour, I'd finally decided to read. It was an adventurous tale, filled with scandalously dirty romance and a dashing prince. A perfect escape from reality. I hadn't packed the book myself, but found it jammed into my pack, wrapped carefully in a tunic so as not to bend or scratch.

My heart had warmed. I knew without a doubt Eszter had packed it. She was always so thoughtful. Maybe she knew I'd need a little fantasy in my life. To live in someone else's shoes for a while.

Gods bless that girl.

I'd found a skin of wine stashed within the musty cupboards in the kitchen and filled a goblet to the rim. The heavy-bodied red had warmed my insides, dulling the keen edge of my anger. It had also made me drowsy so close to the fire. I'd been rereading the same sentence repeatedly, still too guilt-ridden to focus yet too emotional to sleep. Thoughts of my throat being slashed or my blood being drained in a cult ritual kept haunting me. Would they drain me like they had Hanna and the others? Would they feed from me like vampires or simply suck the soul from my skin like the harbinger himself?

But worse than that I'd kept picturing Dante's face when I'd blamed him for the loss of his men. It was cruel and cold. And I hated it.

Wordlessly, he poured himself a cup and sat down on the sofa, scrubbing a hand over his face. His cheeks were flushed, brown hair tousled, but his eyes were dark. Filled with a lingering anger. I suspected it was more at himself than me. There was much to learn about Dante, but I knew he felt the deaths of his men keenly. They weren't just his soldiers, they were friends. Brothers.

A pang of sorrow cleaved through my chest. When he caught me watching him, he stared me square in the eye. Unyielding.

I straightened, squaring my jaw, opening my mouth to speak.

"What happened tonight?" he asked quietly before I could get a word out.

Clenching my teeth, I looked away, silent for a moment. "Everything." A muscle ticked in his jaw, but he didn't push. I closed my eyes, feeling the heaviness settle over me. When I could bear the silence no longer, I asked, "Who's going to tell their families?"

He didn't need clarification. "I will," he replied calmly. "As commander it is my duty to bear the news to the families of the fallen. They will be looked after. My father will ensure they are provided for."

My eyes stung as I bit back the words I wanted to ask. *Who will tell my family? Who will make sure my mother is cared for when she grows old? Who will see to it that Eszter never goes a day without smiling?*

I cracked my lids, travelling the sleek jaw, the curves of his lips, the straight nose. And above, to brown eyes, the reflection of the fire flickering in the golden rim. "So much death," I sighed, pressing my head back into the chair. "The war hasn't even begun yet."

"Is that why you were so angry?" he asked gently.

"Since I met you, my world has been upended, Dante. I'm losing everything I care about and I'm ... changing into something new. It frightens me."

"You're afraid of your power?"

"There is a darkness inside me. A beast roaring to be freed. I'm scared of what will happen when it is."

He reclined against the couch, crossing a leg over his knee while he swirled his wine goblet. He looked every inch a king upon his throne as his lips curved into a grin. "The world should fear your power, Kitarni. *And you.* You are no longer a forgotten, lonely girl. You are a wolf, furious and free. It's time to join your pack."

The way he spoke kindled a fire inside. There was truth in what he said. Power. And, perhaps the most soul shattering of all, he believed every word. Believed in me.

Swallowing a lump in my throat, I leaned forward, closing the book in my lap.

"I'm sorry."

He raised a brow, remaining silent. The bastard was really going to make me say it. Sighing, I set both the wine and book on the coffee table, clasping my hands together instead.

"I shouldn't have said those things to you. It wasn't your fault and I—I was upset about ..." I bit my lip, holding back all the words that wanted to blurt from my mouth.

"What?"

Annoyance flared again. "I'd rather not say."

"Why were you upset, Kitarni?"

"For the love of Isten, I can't tell you!" I snapped, rising. Irritation surged through my veins and I scowled, determined to be finished with this conversation. "I'm going to bed."

His hand snaked out and grasped my wrist quicker than I could blink. "If you're not going to tell your truth, then I will. Do you want to know why your words hit so hard? Why the blame cut so deep?"

I blinked at him as he stood slowly, towering over me, forcing me to look up into his eyes. His face was filled with an old and primal rage.

"When I was younger, the cultists came to Mistvellen. They struck the day after Yule, while the guards were still drunk and the rest of us were sleeping. It was a bloodbath. Scores of innocents were cut down ..."

His voice trailed off and sorrow clutched my heart as he relived the horror of that memory.

The pain in his eyes flared cold as ice. "My father was in Transylvania securing safe trade routes for the witches and táltosok, so he wasn't around to protect us. I was just a boy, so when they came for her, she didn't stand a chance. The guards tried to reach us in time, but they were too late. She fought for me with everything she had until they stabbed her. That whole time I just watched, too frightened to move. When they took her, screaming and bleeding, *I did nothing*."

Regret coursed through me at those three little words. The same ones I'd snarled at him earlier, not realising the trauma they could cause, the memories they'd rehash.

Silence blanketed the room as we stared at each other, neither one moving a muscle.

"I've never spoken to anyone about her, but it's taken me a long time to forgive myself for not acting that day. I've struggled with her loss ever since. So, you can hold on to your truth, you can lie to yourself and shove down your fears, but it will only eat you alive if you let it."

He'd offered me a glimpse into his past, shared one of his darkest secrets, and it meant too much. He looked at me with a kind of defeated expression and my stomach flipped at the sight of it. Was our little game worth it? Did he really hate me?

Because I didn't hate him. Not even a little and maybe I was done pretending that I did.

"You don't understand," I rasped, emotion clogging my throat. "Saying it out loud will make it real. I can't deal with this right now. I will *break*."

He lifted a calloused hand to my cheek. "Then we'll put you back together, piece by piece."

My skin hummed under that touch, tingling with awareness. "I ..."

His thumb swept over my lips and I parted them softly, lost in eyes sparkling with mischief. He leaned in, sweeping my hair from my shoulder as he whispered in my ear. "I am not afraid of you, Freckles. And you are not alone."

My breath hitched as his own sent shivers down my neck and, gods help me, I threw caution to the wind, forgetting my fears, letting my walls tumble and igniting the need deep inside.

I couldn't unleash my anger on the world, but I could ignite passion with another.

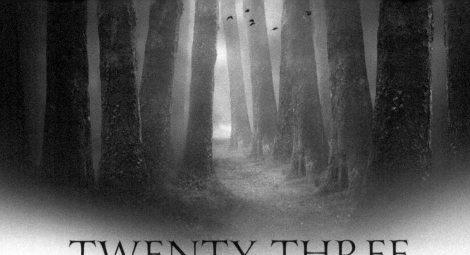

TWENTY-THREE

Curled my fingers in his shirt, clutching the fabric in my fists as I tugged him closer. His lips crashed into mine, hard and bruising with need. My heart thundered in my chest as the world rippled to nothingness—nothing but him and me in my bubble of awareness.

His hands felt like fire when he lifted me into his arms, setting me down on his lap as he sat back against the cushions. I straddled him, wrapping my legs tight around his body as he lined up beneath me. I rolled my hips against him, my core turning molten at the hardness pressed against me.

I opened my mouth and his tongue curled in, exploring and eager, glorious and devouring. He tasted like red wine and embers, and I squeezed my eyes shut at the sensation.

A moan escaped my lips, the sound stirring him even further. His fingers fisted in my hair, clenching the roots to angle my head and expose my throat. Warm lips travelled my jaw, his teeth scraping over my trembling pulse then back up to claim my mouth.

Desperation filled me and I roved my hands under his shirt, sliding them over rigid muscle and smooth planes. He was built like a god, the olive tone of his skin gleaming in the firelight.

I lost myself to the deepening kiss, growing hungrier as my fingers dipped tantalisingly low, tracing the vee above the lip of his pants. A low growl rumbled from him and his grip on my hair tightened, forcing my gaze to meet his.

They glinted dangerously in the firelight and I traced a hand gently along the sharpness of his jaw, the angles of his cheeks before plunging my own fingers into his hair. His lips quirked as he plucked leaves and twigs from my hair as I stared at him, a soft and surprising laugh leaving me. His dark locks gleamed with reddish strands as I ran my fingernails over his scalp and he elicited a low groan that thrummed through my core.

His hands dropped to my shirt, making quick work of the buttons until the material opened, revealing plain white undergarments beneath. He looked at me appreciatively, roaming calloused hands over the exposed skin, drifting down my collar bone, my chest, in between my breasts and down dangerously low.

Excitement coursed through me at the proximity of those practiced hands, teasing as I had only moments before. I writhed at his touch, trying to squeeze my thighs together to relieve the need pounding deeper. But he leaned back, a wicked grin on his face. "Take it off."

I hesitated. What would he think if he saw my scars? The writhing stripes of shimmering black slashed across my spine? I'd never shown them to a lover before. Never revealed that part of myself.

Don't hide.

Raising a brow, I tugged on the fastenings of my corset and shrugged out of my shirt slowly, rolling the sleeves down my arms. He appraised my breasts, but I reared back before he could touch them, slapping his hands away.

"You next," I said softly.

His eyes flashed as they drank in every curve. I'd always been relatively fit, built athletically. Slim, yet not waifish like many of the other young women. My ribcage wasn't as tiny, my waist not as small, but I was in good shape. Strong, feminine, and glowing.

I wasn't ashamed to admit it. Seeing the way he looked at me, I felt powerful. Daring. Dante challenged me, excited me in ways other lovers never had.

He peeled his shirt off lazily, shrugging out of it with a crooked smile. The tattoos inked over his chest gleamed, the wolf snarling from his chest, the flowers seeming to shimmer in the firelight. His corded arms rippled as he moved and I traced each vein flushed from heat, from the blood pumping through his body. I kissed his forearm gently before leaning in to claim his lips again.

Taking my neck in one hand, he pulled me closer, crashing my lips to his once more as his tongue swept into my mouth. He pressed my hand to the strain of his pants and a thrill coursed through me.

"Remove them," I commanded, no longer able to tamp down the pounding in my core.

He grinned against my lips, squeezing a hand around my upper thigh before obeying. "So bossy."

My pants dropped to the floor as he tugged his off and picked me up, squeezing my ass before he lay me before the fire. To my relief, Laszlo had long since disappeared, but the brief thought rushed from me as he stared at me hungrily.

"Beautiful," he whispered, right before placing a finger to my centre.

Gasping, I jerked, arching my back as his fingers circled below. He slipped one finger in, then two, and I gasped as my body pulsed with heat, my core tightening around his clever fingers. I writhed against him, the ache mounting, the pleasure surging to the surface. Leaning back on my elbows, I cupped a hand to his length—the considerable size of him in my palm.

Pumping him slowly with my hand as he moved his fingers in and out of me, we matched rhythms until the crescendo quickened, faster, faster, my cries combining with his moans until my legs were shaking and I felt a wave of delicious heat surge through me. My climax mounted, and his breathing came in quick gasps as we came together. I couldn't think, couldn't breathe, overcome with pure bliss so agonising I wanted it to stop. To never stop.

 261

I felt him shudder beside me, but I knew he wasn't spent yet. His brown eyes looked gilded in the dim glow of the fire, his skin gleaming with sweat and dirt and the faintest splatters of blood here and there.

The sight of that black substance on his skin stole the desire from me, made my stomach turn as reality came crashing back hard and fast.

Lying on my back, I squeezed my eyes shut, trying to push the thoughts from my mind. Dante placed a featherlight kiss to my collar bone, his hair tickling my cheek as he bent over me. My skin prickled with awareness at his touch, the very press of his lips sending delightful shivers down my body.

When I opened my eyes, his face was crumpled with concern. "Did I fail to please you?"

Realising the despair had broken through my mask, I sat up. "Gods, no. Believe me, Dante, there's no question of that. It's just ..." I sighed, turning towards the fire, prodding at the dying embers with a poker.

A sharp intake of breath made me realise my mistake. He'd seen them—seen the ugliness scrawled over my back.

"Who did this to you?" he growled. "Who hurt you? I will rip the head off their shoulders where they stand."

I grabbed the closest thing I could find—his shirt, still smelling of leather and embers and *man*—and shrugged it on, the material swimming on me and managing to reveal most of my cleavage. "No one," I said quietly. "Not a man, at least. It's complicated witch business."

He watched me, placing a hand on my thigh in silence. I liked that about Dante. He sensed my moods like the change of the winds, could understand when I needed space. He didn't push like most people would.

"They're beautiful, you know," he said softly. "Whatever happened, it made you stronger. You should wear your scars like armour. Embrace them."

Don't hide.

His words brought tears to my eyes. I'd spent so long trying to be invisible, I had started to believe I deserved it. The pain, the jeers, the jaunts and the loneliness. But he was right. The ugliness was a part of me. Just like the power in my veins.

I took a deep breath, not yet ready to dive into that story right now. "The blood on you reminded me of what happened tonight. What's yet to come."

He stretched his arms out in front of him, frowning at the black splotches. "Ah. Blood and bones I can handle. As long as my wife is satisfied."

Despite the lurch of terror—and a strangely satisfying tingle—at the endearment, I laughed quietly. "I'm not your wife *yet*." I tapped a finger to my lips, a smirk curling my mouth. "And I'm not sure I am satisfied. We barely scratched the surface."

He chuckled, a low hum that made my heart flutter. "Believe me, Freckles, when I'm done with you, you won't be able to walk the next day."

I shivered as his words slid over my skin, settling in my core. My breath hitched. "And what do you plan to do to me?"

He leaned in close, whispering in the shell of my ear. "When I bow before you, I will worship your entire existence. You are a goddess, and I, your humble servant."

His gaze swept over me, shamelessly appraising every inch of my body before he stretched alongside me like a cat. He stroked the curve of my waist with one unhurried finger, drawing idle circles on my skin.

"Then, as your goddess, I demand your prayer. I need every inch to fill me up." My voice was husky, laced with desire. *Who the hell was this girl?*

His lips curved into a knowing smile. "If we started now, we wouldn't stop until the sun was up. And when I claim you, I want it to be in *our* house. In our bed." He paused for a moment to fist the shirt in his hand and flick a tongue over my breast, eyes glinting dangerously.

"As my wife."

I tossed and turned for the rest of the night, conscious of Dante's warm body beside me, the sounds of his breathing filling the stillness. Neither one of us had complained about sharing a bed after our tryst. There seemed little point to hiding our desire any longer.

His words repeated in my mind. *"Our house. Our bed. My wife."* Did he really want these things? Dante was exciting, thoughtful, fun—and stupidly handsome—but was that enough to blur the lines of duty? It felt less like a mutual acceptance of our marriage now and more a spark of interest at what was to come—at what could be.

Rolling onto my back, I stared at the ceiling, diverting my attention from the muscles in his shoulders, the curve of his spine.

We'd crossed a line tonight—one we couldn't go back from.

And maybe ... maybe I didn't want to.

Truthfully, I would have given myself to him entirely tonight but, surprisingly—and a little annoyingly—we'd never made it that far. *My fault.* My stupid brain not shutting off, not letting me have one small moment of reckless pleasure. He wouldn't have bedded me altogether, though. I supposed he still wanted to court me, to earn my favour. Perhaps he thought I'd respect his restraint more.

Idiot. I'd practically tossed aside all reservations.

I'd needed him. Needed a release, if not from my magic, then of simple, sexual pleasure. It had quieted the power, for now. Knowing what he could give me, though, what he promised would come, only kindled the desire even further. But as we lay side-by-side, his hand clasped on my thigh, I realised I had never felt so alive as in that moment.

Knowing my life would soon end had somehow made it more

passionate, more thrilling. That's what I kept telling myself, but I couldn't deny something had changed between us. The anger had thawed, the battle lines withdrawn.

He desired me. Had made every effort to ensure my safety and comfort.

His face was relaxed in sleep, the muscles of his brow softened, the line of his jaw and cheekbones somehow less sharp. Not so dangerous at all. I think, under the killer instinct and the cocky smiles, lay a soft shell. One I might crack open to find a gooey centre. A chocolate to be savoured—and I knew my sweets.

A gentle voice warned where this road could lead. And I promised myself I wouldn't—*I couldn't*—develop feelings for him. But where the mind is logical, the heart is all fire.

If I wasn't careful, I would burn in those flames.

TWENTY-FOUR

It was a quiet ride to Mistvellen. No one was in the mood for chatter after last night's events. The bodies of the two fallen guards had been rolled in sheets from the cabin and secured to their mounts so their families could bury them.

Scarlet seeped from the white cotton, staining the fabric and setting a stark reminder to carry with us. András told me their names were Bela and Csaba. They both had wives and children waiting for their return. Families who would miss them forevermore.

Dante barely spoke as the day wore on, but I saw the hard set of his jaw, the way his eyes darted to them. Guilt fired through me once again at my words from yesterday.

He placed a warm hand on my knee as if sensing where my thoughts had gone. A small gesture of forgiveness. A breath shuddered from my lungs and I petted Arló on the neck, cooing to him gently. The little coward had quite the scare last night, but at least he didn't bolt altogether.

I narrowed my eyes. *This time.*

Laszlo bounded ahead, unperturbed by the gloomy forest, the gnarled roots or the spindly trees clawing at the sky. Even if the canopy wasn't blocking out the daylight, the leaves still seemed grey and lifeless, casting a perpetual shroud over our shoulders.

When several hours had passed without hide or hair of animal, cultist, or creature, I could stand the silence no longer. "What's it like? Mistvellen, I mean."

Dante raised an amused brow. "It's beautiful. The woods open to rolling green hills and on the southern front are rows and rows of lavender bushes. When the sun sets, those hills sing."

It sounded charming. Something an artist might paint to hang in gilded frames upon nobles' walls. Lavender was often used in tonics and spells or, for the upper class, in perfumes and lotions. But I wasn't aware of any witches in Mistvellen. "Why lavender?"

Dante's smile was sad, his gaze faraway. "It was my mother's favourite flower. She suffered from night terrors, so the maid would give her poultices to lie beneath her pillow to calm her. And purple was always her favourite colour. We had some plants in our gardens, but once she passed, I had the rows planted to honour her memory."

My heart constricted and, leaning over, I squeezed his leg. "I'm sure she would love it."

268

His answering grin was a brilliant flash of white teeth. A rare, true smile that I hadn't really seen yet. A strange feeling bubbled inside me at the sight. "I think so too."

"And what's your home like? The town?"

"You won't find a more generous and loving people. Most among us are táltosok, but we welcome others, too. Humans and witches, men and women of all cultures and places. Within the stone walls of our town is a bustling hive. The people support each other. There is no upper or lower class like one might find in human towns. All are happy and healthy. We look after our own."

"You allow humans to live there too?" My jaw dropped in disbelief. I couldn't believe what I was hearing. Humans! The people who cried murder at the very sniff of the word witch. "Aren't you worried they will spread news about the town? Just one gossipmonger could spread word to nearby villages—have raiders with pitchforks and torches banging on your doors."

Dante chuckled. "Our community thrives because we are all equal. Táltos, witch, human, it doesn't matter. We keep each other safe and we work hard to keep a good thing going. The people have homes, jobs, food on the table and fires to keep them warm. They respect my father and his reign."

Blinking, I sat back in my saddle. "I didn't know," I whispered. "All this time, I had no idea just how separated from the world my coven really was. Why?"

He looked at me pointedly. "Can you think of no reason?"

269

My nostrils flared. "Caitlin."

Those brown eyes hardened like steel. "She's still living in the past, afraid to embrace a future where power is shared among the many. I know her. People in positions of power do not share the load lightly unless their choices are taken from them. The girls in your village? She knows many would leave if they knew greener pastures lay beyond."

"So she keeps them penned like animals. Hiding behind a society designed to behold women to their homes, to their petticoats and sewing, pianoforte and a fool's curtsy." I snorted. "What rubbish."

"Have I told you how sexy you are when you're pouting?" Dante purred.

Rolling my eyes, I kicked his shin. "You are incorrigible."

"And you are glorious. I think you'll quite like being the lady of Mistvellen. You've already got the bossiness down. A few fine dresses and jewels and you'll be right at home."

"I don't need dresses and jewels. If you haven't noticed, I'm not exactly a girly girl."

He smiled and a dimple cracked his cheek. "Oh, the gowns aren't for you, Freckles. I like my presents wrapped before I rip the finery off."

A blush stained my cheeks and I aimed a kick at his leg again, but he nudged Arló with his stallion, making me wobble in my seat. I glared as the other dimple popped into place. "You are an arrogant ass."

"And you are a stubborn mule. We make a good match." He leaned closer. "By the way, if you were wondering what the jewels are for, I'd like you to keep them on when I fuck you. Wearing *only* the jewels."

A jolt fired down my core and he urged his horse to trot to the front of the procession, laughing as my curses followed behind him.

We made it to Mistvellen just after sundown.

I'd never been so happy to see the night sky. Stars twinkled from black velvet above and the air seemed fresh and crisp after the confines of the forest. I urged Arló onwards, gulping down clean oxygen and my head cleared instantly, freed from the heady fog of the Sötét Erdő.

Lavender climbed my nose and I smiled to myself, welcoming the calming aroma. I spotted the rows of purple lining the hills to the right. Words hadn't given them justice. They were beautiful and, in the daylight, I knew they'd contrast vividly with the green pastures and the gentle slope of a mountain looming in the distance.

I cast my eyes straight ahead. The trees opened onto a dirt road carving straight through rolling green hills, tulips in reds and yellows and pinks dotting the fields. Beyond, white stone walls with stunning rounded archways cradled the quaint town beyond.

Thatched roofs could be seen from the slight rise overlooking the village, but I was more impressed by the buildings above them. Many had rounded domes in hues of sage green, and even shingles lining the roofs.

The architecture was a testament to the gothic style I'd heard was rapidly developing in English and French settlements. My jaw dropped as I stared at this advanced city. To soften the stone maze, creeping ivy sprawled over walls and roofs, and gardens twined gently through the streets. Compared to my humble village, it was a masterpiece.

But it wasn't the town which took my breath away. Beyond the streets loomed a castle in the same style. Columns of polished marble pierced the sky, arches with shallow divots curved over the courtyards and balconies, windows with round-headed arches peeking out from stone walls.

Raising a brow, I glanced at Dante. "You failed to mention you live in a castle."

András rode up beside me, an amused grin across his pale cheeks. "Don't let it get to his head. It's already fat with self-importance."

"Don't be jealous, András," Dante replied with a smirk. "Petulance doesn't suit you."

His friend's smile only widened. "Why would I be jealous? You can keep your responsibilities, I'll enjoy the merits of coasting off them." He turned to me with twinkling green eyes. "I'm quite fond of the friends I keep within those castle walls."

Dante snorted. "You're referring to the many servants wrapped around your little finger, of course."

"Wrapped around something else more often than not, actually."

I rolled my eyes. "You're both despicable."

My husband-to-be winked at me. "I never promised otherwise."

"And do you have *friends* within the castle too?"

His grin was lazy. "Would it annoy you if I did?"

Yes. Not that I'd admit it. I lifted my chin in the air. "You're annoying me right now."

András leaned in. "Don't tell him that. He'll make it his goal to continue doing so."

I glared at Dante. "Need I remind you I have three throwing knives and a dagger strapped to my person right now. If you're not careful, you might wake up without your precious commodity one morning. I doubt your friends would like you then."

Dante's dimples flashed. "Savage, my lady. So you *do* care."

András shook his head. "You've done it now."

Gods, give me the patience required to deal with this insufferable man. Seething, I clenched my teeth together. "By Hadur's blade, if you don't shut up, I'll stab you right now."

"Bossy *and* violent. I think you were made for me, Kitarni."

My heart fluttered. Was it weird how much I enjoyed this game? I snorted. "You really are depraved."

"Perhaps. But I think you quite like that."

I did. Something must be wrong with me, but I did. He challenged me, brought out a woman I hadn't met before. I liked this new Kitarni. One who didn't shy away from others or hide her true self. With Dante, I could joke, I could cuss, be vulgar and just be *me*.

As I opened my mouth to sling some curses at him, András slapped a hand to my mouth. I noticed Dante had stiffened beside me, holding a hand up in the air. Confused, I looked around, trying to spot anything unusual. A flock of birds took to the sky behind us, making me jump.

Whipping my head around, I peered into the woods, searching the boughs, the fat trunks of the outlying trees. Goosebumps prickled my skin as the unnerving feeling of being watched settled over me.

"We're not alone," András whispered beside me, removing his palm from my lips. His hand hovered over his sword hilt, the other stretched out protectively before me.

Dante's brown eyes narrowed as he surveyed the forest. "The cultists are here," he informed his second. "Take Kitarni, get her behind the safety of the walls. Don't—"

A strange whistling sound sped through the air as an arrow embedded itself in the chest of one of the guards. His lips formed a surprised 'o' before he toppled off his horse with a thud.

Dead before he hit the ground.

TWENTY-FIVE

S hrieks sounded all at once from the woods as cultists in black hoods and robes came charging from the treeline. Arló pranced beneath me, and I squeezed my legs to grip Arlo's flanks.

András whipped his blond head towards me, green eyes blazing. "We need to go. Now."

He lunged for my reins right as a stone whacked into the back of his head, rendering him unconscious ... or dead. He slumped over his horse which, thankfully, had the sense to canter away from the brawl and towards the town gates.

"Shit." I looked between András and the soldiers, panic rising at the flood of cultists. I could have fled like Dante wanted, but as I looked at the bodies on the backs of those horses—at the man who'd fallen to the earth—I set my jaw, welcoming the promise of a fight. I felt, saw, *smelt* red. And I would not cower like some meek maiden.

275

Rounding Arló, I turned towards the commotion, arching a leg over his back before jumping off the stirrup. Dante caught my eye, a murderous gleam in his own. The killer was back and he was *not* happy.

His lips twitched, his jaw like glass as he clenched his teeth. I thought he'd yell at me to leave, but instead I saw a flash of surprise, followed by approval. I would fight for him and his people as he would for me. Because they were my people now. *Our* flock to protect.

Embers sparked to life as I focused on my first victim. A man with stitches holding his lips together, the same frenzied eyes of someone dosed with bloodmorphia. He would burn first.

I lobbed the fireball at his cloak, lighting up the night as the flames engulfed him entirely. The muffled screams of a voiceless man filled the air as he flailed, skin melting off his frame until he fell in a scorched heap on the ground.

The sickening smell of charred flesh climbed my nose, but I had no time to delay. Drawing a knife, I hurled it through the air, the blade embedding in the chest of a girl slightly younger than me. My stomach curdled as I looked at her face. Flat, dead eyes, a waif of a creature whose only taste of the world had been darkness and death.

She choked on her own fluids, hacking up blood. I'd pierced a lung. It was an ugly, painful way to die. Regret washed over me for the briefest of moments, but I turned my back, pawing curly strands from my cheeks to face my next foe.

Dante hovered nearby, his swords glinting in the moonlight, the wolves on his sword pommels snarling as he brought the blades arcing down upon necks and chests. His vest and shirt were already soaked, a testament to a violent, wicked creature.

The cultists surged in waves. Streaking from the trees like rats from a nest. My heart stopped when the last figure stepped into the moonlight. He towered over the others; a muscled, hulking beast of a man with oiled skin and sickles in his hands. And, draped over his neck, the skin from a bull's head, worn as a mask. Dried blood still crusted over the man's skin. It must have been a fresh kill when he'd donned it.

Bile rose in my throat. A sickening tribute to what the Christians called the devil. To dark magic. He lifted a sickle, pointing it at me menacingly and my bowels turned watery. Either he'd singled me out because he believed me the easiest target or they knew now who they hunted.

A screech to my left had me whirling under a serrated blade and kicking my leg out to topple my attacker. My boot connected with a shin, smashing into bone and forcing them to their other knee.

Striking hard and fast, I plunged my dagger into their stomach again and again, surprised by my own savagery. Red soaked my hand as I pulled away, pooling down my sleeve in sticky waves.

A whistle pierced shrilly through the commotion and I turned towards the source. A woman with long black hair and

blue eyes smiled cruelly at me before glancing over her shoulder. I followed her line of sight, squinting into the woods to see wolves yipping and snarling.

They were black like the ones I'd first encountered with Dante, their eyes feverish with the same silver-blue shimmer. They sprinted towards us, hackles raised and maws dripping with saliva.

Dante snarled as he gazed upon those corrupted beasts, his nostrils flaring as he readied himself for the assault. He stepped before me, his towering frame shielding me from their wrath.

I looked around helplessly at the blades plunging and arcing, the spatters of blood laying waste to all around us. Most of the horses had fled towards the gates, but Laszlo remained, snapping at the heels of cultists, snarling and lunging at legs and hands and throats, as loyal and fierce as the oncoming wolves.

All around us, soldiers grappled with beasts and cultists alike, but the bull-headed man stalked towards us menacingly, his sickle carving a path through bodies. "My mistress wishes to send a message," he shouted in a deep voice, eyes flickering beneath the animal he wore. "She knows who you are, what lurks within your blood. And like this bull, she will shed your skin and bleed you dry. We are coming for you, Kitarni Bárány. She will rise."

My breath came in rasps, chest heaving as I watched him slowly lift those sickles. They glittered in the moonlight, as cold and cruel as his message. I glanced at Dante, his face stricken, an emotion I couldn't place flashing through his eyes. I couldn't lose him.

Shouts and gargles rang out around me as men fell like flies. So much death. But it would end now.

Fire sparked through my veins like molten lava and the power surged to my fingertips, sparking out in volleys of crackling embers as they exploded on the backs of wolves, igniting fur like tinder. Cultists' cloaks went up in flames, skin sizzling and spitting like fat dripping from roast meat.

Beads of sweat dripped down my brow at the heat and exhaustion beginning to weigh down my bones. A heavy fog clouded my senses, making me sluggish. Several wolves baled up Dante as he fought to keep the bull-headed man at bay, doing his best to ward them off with his swords. Black tendrils curled like smoke from his fingers and his eyes flashed in a brilliance of gold as he conjured his magic.

The black smoke wafted into the mouths, eyes and noses of the fallen, and their bodies twitched to life one by one, limbs snapping back together, muscles jolting with renewed vigour. The dead cultists now fought under his command—under all the guards now. We were blanketed with the powdery mist.

Bodies dropped around me, but still the cultists outnumbered us. When the last of the reanimated dead tumbled once more to the ground—the energies of all the táltosok spent— we still faced a small handful of cultists, the bullhead man and a few snarling wolves.

My breath hitched as a cultist lifted their blade high, ready to

plunge it deep into Dante's back. Those few seconds were the most agonising of my life as I sprinted to his side, shoving his body out of the way right as the dagger descended and ground into my flesh.

The dagger pierced the flesh above my heart, sinking into muscle with the ease of a knife scraping butter. The adrenaline flooding my body made the strike feel more like a punch—that was until I felt hot liquid spilling over my chest, dribbling down my shirt in slick spurts.

The blade descended again, knocked off course at the last minute by Dante. It sliced my arm instead, sending more streams trickling down my arm. He roared and, as I watched his beautiful face transform into that of a monster enraged, the pain finally registered.

White-hot like a blade from a forge, it surged through my body. My legs had the strange sensation of pins poking into my skin like Mama's needles in embroidery and I crumpled to the ground. Blinking back the pain, feeling my breaths coming short and heavy, all I could do was lie there, watching Dante howl before gutting the cultist like a pig.

His clan members howled right back, the sound seeming to give them a new burst of energy.

Hot, sticky splotches rained on my face, but I couldn't focus, couldn't see properly as the pain blurred my vision. I heard him speaking vaguely, asking me to "Stay with him, to hold on."

As I saw the silhouettes of my comrades rushing forward to

protect me, the flash of a bull's head drawing closer, the bodies littering the ground, I felt something shatter. My restraint snapped and that darkness I'd forced deep inside scrabbled to the surface.

Rage. Sorrow. Fury. They drove that power to my fingers, shuddering until I allowed the final release. I glanced at Dante's shouting face, not registering the words coming out of his mouth. But fear filled his eyes, pulled the curves of his mouth taut. We were losing this fight. Our party was too small, too exhausted to hold on.

And the thought of Dante being gone? It was not something I would allow.

I squeezed my eyes shut, willing my magic not to harm him and the others, commanding it to destroy only that which sought to kill us. And with one shuddering sigh, I let my power go, and felt myself fade into oblivion.

PART THREE
THE BLOOD OF WOLVES

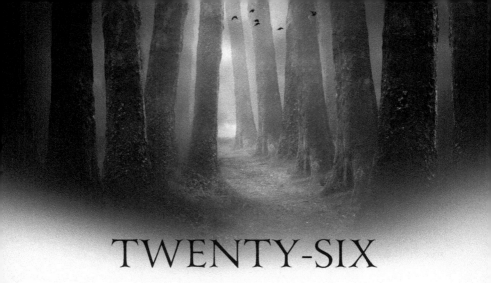

TWENTY-SIX

gasped, struggling to claw my way out of the abyss, only to find my enemies were little more than an excess of quilts swaddling me. Laszlo lay at my feet, curled up in a ball. I breathed a sigh of relief. The lazy hound didn't have a mark on him.

The room I was in appeared to be a guest suite, furnished tastefully in hues of cream, gold, taupe and the warm tones of reddish woods.

Beyond the bed lay a wall of beige and gold brocade, a chest nestled against it, and a simple seat trimmed in gold sitting in the corner. To the other side was a small sitting area that opened onto a balcony. Gold light filtered through the room, glowing as it settled on the curves of Dante's face, contouring every sharp line into gilded bone.

I relaxed at the sight of him, feeling safe and comfortable in this strange place. He smiled down at me from his perch by the

285

bed.

"Hello, Freckles."

"Hello." My voice was raspy and I licked my cracked lips.

His eyes followed the motion for a moment before dragging up my face and settling on my gaze. It felt intimate and searching, and my cheeks heated from his stare. Finally, he turned to the bedside and offered me a cup of water from a carafe. I drank it greedily, wincing as I twisted my body.

Shoving the blankets from my chest, I peered at the bandages plastered over the stab wound and wrapping around my arm. Someone had dressed my wounds and changed me into a simple white shift while I'd slept.

"How long have I been out?"

Resting his chin on his hands, he leaned forward on his elbows, a grim line set on his face. Shadows darkened his red-rimmed eyes and his hair was mussed. With a start, I realised he was still dressed in last night's clothes, soaked through with blood and grime. My heart jolted, stomach flipping. He hadn't even left my side to freshen up.

"You were in and out of consciousness while the healer attended you, but you slept for most of the night. It's now around midday."

I pushed myself up, grateful as he propped the pillows comfortably behind me. "How many?" The whisper was still too loud for the silence of the room.

His silence was answer enough, but with a long-winded sigh,

he confirmed, "Twelve in all. If you hadn't intervened, we'd likely be dead, Kitarni."

He usually used my proper name in serious situations, but this time his tone was laced with admiration and ... something else. It made my heart do a little dance, but panic quickly flooded in and my eyes widened. "My magic! What happened? Did I hurt anyone? Did I—"

Pressing a finger to my lip, he swiped his thumb across my mouth, tracing the curve of my cheek until he cupped my chin in his hand. "You were incredible. Your magic decimated the cultists and their wolves, turning them to ash without so much as a blink. I've never seen anything like it. The power misted over all of us, but when the dust cleared, not one of our men was harmed." He shook his head, looking at me in awe. "How?"

It was my turn to stare, dumbfounded. "I don't know," I whispered. "I remember feeling so desperate, so *angry*, I just willed it to do what I wanted. Apparently, it obeyed." Relief flooded over me, drowning out my panic and anxiety. Perhaps the power was a boon after all. Something I could control. If I could master it, then we might stand a chance against Sylvie.

The thought quickly soured, and I grimaced. First, I'd have to raise her from the dead. What came next ... I wasn't sure of the particulars. Fate had said my blood was the key. Once spilled, it would resurrect her. But how could I destroy her in her supernatural state if I was already dead? Or if I'd been sent to the Under World?

A sliver of hope inside me sparked. Perhaps I would have a second chance, too. If the cultists could bring their leader back, why couldn't I return? How else would I be able to deal the final blow? It seemed logical enough, in a dark magic, what-the-fuck-will-I-return-as kind of why, but it was all I had to go on. I needed answers.

Dante's warm hand squeezed my own and I jumped at the touch.

"Where'd you go just now?" he said softly.

My throat bobbed. "Just groggy from the pain."

He saw through my lie, his brows pinching ever so slightly before smoothing out. "I'll let you rest."

"Wait," I squeaked, latching a hand onto his arm. "Is András okay?"

Dante grinned. "Aside from being furious that he missed the entire fight? He's sporting a rather large lump on his head, but he's fine. Taking solace in the company of his *friends*, I believe."

I rolled my eyes. "Good for him, I suppose."

A faraway look settled in his gaze. "We all deal with grief in different ways. András prefers to drown his in the throes of pleasure."

"And you?" I whispered.

His eyes snapped to my own. "I train. And when I'm faced with my enemy, I kill what threatens my own."

A shiver ran through me at those words—the hard set of his jaw. I knew he was thinking of his mother now. I wondered who he might have been had he not witnessed her death. Trauma like that leaves a scar. Would he still have been a blade of justice for his people? Would he be the killer he is today?

"I'll let you rest," he repeated quietly. Rising, he padded over towards the door, but halted, shifting towards me again. "When we first met, you were able to heal Laszlo. Can you use that power on yourself?"

Scowling, I shook my head. "Beyond simple tricks and spells, most witches have an affinity for a singular magic, such as earth or fire. Witches dwell in covens of the same power to practice in peace and unity. As a fire witch in an earth village, I'm sure you can appreciate how much flack I copped when a wayward spark would set fire to anything of a flammable nature, such as, oh I don't know, crops, plants, vegetables ... everything!?"

Amused, he shot me a crooked smile. "You set fire to their work, didn't you?"

It was more of a statement than a question and, by the twinkle in his eyes, he was enjoying this immensely. Huffing, I turned my nose up. "Not on purpose. What do you expect? I was young and had no one to train me."

Chuckling, he leaned against the wall. "Go on."

Grinning despite myself, I tucked my hair behind my ear, conscious of the knotted tangles housing god only knew what. I groaned inwardly. I probably smelt like the dead, too.

Sucking in a breath, I shoved my insecurities down and continued. "Healing magic requires sacrifice and balance. I can

only heal others by bloodletting or taking on the pain of their injury."

Intrigued, he crept closer, because *of course* that would be what piques his interest. "Is that why you cut yourself to heal Laszlo?"

"Yes. A sacrifice in exchange for power," I explained. "For small hurts or broken bones, it usually only takes a slice to the palm, but larger wounds like this? It's too costly. I can't heal myself without inflicting more damage or risking death. Healing magic seems to be more costly than my blood magic. I don't know why. It was a gift from my father—I never got the chance to ask him about it."

"Before he passed away?" he asked gently.

I nodded. "It was the last thing he did. His way of preserving the line, I suppose."

"Or preserving *you*," Dante said. "It takes a skilled táltos to summon magic like that—to harness the spiritual energies and weave it like so. Your father was a powerful man, but perhaps the payment of using that magic is steeper than most can afford. If you only have a kernel of that power inside you, that might explain why it's harder to use. Your blood magic was gifted by birth—it makes you who you are. Healing magic contradicts the destructive nature of your other gifts. It upsets the balance."

I'd never thought of it like that before, but it made sense. All power came at a price. A flicker of sorrow coursed through me and I wondered if my father had given me this gift knowing I'd need it to protect myself—or my family—when I grew older. A kind of safeguard if evil came knocking. And it had blasted down the doors by now.

Dante chewed over this knowledge, his brown eyes sparkling with a new idea. "If you can't use your magic on yourself, what if someone else assisted?" When he looked at me with all the curiosity of a cat, I understood where he was going with this immediately.

"No fucking chance," I replied firmly.

"I have blood to spare," he said with a disarming grin. "You need to heal. Unless you'd rather stay here while we hunt for the cultists' base, of course."

My nostrils flared. "You wouldn't dare."

"Oh, I would. They were following us the whole time, waiting to strike. You heard the bull. They know about your power—who you are, Kitarni. I don't know how, but they know. And they're coming." He ran a hand through his hair. "Our soldiers are strong, but we cannot prepare for something we know nothing about. We need numbers, locations. We need to know the threat they pose against both our homes."

True, true, true.

"I'm fine," I insisted, swinging a leg over the side of the bed. Gritting my teeth together, I bit back a cry, trying and failing to ignore the burning pain in my chest.

He was there in an instant, calloused hands grasping my calf and propping me back on the bed. His touch inflamed my bare skin. "You are *not* fine. You could have died yesterday and I ..." He looked away with a frustrated growl. "I promised no harm would come to you. I failed."

I raised a hand to his chin, tracing the stubble that had grown over the last few days. "You can't protect me from everything," I whispered, feeling miserable. *You can't protect me from myself. From what I must do.*

His brows pinched as he studied me. "I can and I will. *I must.*"

Shaking my head, I sighed. "I can look after myself. I'm the only safeguard your soldiers have got against the cultists."

"I can't deny your magic is incredible, but even you have your limits. With this injury, magic is firmly out of the question." He looked me over studiously. "Still, you wield a blade far better than I'd expected. You're fast, but you can't rely on throwing knives or daggers in a sword fight. I think we'll have to amend that."

"I've been taught swordplay," I said indignantly.

His grin was devilish. "Not by me you haven't."

I pursed my lips. "Are you always so arrogant?"

He crossed his arms, that damnable dimple winking back at me. I supposed more training couldn't hurt and he handled a blade like the god of war himself. Hadúr would be pleased. "Fine," I groused, blowing out a breath. "I accept your proposal."

Dante chuckled. "That'd be a first. Unfortunately for you, you're not going anywhere until you heal." He looked at me pointedly.

Huffing, I rolled my eyes. "I'll sleep on it. But no promises."

Leaning in, he placed a gentle kiss on my mouth—barely a brush against my lips—before walking out the door, leaving me alone to my thoughts.

Groaning, I shook my head, burying myself carefully in the silky sheets. Even that slight movement sent pain rippling up my shoulder.

Dante was right. I'd be out of action for weeks, if not months. As far as I knew, healing magic was not a common gift. If what Dante said was true, it took a skilled táltos indeed to claim spiritual energy as their own and, apparently, they were in short supply. Dante would have had a witch or táltos tending to my needs the instant we made it back to the keep otherwise.

So how, then, had my father claimed such power? He'd gifted it to me before passing from this world into the next, so I'd never know. But perhaps there was a way to train that skill or find someone to learn from. I set that thought aside to revisit later.

Between the very contrasting gifts of healing and destruction, I was a puzzle. An anomaly. Mama never should have kept me in the dark. I might have gone to the banya for help, might have—

I sighed. There was no use for dreaming or laying blame. Even if I'd searched for the banya, Baba Yana, I wouldn't have found her. She was just as puzzling as I was, and far more mysterious.

I had little in the way of options. Both my fire and blood magic were useless if I couldn't heal myself. I clenched the quilt

293

tightly. Would it be so bad if Dante scouted the woods without me? We needed to act. Soon. I grimaced, thinking of the corruption in the Sötét Erdő and how quickly it was spreading.

We had more than cultists to worry about now. The creatures were volatile, but time was our greatest enemy. If the cultists' dark magic continued to flood the earth, our families—our homes—would fold beneath its touch. That could *not* happen. Eszter and Mama were still my priority.

I didn't want to send more men to die, didn't want to think of Dante hurt or worse. Their shamanistic power wasn't enough to quell the tides of fanatics overdosed on bloodmorphia. Which left me with the most important question.

Was I ready to face my demons in the woods? Was I ready to die to save the ones I loved?

I woke to the sound of humming as gentle hands busied themselves with my bandages. Cracking my eyes open, I found a beautiful woman slightly older than me applying salve to my wounds. My skin tingled under the cool balm, but her fingertips were so gentle I barely felt them.

"The prodigal princess returns to us at last."

Not a blemish or sunspot marred her light skin. Her blue eyes sparkled as she looked down a button nose, bow lips smiling as she appraised me. Her raven hair was braided in a coronet upon her head, the sleeves of her royal blue dress pulled back to work.

Groggily, I studied the craftsmanship of the taffeta, the fine needlework of the silver whorls swirling over the bodice, the square-set sapphire dipping into her decolletage. If anyone here was royalty, she fit the description. Raising a brow, I studied the stranger. "Princess?"

She smirked as she twirled one of my locks in her hand. "Your heretic ancestor labelled herself a queen. Given your power stems from the bloodline, I figured it was only fitting you bear such a title, too."

This one didn't mince words. I liked her already, but there was something about her I couldn't quite place. A strange aura that spoke of something ancient. Something otherworldly.

A shiver ran down my spine and the hairs on my arms raised, but just as quickly as it came, the strange feeling was gone. I shook my head, shifting to sit up.

It was probably just my sluggish mind playing tricks.

"Forgive my forwardness but ... who are you?"

She pouted, taking a seat on the edge of the bed. "He didn't mention me? How disappointing. I'm Margit, your betrothed's cousin." Frowning, she smoothed her dress down. "Honestly, after everything I do for the Sándor family, I deserve a medal or a crown."

A voice interrupted from the door. "For emptying the coffers to fund your numerous closets?"

Dante leaned against the threshold, one perfect eyebrow raised in amusement. He'd bathed and was now dressed in a

white shirt, a charcoal-grey doublet, and black slacks. His olive skin gleamed in the candlelight and his wet hair was raked back. By all that was holy, it should be a sin to be so handsome.

Margit straightened. "Someone has to run the place while you and Farkas are off gods-only-know-where. I deserve to treat myself."

"Do all of your treats come with gems the size of eggs?"

She grinned wickedly, dismissing the question with a wave of her hand. "My nest eggs serve me well. Not all of them were born from your pocket, I'll have you know. My suitors come bearing gifts, too."

Dante snorted. "Poor souls. I hope you let them down easy when you're finished with them." He turned to me. "How are you feeling?"

"Like I've been stabbed," I retorted with a smile.

"My brave girl. Have you thought about my request?"

Straight to the point, then. Margit gazed at me curiously while the silence stretched. I'd made my decision last night but saying the words would make it real. My throat bobbed as I swallowed.

"I ... I'm willing to try the bloodletting. Under one condition. If I say we stop, you are to obey without question. I'll not heal myself by putting your life at risk."

"Done," he replied without hesitation. "Let's get started."

"Now?" I squeaked.

His eyes flashed devilishly. "Unless you have a prior engagement?"

My only defence was to send him a withering glare.

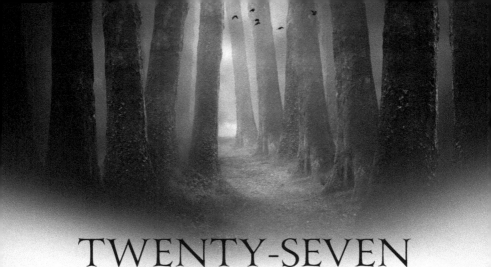

TWENTY-SEVEN

"**S**houldn't someone else come with us in case, you know, you start dying on me?" Snakes slithered in my belly, writhing into one big tangle of nerves. I was anxious about bloodletting with Dante, but I was strangely calm. I should have been terrified, but he made me feel safe, capable. *Powerful.* I shivered in his hold as the chill air of the castle caressed the bare skin of my arms.

He held me tighter to his chest as he stalked down the corridor, his strides purposeful as he carried me to his quarters. I'd insisted on walking, of course, but he refused to give in to my complaints. And truly, I could think of worse things than being cradled by his warmth—the corded muscle of his triceps.

"I have every faith neither of us is going to die tonight."

"How do you know?" I breathed.

He glanced at me, his dark brown eyes bathed in an indecipherable expression. "Because I have faith in you."

My insides warmed at the comment. Whether it was the sincerity of it, or that he'd said such a thing to *me*, I didn't know. I remained quiet and we lapsed into silence as he walked.

The castle corridors were lined with smooth, sandy-coloured stone and dotted with sconces creating flickering ambiance as the moonlight crept through the slitted windows. Art depicting battles and feasts lined the walls in gilded frames, and the stone floor was laid with running red carpets trimmed with gold. The castle was bright, cosy and surprisingly busy at this time of night.

Guards were few and far between, but the many rooms we passed were filled with people. Laughter bounced down the halls as servants finished up their nightly rounds and nobles strutted past with bright eyes and gentle smiles.

If they were intrigued by their lord carrying a dishevelled woman in his arms, they didn't show it. Were such oddities a common occurrence around here? My stomach coiled for the briefest moment and I blinked. Was that jealousy? I almost scoffed. *Oh, Kitarni, foolish girl.*

Dante greeted everyone we passed by name, bidding them a good night or a pleasant evening. All smiled in return. I looked at him in awe. He hadn't been lying about the ideals of equality. He was obviously given the respect deserved as the lord-in-waiting of the castle, but no one—not one soul—seemed indifferent or angry or jealous about his standing.

"You really weren't lying about the way of life here."

"I don't lie," he said matter-of-factly.

Glaring up at him, I replied haughtily, "Oh, that's right. You merely omit information."

He smiled down at me and my chest hitched at his full lips, the angle of his jaw. "What can I do to make it up to you?"

"I can think of a few things." The words left my mouth before I could stop them. *Oh my gods. Kill me now.*

"Well then," he purred. "I'll be sure to satisfy your needs in full once you're healed. Wouldn't want to hurt you as you are."

"Hurt me?" I squeaked.

He shot me a crooked grin, but he set me down on the floor before I could enquire further, opening the door to his chamber.

Stepping inside, I looked around the room tentatively. It was much the same as the guest suite, only bigger, with a mahogany desk piled with missives and a plush navy and gold brocade armchair situated in one corner. The sitting area was larger too, with black lounges on a cream rug encircling a fireplace. Above the mantel sat a portrait of his family. His father, proud and regal, a happiness softening the usual stern lines on his face. Beside Farkas, a beautiful woman with long, chestnut hair and dark brown eyes cradled a young boy in her lap.

His mother. Her skin was slightly darker than Dante's, but she bore a nearly identical set of eyes and full lips that mirrored his own. Her brown curls were streaked with the same russet glint as Dante's too.

My heartstrings pulled at the love in that frame—at Dante's broad, boyish smile, complete with two dimples. They'd been so

happy and that joy had turned to ash because of the cultists. My jaw hardened at the thought of more bloodshed, more lives lost and families broken should their darkness spread.

No. Not if I could help it. I turned to Dante, avoiding the shadows of his bedchamber in an adjacent room. What I wouldn't do to get a peek in there. To see a side of him usually hidden behind the mask. Shaking my head from sentiments, I gazed at Dante.

"Where are we going to do this?"

He smiled. "That depends. Where would you like to bleed me out?"

"Would you take this seriously?" I snapped. "I've never done this with another person before. It could go badly." I raised a hand as he opened his mouth, probably about to make fun of my virginity over bloodletting.

His mouth snapped into an amused line, but he lifted his own palms in defence. "Follow me."

He padded towards his bedchamber and my stomach thrilled at the sight of the four-poster-bed shrouded in smoky swathes of silk and plush quilts in charcoals and silver. If I'd thought the guest suite bed was big, this was huge. My brain started thinking of what activities could take place in that bed and I jerked myself away from the sight.

Dante's chuckle was low and deep, as if sensing where my thoughts had gone. He followed my movements with hawk eyes, watching as I strode towards what appeared to be a bathing chamber. Conjuring my fire, I snapped my fingers, lighting the candles lining one side of the room. A sly grin crept over my face. It seemed Dante was something of a romantic.

As light flickered in the chamber, I found a large, smooth hollow inset into the stonework. I gasped as I realised what it was. "Is this—"

He grinned. "Rather than using those primitive tubs, we built a more permanent solution. There are hot springs beneath the castle, and we have a mechanism to hoist up buckets of hot water. We still need maids to run the water back and forth, but it's a hell of a lot better than wallowing in a child-sized bucket."

I pointed to a circular hole at one end. "How do you keep the water from running down that hole? What do you do with the dirty water?"

He rested his hands on my shoulders, steering me closer. "I've never heard you so inquisitive. We use this little baby to seal the gap and hold the water. When we're done, you pull it out and the water drains down a series of stone tunnels and out onto the fields surrounding the castle."

Dumbfounded, I stared at it, tentatively touching the stopper. "What witchery is this?"

He chuckled. "No magic at all, it just seemed logical. But, admittedly, we made the first with the help of your kith. I can't figure out how to get fresh water sourced to the bath itself, but I have a few ideas." His brows pinched. "Our local seer has termed it 'plumbing'. It's going to be big." He frowned. "She also said

someone else would claim its invention years from now."

I eyed it longingly. What I wouldn't do for a bath.

"You can wash later," he declared behind me, his breath tickling my neck. "More blood needs to be spilled yet."

I glared at him as I swivelled, feeling a bite of pain travel up my shoulder. "For the person doing the bleeding, you seem awfully cheery about it."

He shrugged before prying the doublet from his chest, slipping it over his head casually. The shirt came next as he untied each button painfully slow. The soft hairs of his chest peeked over the collar, the hint of sweeping black ink. I swallowed, transfixed with the wolves emblazoned on each silver button, then the skin beneath it.

"Why are you undressing?" My voice was husky and I cringed inwardly at the tone. The obvious desire in it.

He looked at me innocently. "I happen to like these clothes. No use ruining them."

I raised a brow. Where his cousin hoarded jewels, it seemed Dante was a clothes-coveting drake. He was always dressed impeccably but, in his defence, fine attire like that was made for his body. His outfits were fitting enough to reveal the muscles in his sleek torso and sturdy legs but left much more to wonder about. I'm sure I wasn't the only woman to think so.

When he noticed me staring, he drawled, "Care to join me?"

His shirt slipped from his torso, revealing the wolf tattoo, the flowers encircling the sword slicing down his abdomen. I had to double check I wasn't drooling. I thwacked him on that ridiculously hard stomach. "Just hurry so we can get started, asshat. You're making me feel murderous."

"As you wish." He withdrew a blade from a sheath at his hip before stepping into the hollow, stretching lazily in the bath. I blinked at the dagger, fascinated by its make. The black hilt was carved in a figure eight of a snake eating itself, two tiny rubies inset into the eyes. The blade itself was wavy, rippling down into a sharp point.

It reminded me of the cultists' weapons. Ceremonial in style.

I flicked my gaze to Dante's as he offered it to me. "What are you doing?"

"Less mess in the bath," he explained. "I don't want the maids to think I've killed someone in here. It would be quite the scandal." The mischievous glint to his eyes suggested he'd enjoy that very much, in fact. He patted the space between his legs suggestively.

Panicked, I gaped at his calmness. "How much blood do you think it's going to take?" Shaking my head, I amended, "Don't answer that. Let's just get this over with."

He nodded, pinning me with his stare as I wiped sweaty hands on my thighs. My skin flushed with heat, the nerves inside my stomach writhing once again. How different would this be, really? The magic was simple enough to conjure, easy enough to manage. Yes. I devoured positive thoughts, rifling through them one after another as I inhaled, exhaled, steadying myself through

  303

simple breathing.

Dante watched me all the while, head cocked curiously, but he sat perfectly still as I reached for the outstretched blade. Running a thumb over the snake, I swallowed my fear.

And then I cut.

Just a small slice to his palm. The blood welled and bubbled, sliding down his hand and plopping onto the bath. Pitter-patter. It sounded like rain as they dropped one after the other. My stomach roiled at the sight, so I closed my eyes.

Burrowing into my power, I focused on the energies within my core. The strength of my ancestors coursed angrily in the cage I kept locked and shoved down deep, the beast within leashed until the next battle would come. Breathing slowly, I shied away from that darkness, finding the subtle golden glow of my father's magic. The gift of healing—and the curse.

I yanked the thread taut, finding the magic flexing in my fingers as I snapped my eyes open. Nodding to Dante, I held his bloody hand in my own, wincing as the simple movement sent pain down my arm and firing in my chest.

Once his fingers twined around mine, I *pulled*. Soft, golden light filtered through our clasped fingers as his energy combined with my own.

My body tingled as his life trickled into my body, slowly, surely, little more than a steady drip. The tension in my ribs eased and the skin warmed as the bruises there began to melt away. I held my breath, waiting for it to course to my stab wound, but it sputtered out.

Disappointed, I glanced at Dante. "It wasn't enough," I said quietly.

Before I could blink, he took the blade from my free hand and sliced deep into his bicep. He gritted his teeth, but not a sound escaped his lips as he stared into my eyes, not shying from the pain. I had the vague feeling he almost welcomed it, as if ... as if punishing himself. For failing to protect me? Or something else?

I slid my hand up his arm, slick with sticky, hot blood. Jolting at the power surging through me again, I gasped, blinded by the gold now flooding the room. I squeezed my eyelids shut as his energy soared into my veins, coursing towards the wound, cleansing it.

His blood was intoxicating, whispering like smoke, dark and dangerous and strong. A strange connection to the spiritual glided through me. Was this what táltosok felt when they called on their magic?

Giddy with elation, my mind blurred, skin heating under his touch, body singing with power and life. My eyes rolled back in my head as it surged into me, the hole in my chest knitting closed. I was drunk on his power, consumed by it.

More.

I drank him in greedily, feeling more alive than I ever had before. Taking, taking, taking until I was high with magic, with *power*. When the wound was nothing but a memory, I at last

opened my eyes.

"Dante!"

His head lolled back on the tub, eyelashes fluttering as he struggled to stay awake. Blood soaked his arm, dripping from splayed fingertips and pooling into the copper base. So much red everywhere. The slash on his arm was deeper than I'd realised. How long had I drawn from him for? How much did I steal?

"Kitammnee." My name was but a slurred murmur on his lips.

"Fuck." I hurried to the stone bench, dragging a fresh rag from the counter, putting pressure on the wound. The rag quickly soaked through with red. "Fuuuckkk." Running blood-soaked hands through my hair, I gazed at his sagging form, tears burning my eyes.

"No one is dying today, alright? You said so yourself, and you're a stubborn ass so it must be true." A single tear splattered on his cheek as I leaned over him. Desperate, I hefted his frame under my armpits, straining under the weight as I shuffled him forwards.

I squeezed into the space behind him, laying his head against my chest with one hand while I compressed the rag over his wound. He'd given too much. No. I'd *taken* too much, drunk on his blood and the vigour now surging through my veins.

Perhaps I couldn't heal myself, but I now had more than enough power to at least seal his wound without inflicting damage on myself. Dante had spoken of an imbalance of magic

306

yesterday and that's exactly what I'd caused.

It was time to give back.

Snatching the dagger from the floor, I sliced my palm and discarded the blade, holding my hand aloft while I squeezed his arm with the other.

"Please," I sent a prayer to the gods, the magic—anyone and everything—to listen. "Please."

Closing my eyes, I willed some of that golden light into his veins. It burrowed into his flesh, flashing beneath his skin as the power began to work. Slowly, the blood stopped flowing and the tissue began to rejuvenate until the skin sealed and a pale sliver of a scar remained.

"Come back to me," I whispered in his ear. His lips twitched, his breathing evening out into a steady rhythm. Sighing, I slumped behind him, shifting his head into my lap. He was going to be okay. Weak and groggy from blood loss, perhaps, but I trusted my power was still at work inside him, doing whatever was needed to combat the effects of blood loss.

Closing my eyes, I lay there, relishing every pump of his heart, every rise and fall of his chest.

I cried for the rest of the night.

TWENTY-EIGHT

"Sweet mother of mercy. Please tell me I don't have to remove two bodies from the tub."

The voice jolted me awake and I lifted my head, wincing at the twinge in my neck from sleeping in a bloody bathtub of all places. Dante still slept in front of me, so quietly I had to press a finger to this throat. His heart was pumping. Stronger than I'd expected after last night.

Sighing, I swivelled to face the intruder. Margit stood at the threshold, carrying a tray of fruits drizzled in honey as well as two porridge bowls. A carafe of what I prayed was water perched on top and I eyed it greedily.

"Margit." My voice cracked, hoarse from sobbing all night. Her head was haloed from buttery sunlight pouring through the windows in the bathroom, giving her an angelic aura.

"You look like shit," she grumbled, sniffing the air. "Smell like it, too." One perfect eyebrow rose as she peeked into the tub, roving over the puddles of blood. Her gaze clouded with worry. "Is he ... okay?"

"Mercifully. But we shan't be repeating that anytime soon."

Her sharp blue eyes pierced my own, and she clucked her tongue. "I like you, Kitarni, but you'd better be worth the trouble. If he'd died, I would have had your head."

I didn't doubt it for a second. "I would have laid it down for you," I admitted. "I don't—I don't ever want to do that again."

Watching him almost die last night was the scariest thing I'd ever witnessed. The memory of it—of his pallid skin, the blood dripping down his arms—sent a shiver down my spine. My heart ached at the thought of him hurt and my stomach felt like crows nipped at my flesh from the inside out at knowing I'd been the cause of his pain.

Never again. I couldn't bear it and, right now, I was too relieved to dig deeper into what that meant.

Margit set the tray down on the bench and poured two goblets of water. Her face softened as she looked at the tear tracks down my cheeks. I could only imagine how frightful I looked.

"All that matters is you're both alive. Here," she passed the cups to me. "Drink this."

I sculled the water in one go, licking my lips in relief. The movement stirred Dante and he mumbled something incoherent before his long lashes fluttered. He groaned as he woke, eyes cracking open slowly.

"Thank the gods," I whispered.

"You weren't lying when you said you were feeling murderous, Freckles," he breathed, sitting up slowly.

Tears pricked my eyes. "I'm sorry, Dante. I—"

"I'm needed in the apothecary," Margit said quickly. She turned on her heel, casting us a sly look before disappearing. Her lips curled with the slightest hint of amusement. If she wasn't worried, that was a good sign, right?

I turned my attention back to Dante, who had shifted in the tub and was now leaning against the opposite end. His smile was smug. The kind of shit-eating grin only a noble's son could conjure. Normally, I'd want to punch a hole in it, but I wilted in relief. Miraculously, his skin was flushed with colour and his arm was smooth, nothing but a scar to mark last night's events.

"Why, pray tell, are you so pleased with yourself right now? You almost died, Dante!" My voice rose a few octaves, betraying the fear and distress from last night. I buried my face in my hands, trying to block the images from my mind's eye.

I still recalled the power surging through me—his power. Fiery and bright and all-consuming. But the sight of seeing his blood running so freely, the way his body had sunk in on itself, that memory would haunt me. I had almost killed him. It was one thing to fight in self-defence, but something altogether different to see someone you cared about dying.

Shit. I did care. Maybe a little too much. My plans to keep things strictly sexual were not going well at all.

He swiped the other goblet still full of water from my hand, drinking it to the dregs. I eyed a bead of water dribbling down his chin. "You did it," he said victoriously. "Your power is ... you're phenomenal, Kitarni."

A blush stained my cheeks and I peeked up at him, shyness gripping my heart. "You're ok then? I thought—" I choked on the words, too cowardly to admit just how much the lure of power had consumed me.

He scooted closer, tilting my chin up with one finger. "I am better than okay. The wound is gone. After losing so much blood I'd expected to be weak, but I feel great. I can feel your magic lingering inside me. Your fire burns through my veins, giving me strength."

I blinked several times. "You can feel it? I'd thought I was just imagining it but for the briefest moment last night, I swore I felt a glimmer of yours, too."

He nodded. "I told you we'd pull through. We make a good team, Freckles." He tugged my waist, pulling me gently into his arms. Left with no room, I was forced to wrap my legs around him as he lifted me into his lap.

My body sparked at his touch, my breasts pressing against his chest. I still wore the simple shift, now streaked with blood and grime and, beneath the crusted blood on his own skin, his abs were hard and ridged against my body. My breath hitched as I looked into his brown eyes, the gold flickering dangerously now.

Placing a featherlight kiss to my brow, he stroked the planes of my cheeks, exploring every sweep, every hollow and the dip of

311

my lips. His fingers swept down my neck and under my shift, the pad of his thumb tracing the place my wound had been. Nothing but smooth skin remained and the glimmer of a white scar. We both wore a scar from last night.

With a crooked grin he said, "Seeing as we've been in this tub for hours on end, maybe we should utilise it."

A soft laugh escaped my lips. I wasn't even sure why I was laughing. Maybe it was just the elation of being alive—the sheer stubbornness we shared and the refusal to allow the other to stay hurt.

He stared at me with something like awe on his face. "What?" I asked nervously.

Dante shook his head, a dimple emerging on his cheek. "I've never heard a more beautiful sound."

I snorted, flicking the end of his nose playfully. "Okay, lover boy, I think you're still a little disoriented from blood loss. Let's get you washed up."

He lifted me in his arms without another word and I yelped, squeezing my legs harder around his midriff. The other dimple popped into view as he set me on the edge of the hollow, pressing himself against me before leaning down.

His hand slid dangerously high up my thigh and his thumb circled the area lazily. "What are you doing?" I breathed, my core instantly responding to his touch.

He leaned closer, still circling that damned thumb as he shot me a feline grin. The next second I heard something scrape

against the ground. The bath stopper. Ugh, he was such a tease.

"I'll be right back," he announced, pulling away suddenly and loping towards the door.

"Where are you going?" I barked. My core was tight and I had to squeeze my legs together to quell the rising need. Was I deranged? What kind of madwoman felt like this after everything that had happened?

Passion, I realised. Elation. Gratitude. Sheer dumb luck at both of us living. We were alive and I planned to make the most of it while I still had blood in my veins. To make every moment count.

"Be patient, Freckles," he purred, disappearing from the room.

I sat there for what felt like an eternity, twiddling my thumbs, even considering satisfying my needs. The morning was fresh, despite the sunlight filtering through and my arms prickled. Irritated, I jammed them under my armpits, trying to warm myself.

Just as I was about to storm out, a swarm of maids bustled in, each offering me a polite "How-do-you-do" or a "Good morning, my lady". All of them trying vainly to control the wide eyes and gasps of shock upon seeing puddles of blood in the tub.

I waved a hand awkwardly and found myself dragged into the tub, a few bucket loads poured over my head. I squawked when the water drenched my skin, but at least it wasn't icy. The women massaged my head, plucking sticks and leaves from my hair as they

 313

scrubbed at the caked blood and dirt over my body. They kept my shift on as Dante was present, but the white material did little to hide my breasts.

Dante popped his head around the corner as they splashed bucket after bucket of water over the tub, flushing all the grime from the surface—and *me*. They filed out one by one, presumably to bring fresh water for a bath.

"You didn't think to warn me?" I hissed as he stepped back in. I covered myself with my arms but, truthfully, I was more worried about looking like a drowned rat.

He assessed me from head to toe and laughed as he plucked a slivered apple from the tray and popped it into his mouth. I watched with narrowed eyes as he licked the honey from his lips. "Don't worry about the maids," he drawled, selecting a handful of morsels before approaching me. "They've seen blood plenty of times before."

I raised a brow. "Just how often do you nearly die in your quarters?"

His eyes glinted. "There have been incidents in the past where I've needed stitching up. But I've never been at a lady's mercy before. A treacherous witch at that."

"Treacherous!?" Frowning, I poked a finger at his chest. "The day is young. I can still stab you or set you on fire."

"But you won't." He popped a date into his mouth, studying me. "Fig?"

My stomach grumbled before I could reject his offering, so I

snatched it from his hand eagerly. I moaned at the explosion of sweetness and Dante twitched beside me.

"Don't do that unless you're prepared for the consequences," he said slowly.

"What, enjoy my food?" I teased, rolling my tongue over my lips. For good measure I plucked a slice of pear from the tray, taking extra care to lick the honey slowly from my fingers. "Mmm."

He shuddered. Actually shuddered! "For the love of Istenanya, I swear I will take you against that wall right now."

Pouting, I ran a finger along his chest, then dropped it with a shrug. His desire strained against his pants. "If you can't control your urges, I'll be forced to believe you're not worth the effort."

He pulled me out of the tub and pushed me against the far wall, running a tongue over my lips, sinking his teeth in just hard enough to hurt as he kissed me. The pain sent a thrill to the juncture of my legs and I crashed my lips against his own.

Pulling back, he whispered against my ear, "Before I'm done, you'll be begging me to give you release."

My body betrayed me, shivering beneath his touch. Damn it all. My breasts felt heavy, my nipples scraping against the silky shift. I wanted him to rip it from me, to taste me, be inside me.

Scuffling steps broke us apart and I flattened against the wall, covering my modesty with my arms, trying to sink in on myself.

Dante leaned casually against the bench, lips smirking

315

between every bite. I grabbed a bowl of porridge and wolfed down the now cold contents, if only to give myself something else to focus on instead of the need still thrumming through me.

It was my turn to laugh when the women advanced. "My lord," they giggled as they dragged him into the tub, dumping the cold water over his head. Blood sluiced down the drain and I cackled at his bemused expression. His hair hung limp over his face and his arms trembled at his sides. *Who's the drowned rat now?* I thought gleefully.

One maid popped the stopper in the tub and they all began pouring their buckets into the now clean surface, taking a couple trips to fill it until marching out like soldiers once done. All the while, Dante's eyes never left my body as he consumed his breakfast without a care in the world.

He grinned through a mop of hair, but when the last maid had filed out, we stood staring at each other, each having eaten our fill. A different hunger filled our bellies.

"Take them off," I commanded, pointing at his pants.

He obliged, fingers working at the leather ties before he stepped one foot then the other out of the sodden slacks. I clenched my jaw to avoid gaping at his length. The sheer size of him, even after being drenched with cold water.

"Come here." His voice brooked no room for argument and, dreamily, I stepped into the tub, drawn by his magnetism. His fingers clutched the bottom of my shift, peeling it up, up, up until it caught on my breasts. I laughed nervously, then squeaked as I felt his lips press against one puckered nipple then the other.

The shift tugged free as I wriggled out of it. It took a moment to register I was once again naked before him, but it felt different this time. My lips trembled as I gazed at him, suddenly feeling self-conscious. We'd shared a connection last night—something that had bound our bodies through magic.

He'd touched my very soul. What had he found there? I wrapped my arms around my breasts again, tilting my head away.

"Don't shy from me," he said softly, placing a hand on my cheek and gently shifting my gaze to his own. "You never need to hide from me, Kitarni. You are beautiful, inside and out. And you are mine."

His lips swept down on my own, bruising with need, claiming me as he so suggested. Warmth flooded through me at hearing those words—the conviction in them. I clasped my hands over his own and we sank into the water.

Still shivering from being soaked earlier, I hadn't noticed how cold it was, but as my bottom touched the surface, I yelped. Dante laughed and I couldn't help but grin too. "Why don't we see about this temperature?" Conjuring my flames, I plunged my hand into the bath, heating the water until it was pleasant. "Much better."

He submerged himself in the water—which only just covered his hips—and groaned as he rotated his shoulder blades, leaning against the tub. "You, my dear, are a saint. Witches don't get nearly enough credit."

That we could agree on. Sighing, I settled into the bath, welcoming the heat as it warmed my bones, sapping the tiredness from my body. He prowled closer, tugging my ankle until I sat before him and curled my legs around his waist. "I could think of ways you might show your gratitude."

He rumbled his agreement against my shoulder, planting kisses across my collarbone, down my chest and to each breast. I arched my back, leaning into his touch. His tongue flicked over my nipples, a hand snaking down to my centre. I gasped as his fingers circled over me.

A sigh escaped my lips and I closed my eyes, grinding against his touch ... until it stopped. He laughed as I scrunched my nose up. "I said I'd worship you, Freckles, and I plan to cover every inch. But you have to be patient."

Snapping my eyes open, I frowned at his smirk. He was enjoying this immensely. Ignoring my protests, he swiped a bottle of oil and a comb from the tub's edge. The maids must have left it in their wake. The scent of lavender washed over me as he rubbed the oil in his hands, working it into a lather before slathering it over my arms, my breasts, my shoulders. Coiling my hair over one shoulder, he worked the muscles in my neck, kneading out the knots that had formed over the last few days.

I groaned as his fingers threaded into my hair, massaging my scalp. "I feel like I haven't bathed in weeks," I sighed.

"You smelled like it too," he chuckled.

I elbowed him in the ribs and he snatched both of my hands,

lifting them up to clasp around the back of his neck. His palms wandered down my chest, cupping the swell of each breast before sinking beneath the water. I felt his desire press against my back and parted my lips as his fingers slid inside me.

I squirmed beneath his touch, heat flushing my skin, need rising until I was breathless and moaning. "So impatient," he whispered in my ear, shuffling my body around so he could access me easier.

His pace quickened to a crescendo, my breasts heaving with every breath, my back arching further still as I leaned into his touch, riding his fingers. I'd thought the water would dull the sensation but my desire for him went beyond simple lust. Heat and dizzying pleasure flooded my body in waves as I climaxed and he groaned as I shifted, clamping down on his thighs, needing something to ground me.

When the pleasure ebbed, I shuffled to face him, a hungry smile on my face. "Your turn."

I started slow, rubbing the soap over the broadness of his chest, the muscled ridges and the smoothness of his stomach. He bent his head so I could reach his hair and the dark locks turned glossy as I ran my fingertips over his scalp and down each strand.

When I'd finished massaging his hair, I swept my fingertips down his chest, his stomach, until I gripped him in my hand, working his cock, sliding my thumb over the head in teasing strokes. He closed his eyes, folding his arms behind his head, a happy sigh escaping his lips.

I quickened my pace, pumping him faster, tightening my grip ever so slightly. His dark eyes snapped open and he stared at me hungrily, a moan escaping his lips as he watched me work him.

My core thrilled to see the lust in his eyes, his cock throbbing beneath my touch. He grabbed my waist and reeled me in, crashing his lips against mine as he came, his body jerking, his moan whispered against my lips.

I kept kissing him, stealing small kisses as he held my cheeks in his calloused hands, his fingers sliding to the base of my skull. He drew me closer, cradling my head to his chest and I revelled in the beating of his heart, the flushed skin.

Alive.

We lay there for a while, simply enjoying the quiet and the warm embrace of our bodies folded together. I couldn't remember the last time I'd felt so safe or *wanted* to stay still for so long.

He smiled as I leaned back—a lopsided but happy grin. I studied the man before me, looked into his eyes.

All traces of cockiness or the haunting glimmer of his past were gone. He was the most relaxed I'd ever seen him, his arms resting on the bath's edge, his legs sprawled out lazily either side of me. And that smile, that gaze—I might have drowned in those eyes. His walls were crumbling, allowing me to see the man beneath. Bearing his true self. Could I say the same for my own defences?

Swallowing the lump in my throat, I pushed down the

strange fluttering in my stomach. A mixture of emotions flooded over me. Everything I was. Everything I couldn't be. Hysteria bubbled in my chest as I dropped my hands. "What's wrong?" he asked, pulling me into his arms.

Trying to push past the knot lodged in my throat, I tried to speak, tried to give voice to everything I was feeling. But if I told him the truth, could I come back from that? Could he? "I ..."

"It's okay." His chest rumbled against my cheek as he spoke. "I'm here. You don't have to tell me now, but I'll be here for you when you're ready. I'm not going anywhere, Freckles, I promise."

But I am. Sobs wracked from my chest and I burst into tears, allowing them to flow in rivers down my cheeks. Cleansing my soul of yesterday so I might have the strength for a tomorrow.

He held me silently until I was ready, cradling me in his arms, protecting me from the world. His hand stroked my hair idly, and I focused on that simple motion to get me through. I hadn't shared such rawness with someone besides Eszter and my mother for the longest time.

Hadn't been hugged by a friend, shared promises or secrets. No one except perhaps Erika had ever bothered to get to know me—the real me—the fragile girl beneath the hot-headedness, the fire, the magic.

As if sensing where my thoughts had gone, he lifted my head gently, placing his palms on both of my cheeks. "I see you, Kitarni. I see you, and I'm staying."

A fresh wave of tears pricked at my eyes and he swiped his

thumbs across my cheeks tenderly, all the care in the world lighting in those brown eyes, in the golden ring that seemed to glimmer in my presence.

"Kiss me," I breathed.

He obeyed, one hand sliding round the back of my neck, the other tenderly cupped around my jaw. His lips were bliss as he kissed me, not fiery or passionately like before, but gentle, searching. His tongue swept in tentatively and I opened to his touch.

My heart flickered in my chest and I placed a hand over his own, the rhythm pumping steadily, gloriously. *"I see you. I'm staying."* Something inside me shattered at those words, freeing a girl with the wilds in her heart and adventure in her soul. A girl who had been overlooked for so long she hadn't known what it felt like to be seen and heard.

For someone with eyes only for her.

That girl cracked free from a mould that day, opened her wings and shifted her eyes to a new world, one where she would be unapologetically her.

Fierce and free.

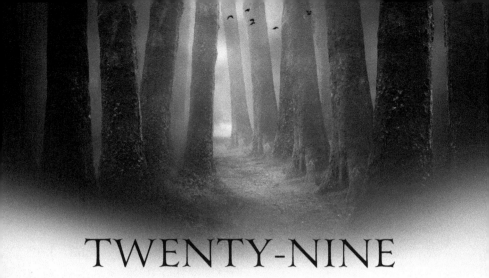

TWENTY-NINE

ante walked me through the streets of his town and, the more I came to know of Mistvellen, the faster I fell in love. The cobblestone streets were bustling with activity, townsfolk coming and going as they went about selling their wares or running errands for businesses.

The streets nearest to the castle were clean, with boxed tulips in pinks and creams blooming from their nests and wisteria creeping over the stoned walls of manors and odd shops. Everyone bowed and smiled as Dante passed, many glancing at me with curious gazes, their eyes lingering on my attire.

I ran a hand over my skirts, smiling to myself. I was a vision today, so I couldn't blame them. After running around in pants for much of my life—a fact Caitlin had despised and fellow witches had turned their noses up at—it was nice to wear something feminine and well made.

A tour of Dante's quarters after our bath had made me gasp

323

in shock—and I wasn't so easily surprised. He had a dressing room lined with storage chests which had been teeming with the finest silks and velvets, furs, cottons, and taffeta, and that was just for him. But on the other side of the chamber, he'd arranged a set of storage chests, each filled with gowns for all occasions, gloves, furs, boots and, even better, a storage chest filled with gear for training and battle.

"Fucking hell. You have—you have a dressing room?" I'd remarked, eyes wide as saucers as I'd stared at all the finery in the one room. More than I'd ever expected to see in one place.

Dante had laughed. "If you're going to be a magical entity, you may as well milk it. We might not answer to the Kingdom, but we reap its rewards. My father offers certain ... benefits ... to the neighbouring kingdoms. Black market, of course, but his deals barter gems and coin, silks and the like in exchange for certain spells and tonics our witches can concoct. His connections spread as far as the Middle East."

I'd blinked several times. "*Certain spells?* Whatever could you be offering that's worth that amount of coin?"

"Tonics to heal severe ailments, to make someone's hair shinier, catch the eye of a potential suitor, produce better yielding crops, that kind of thing. You'd be surprised how deep nobles will dig in their pockets if they think it will increase their standing in court or to find themselves on the arm of the wealthiest bachelor. It certainly fills our coffers."

"You heathen," I'd giggled, punching him in the arm. "I love

324

it."

As I swished down the streets in a sea green dress in the finest taffeta I'd ever laid a hand on, sliding a finger over the golden embroidery lining the seams, I couldn't help but appreciate such a swindling. Such spells did exist, though they weren't always the most reliable, but perhaps the Wolfblood Clan really was helping others while helping themselves.

The people here, at least, were healthy and happy, and the children were well-dressed, their cheeks flushed as they scampered through the crowds, playing hide-and-seek and getting up to mischief.

I gaped at the many shops within the town centre. We passed an apothecary with curiosities lining the window. Everything from newts' eyes to lidérc hooves to garabonc teeth—creatures much like táltosok. Old wives' tales told of them wandering the countryside in search of milk from humble villagers. If the villager didn't provide at least a full jug, it was said the garabonc would summon storms or blizzards and ride on dragons to wreck the roofs and tear the trees from their roots.

I'd yet to see one, but I'd always been sure to keep milk freshly stocked.

The smells of cinnamon, sugar syrup and fresh bread wafted up my nose, causing my stomach to grumble. I sighed, dreaming wistfully of Mama's cooking. I missed her so much already. What was she doing right now? I imagined her in her garden, weaving her magic to tend to the flowers and vegetables, her apron

smudged with dirt and her brown locks spilling from her bun. Eszter would be beside her, basking in the golden sun, weaving her needle and thread with practiced fingers.

Perhaps Eszter could open a store in Mistvellen one day, especially if she found a suitor here. A charming, handsome young man by the name of Lukasz. Wouldn't that be lovely? But such dreams would never come true unless we triumphed over the cultists.

My eyes stung. Best not to imagine a world I might not exist in.

Dante's arm looped through mine, his weight a comforting presence at my side. "Are you hungry?"

Peeking up at him from under my lashes, I smiled, forcing back the pain. "Always."

He veered us towards the baker's shop—a stone building with a cherry red door and matching windows. A ginger cat sat on the sill, watching everyone with inquisitive green eyes.

It arched into my touch as I smoothed a hand over its back. "Hello, little one." A cornflower blue collar around its neck read 'Salamon'. "One who brings peace. What an apt little name for you," I cooed.

Salamon chirped back, his tail twirling as he prowled the sill. To my surprise, he leapt at Dante, climbing his arm and settling on his shoulders, blinking those green eyes at me. Cocking my head, I raised a brow at Dante.

He chuckled, patting his small friend. "Salamon and I go way

back," he said with a cheeky grin. "Come, there's someone I want you to meet." He paused, adding, "He makes the best *bejgli* in the Kingdom."

"Why didn't you say so earlier?" I grinned, dragging him by the wrist through the door.

The bakery's interior was just as quaint with a fire crackling merrily in the corner, a workroom at the back and a long bench displaying treats. My tongue salivated at the sweets. *Kakaós csiga*, rolls in spirals of melted chocolate called cocoa snails; *kürtős kalács*, a spit cake made from sweet dough and rolled with sugar; *bejgli*, walnut poppy seed rolls; and an endless row of cakes.

"Dante, my boy," boomed a voice from behind the counter. Startled from my food hypnosis, I stared at the owner. A rounded man with black hair tied in a leather strip and an apron dusted with icing grinned broadly. He scooted through the bench gap—sideways, to allow for his girth—and chuckled as he slapped his meaty arms around Dante.

"It's good to see you, Imre." Dante's voice was muffled and I couldn't help but laugh as his towering, bulky frame was now dwarfed by the baker. When they broke apart with a few claps on the back, Imre turned to me expectantly.

Dante smiled. "I'd like to introduce my—"

"Kitarni," I interjected, holding out a hand. Imre tugged it and swept me up into a bear hug. My legs dangled like a child's as I was lifted off the ground with a squeak. It was kind of nice to be held with such warmth. I liked Imre already, even if he was squeezing the breath from my lungs. He smelt like chocolate and berries and felt like home.

I coughed a cloud of flour as he at last set me down gently and took me by the shoulders. "My, you are a treasure," he said with a kind smile and brown doe eyes. "Beautiful as a spring day and eyes full of fire. What poor luck has stuck you on the arm of this one?"

"Our parents saw fit for us to marry," I drawled, smoothing my skirts down. "My magic is ... sought after, you see."

Imre nodded, catching on, but thankfully he bypassed any talk of siring heirs or bearing children. "Ahh, a binding of our peoples. Well, should you ever need an escape from this one"—he jerked his head at Dante—"you may find solace in my shop."

"I'll keep that in mind," I chuckled. "Though you should know I have a sweet tooth that might eat you out of house and home."

"A baker's greatest delight is to see his work enjoyed." He eased his way behind the counter once more, gathering a collection of sweets and wrapping them in cloth. "My gift to you, my lady."

"Just Kitarni," I said with a smile. "But thank you, you're too kind."

Dante took the bundle of sweets from my arms, raising his brow at the baker. "You aren't trying to butter up my bride, are you?"

Imre lifted his hands in supplication but looked slyly at me.

"If I was, did it work?"

Grinning, I pressed a kiss against his cheek, fluttering my lashes. "Everyone always says food is the way to a *man's* heart, but bakers know best."

His laugh roared through the building and Dante latched onto my arm, rolling his eyes. "Be seeing you soon, old friend."

"Keep her safe, wolf lord. Such a jewel should not be tarnished," Imre called after us.

Dante's reply was so quiet I barely heard it over his breath. "She is much too precious for that."

I'd never seen so much purple in one place. The lavender fields seemed endless as they sprawled over the sloping hill, row upon row stretching towards the mountains in the distance. The distinct floral and herbal scent climbed my nose, laced with a woody undertone, instantly relaxing and calming all at once.

Bumblebees hovered overhead, their fat little bottoms swaying in the soft breeze, flitting in yellow and black stripes under the sunny sky. Gazing at the castle town behind us, I might have believed myself a girl living in a faery tale.

This was my home now. A concept which had seemed impossible to believe mere days ago, yet the man beside me was doing his best to make that transition easier. His head was upturned, eyes closed, long dark lashes fanning over his bronzed

skin as he basked in the sunlight.

He seemed so human now—so normal—I could almost forget the killer inside him, the wolf of Mistvellen. But I wouldn't. I needed that beast now more than ever. Needed him to build an army, to protect the ones we loved, to see us to victory once ...

Once I was gone.

Or wasn't. I would not go down quietly, but I still didn't know what lay ahead.

Refusing to ruin the serenity of this place, I took a bite into my *bejgli*, ripping my teeth through the roll mercilessly.

"Does it pass the test?" Dante drawled. I hadn't realised he'd cracked an eye open and was watching me with pure amusement dancing in his eyes. The sunlight gilded them and highlighted the red in his brown hair.

"Verff—guff." I swallowed my mouthful, grinning. "Imre might be my new best friend."

He smirked but grabbed a pastry for himself, taking a generous bite. Even the way he ate made something in my chest jolt. My throat bobbed. I would not think about what else he could do with that mouth. I would not—

He groaned and that nearly undid my restraint—until he smiled at me. I tried to suppress my smile as I pointed at his mouth, shaking with bottled up laughter. "Um, I think you've got something in your teeth."

His brows creased together and, unable to withhold the dam any longer, I cackled at the poppies stuck between his teeth. The

utter look of confusion on his face had me doubling over until tears leaked from my eyes.

Dante laughed too, sprawling back on his elbows and flashing me a lazy, poppy-filled grin. I struggled to breathe as he quirked his brows suggestively. "Please stop," I wheezed. "It's too much."

Making to turn away, I yelped as he pulled me into his lap instead. He was warm, solid, and I allowed myself to sink into his touch. He coiled a strand of my hair around his finger absentmindedly and we sat there for a time, sinking into comfortable quiet.

We spent the afternoon just talking and I realised it was the longest time we'd spent together where we hadn't been doing unsavoury things or hacking at monsters. He asked many questions—simple things at first, like my favourite colour, food, hobbies. Sage green and, ironically, lavender; anything sweet; and riding, reading, and cooking.

He grinned. "You're as much a kitchen witch as you are full of fire then."

"The *best* memories are made with good food, good company and a stiff drink," I replied.

Easy and distracting questions, but I liked that he asked. I quickly realised the small details were things I was most eager to learn. Simple treasures or daily habits of a normal person with a normal life.

Dante liked red; goulash and paprikash; and training,

strategy games, riding, and reading.

"No, really?" I exclaimed at the latter, brows drawing together. "What do you read?"

I felt him shrug behind me. "Historical anecdotes on supernatural beings, grimoires, tales of knights saving damsels in distress, slaying monsters. All the fantastical. Though, if I'm in the mood for something scandalous, I have a few books on ... leisurely activities."

My cheeks heated. "You can't be serious."

"When it comes to pleasure, darling, I'm deadly serious."

His right hand began creeping up my leg, pushing the skirt up higher, higher, his fingers splaying over my thigh and curling round towards the junction of my legs. My breath caught in my mouth, but his comment about books had my mind distracted.

"Do you—do you have a library?"

His fingers stopped circling and I peeked up at him from his lap. His eyes were bright, his smile genuine. "Of course. It's all yours, should you wish to use it."

An idea formed in my head. "Yes. Yes, I would like that very much."

I chose to sleep in Dante's bed again that night—but I loved that he'd given me the choice to stay or sleep in the guest suite. It struck me how different things were here. No one looked at me strangely for being alone with my intended. I didn't need a

 332

chaperone, didn't have someone watching my every move. It was nice to not feel judged or indifferent.

The witches here smiled freely and táltosok were polite. I had seen families walking the streets together today and my heart had soared to see such a simple, precious thing. So very different from my home and so much *better*.

My thoughts turned to the future. Of all the things I could do with my title—with the táltos at my side. I was playing a dangerous game, flirting with Dante, sharing small secrets, learning the man beneath the mask.

It was dangerous to *hope*.

Dante was with his father and András tonight, planning all things military and preparing for the days to come. I'd decided not to attend, giving myself some time alone to adjust to my new environment, and truthfully, Dante seemed like he needed some space. After hearing the message from that creepy bull-headed man, there'd been an undercurrent of tension running through him. He did well to hide it, but I knew he worried for Mistvellen. For me.

While I still refused to entertain the notion of falling for him—that our relationship could remain strictly sexual—there was no denying the crackling embers of something unfamiliar. A new feeling beginning to bloom. It was something I couldn't think about, didn't have time to nourish. I couldn't water that seed, *not yet*.

The táltosok could tend to the castle's defences and armies

 333

tonight. I had my own scheming to do, away from Dante's distracting dimples or the warmth of his embrace.

Bigger games were afoot and I planned to have a winning hand. Fate demanded sacrifice, but the more I came to explore this new world, the more I realised how much I wanted to fight for it. To *live* in it, when the dust had settled.

Mistvellen was magical. A place I could belong, truly *belong*, and live a happy life. No longer as a pariah or the town oddity, but a woman welcomed with open arms, whose magic was a gift, not a curse.

I was no longer that broken girl. I was a witch, powerful and strong and ready to burn every cultist to cinders if it meant saving my family. But first I had to imperil them even further by bringing her back.

My stomach twisted. Damn Fate. Damn Death and every supernatural fucking entity who would use me like a pawn. I am *not* a pawn. I would be a queen and I would conquer.

Dante had mentioned a library with grimoires and history books, so I'd start there. I'll comb through every tome and find a way to survive what's coming. A grim smile graced my face. When Sylvie rose, I would be ready.

Plotting her demise put me in a rather good mood. I smiled to myself as I sat on the bed, removing the pins from my hair and brushing my locks. A stunning porcelain hand mirror carved with blooming roses caught my eye on a nearby table. Dante's mother's, perhaps?

I peered at the girl in the mirror. She seemed older, somehow. Stronger. My olive skin glowed from the energy Dante had given me, the freckles splattered across my nose winking in the firelight. I thought of his nickname for me and smiled. Maybe I didn't hate the endearment.

I paused. Lodged between multiple teeth were little black dots. Horrified, I pulled the mirror closer, only to realise the little blurs were poppy seeds. They must have been there all day and Dante hadn't said a word.

I laughed, feeling a warmth rising in my stomach. *The little devil.*

The wolf pup liked to play and the next move would be mine.

THIRTY

spent the next few days poring over tomes and I'd never been more thankful Mama had taught Eszter and me our letters. The library was a dream. Tables upon tables in a dark, reddish wood housed books and a cosy fireplace crackled in the corner. Couches and armchairs in sapphires and golds dotted the room, and sconces lined every wall.

I'd stay forever if I could. What more did a girl need when multiple worlds were at her fingertips? Dante had understated the selection. There were indeed several cases of fantasy and romance alone, while the rest were filled with history, poetry, the sciences and the magical and mystifying.

After initially scanning the romance selection and pocketing a few for later—my, my, he wasn't lying about scandalous—I had hurried on to a section about the supernatural, stacking grimoire after grimoire and historians' accounts of creatures great and small. Anecdotes of the gods, of the middling world and what lay below, simple spells and tricks. I'd flicked through all of them.

Days had passed and still I had nothing. I tossed the book on the used pile, where it puffed out a cloud of dust indignantly.

Raking a hand through my hair, I sighed, annoyance simmering just under the skin. "I'm doomed, Laszlo." I hadn't seen much of my four-legged-friend since arriving in Mistvellen. He'd been spending time with the pages and grooms charged with caring for the horses and hounds of the castle. He padded over to my chair, laying his head in my lap and looking up at me with those big brown eyes. I scratched his ears absentmindedly, shuttering my lids as I leaned back in the chair.

"Anything I can help with?" A voice sounded from the landing above and I peered up to find Margit smiling down at me, the same mischievous expression in her eyes I'd come to expect from Dante.

I scowled. "Unless you can conjure a spell to wipe out a horde of cultists, probably not."

She glided down the stairwell, taking a seat at the table overflowing with tomes. Laszlo bounded over to her, snuffling at her hands and she laughed, scratching his ears. Her attention turned to the stacks of books. "Dante said you loved to read, but this is ... ambitious. What are you searching for?"

I bit my lip, unsure how she'd react, so I offered a half truth. "I'm looking for dark magic. If we're going to fight the cultists, we'd be better prepared if we knew what to expect."

She nodded, seeming to accept the answer, but the glitter of

her eyes told me she didn't fully believe me. "You won't find knowledge on dark magic within these shelves." My heart sank and I slumped deeper into the chair. "I didn't say such books didn't exist," she added with a grin. "You just need to know where to look. Follow me."

Rising in a sweep of red velvet skirts, she led me to an alcove in the shelves. There was nothing unusual about it until she pulled on a tattered old tome and hefted the shelf aside. It revealed a hidden passageway descending into the bowels of the castle. I hesitated at the precipice, but she winked. "After you."

Summoning a fireball to light the way, I progressed into the musty tunnel, focusing on placing one slippered foot in front of the other. Cobwebs clung to my hair and skin and I clawed at my face in disgust. The tunnel had been abandoned for some time. The passage was cold and smelt stale, but that didn't seem to deter Margit. "What is this place?" I whispered.

Only the silence of tombs answered, thick and heavy. The deeper we went, the more my bones chilled and my stomach roiled with panic. Anxiety slithered into my heart, causing beads of perspiration to film over my palms and forehead. An old magic seeped from this place, curling around my shoulders, tugging me closer.

At last, when the walls began closing in and my breaths turned ragged, a chamber emerged into view at the end of the tunnel. A bookcase stood covered in cobwebs on the far side and a table laden with a cauldron stood in the centre, surrounded by rickety old chairs. Potion ingredients lined the walls—everything from animal skulls to dried herbs, soils, chalks and candles. *Black candles.*

The subtle smell of copper tinged my nostrils and an otherworldly feeling washed over me, tugging at that power curled deep inside my gut.

I whirled on Margit, narrowing my eyes. "You practice dark magic," I hissed. "I could feel something strange about you. I smelt it on you the moment we met. Working with the cultists, are you?"

She scoffed. "Please, those fanatics? Nothing but addicts and religious zealots, the lot of them. So drunk on bloodmorphia cups, their own magic abandons them. Pitiful creatures."

"So what is all this?" I gestured at the chamber.

She sighed—a long, world-weary sound of a woman far older than her years. "I am no ordinary witch. The elements forsook me and I am cursed with the vision instead."

I blinked. "You're a seer?"

Margit pursed her lips, taking a seat at the wooden table. "As you say." She pulled a vial with ruby liquid from her skirts and took a long draught, body shivering as her eyes rolled back in her head.

I looked on in disgust, realising at once what the liquid was. "For someone swearing they aren't in league with the cultists, you seem pretty comfortable sipping on bloodmorphia like it's fucking wine."

Her blue eyes pierced my own when they opened, her cheeks flushed with warmth. "Do not judge me, girl. We all have our vices. Mine keeps me sane, and I only use a small amount to take the edge off. When the visions come, they drown me in waves. After a while you learn how to swim."

"So, the drug helps to, what, calm the storm?"

"In a word." She smoothed back a lock of raven hair. "My parents were killed in the siege led by the cultists. Mama told me to hide down here until someone collected me ... Nobody came. When I finally emerged, I found their bodies growing cold in the castle corridors. The very same night, the first vision occurred. I couldn't stop it, couldn't be free of it. And that's not all. I ... see them. The dead. The souls who wallow in their grief or their vengeance instead of passing on."

"My gods." I sank into a chair, horrified by her story. For a child to have suffered so much—to see the unseen with no explanation why—I couldn't begin to imagine the trauma of such a gift. No wonder she returned to this chamber. It was a safe house, a place she could hide away from the world. Or perhaps just be herself without the sideways glances and quiet titters of people who didn't understand her magic or might judge her for it.

I could understand that, knew the consequences of indifference all too well. My mother had died before I ever knew her. I'd never known her love, or the lack of it, but Margit and I weren't so different. She'd been through hell and came out stronger. I was still caught in the middle.

 340

The thought of her waiting down here while the cultists butchered those in the castle made bile climb my throat. That was something no child should ever see. I placed a hand gently over her own.

She flinched under my touch but did not pull away. Instead, she hefted her chin, looking into my eyes. "Do not pity the child. She died long ago. A witch was born in her place, one who knows the path you walk."

I stared at the woman before me. She wore her wounds like armour, wielded words like swords. She was a warrior in her own right, a woman worthy of admiration. Her tale was a test. One I planned to pass.

She did not want my sorrow, so I would show her my strength. Grinning slyly, I sat back in my chair, folding my arms across my chest. "It's as Mama always said. 'In dark times, deny not the hand of friendship. Fill it with the flame of fury.'"

A wintry smile settled over Margit's face. "Then let me be your ally, Kitarni, for the gods know you'll need one."

"Aye. I'd settle for a friend. I'm a little short on those."

She shrugged, tossing her hair back. "I'm a black-hearted bitch, but I'm the best one you've got."

I smirked. "I think you and I are going to get along famously."

She gulped the remaining bloodmorphia from the vial, wiped a hand over her lips. "Right ... I think it's time you and I had a little talk about our dear friend, Fate."

THIRTY-ONE

"Can't believe we're doing this," I muttered, placing black candles at the seven points of the pentagram Margit had drawn. "Death is going to be very unhappy with us."

She shrugged a delicate shoulder. "He'll get over it. He has eternity, after all."

Despite my trepidation, I barked a laugh. "These beings will hold a grudge for an age. Isn't that why we're in this mess in the first place?"

"Correction." She lifted a finger. "*You're* in this mess. I'm merely an aid for when shit goes sideways."

I glowered at her as I ignited the candles with a click of my fingers. "I'll be sure to remind Death when he's nice and snug in our little trap here. Right. What do we do now?"

"Strip," she ordered.

I blinked. "I beg your pardon?"

"You may beg, but it won't cure you of your curse. Now remove your dress so I can get a look at the mark."

A shiver ran down my spine. "How do you—"

"I've seen it in my dreams. It binds you to him but, equally so, it serves as a tether for *you* to tug on. I'll need it to summon Death within the devil's trap."

Grumbling, I peeled my dress over my head, thankful I was wearing a simple velvet gown without stays or ties. Setting it down on the table, I shivered in the thin under-shift as Margit directed me to the edge of the star, her fingernails making quick work of the tie at my neck. She peeled it back from my shoulders, revealing the upper stretch of the three rippling scars upon my flesh. "Gruesome," she remarked with fascination.

I flipped her the middle finger in response. "Hurry up, it's cold as a witch's tit in here."

"Cute. But it's about to get colder." She began intoning in what I presumed to be Old Latin, a dialect unfamiliar to my ears. The scars pulsed, throbbing down my back. Frost speared down my spine, leeching into the floor and filling the chamber with a low fog roiling at our feet.

The hairs on my arms raised as the temperature plummeted and her words grew louder, urgent. The candles flickered in response, sending eerie shadows scattering over the walls. I gritted my teeth as my shoulder blades trembled, my back arching. It felt like a demon clutched at my spine, ready to rip it from my body.

Tears pricked at my eyes and I doubled over, but Margit kept

her palm on my back, a force immovable. "Make it stop," I gasped. "I can't ... it's too much. Make it stop."

The pain stopped abruptly and Margit stumbled backwards, the breaths heaving from her chest. An unmistakable presence washed over me, an aura of darkness and despair. He was here.

"You could have asked nicely," Death purred from behind a blackened cloud. When at last he appeared, I was face-to-face with a void of black, only this time eyes glinted dangerously in the shadows within. Not pupils or irises, but a shifting of light that somehow portrayed his anger. His aura rippled with it and I shrank despite myself. "You dare to summon me," he whispered, his voice so low it pierced the stillness.

"I-I—" Words failed me. I bent my head in supplication, throat bobbing as I forced my tongue to untie and my lips to loosen. "I only wished to ask for your guidance."

"Do you think you're clever, trapping me in a circle of this chalk? I may not be able to intervene while you're alive, but I can make your soul suffer in exquisite ways when you're dead."

I suppressed a shiver at his threat, forcing myself to breathe, to remember why we'd called him. "I have some information you might find most intriguing."

He paused, his robes billowing in shadowed tendrils. "In exchange for my assistance, I presume."

"Nothing comes without cost. Witches know that well, as do you."

He paused, considering me. "Very well. Speak your piece. If

I find your knowledge valuable, I shall offer my wisdom in return. But if you waste my time"—he lifted a bony finger—"you *and* the seer will suffer the consequences."

I felt Margit move behind me, but I didn't turn away, wouldn't give him the satisfaction of seeing my fear written in sweaty drops upon my face. "There is a priceless artefact Fate seeks, hidden by Sylvie before she died. With it, one holds the power to rule over the Under World."

"I already know this," Death said coolly. "I was the one who promised it to her. A crown for the weaver of time, a ring for the ruler of the dead. A gift for my bride to be, before that wretch of a witch stole it when she summoned me last. Fate refused to be wed without it."

"That must have angered you greatly," I said carefully. "But why not take your hand without it? Surely she could have no better match in hell."

Death hissed, his raspy breath filming over my face. "My patience wears thin, little witch. You did not summon me to discuss my marital woes. What's it going to be, a time loop of your worst nightmare or torture at the hands of my minions?"

"Wait," I blurted. "Once she obtains the crown, she plans to overthrow you and rule over hell alone."

Death went preternaturally still—even his robes ceased their floating. "You lie." His rasp sent a thousand bugs skittering over my flesh, his skeletal fingers stretching for my throat.

"She speaks truth," Margit cried, stepping past me. "I have

seen it."

"Show me."

She held her chin high, jaw set stubbornly as she approached the demon before us. The barest shiver prickled over her skin as she placed one hand in his own, her disgust visible in the slight twitch of her lips upon contact.

Eyes rolling back into her head, mere seconds passed until she gasped back into herself, and Death withdrew his hand with a hiss. "Blasphemy," he shrieked. "Betrayal." His robes thrashed against his trap, slamming against an invisible barrier as his wrath lashed again and again. "Speak, witch, and you shall have your answer."

Breathing a sigh of relief, I stepped toward the star. "Fate said my blood would bring Sylvie back. That it was the only way we could destroy her once and for all. But she said I'd have to die first."

Death stopped his thrashing, falling silent. I could have heard a pin drop. It was so quiet. To my surprise, he laughed. Cold and cruel and hollow. Margit and I exchanged a baffled glance.

"My darling Fate, what a web of lies she spins with her needle and thread."

"I don't understand."

"Foolish girl," he remarked, still chuckling. "It is true the cultists' dark ritual can revive Sylvie from her grave, but it takes little more than a cup to bring her back."

"Gods," Margit said softly. "But my vision ... I saw Kitarni. She was bleeding on an altar."

Death turned to her. "Visions are not set in stone. Your little trick today has altered the course of your futures."

Relief washed over me, lifting a weight from my chest. "I'm not going to die?"

"That remains to be seen," he replied flatly. "But no, you needn't die so that she may live. Your blood is strong and like calls to like. Her essence will latch on to the power in it, drag her back to the living."

"Why? Why would Fate lie about that?"

"It would seem my spider has several plans up her sleeve. Do you not see, little witch? She was using you for her own gains. You were naught but a shovel to dig for her spoils, a gift for an unlikely ally."

My nostrils flared and I gritted my teeth. "So she planned to cross me, have me killed so I wouldn't stand in the way of her game."

Death watched as I paced around the circle. "Should you survive the ritual, Fate will do everything in her power to ensure your death. She needs the crown to rule hell and what better friend to keep than the most powerful witch of your time?"

"Someone to commandeer the Middle World," I said softly, catching on. Halting, I stared at him incredulously. "She wants to rule Earth as well?"

Death nodded once. "A goal threatened by the last living

347

witch with blood magic in her veins. She cannot touch you on this plane. While you live, she is powerless to intervene. But Sylvie is not."

"Holy fuck," Margit breathed.

I twisted a curl around one finger, chewing over this information, already scheming my next moves. "I've a proposition for you."

Death waved a bone finger and, if he had a mouth, I'd bet it would be grinning devilishly now. "Go on."

"When Sylvie returns, what say I find the crown for you? You will have the means to keep Fate in check and remain ruler of the Under World. Earth will remain safe and almost everyone has a happily ever after. What say you?"

"I'd say you're quite possibly my favourite witch."

I snorted. "Of course I am. Your assistance has been enlightening. Thank you, Death. I trust a continued alliance is mutually beneficial, then?"

He sighed. "I will refrain from skewering you in the next life, if that's what you're asking."

I grinned. "You are a saint, truly."

"Angels would weep to hear you say that," he purred. "Now let me out of this blasted chalk. I've schemes to plot and a wedding to plan."

THIRTY-TWO

The wind howled, tearing at my shawl as I stood upon the balcony of Dante's suite. The evening air was chill, biting at my skin, but I didn't mind. It reminded me I was alive, that the blood running through my veins still thrummed with life.

His chamber was located on the south-east wing, providing a clear view of the lavender hills and the woods. The purple flowers were stunning in the setting sun, kissed with pinks and oranges in a swath of golden, silky sky. But I stared upon the treetops now. Deep within, cultists writhed in snake pits, venomous and volatile. They would taste my blood on their lips, drain me dry if they could.

But I knew better now. My heart felt lighter after Margit's and my meeting with Death, and a sly grin curled my lips. It couldn't have gone better. The horseman himself had given me hope I'd not been able to muster. I didn't need to die. I didn't need to—

Fuck. I could dare to dream after all. As I gazed upon the sprawling woods, a flutter of hope brushed featherlight strokes in my chest, easing the tension that had burrowed deep. *What might I do with my life?* I wondered. *What lies beyond the cold clutches of cultists and curses?*

I would be a wife, a mother, a lady of a castle. But what of the girl behind those duties? I gripped the cold stone wall, leaning forward, feeling the rush of air upon my face. I could do anything I wanted. Write an epic tale, hone my skills in the kitchen, explore the world beyond our borders.

Yes. I wanted to walk among sands, feel the spray of salt upon my skin, climb mountains, taste delicacies unknown to the Kingdom of Hungary. I wanted it all.

Calloused hands reached around my front, cradling me to a warm chest. I smiled at his touch, the familiar scent of leather and wood, the warm breath upon my cheek. He nuzzled into the crook of my neck and a jolt fired through my body. There was something else I wanted too. *Someone.*

If we survived what was to come, could we be more than lovers? Would we grow together, embrace a future not just as man and wife, but partners in every endeavour? Perhaps I was a fool for denying it, but a part of me felt we were walking towards that destination already.

And for the first time, I wasn't afraid. The thought of opening myself to him, to bearing every part of my soul wasn't frightening anymore. Dante made me feel alive. Strong, powerful,

 350

worthy. The last thought nearly broke me. In his eyes, I was worthy. Of not only him, but his people—the world.

"Did you find what you were searching for in the library?" he asked, grazing my cheek with his lips.

My eyes stung, and I sank into his embrace. "Yes," I breathed, almost choking on the word. "Yes."

Turning, I reached up on my tiptoes and kissed him gently. Searching. His answering kiss was tender as he opened to me, exploring my mouth with his tongue, pressing his full lips to my own.

I lost myself to that kiss, my hope and joy surging through every twist of our tongues. When at last we pulled away, breathless and hot, he smiled at me. A true smile—one unmasked and innocent in its entirety. His eyes were soft, gentle, and my heart might have hitched at the sight of them.

"What was that for?" he asked softly.

Squaring my shoulders, I lifted my chin. "I was so angry when I learned of this marriage. The thought of being worn as an accessory on the arm of a noble's son, to be trapped in a cage, however gilded that may be. I wanted to run. Far, far away."

"But you stayed for your family."

I nodded slowly. "They are everything to me. I would bottle the sun to give them warmth, steal the stars to fulfil their dreams. Knowing they would be cared for and kept safe was the only reason I stayed the course, especially after learning of the cultists. Of Sylvie."

The light in his eyes banked at my words. Was that disappointment etched into the lines of his face? Taking his chin in my own, I forced him to look at me. "That was before I met you, Dante. You reminded me of my worth, bolstered my strength and gave me armour. I ... I want to see what this is between us. I want *you*."

"I don't deserve you, Kitarni." His voice was so quiet I barely heard it over the wind. "I'm not a good person. I've made terrible choices, done horrible things."

The sorrow in his voice quavered, but I refused to let him sink. "You're an insufferable, stubborn asshat with a penchant for scandals and unruly women. And I wouldn't have you any other way."

A ghost of a grin lit his mouth at that. "A devilishly handsome, insufferable, stubborn asshat," he corrected. Laughing, I rolled my eyes, but my mirth sputtered out as he brushed his knuckles across my cheek, his eyes glinting with something I couldn't quite place. "You could conquer kings, you know that."

Splaying my hand across his chest, I pushed him inside the chamber until the backs of his knees met the bedframe. His eyes widened in surprise as he tumbled back on the bed and I unbuckled his pants. "I'll settle for a lord-in-wait."

Slowly, I bent down, clasping the folds of my gown and peeling them up over my head. His eyes roamed my bare skin, turning hungry when seeing the chemise underneath. It was a

silky black slip of a thing, hugging my curves like a second skin and cutting dangerously low at the front, leaving little to the imagination.

"Oh, I like that one," he whispered. "I'd like it better if it were on the floor."

"Patience," I crooned, toying with the spaghetti straps at my shoulders. "What else would you like?"

A low hum rumbled through him as I lifted the chemise over my head, exposing my breasts. He pounced, dragging me onto his lap and seizing one nipple in his mouth, flicking a tongue over it before moving to the next one.

I curved my back, leaning into his touch. His palms were warm as they slid over my skin, curling around my waist and rubbing over my breasts. "I want to see you touch yourself," he whispered in between kisses. "Show me what those clever fingers can do."

Need flared hot and heavy in my core as I shoved him further back, trying not to tremble at the hunger in his eyes. I was already wet for him, the heat surging through my stomach, pulsing in my core. He shuffled back, leaning against the pillows like a king lounging on his throne.

Those brown eyes flashed with gold, following my movements as I faced him, reclining on the edge of the bed. I trailed my fingers down my stomach, down my centre, circling two fingers over the bundle of nerves idly.

His cock bulged against his pants and he edged closer, but I

pressed one foot against his chest, shaking my head slowly, a smile carving my lips. "You can watch, but you can't touch. Not me, not yourself."

He sucked in a ragged breath as I kept circling, kept teasing, speeding up my momentum until, ever so slowly, I slipped those fingers inside me. I moaned, tilting my head up.

At my pleasure, he shivered, a pained noise escaping his lips, his hand creeping towards his pants. I smiled, rocking my hips seductively. "I've thought about what it would feel like to have you inside me," I whispered. "What we could do together."

"Tell me," he said breathlessly. "What did you imagine?"

I pulled my fingers out before sliding them slowly downwards again. "You'd put your fingers inside, taste me, and then you'd take me over and over again. I want to feel you inside me, hard and fast and holding nothing back."

"Fuck, Kitarni. I will do anything for you."

I smiled, easing myself fully back onto the bed, opening my legs. "Then do it, Dante. I want it all."

He drank me in greedily, appreciatively and then his fingers were upon me, splayed in circling, teasing motions. I gasped as he knelt between my legs and tasted me, his tongue flicking until I was writhing, moaning.

"Gods," I breathed, my skin heating as the wave of pleasure built inside me. He crashed against me like a dam, shaking my foundations as I rocked against him, grinding against his mouth.

I cried out as my climax swept over me, breaking me apart as my legs quivered. *More.* I wanted more of him. All of him. He looked at me, smiling lazily, a questioning glint in his eyes.

I nodded and, on a breathless whisper, I commanded, "Yes."

He removed his shirt and shucked off his pants. I stared at his length, the powerful thighs beneath. The muscles bunched in his arms as he reached down between us, grasping his cock and running the head over my clit.

Dante lined himself up with my centre, easing in gently before slamming fully inside me with one thrust. We both gasped and he allowed me a second to adjust to his size before he began to move. Dante gave no quarter, filling me up, thrusting deep. I arched beneath him, hands clasped to his shoulders, nails digging in so hard he clenched his jaw somewhere between pleasure and pain.

His lips swept down to mine and I could taste myself on his lips. He dragged his teeth over them, biting down hard enough to hurt before flicking his tongue over the pain, then the exposed column of my neck.

It only made me want him more. I writhed against him, wrapping my legs around his waist, locking my body to his own. We fit so perfectly together, moving in tandem, grinding in a whirlwind of pleasure.

I met his need with every stroke, angling myself so he could thrust deeper still. He moaned and the sound had my core thrumming deep. He kissed me, our tongues twisting, our need devouring. I savoured every inch of him, rocking harder and

 355

faster, releasing my legs from his waist and stretching my hands out to grasp the edge of the bedframe.

He latched one hand to my hip, the other clamped tightly over one of my hands and I arched, dropping my head backwards. He thrust faster, faster, until I was screaming, his groans filling every crack in the silence of the bedroom.

"Dante," I whispered, and his name on my lips was his undoing.

He pounded, jerking against me as we both climaxed, my pleasure coming in dizzying waves as vertigo flushed to my head and warmth spread from my core. Our bodies were slick with sweat, my heart pounding with adrenaline as I lay gasping.

When he finished, he lay on top of me, wrapping me in his embrace and I didn't want to be anywhere else, do anything else in this moment.

There was only him.

THIRTY-THREE

"You're the most beautiful creature I've ever seen."

"Flatterer." I punched Dante in the arm before turning to the mirror, unable to wipe the stupid grin from my face. I felt like a queen, swathed in black silk that cinched in the bodice before spilling out in smoky waves to the floor. The fabric had a sheer layer sweeping around my arms, giving a fluttering cut-off sleeve.

Margit helped pin half of my hair up with a snake clip, its eyes beaded with jet black gems. My hair hung in gentle curls, smelling of orange blossom and almonds—a tantalising lotion she had gifted me earlier.

She painted my lips with a subtle rouge and dusted my cheeks. "There," she said with a flourish of her brush. "Perfection."

I blinked at the reflection staring back at me. Someone wholly different, yet wildly familiar. Her hazel eyes burned with resolve, her spine was straight and she smiled. A fierce thing from a fierce witch. "Margit, I'm ..." I trailed off, unsure how to thank her. Not just for the small gestures, but for the friendship she'd offered. The kindness, despite my hasty judgement yesterday.

She swept my hair over one shoulder and leaned in close, whispering so only I could hear. "In my mind, you're a queen, Kitarni. The only one keeping her caged was you. It's time to open the door." She smiled knowingly and turned away, placing a gentle hand on Dante's sleeve before exiting the room.

"There's just one thing missing," he said.

I frowned at him in the mirror, brows pulling down as I smoothed my palms over the dress. What could top Margit's efforts? Something glittered in his hand, catching the light of the sconces. Gold and red, swinging in a pendulum from his fingers.

Turning, I gasped at the sight of the necklace. A ruby teardrop the size of my thumb nail hung from a chain of gold, caged within golden filigree.

"May I?"

I nodded dumbly as he placed the chain over my neck and the ruby settled between my breasts.

It glimmered like a scarlet pool, soaking up the firelight. "It's beautiful."

"I had it commissioned by the castle jeweller. A reminder that you are more than your magic. Your blood may be different, but you are more precious than any power attainable. Your kith may not realise that, but I do."

 358

Tears pricked my eyes as my throat closed over, emotion bubbling up within. The more I saw this side of Dante, the more I wanted him. The softness beneath the muscled exterior. The smooth creamy goodness of a bejgli. And gods, did I want every part of him even more after our bedroom session. I tried not to glance at the bed behind us, but my eyes defied me.

Dante caught my gaze and smirked, already knowing where my mind had gone. "My good girl, I promise you'll get *that* reward later."

I licked my lips. "I do recall you said something about wearing only jewels to bed ..."

His eyes flashed. "On second thought, perhaps we have time before the feast."

I laughed, shaking my head and turning to the mirror again. My throat thickened with emotion suddenly at how easy this felt. How nice.

"Thank you," I breathed.

I didn't have to clarify just how deep that went. Dante only nodded and offered his arm. Squaring my shoulders, I didn't spare a thought for the girl I'd left behind.

Only the woman I'd become.

I had eyes only for the food when we arrived at the feast. The hall was beautiful, with giant tapestries depicting scenic locations

lining the walls and fireballs suspended with magic hovering beneath the domed ceilings. The table swept down the length of the room, where men and women in glittering finery laughed and drank.

But it was the dishes and the smells that caught my attention. Roast meats and vegetables drizzled in gravy, small poultry, freshly baked bread, endless carafes overflowing with wine. The spices coating several vegetable dishes were heady and consuming; I let each ensnare my senses, noting imported saffron, sweet cinnamon, ginger, and more.

Dante offered me a seat by the head of the table. Farkas hadn't arrived yet, but his chair seemed imposing in the bright space. All the nobles in attendance smiled and laughed, but I couldn't help but notice the sideways glances at his chair—the taut lines as they spoke.

A darker power had reared its ugly head and Mistvellen was under threat once again. I supposed anyone would be frightened of that. Many would have lost loved ones the last time the cultists came calling.

I took a large gulp of the red wine, trying to focus on the conversation, nodding and smiling politely to the gushing of the noblewomen seated closest to me, but I couldn't help lapsing into thoughts of the Sötét Erdő. They were hiding there, biding their time to strike or for us to walk into their net.

At last, Margit entered the hall, saving me from my thoughts and the idle conversations of the women in court. I'd rather fight

a lidérc than pretend to know the first thing about sewing a hemline or what the fashion of the week was.

My heart jolted. Eszter would be in her element if she were here. A boot slid up my thigh under the table and I choked on my wine, throwing Dante a glare. The rascal just smiled, his cheeky grin sending welcomed shivers up my spine.

Margit slunk into the chair beside me, her eyes a little too bright. I raised a brow, searching her face. She looked drained since the half hour I'd last seen her. Drawn, pale skin and eyes lined with dark circles even makeup couldn't hide.

"Are you okay? You look like you've seen a ghost." I rested a hand on hers and she startled at my touch. Her skin was cold as ice.

"A ghost," she murmured, so quietly I didn't hear her. "Yes, a ghost." She blinked rapidly, seeming to return to the present. "I—I had a vision."

My heart jolted, but I pulled a wine goblet and wrapped her fingers around it. "Drink. It'll help calm your nerves and warm you up."

She took it gratefully, sculling it to the dregs. Colour seemed to return to her cheeks almost instantly and she sank deeper in her chair, twisting anxious hands into the folds of her navy skirts as she leaned closer.

My eyes met Dante's from the other side of the table and one look was all it took until he was by our sides in an instant, crouching between us. He spared a concerned glance for his

cousin, eyes narrowing suspiciously.

"I saw her, Kitarni. Risen from the ashes, as alive as you and me. There's no escaping her return. I know deep in my bones there's no stopping it."

Straightening my spine, I looked her in the eyes. "I know, Margit. Death warned us this was inevitable. What matters is what we're going to do about her return."

She nodded, grabbing another goblet from the passing waiter's tray. Under the table she discreetly emptied her flask into the cup, stirring it with a black painted fingernail. "She will destroy the world if she comes to power. I have seen it—what will come to pass should she triumph. Mistvellen, your home, all of our kingdom will rot or burn."

"We won't let it come to that," I said sternly. "I swear it."

Margit squeezed my hand, her brows pinched with sadness. "You will not be the same when you are done."

Frowning, I studied her face. "What do you mean—"

A bang sounded from the far end of the room and Dante returned to his seat as everyone rose, bowing and curtseying as Farkas entered. All waited until he was seated before resuming their positions.

The wolf lord's dark eyes swivelled to me.

"My lady," he said with a polite nod. "I trust you're enjoying your stay thus far?"

"Mistvellen is a beautiful place, my lord, rich with culture. Your people seem well cared for … happy."

He paused, sipping from his goblet before steepling his fingers. Every action he took seemed measured, precise. I wondered if he ever relaxed behind closed doors or if he was always so stern and straight-backed. The wolf lord's eyes always seemed to search for danger, even as he scanned the room now, his gaze sweeping over every guest.

Farkas stared at me thoughtfully and I wanted to wriggle under the weight of it. He seemed tense, his posture stiff and tiredness rimming his eyes. "Happiness is a by-product of feeling safe and knowing one has stability and security. The cultists threaten what we've built here, but I will not let my city feel the sting of loss again."

I nodded. "These will be my people soon, too. I want to protect them as much as you do."

Surprise flickered over his features and he glanced between Dante and me carefully. "There is much to lose in times of war. As commander of the Wolfblood army, my son will fight beside me in the days to come. Every day he rides to battle, my bloodline is at risk—my son—and it is every father's fear to lose their child."

He sighed, scrubbing a hand over his face. "I would sleep better knowing you weren't out there too. As Nora would."

I stared at him, a little bewildered at the sentiment. My heart warmed as I glanced between him and his son. Farkas was an honourable man, but I had my own honour to uphold. Placing a hand on his arm, I offered him a grim smile. "I can't sit by while the men go to war. I am a witch and I will not cower behind stone

walls while the táltosok fight. Not when there is so much at stake and certainly not when I have the power to defend our people."

He leaned back in his chair and, to my surprise, cracked a smile. "You are your father's daughter," he chuckled. "Nora said you wouldn't listen."

I raised a brow. "I'm a Bárány. Stubbornness runs in our blood."

"Do your mother and sister share your temper and charm, too?" Dante drawled.

I kicked his feet under the table and Margit snorted into her cup as she feigned drinking wine beside me, but I ignored her.

"My mind is made up," I said to Farkas, my tone turning serious. "I will join the scouting party tomorrow, but you should know, events are set in motion that cannot be avoided."

"Margit has had visions, Father," Dante added quietly.

She stiffened beside me, casting her blue eyes on the lord. "It's true. Sylvie will return. Whether Kitarni seeks her out or waits for the cultists to come, they will take her. It is written in blood. But know this, my lord. Kitarni is all that stands in the way of the Dark Queen's reign."

Farkas swore, spouting a string of curses that would make a sailor blush. He glanced at his niece, his jaw ticking. "Is there no way to prevent this from happening? No means of altering the vision's outcome?"

"It's possible, but highly unlikely," she replied. "My visions aren't set in stone but it's more a glimpse of the future. They haven't failed me yet."

"Yet," Dante said, grasping at the word. His eyes gleamed with a kind of desperation I hadn't seen from him before. "So there's still a chance we can stop this?"

Margit said nothing and my heart sank. He really believed we could. I wanted to hold him to my chest, to tell him everything was going to be all right, but it was a lie—a damn lie—and Margit knew it as well as I did.

"Dante," I began.

"You can't go," he said abruptly, the muscles in his face tensing. "If there's even a small chance that we can keep you from her clutches ... we'd be fools not to be cautious."

Despair settled in my gut, curdling like dated milk. I wanted to believe there was another way, but I knew it wasn't so. I took a deep breath, feeling myself breaking apart inside. "Before I ventured to Mistvellen, you agreed I would be included in this war, that my choices are mine to make. I hold you to your word. All my life I've felt useless compared to my witch kith. Now, I have the chance to do something with my power. Don't take that away from me."

My last words almost broke and Dante's face fell as he took my hand. He understood me better than anyone—perhaps even myself—and he would never, *never* ask me to make myself smaller or to hide from my worth. He'd taught me to embrace who I was, helped me understand how strong I could be, how powerful. He'd been right.

365

The darkness inside me had terrified me at first, but I finally realised it's what makes me stronger. We all had monsters under our skins, but my anger, my sorrow, my past—and even my blood—made me who I am.

I reached out to the beast inside, stroked its black scales, didn't shy from its talons. It was just a piece of me—a lonely, misunderstood creature. But if I fed that power, showed it its worth, I could be even stronger.

And that was empowering. Freeing.

When the cultists had attacked us at Mistvellen's gates, I had trusted myself enough with that power and I would do so again.

THIRTY-FOUR

"You're too easy to read," András said with a cocky grin as he watched me mulling over my next move. "Like an open book."

I studied the chess board, scowling at the wooden figurines carved in the likeness of wolves, táltosok and witches. "This is my first time learning the game," I groaned. "You set me up to fail before we even began."

He laughed, his blond curls dropping over his face. His green eyes flashed, reflecting the fire from the hearth. "It's a game of strategy. You have to think several steps ahead, rather than charging into battle with fire blazing and no thought for the outcome."

I raised a brow. "I recall my tactics having served me well in battle so far."

A soft chuckle escaped his lips. "Fair point. Unfortunately for a grunt like me, I wasn't born with the power to decimate my

 367

rivals."

He said that like I should thank my lucky stars and I plucked the wine goblet from our table, hiding behind it as I took a sip. "I suppose everyone has been talking about my magic? What happened outside the gate?"

He grinned. "Naturally. Should they not be?"

"It's not that," I said slowly. "It's just ... until I met Dante, I'd always thought about my gifts as a curse, not a blessing."

"All magic is a gift. It's up to the host how they use it. Why do you use your power, Kitarni?"

I blinked. No one had ever asked me that before but, as I thought about it, I realised I'd only ever used my fire and blood magic in times of need. Fire was dangerous, but it was necessary, too. Fire meant warmth, comfort and full bellies. And my other magic?

I lifted my chin with conviction. "I use it to protect the ones I love. To keep my family and my people safe."

András leaned back in his chair, resting his boot over one knee, a sad smile on his lips. "You proved that before you even stepped foot in Mistvellen. You gave yourself to the cause without a moment's hesitation. What could be more honourable than that? Your magic is a gift, Kitarni. One you're worthy of."

I settled into my chair, feeling that warmth spreading in my stomach. He'd put it so simply, but it was perhaps the biggest compliment I'd received in a long time. More of a lesson—a reminder that I had the power to make change.

368

His expression drifted and I wondered what had caused the haunted look in his eyes as he lapsed into silence.

"Do you have family in Mistvellen?" I blurted, wishing I hadn't been so forward, but András didn't shy away.

"Not in the way you mean," he replied, his demeanour darkening. "My mother died giving birth to me and my father abandoned me to sail the seas. Lord Sándor took me in when I was just a squalling babe. Dante's been like a brother to me ever since and Margit a big sister, though certainly not a safe one to have."

I smiled, imagining them playing as children. András with his golden locks and bright smile, Dante with those big brown eyes and air of haughtiness about him. Margit, of course, would have been the one getting them into trouble.

"Are you still spinning that sob story? You were such a sensitive child, you balled at every little thing," she said, swishing into the room with a teasing grin. "Someone had to forge you into stronger stuff."

"You shoved me off the wall and broke my arm and leg," András said with a glare as she sprawled over the couch.

"Nudged," Margit said innocently, batting her lashes. "You were just too slow and chubby to move fast enough." She turned to me, a knowing grin on her face and a dangerous glint in her eye. "He had a fondness for sweets, it was a vulnerable time for him."

"The cooks used to give me extra treats," András whispered

behind his hand with a wink. "I was the apple of their eye, even then."

"Yes, and I'm sure everyone's had a taste since," Dante smirked as he strolled into the room.

I laughed, letting myself fall into the ease of their company, the gentle teasing and jokes. Dante settled on the arm of my chair, his presence warm and comforting beside me. I watched the group eagerly, feeling drawn to the soft tug of happiness pulling at my heart.

They were a strange lot, but they were family in all the ways that counted. It made me miss Mama and Eszter even more, but it also gave me hope that one day soon I might find my place among this pack.

Dante was the leader, the foundation that made them strong and united; Margit was the clever one, sophisticated and unyielding; and András was the hope and adventure, the light that guided their way.

So where did I belong?

THIRTY-FIVE

Dante and I made love again that night, just as rough and passionate as before. There was no denying how much we wanted each other—how much we needed each other's touch. I was fire and brimstone, Dante was smoke, shadow and warmth.

Perhaps it was the unspoken fear that we would find more than we bargained for after setting out tomorrow, but it made the sex even wilder. He was unchartered territory, an adventure—and I planned to explore the whole map.

Margit had given me a tonic to prevent any accidents. So long as I took it once a month on a full moon, I would not be with child. The time would come where I would do my duty and honour my agreement with Farkas, but not until the dust had settled and we were all safe.

When at last we'd flopped onto the bed in a tangled, sweaty mess of limbs, I turned, gazing into his dark brown eyes. They were clouded with concern, something unfamiliar flashing in those depths.

"What's wrong?" I whispered.

He hesitated, his face falling blank as a mask slid into place. "I can't stop thinking about Margit's vision. Please, Kitarni. Don't go tomorrow. It's too dangerous."

I sat up, gaping at him. At the wall he'd just erected. "Ever since we met, we've been facing all kinds of monsters. Now, you're doubting my abilities?" I elbowed him playfully at an attempt to lighten the mood, but he sighed.

He shuffled up the bed, leaning against a bundle of pillows. "It's different this time. Margit said the cultists would capture you ..." He shook his head. "We can't allow that to happen."

I narrowed my eyes, studying his face. "You knew it would come to this eventually. Did you really think I'd stay home while you risked your neck?"

He ran a hand through his hair, shooting me an exasperated look. "We didn't exactly start off on the right foot, Kitarni. When we first met, I wouldn't have given two shits about the choices you made. But you've found a way to burrow under my skin, and now? It feels like we're giving them what they want. Why send you straight to them? Why allow Sylvie to rise at all?"

"Allow it?" I scoffed. "You're a fool if you think us mere mortals have a choice. If we leave them be, they will only grow stronger and the corruption will spread. If Sylvie wasn't here to lead the fight herself, we would only die by the inevitable plague spilling over the land."

He jumped out of bed, shoving a pair of pants on as he paced. "Is there no spell capable of fighting it? What about your village? They are earth witches, surely they can do something to stop the spread."

"It doesn't work like that," I replied, pinching my brows together. "This is dark magic we're talking about, Dante. Earth magic is used to grow, to nurture, not to destroy. I wouldn't have the slightest clue how to fix this and I'm sure, if there was a way, the council would have tried already."

He snarled in frustration and I sat up straighter, covering myself with the sheets. "I know you're afraid of what the cultists are capable of. So am I. But what happened when you're a boy, what happened to your mother—"

"Don't speak of her," he snapped, whirling on me.

I shrank back, a pang of hurt spearing through me. He'd never spoken to me like this before, never been so angry in my presence. My own annoyance flared, rising to the surface. "What is *wrong* with you? The Dante I know would never cower from a fight."

"Maybe you don't know me at all then," he muttered, so quietly I almost missed it. Resigned, he sat down on the bed and I scooted over to him, refusing to let him drown himself in emotions.

"Hey," I said quietly, running a hand through his hair and down to his neck. "You can talk to me. Tell me what's really going

373

on. Don't make me burn it out of you," I said with a wiggle of my fingers.

He smiled softly, but it was a small, ghost of a thing. When he looked at me, I saw pain and sorrow and fear there. "Kitarni," he began. "I need to tell you—"

Something banged in the corridor outside and he jumped, immediately on alert, a dagger in his hand. I crept behind him to the door, a fireball hovering in my palm. When I nodded at him, he threw open the door, blade brandished, but it was only András and another man further down the hall.

He was laughing, stealing kisses with another táltos, a wineskin in hand and a grin that lit up the room curving his lips. When he saw us, he lifted the wine in salute and the man beside him laughed as András fumbled with the door handle.

"See you in the morn," András sang. "We go to hunt some cult—" He hiccupped, giggling to himself. "Cultists."

I rolled my eyes. "Trust you to be absolutely buggered the night before we leave."

He raised his brows suggestively. "Not y-yet."

"Gods," I mumbled under my breath, turning to Dante. "I'm going to help him get to bed. I think he's a little too far gone to do anything at this stage."

Dante opened his mouth, but he shut it again without a word.

"I'll be back soon, I promise," I said. "We can talk more then."

It took longer than I'd expected to get András into bed. The idiot kept veering around the room, playing a game of cat and mouse. I had half a mind to bludgeon him with a candleholder, but thought better of it. He'd need a miracle in the morning to deal with the consequences of drinking, let alone the headache of an injury he wouldn't remember receiving.

When I finally got him to lay down, he was unconscious the moment he hit the bed. His friend had proven no help at all, flopping beside him and snoring immediately. I smiled fondly. "Hopeless," I said to the sleeping pair.

By the time I made it back to Dante's room, I found him looking sheepish, sitting on the edge of the bed, a couple goblets of red wine in his hands.

"A peace offering," he said morosely.

I couldn't help but laugh at his puppy dog eyes, taking the cup from his hands and strolling back to the balcony. The city slept peacefully, the odd hearth lighting up the darkened homes in the square below. A curl of lavender climbed my nostrils and Dante came up behind me, wrapping one of his big bear arms around my waist.

This was my city now. My home. And I was damn well going to fight for it.

"To Mistvellen," I said, clinking my goblet against his.

"To victory," he replied, and we both sculled our drinks.

 375

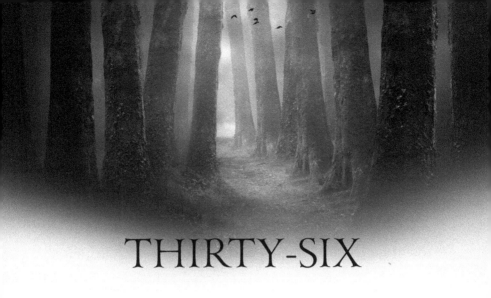

THIRTY-SIX

didn't remember falling asleep, but I woke to sunlight streaming through the windows, casting a bright glow around the room. I glared at the dust motes as they filtered through the rays. My head pounded and my throat felt dry as dirt. I licked my lips, patting a hand around in the bed for Dante. The bed was cold everywhere my palm landed.

"How late is it?" I croaked, but only silence answered me. "Dante?"

I rolled over, but the space beside me was empty. My gaze caught on one of the goblets and, shuffling over, I peered in the cup suspiciously. A powdery film lined the bottom and I suddenly realised why I was feeling like a horse had kicked me in the head.

He'd drugged me. The fucking ass had drugged me.

Shooting upright—my head blazing in response to the sudden movement—I winced, running to the bathing chamber and then to the settee out in the main room.

Dread pooled in my stomach, slithering through my sluggish veins. "No," I whispered. "No, no, no." I ran to the chamber filled with chests and my heart dropped to my stomach. Dante's armour, his swords, his travelling cloak ... all gone.

Frustration flared and I curled my fingers, my nails biting into the skin with a sting. "You stupid fool." Tears filled my eyes. He'd left me behind, still believing he could prevent the inevitable.

I folded in on myself, crumpling to the ground. Hopelessness pulled at my nerves, unravelling the threads of my mind. How would I ever find them now? I was a halfway decent tracker, but who knows how deep into the Sötét Erdő the cultists' lair was? And what if—

My breath caught in my throat. What if Dante and the others were captured? Panic clawed at my heart, making my chest tighten.

A gentle knock sounded at the door and I whipped my head up to find Margit entering. She carried a box in her arms and looked down her nose at me. "You're a sight for sore eyes," she huffed.

I could only stare at her with blurry eyes, reaching a hand to her in desperation. Her lips pressed together and she set down the box on a desk and glided across the room like smoke.

When her eyes softened, I thought she might embrace me— lend me a shoulder to cry on—but instead I was met with a resounding *smack*. I clutched my cheek and blinked several times,

the panic seeming to ebb out of me in waves as air filled my lungs once again.

She raised a brow. "Better?"

"Yes. Th-thank you," I stammered. Her hand found my own and she pulled me up with a surprisingly strong grip for such a petite girl.

"I had a feeling my idiot cousin would do this. Lucky for you, I took extra precautions," she said, taking out a crystal from the sleeve of her dress.

My despair dissolved as I realised what she held in her hand. "Oh my gods." Excitement bubbled in my stomach as I snatched it from her. "You didn't!?"

It wasn't an ordinary crystal, but a wayfinding stone. A talisman that, once spelled by a witch, will lead her to its partner crystal. If Dante had the other in his possession, the spell would lead me right to him.

"Of course I did," she scoffed. "I sewed its sister into the lining of his boots last night."

I blinked. I'm not sure I wanted to know how or when she'd managed that, but it didn't matter. I pulled her into a bone crushing hug, ignoring her muffled grumbles. "You're a saint, Margit, you know that?"

She smoothed down her dress when I let go, but she cocked her head. "Obviously. But we don't have time for sentiments. I have something for you."

Her gown swished along the ground as she opened the box

and turned, a sly smile on her face as she held the item out to me. I gasped, eyes widening as I beheld a black breastplate.

It was of fine make—far superior to anything I'd ever worn—fitted to a woman's form so the top would finish just above my breasts. Howling wolves were engraved in silver on the front, surrounded by sweeping vines and flowers in traditional Hungarian style. It reminded me of Mama and Eszter's embroidery, while representing the wolves of the Wolfblood Clan.

Tears pricked my eyes as I took it reverently from Margit. She offered me a natural smile and I thought it might be one of the loveliest things I'd ever seen. "You're one of us now, little wolf," she said softly. "Wear it proudly."

I set the armour down and swept her into another hug; this time her arms wrapped around me tightly. She was warm, comforting, and I thanked my lucky stars to have found such a friend in this new world—in my new home. "Thank you," I whispered. "For everything."

"Don't thank me yet," she said softly as she pulled away, looking me sharply in the eyes. Her eyes were bright, but sadness showed in the taut lines of her face. "And don't you dare fucking die on me."

"I won't," I said softly, and then a little louder, "I swear it."

We both knew what I was walking into. But damned if I was going to let fear stand in my way. *For my people*, I reminded myself. *For my family.*

 379

"Go," Margit said. "Tear those cultists limb from limb."

I nodded. She didn't need to tell me twice.

Arl thundered out of the gates of Mistvellen like a storm born on high winds and I bent low, my gaze set on the trees in the distance. Laszlo bounded beside us, his velvet ears flapping with every bounce and tongue lolling out.

Somewhere inside the Sötét Erdő, Dante and the others were tracking their prey, but I was on a different scent. I glanced at the crystal in my hand. It was now glimmering a faint blue and, the closer I came to its sister, the brighter it would glow.

They had a couple hours head start on me, but I was determined and I had magic on my side. "Woah, boy." I pulled Arl to a stop beside the treeline, jumping down and squaring my shoulders.

This was it. As soon as I stepped into those woods, there was no telling what would happen. I turned, stroking Arl's muzzle. His hair felt like velvet beneath my fingertips and I leaned my forehead against his head.

He knickered, nibbling on my fingertips softly as I pulled away. I smiled, leaning down to scratch Laszlo behind the ears. A low whine pulled from his throat, as if he already knew he couldn't come.

"Not this time." I savoured his warmth, the cuddliness of his coat as I forced him into a hug. He allowed it begrudgingly,

licking my cheek. "Go home," I said, jerking my head towards Mistvellen. Margit had promised to look after them both and I was certain Laszlo would have a fine throne on her bed while I was gone.

He whimpered once more and the sound pulled at my heart, but I couldn't risk him getting hurt again and the deepest part of the forest was too tight—too dangerous for them both. "Go," I demanded sternly.

Arló pawed at the ground, tossing his mane, but he began trotting home, Laszlo by his side. The latter looked back at me like I'd wounded him, but it was for the best.

I turned to the forest, taking a deep breath before I entered and, without looking back, I stalked into the trees, headed to the place where darker things dwelled.

THIRTY-SEVEN

It had taken me half a day to find the group and Dante fumed upon seeing me. When I'd explained how I'd found him so quickly, he had sworn a string of curses that had made even me blush, while András had laughed like it was the biggest joke he'd heard all year.

At least the latter had been happy to see me, I thought miserably. Deep down, Dante must have known I'd follow. Short of locking me up, there wasn't much he could have done and he would never stoop so low. My freedom meant everything to me—my choices. He respected that, even if he hated what it could cost him.

Days had passed and still we'd seen no sign of cultists lurking in the woods. The branches tangled above, blocking out the sun and stars alike. All remained quiet. Deathly silence enveloped us, as if those inhabiting the Sötét Erdő had fled its boughs and burrows.

382

I hoped the animals had escaped the sticky grasp of corruption spreading within. We were careful not to touch the tar-like substance dripping from branches and pooling in leaves—keeping fingers firmly by our sides, our strides cautious and measured.

András stayed close, his mouth firmly set in the flickering firelight. My heart warmed at his protectiveness. I felt pulled to him. His charming smile and wit made him easily likeable and he was someone I could see myself growing close to in time. He'd grown uncharacteristically gloomy over the last few days, but I supposed the woods were to thank for that. This place had a way of wearing down the spirit. The trees seemed to huddle together the farther we walked, bearing down on our hearts and souls, ensnaring us in their roots.

Dante tracked the forest floor, searching for signs of boot prints, snapped twigs and damaged foliage. A bloodhound on the scent. He'd been distant since we'd left, a worried frown always marring his features. We'd never finished our conversation back at Mistvellen. He'd been about to share something important and that thought still hung over me like a cloud, but we hadn't broached the subject again. Truthfully, I think he was still too angry to be around me. Whether that was at me or the situation we were in, I didn't know.

I couldn't blame him for being angry. The price of being caught by the cultists was steep and our mission came with many perils. It angered me, the thought of Sylvie's resurrection. Why

must she come back? A war loomed on the back of one woman. A single witch whose words had the power to wield lies and instil blind devotion in her followers. And yet, Fate and Death both promised her return was necessary. Margit had her visions. It was written.

Sighing, I smoothed a hand down my braid, sparing a glance at the wolf lord snuffling at trails I couldn't see. Before we'd arrived at Mistvellen, he'd had no qualms about my joining the scouting party, but Margit's vision had changed everything—our whole relationship had.

What did he expect? I knew he didn't like me when we first met, but regardless of how things had developed, I was my own woman and was free to make my own choices. He knew that—hell, he encouraged it. Other men might have locked me away, threatened me with violence or worse, but Dante had not stood between me and the horrors that awaited and that meant ... it meant everything.

So why the distance? Why the cold shoulder? I bit my lip as András bumped my elbow, jolting me from my thoughts. I flicked a tongue over my lip, the tart taste of metal in my mouth.

He shared an apologetic look, his green eyes softening. "A coin for your thoughts?"

I flattened my palm against the blade sheathed at my thigh, comforted by its weight, the cool hilt against my skin. "We've been wandering aimlessly for days. I just ... I thought we would have found them by now."

He nodded. "Time passes slowly in this place. The rot festers, clinging to all living things. Do you feel it?" His lips turned down, puckering in distaste. "It fogs the mind, weighs heavy on the shoulders. I fear time spells our ruin should we linger much longer."

Tension bracketed my neck, pressing uncomfortably down my spine. He spoke true. I felt sluggish, my bones brittle and muscles slow. I glared at the surrounding trees slick with crawling black, the sticky sap dripping from their branches. A root snagged my boot and I stumbled forwards, András holding me upright in his firm grip.

Anger and embarrassment surged through me like lightning. "Mother mercy, this fucking place—" I blinked rapidly, leaning down to study the offending root.

"What is it?" András asked softly, his hand still clenching my arm as if afraid I might murder the trees.

"I recognise this tree. I've tripped on it once already," I breathed, shooting daggers at the root. I remember looking at it earlier this ... morning? I couldn't tell what time it was, but it didn't matter. Sure enough, I spotted the whorls and cracks of a mark resembling a hag with a bent nose and an evil grin. I'd thought it amusing earlier, now it just seemed to mock me.

"Are you sure?" András said, brow raised and scepticism crinkling his fine features.

"Oh, don't give me that look," I snapped. "I swear on my father's grave we've been here before. Don't you see András?

385

We're going in circles."

"Kitarni," he started, but I ignored him, storming towards Dante.

"Do you have anything you'd like to share with the group, *tracker?*" I hissed in his ear.

He looked at me, amusement quirking one side of his lips. "What have I done to earn your ire now, dear one?"

I jabbed him in the chest. "Pack your pretty boy smile a bag because it's going on a trip. You're stalling, Dante. Why?" His smile faltered and surprise lightened the depths of his gaze. "Did you think you could keep us in the dark forever?"

"Nice," András muttered behind me. I gifted him a glare and he quieted, crossing his arms over his chest. The other scouts shuffled awkwardly, finding anything other than Dante or me to look at. All except András, who grinned like a king's fool.

Dante sighed, grinding his teeth. I knew that look—the frustration it would cause me. "I might have dragged my feet at first, but I suppose there's no hiding it any longer. We're lost. The trail just ... vanishes."

"You've got to be kidding me," I groaned. "Fuck me, this is bad."

He raised his hands in supplication. "Any other time, any other place, darling, I'm yours. But as it stands, your assessment is apt."

My nostrils flared. "Táltos ass."

"Stubborn witch," he said.

András stepped between us. "If I could just—"

"*Insufferable* oaf," I snapped.

András lifted a finger. "If I might interject—"

We both turned on him and snarled, "NO."

The word seemed to echo in the wood, harsh and loud. *Too loud.* An uneasy feeling skittered down my spine as I stared into Dante's eyes. The browns were so dark they appeared black in the gloom, if not for the golden ring encircling his irises. His own trepidation blinked back at me and, slowly, his hands reached over his back to the twin blades sheathed there.

From the shadows beyond the firelight, flashes of silver-blue gleamed through the foliage. One by one, they popped into view, the orbs shining with a madness akin to the lidércek and the wolves we'd faced. They stepped from the darkness, bright white dresses dragging on the ground, catching on the teeth of trees.

My heart soared into my throat, the claws of anxiety digging deep into my stomach. At first glance I'd thought them cultists, but as they stepped closer, my gut twisted with fear.

"Tündérek?" Black crept up their fingernails, pulsing in their veins. The faeries had fallen to the cultists' corruption, their minds no longer their own. I wondered if their power still lingered, or if that, too, had been stripped from their bodies.

András uttered a world-weary sigh. "I tried to warn you."

"Shush," I hissed, tilting a head at the faeries as they approached. Defeated, he lifted his hands in the air, but I ignored him. They were beautiful in a classic, yet strange fashion. All sharp lines and symmetry, hard and yet heartbreakingly mesmerising. Their white gowns were brown and bloodied, their nails jagged and sharp from the gods only knew what. All had long hair that tumbled to their waists or lower still, and all looked on with blank expressions. Except two.

A woman with sable skin, the other with flesh pale as her namesake. One with tight black coils, the other with flowing white hair. Both were tattooed with flowing vines and flowers. Both wore veils covering their faces, but I knew immediately who faced me.

My faerie friends. Jazmin and Lili. "Not you, too." My voice was little more than a whisper, heart plummeting into a well of despair. "Why didn't you get out? Why didn't you leave?"

They lifted their veils in unison, peeling back the delicate cloth to reveal blank faces. Their eyes were not the silver-blue of their kin, but blackened pools, the surrounding skin streaked with the corruption that had infected them.

They didn't answer, only outstretched their hands, beckoning me to take them. My body moved of its own volition, even as every instinct prickled with awareness. *Danger*, it screamed. *Run, run, run.*

I gritted my teeth at the sensation of my hands being pulled on puppet's strings. Were they using magic against me? Was the wood itself urging me forward?

"Let her go." Dante's growl was pure command, dripping with warning as he ushered me behind him.

The sisters blinked, their focus turning to him, lips pulled back over their teeth. They hissed, the sound echoing as their brethren changed their stances, like snakes uncoiling to strike.

Dante raised his swords, the blades glinting in the firelight. For the first time, I caught the text engraved on those blades. *'Be not the shepherd of sheep but a leader among wolves.'* The scripture struck a chord deep inside. A bell named clarity.

I had been that shepherd. A girl devoured by the opinions of many, consumed by sorrow and loneliness. I would not make the mistake of bowing before sheep again. I was a wolf now and I'd found my pack.

He caught my eye and I nodded my head just once. Reluctant at what duty asked of me. "Do not kill them," I said loudly, my voice radiating authority. "We will not spill the blood of innocents today."

Dante paused, warring with the killer within. But whatever he saw in my eyes, it softened the hardness to his face, the mask of the soldier. "As you wish." The whine of swords unsheathing answered as the scouts pulled their blades and it shocked me to realise their lord had given me power. They answered to *me*.

Lili struck first, her fist colliding with Dante's chest, sending him flying backwards into a tree. He fell to the ground, the air wheezing from his chest. I didn't have time to attend to him, ducking under a swipe of Jazmin's jagged nails. Her face was empty, soulless, and it hurt to look at her this way. To see no sign of the friend who'd once welcomed me among her people,

supped with me, shared the secrets of a forest once gilded in sunlight.

"I don't want to fight you," I breathed. The sisters ignored me, converging on both sides, water pumping from their hands just as András lunged for me, heaving me into his arms and spinning. I lashed out with a boot, landing a blow square on Lili's jaw, another on Jazmin's nose, the latter resulting in a loud crack.

I cringed at the pain I was causing, but I would not go down without a fight. Water crashed upon us from all directions, drenching every soldier fighting. Theirs was a storm of fury and we were its target. Soldiers flew back one by one as the faeries' magic blasted with the crushing weight of waterfalls, surging again and again, tempestuous and unforgiving.

András, the crazy bastard, laughed as we battled side by side, using the hilts of our blades to clock our enemies in the head and render them unconscious. "You know," he said a little too cheerfully given the circumstance, "I think you need to work on your hospitality. Why is it we're always butchering our guests?"

"Less talk, more bludgeoning," I yelled through the torrents of water, blinking the moisture rapidly from my eyes.

He only grinned, somehow still charming in the grips of a battle. Honestly, was anyone around here actually sane?

Men and faeries alike sprinkled the ground before us. True to their word, the men hadn't dealt any sword blows, but some faeries were alarmingly still. A problem for later, if we could get through this.

Swiping the water from my eyes, I peered frantically around the moving bodies until, finally, I spotted Dante clutched in the hands of Jazmin and Lili. His head lolled and blood streamed down his face in the rainfall. He'd taken a bad blow to the head.

Lili held her hand up to his neck, one finger raised threatening to the soft skin of his throat. Her nail was sharp as knives, poised carefully. One slice and it would be over.

"Stop," I cried, whether to the faeries or the men, I didn't know, but it caught everyone's attention. "Lower your weapons."

The scouts saw their lord and complied immediately, András following shortly after with an unhappy grunt.

Lili looked at me, her black eyes narrowing as I took a cautious step closer. Sheathing my dagger, I raised my hands. "What do you want? Let him go—let them all go—and I'll do it."

"They wait for you," she hissed. "Your blood calls to them."

My skin prickled at her tone, the eerie sing-song voice in which she spoke. Whatever or whoever this was, my friend was long gone. I took another tentative step, but she hissed, clutching Dante's jaw in her fist and pressing her claw to his throat.

A panicked chill flooded my veins. "Okay," I said, raising my hands. "I will come with you. Just don't harm them."

"Like hell," Dante snarled, writhing beneath her touch. They must have immeasurable strength if they could hold him back. His muscles bulged with effort, straining against his shirt as he struggled. "If they take you to the cultists, they'll eat you alive. They'll drain your blood to bring her back." His outburst earned

him a prick of the nail, blood dribbling from the small slice.

"I must," I said softly, the words still firm as I stepped around him. "I will meet my fate with iron in my heart and war song in my blood. The time for hiding has passed."

"Kitarni, no. You don't understand what they're capable of. What they plan on—"

Jazmin struck him across the face and he sagged against her, blood dribbling down his face as he fell unconscious. "Silence, worm. You will learn your place soon enough. Rotting and writhing beneath the ground."

I cringed, aching to hold him in my arms. My fingers itched to heal him, the power sensing my need, swirling frantically within my blood. "Please. Do you not remember me? We were friends. I was—"

"You are nothing," Lili sneered. "A vessel holding the key to her resurgence. With your blood, she will rise. Now come. They wait."

I felt András's hand on my arm, saw the fear and fury etched in his face. Not just for his lord, but for me. Somehow, it gave me the strength to face my own fears. I squeezed his arm, nodding just once as I looked over his shoulder at the man I'd come to care for.

He wilted beneath my touch but relented with a backward step. Dante would be safe under his watchful eye if I didn't make it. Squaring my jaw, I looked at the surrounding faeries, landing finally on Lili's face. "I will go with you, but I need assurances my friends won't be harmed."

The sisters paused, seemingly conversing with little more than a cock of their heads. Lili turned to me. "We will not harm your friends, but they *will* join us. They will watch."

My stomach twisted at the unveiled threat. Gods. They planned to truss me up like a pig to slaughter. A carcass to feed from while my friends looked on helplessly.

A flutter of satisfaction filled me and I smirked defiantly at my captors. At least we'd have one advantage after this. The táltosok would be led right into the viper's nest. We'd know the lay of the land, gather numbers and critical intel to use in the days to come.

If we survived the day.

As if sensing my thoughts, the sisters hissed and their kin set to work, binding the soldiers and shoving sacks over their heads. Where the fuck had they hidden those?

Jazmin grinned, the once mesmerising expression now terrifying as she tilted her head. A predator sizing up her prey, mocking me with a cruel sneer because, of course, they had no intention of giving away any secrets.

"I swear on all the gods, if you hurt them, I'll rip those pretty heads from your—"

Words failed me as something hard hit the back of my head. Stars burst behind my eyes, blurring the world as I slipped hard and fast into a realm of black.

THIRTY-EIGHT

woke to the sound of buzzing. An insistent humming that grew louder and louder, causing my temples to throb violently. Wincing, I lifted my head, immediately regretting the movement as nausea rolled over me in hot flushes.

Cultists surrounded me, their hooded heads bowed, their hands outstretched in a circle. Finally, I realised they were chanting, not humming. At least, those who had tongues left to speak with. Muttering words in an unfamiliar tongue, they sang discordantly, their off-tonal cries raising the hairs on my arms. Somehow, the sounds emanating from those with stitched lips were worse.

Everything about these people was wrong. Sickening. I gasped as they lifted their heads all at once. Not only had many of them removed their tongues or threaded their mouths shut, but others were missing eyes. Their organs replaced instead with ugly red crosses seared into their skin.

Bile threatened to erupt and I forced myself to look away—anywhere but at the height of desecration. I knew they had defiled themselves for her, sacrificing mind, body and soul for their dark leader.

A body swam into view and I blinked rapidly, trying to focus on the source. "Awake at last," the voice crooned. A woman's. Lilting and elegant but underlined by a hardness too. She wore a red gown that clung to her hips and thighs, the fabric cutting a sharp vee, exposing the curves of her breasts.

I craned my neck to peer at her groggily, wincing at the shooting pain in my head, but she placed a hand on my cheek, pressing down hard. The cool surface seeped into my flesh and I squirmed under her touch. Cold, hard metal bit into my wrists as I struggled and panic flooded my senses upon realising I was chained. Not trussed up like a hog but bound to a cold stone slab instead.

Just as Margit had foreseen.

"The more you struggle, the harder the metal will sink its teeth," the woman whispered, almost pitifully, but I could hear that cruel delight again. She wanted this—wanted me to *hurt*.

I hated her already.

"Who are you?" I croaked, moistening my lips. My skin was cold as ice, the clothes clinging to my body still soaked through from the faeries' magic. It plastered the hair to my head, clung to the swell of my breasts. Shame washed over me. They'd ripped my shirt open, bearing my nakedness to the world.

I caught András's eye from across the clearing. His handsome face twisted with rage. He was bloody and bruised, purple and yellow, but he was not otherwise hurt. I was thankful at least that he looked at me, not with pity, but murder in his heart. Fury that his future lady had been so shamed.

The woman ignored my question. "Poor child. You might have been my daughter had Fate's threads been weaved differently."

I tensed, muscles straining taut as a bowstring. My blood mother? But she was dead, rotting beneath the ground somewhere. So who ...?

The woman withdrew her palm, stepping around the slab to stand before me. Long brown hair streaked with russet, bronzed skin and a slender frame, but it was the set of her eyes and lips that had me jolting. The familiar features of one I knew so well.

I'd seen this face before. Twice now. I'd learned every line of that canvas, relished in every secret, sexy look or word from his mouth. But this face, though older now, had stared back at me from a portrait in Dante's bedroom.

"My gods," I whispered. "It can't be. You're supposed to be dead."

She laughed, clapping her hands in delight. "Is that what he told you? Oh, how delicious." Snapping her fingers, she motioned one of the cultists over. "Bring him."

Fear fluttered in my stomach, my hands turning clammy. I craned my neck to watch her minion disappear into the mouth of a cave just beyond the clearing.

I called my magic but found myself blocked by an invisible wall. The power lay dormant, coiled just out of reach. Sweat beaded my forehead as I concentrated, the muscles in my neck straining with effort.

The woman watched me with eagle eyes. "It won't come. The chains binding you are fused with magic. Your power is all but useless to you now." She ran a nail down my cheek and I jerked away from her touch.

"Don't touch me, or I swear, the second I'm free I'll ram my fist down your throat and burn you from the inside out."

She smiled with closed lips, eyes flashing with amusement. A single dimple cut the sharp angle of her cheek. Pain filled me, disgust surging at the familiarity of that smile—of the golden ring in her eyes. "It's a shame to waste such power, such spirit. You might have been my best student if things were different."

"What are you talking about?" I spat. "Who *are* you?"

"My dear girl. Do you still not see?" She raised her thin arms and smiled widely. My belly flipped at the sight of teeth filed into fangs—fashioned like a fucking vampire's.

Bile climbed my throat, realisation sinking in. A vision of Hanna flashed before my mind's eyes—the image of her deflated body, the strange teeth marks on her skin. They matched this woman's teeth perfectly. "You're the one who's been killing the girls. You fed on Hanna like an animal!"

She flicked a tongue over her teeth. "Yes. I devoured them,

body and soul. I took only what was rightfully mine. A blood sacrifice in exchange for my protection from the humans."

I failed to suppress a shudder, the chill on my back sinking deeper beneath my skin. This woman was insane. Drinking the blood of her victims and no doubt getting high off their magic. Bloodmorphia, only she didn't need the drug. She took it direct from the source.

My stomach roiled. The worst part was that she was still a witch, not a vampire or something other, but a witch driven mad by her cult. And she thought she was owed sacrifices in exchange for—

"Protection?" My brows knitted together. "What the fuck could you possibly—"

My words trailed off as it all came tumbling into place. The strange disappearances of the girls, the sacrificial rituals, the fabled warden of the woods, whom no one had ever laid eyes on in the flesh.

There was only one person charged with protecting my coven from the humans. Only one who was said to have erected the wards protecting our village from wandering eyes. *The banya. My coven's beloved Baba Yana.*

It was her. All along, this witch, this *thing*, had us worshipping her like fools. She was a false prophet. A killer of her own kind. And we'd all been stupid enough to believe her lies.

"Come now, pet. I see the cogs turning in your mind. Say it. Say my name." Her lips curled back from her teeth, her eyes

darkening with glee.

Two breathless words wormed their way from my tongue and I almost choked on the name, the countless lies built on the term. "Baba Yana."

The witch picked at her nails, feigning boredom, but I knew it thrilled her to see my despair. To watch me squirm. "Yana is dead. It's Baba Yaga now."

A sob escaped my lips. How long had this gone on for? How many souls had died for nothing? Of all the hateful things I wanted to shout at her, my mind just kept coming back to one question. "Why? You had family, prosperity, love. Why join the cultists?"

Baba Yaga sneered, an ugly, cruel thing that distorted her face, making it appear almost inhuman in the flickering firelight. The cultists still hummed around us, bowing and scraping at the earth. "I'd always been fascinated by the darker magics. I grew up in your village, did you know? Before Sándor swept me away to Mistvellen, I was educated under Caitlin Vargo herself. Oh, how she despised my power. That old wretch always knew I was stronger than her and to keep me in my place she ridiculed me, made me look the fool in front of the other witches. No one ever helped. No one offered a kind word."

Her fingers curled into fists, shaking with her anger. A pang of sorrow speared through me at her pain. I knew what it was to be laughed at and shunned. To be feared for being different. But that didn't excuse the choices she'd made. The terrible things

she'd done.

"Do you expect me to feel sorry for you?" I spat, my words dripping with venom. "You found a way out. Started a new life." I stared at her in disgust, shaking my head. "What happened to make your heart so hateful?"

She smiled, flashing me her filed teeth. "When the cultists came to Mistvellen, my life was forever changed. They showed me a new world—one where I could harness my power to do unimaginable things. They taught me dark magic, showed me the Dark Queen's teachings. Not once did they judge me or hold me back. This is where I belong—not among the mindless sheep of a coven. These people are my family now. This is the true path, child. *Her path.* I've never felt stronger, more in control and, when the Dark Queen rises, we will reclaim this world as our own."

I stared into her eyes, watching them cloud over with wonder, with *love*. She was mad, I realised. Brainwashed to believe what she and the cultists were doing was good—that murder in the name of religion was holy or just. And that's what this was. This cult was a religion based on power and lies, and they were wholly devoted to its cause.

"So you harnessed your power and used it to seek revenge on the coven?" I scoffed. "Even someone as powerful as you couldn't have acted alone. Who helped you?" I asked, writhing in my chains. "The witches in our village believe in the good banya. Of her so-called protection. So who betrayed us? Sold the girls like cattle to slaughter?"

She raised a perfect brow. "The banya is a lie, girl. Baba Yana is a myth—a bedtime story spoon-fed to you for so long, your precious elders aren't even aware of the untruths they spill. They believe in the banya because it makes them feel safe, helps them sleep better in their beds at night. The truth is, there is no single entity that becomes the banya. Many cultists have worn that cloak over the centuries and it is my turn now to pose as your gods given saint. We are all around you, child. We have always been watching."

Oh, mother of mercy. All this time, we'd blindly believed in a falsehood that had eaten away at our coven for years upon years. How easy it must have been to sew such lies. That it "was an honour to be chosen by the banya as her apprentice", that "her holiness must not show her face, for it is too divine for a witch's eye". We were *fools*.

I clenched my fists so hard the nails drew blood in half-moon circles. "How could you leave your son?" I shouted. "How could you kill innocents for this? You're a monster!"

She smiled softly at me, pressing a kiss to my forehead. I spat on her face as she pulled away, but she only laughed. "Who said I ever really left? Your precious lordling has been helping me this whole time. Right from the moment you met."

Panic flooded through me, icy and paralysing. No, he couldn't have helped her. He wouldn't stand for this. My lips trembled, my hands shaking from anger.

"You're lying. Dante wouldn't do that to me," I said, the

words cold and flat, but she'd burrowed into my insecurities, had already begun spinning her web.

Gifting me a knowing smile, she cocked her head at me. "No one is innocent, Kitarni. We're all monsters deep down, we've just learned to embrace it." She ran her hand down my arm, ripping the tattered shirt even further as she leaned in.

Pain seared through me as she sank her teeth into my flesh and I screamed as those daggers sent tremors down my arm. When she rose, peering into my face with cold, dead eyes and a face painted red, I felt helplessness take hold. For the first time since waking, I was truly afraid.

"Delicious. I can taste your power," she said, wiping my blood from her lips with delicate fingers and turning towards the cave. "My dutiful son. You performed your task well. Perhaps too well, in fact. It seems our guest has quite the soft spot for you."

I swivelled to find Dante walking into the clearing, his expression darkening. "What have you done?" he said coldly to his mother. "This was not what we agreed on."

My heart sank at his words, plummeting to the cold, dark depths of my stomach. "You knew," I whispered. "You were working with her all along. Everything was a lie."

His beautiful face flickered for the briefest of moments before an emotionless mask slid into place once again. "Not everything. What I shared with you about myself was true. I—"

Betrayal seared through me, poking red-hot holes where my heart should be. My anger bled from me in waves and I drowned

in it, the sorrow of letting him in. I should never have been so trusting, never have made space for that monster.

Unwanted and unloved.

My eyes burned, but I refused to bend. I was a cursed and broken wretch, but I would pick up the shattered pieces of my heart and I would get through this. Setting my jaw, I took that pain and used it to harden my heart. To solidify that melted steel and make it something stronger.

"I'm going to kill you," I said, raising my chin as I stared at him. "When I get out of here, I am going to rip your heart from your chest, Dante Sándor."

He blinked and I thought I saw a glimmer of surprise. "I didn't have a choice," he said softly. "She was going to kill him, Kitarni. I had to protect Lukasz, I had to—"

"*We* were supposed to do that," I shouted, spearing him with every ounce of my pain. "I gave myself to you. I committed to the cause. We could have saved him together." The agony I felt was unbearable, like my insides were being picked apart, the threads tearing loose. Why? Why did it *hurt so much?*

"Would you have done anything less for your sister?" he said softly.

My breath caught in my throat, the anger flooding my system retreating just a little, because he was right. There is nothing I wouldn't do for Eszter. *Nothing.* His eyes bored into my own, pleading, full of all the things he couldn't say. I opened my mouth, but his mother cut in before I could say anything.

"Oh dear," Baba Yaga said, angling her head at her son, glancing between us with hungry intrigue. He gritted his teeth so hard it seemed they would break. "Now this is interesting. Could it be you return her sentiments?" Her red lips slashed into a cruel smile. "Foolish boy. The wolf cares not for the sheep. We devour it."

He said nothing, turning away from her with a sickened expression. "I did as you asked. Hand the vial over."

She pinned him with a look of annoyance, her lips twisting. "After the many cultists you have killed, I'm not sure I should honour that bargain anymore." She gazed at me thoughtfully, her shoulders losing their stiffness. "Still ... their sacrifices weren't in vain. We have the vessel now. Once our queen is reborn, you may leave."

Something glimmered in her hand as she pulled it from her cleavage. A small bottle filled with red liquid and a strange black smoke that seemed to writhe around it. Dante snatched it without hesitation, his face betraying his disgust as he looked at it.

"And there are no more spells beholding him to you?"

She raised a brow, pursing her lips. "Your bastard brother is safe so long as his blood is in your hands. Burn the vial in purified salt and the dark magic will dissipate."

"How do I know you don't have any spares?" he growled.

She rested a hand on his arm and crooned, "Come now, my son. When have I ever lied to you? Lukasz was merely collateral to ensure your cooperation. You understand."

The breath shuddered from my lungs. She'd been using Dante against his will by holding Lukasz under a spell. But how? My eyes followed Dante's movements as he slipped the vial into his pocket, and I realised. *Blood magic.* Whatever she'd done, it had been serious enough to force Dante's hand.

Everything he'd done, he'd done for his brother. Understanding warred with the pain roaring inside me. I would do the same for Eszter in a heartbeat, but surely he could have told me? Surely, he could have done something, *anything* to make me understand? I was at his mother's mercy. And the fate of the Kingdom rested in her hands. He'd fucked us to the point of no return. He'd fucked us all.

Dante's teeth gritted, but he nodded, averting his gaze as if it pained him to look upon the creature his mother had become. It was clear by the softness to her eyes, the way her hands hovered about his shoulders, that she cared for him. Judging by the shadows curling around his frame and the grimace curving his lips, the feeling wasn't mutual.

Something I could use? But ... no. He'd already begun to walk away. Anger burned through my veins, extinguishing my sorrow and replacing it with hate. "Will you not stay and watch the show?" I hissed. "Are you too much of a coward to see them bleed me dry?"

His shoulders stiffened and, slowly, he turned, returning to his mother's side. His face was blank, utterly devoid of emotion.

 405

"I tried to tell you, Kitarni," he said. "I tried to keep you at Mistvellen."

My nostrils flared. He had tried to tell me something, but András's drunken revelry had interrupted our conversation. And his little delay with the sleeping powder was obviously never going to stop me. I scoffed. Too little, too late. He'd walked me right into the cultists' snare. I stared him down with eyes of molten fire and hissed, "You should have tried harder."

The rippling anger fizzled into anguish as my bravado slipped. Tears threatened to fall, but I held them in—they were pointless now.

His mother pressed her fingertips together, clasping them as if in prayer. "It is time, my son. A new dawn awaits and the Dark Queen will rise above it all."

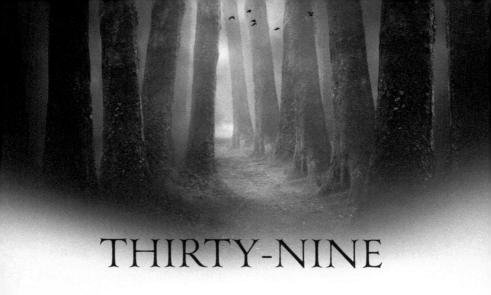

THIRTY-NINE

The humming stopped and silence blanketed the air as everyone in the clearing stared at me. Four cultists wearing ram heads approached, bending a knee at each corner of the slab. I could smell the death still clinging to the masks they wore, the blood dribbling down the hems of their black robes.

A girl in white stepped from the cave, her angelic face vacant and dreamy, as if lost in another world entirely. She clutched something in her hands. A simple chalice, though I had no doubt of what it would hold.

She held it aloft, bowing to Baba Yaga as she backed away, kneeling on the ground. Yaga drew a blade from her belt and I stiffened as it veered towards me, but she kept turning.

The blade flashed, her eyes like black glass as she sliced in one swift motion. The girl's creamy flesh opened, blood pouring from a deep gash in her throat. It flowed into the cup, held now by a fellow cultist, the chalice positioned just so to catch the liquid.

Still smiling dreamily, the girl crumpled to the ground, the light in her eyes winking out as the blood spurted in small gouts, soaking the ground beneath her.

My throat bobbed. What in hell did I just witness?

The male cultist with the goblet set to work, drawing complex symbols on the ground from the girl's blood. My stomach threatened to empty its contents on the stone beneath me and I swallowed, forcing the bile down.

I squinted at the cultist's work. I'd seen nothing like it in the texts in my village. Once done, he scattered black candles around the glyph, as well as sprigs of herbs and tiny animal bones. At the very centre, he placed a black urn almost reverentially.

Not just any urn. Sylvie's. Her ashes must rest inside it. But what dark magic could remake blood and bone? I turned my head to survey Yaga, whose black eyes glittered maliciously. She now carried a tome and I knew, *I knew* it had to be the tome Sylvie had once used to record her dark spells. The power that lay in the book, the demonic influences.

"It is time," she said, her voice euphoric with excitement, her fingers trembling as she beheld the urn. Where her hands shook, her voice was steady, ringing clear and loud across the lake of bowed heads.

The words were unintelligible as she recited from the book. Ancient and old, dripping with power and the promise of

darkness. I pulled at my restraints, my eyes fixed on the blade still clutched in one of her hands. Darkness swirled like smoke above the altar, the clap of thunder booming somewhere far above the twisted branches of the woods.

Panic seized me as Yaga's voice rose, the firelight flickering, the earth rumbling as if readying to open the gates of the Under World and unleash the scourge that was Sylvie.

The blade shifted, descending closer, closer. I squeezed my eyes shut, not wanting to see it fall. My skin prickled with awareness, my body preparing itself for the pain. Faintly, I heard the metal slide of a sword pulled from its sheath.

My eyes snapped open as Dante cried out, his blade descending upon Yaga's neck, András and the other men roaring as they moved all at once. Time moved slowly, yet all too quick. Yaga's eyes widened with surprise, her hand flying out as some darker power halted his blade mere inches from her flesh.

"You would slaughter your own mother?" she screamed, fury swelling her pupils, turning them black with murder.

He sneered at her, his shadows uncoiling with rage around his form, his hand quivering as he fought against her power. "You stopped being my mother a long time ago."

With a flick of her wrist, his own snapped, the blade clattering uselessly to his feet as he cried out in pain. His eyes darted to my own, then to the blade still in Yaga's hand, panic overtaking the usually stoic facade of the warrior.

His soldiers surged over the cultists, many of them equipped

with new blades in hand. But how? More roars filled the space, and táltosok surged into the clearing, blades drawn, many tossing weapons to their still unarmed kith.

Among them I saw Erika and—my heart surged—my mother, twisting and arcing with the practice of a skilled warrior. Tears streamed down my face at the sight of her, fierce and unyielding. Dante must have alerted them ahead of time. My stomach flipped as hope soared through me. He'd had a backup plan all along.

Mama caught my eye, changing direction to crash like waves upon the cultists. Trying to break through, trying to reach me in time.

In the chaos, I swore I saw Fate standing within the treeline, little more than a blur of shadow and wisps as she watched the violence with a smile on scarlet lips. She couldn't intervene in Middle World affairs, but she certainly seemed to enjoy watching the carnage.

That bitch ... that mother fu—

A shout dragged my eyes back beside me. Yaga still had Dante firmly rooted in place, his face twisting, fighting whatever magic fixed him to the earth. The urn within the pentagram shattered as someone kicked it over and her beautiful face morphed into an all-consuming rage.

The knife shifted in her palm, angled to slice my torso, and she shrieked in anger as she plunged it into my flesh. My mother screamed with fear. And I ... *I screamed in pain* as that blade pierced my skin, slicing a deep cut down my chest. My skin

burned as though someone had taken a poker to it, raking through the flesh in one long, boiling stroke.

Yaga murmured those hateful, ancient words and the blood swelled, surging from me in misty waves, swirling into that pile of ash scattered beside the urn. Beyond the pain I had the vague sensation of my power stirring deep within.

The beast was awake and it was angry. A presence stormed into my body, sucking at my blood and paralysing me with venom. I felt the darkness in me stirring, ripping inside me like a hurricane as it fought against the bonds restraining my magic.

Everything burned, everything *hurt*.

Mama ripped Yaga from her feet, long vines curling around her legs and snaking over her throat. *Too late. Too fucking late.* I watched in horror as the blood kept pouring into the ashes until they seemed to shiver with a pulse of magic, the ground beneath that pile of dust crumbling and cracking.

Yaga faced me, a triumphant smile curving her lips, her eyes still black with the lustful swell of dark magic. She bared her teeth, slicing at the vines around her feet and throwing herself at my mother. The two writhed on the ground, grappling with each other.

"Mama!" I shrieked, watching helplessly. I thrashed against my bonds, the manacles sending hot blood trickling down my wrists and ankles. Panic clawed at my heart as Yaga slashed Mama's face with dark magic, tendrils of black piercing her skin. *No, no, no.*

"Death," I managed to choke out, blood dribbling from my lips. "If you're watching, now's the fucking time."

The scars at my back rippled, surging with a cold bite of pain. He popped into existence, black robes swirling madly, his skeletal hand outstretched. With a click, he parted the sea of bodies fighting, throwing everyone back until they sprawled on the ground.

He pulled a smoky rope from his pocket and, with a snap, it speared through the clearing, past the cave and into the trees. A hiss sounded as the cord went taut and he hauled, piece by piece, until Fate came into view, arms bound and teeth bared.

She shrieked, her beautiful face contorting, eyes narrowed as she stared at the commotion. When her eyes met Death's face, she stiffened, fear clouding those hard blue gems.

"Darling," he purred. "How I have missed you so." Coiling a lock of golden hair around one bone finger, he tugged her to his chest. "You've been ever so busy, scheming your treachery in the Middle World, but I think it's overdue you took a little trip downstairs, don't you? We have *so much* to talk about."

His voice deepened, rumbling in warning and her eyes hardened to chips of ice, darting to the blood still misting over Sylvie's remains. I'd expected anger in that lovely face, but her lips cut a harsh line as she looked pointedly at me.

"I will return, mortal. That crown will be mine and I will rule this world. And the next."

Death gagged her mouth with a smoky cord, then looked at

me, cocking his head. I nodded in understanding. He had dealt with one threat and would call on the bargain I'd struck. But finding the lost crown was a problem for another day.

The last thing I saw was Death whisking them away on smoky wings, the shadows of his face forming a demon's smile. As I watched the cloud of blood above the urn turn to darkness and shadow, my heart sank, the faint outline of a body taking shape behind that whirlwind.

Sylvie was back. Fate had won.

I scanned the clearing. Mama was still battling with Baba Yaga and Erika was in the thick of the battle, her blades glittering in the firelight as she swirled and slashed like a dancer. Her beautiful face was set in a stern mask. Unfaltering, unforgiving. I watched as she wielded blade and power, her earth magic rupturing the ground beneath the cultists and sending many to an early grave.

András roared beside her, his eyes black as night as he summoned the dead to his bidding. All around, men and women fell in droves. A bloodbath, a massacre.

There was only one person left to call on.

"Dante." I hated myself for the whimpering tone, for asking anything of that traitor. But fear washed over me, sinking into every pore, my hands trembling beneath the restraints. I was vulnerable, trapped. My chest screamed with agony and my vision was failing. I looked at the world through a blurry lens, my pulse fading, my heart beating a little less bravely with each passing

413

moment.

Blood seeped from my wound, pooling on the stone and dribbling down the slab. The cultists outnumbered the táltosok, spurred by the sight of their mistress, the triumph of their queen returning.

"Dante!" I screamed, seeing the flash of skin and bone behind that whirlwind, the blood used in that ritual now morphing into flesh.

"I'm coming," he shouted back, running to his mother's side. Mama had pacified her with vines, but she laughed manically, the sound echoing around the clearing. "She has risen," she sang. "She's alive!"

Dante knocked her out with the hilt of his sword, clawing at her throat and ripping a necklace with a key suspended on the chain ... the key to my restraints. With steady fingers, he pried the locks open at my wrists and ankles, gently pulling me to his arms.

I stumbled from the stone, allowing myself a few precious seconds in his warmth before shoving him away, barely managing to stay upright. He pulled the shirt from his back and I took it begrudgingly, covering up what little remained of my dignity.

Mama ran to my side, her brown eyes wide, curly hair standing at odd ends. "We need to go. Now."

I didn't need telling twice. I took a step and collapsed, clutching Dante's slick arms. He swung me into his arms and I didn't have the strength to protest. My vision spotted from blood loss and pain, and each step he made sent agony down my chest,

but we had to carry on. We had to—

Cultists blocked our path and I set my jaw, calling my power to my fingers. I almost wept in relief as it flooded through me, surging up, up, up. The beast inside me roared and thrashed and, for the first time, I didn't hesitate. I unleashed that dark creature and set it free.

Red. It surrounded us, enveloping us in a different mist, the smell of copper singeing the air, the taste of blood on my tongue. The cultists in our way winked out of existence and I pushed the power onwards, letting it curl around every enemy, destroying organic matter like fire blazing through a forest.

The power surging through me filled me up like a pleasure I'd never known. Addictive, enthralling. I wanted to drown in its ecstasy. A small part of me warned that this wasn't right, that killing was wrong, but the bigger part—the stronger part— delighted in every cultist I wiped off the face of the earth.

The power surged towards Sylvie, crashing upon her like a wave against the shore. It seemed like time stopped as everyone watched that mighty red arc slicing through bodies and air alike, and I dared to hope, dared to think that perhaps it might be enough. *I* might be enough.

She held out a hand and the power just ... stopped. Bursting like a cloud, drops of red splattering and turning to fog upon the ground. The mist cleared and a figure stepped out, whole and terrifyingly alive.

Sylvie Morici. She was the embodiment of beauty—or would

415

be in perfect health. Her skin held a sickly pallor, her flesh sagging over bones still lengthening and adjusting into shape. She had tawny skin, long legs, brunette hair falling in a straight sheet to a narrow waist. Her eyes were a mystery, her mouth was sin, and she smiled with bow lips. She was utterly naked, but she wore power like a crown, even in her weakened state. The Dark Queen, risen from the ashes.

Her eyes met mine and it took everything in me not to tremble at her form, the ancient, wicked weight of her very presence pressing down on me. "Not your power," she hissed.

My skin prickled, every cell in my body shrivelling at that voice.

Dante turned to my mother, to the táltosok, fear swimming in those brown eyes. "Run."

We bolted, the path now emptied of cultists as András, Dante, my mother and the soldiers ran for our lives, scurrying towards safety. I glanced over my shoulder, waiting for the strike to fall, but Sylvie watched eagerly, drinking in every detail with glittering eyes. Why didn't she follow?

Because she was too weak, I realised, watching the skin still bloom over her bones. I had sacrificed blood, but it wasn't enough. She needed much, much more.

Sylvie's laugh followed me, her power licking at my heels. "Fly, little bird," she called. "I will find your nest. I am the black within your heart. The hatred in your soul. You will take my hand and kneel or be the blood against my lips. Fear me, mortal. For I

416

am coming. I am already with you."

A coldness swept over my bones, settling in the pit of my stomach as we ran and ran and ran. We might have won the day, but those words, they repeated in my mind, haunting my every aching step.

The Dark Queen had returned and the battle had just begun. We might have won our lives today, but the fight for the Kingdom of Hungary would be long, brutal, and bloody.

"*I am coming.*"

My fingers curled into fists, my rage amplifying with each step through the dark wood. I had been stabbed, drained, betrayed and used by táltos, witch, cultist, and demon.

I would not bend.

I would not break.

And I would stop at nothing until that wretch was rotting in immortal hell in Death's dungeons. She wanted a war?

Fine.

Bring it on, bitch.

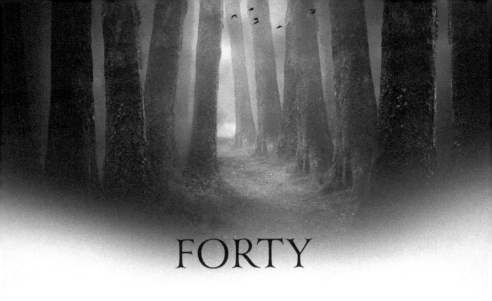

FORTY

slept for three days, waking intermittently to hushed voices and a faint tingling in my chest. I tried to latch on to their conversation, to determine the magic trickling into me, but each time the weight of sleep would pull me under.

When at last I broke free of its embrace, I woke gasping and spluttering, a hand raised to my chest and terror clenching my heart in its fist. I still recalled the pain of that blade slicing me open, the hurt of Dante's betrayal ... and fear. Fear like I've never known as I had looked upon the Dark Queen.

She was back and she was coming for me.

"Shh, you're safe now," Mama said from beside me. Her hand clasped my free one and I sank back into the bed, feeling suddenly at ease as her power seeped into me. I studied the green mist that wreathed her hand and relaxed.

I traced a finger beneath the hem of my nightgown, feeling a raised bump that carved between my breasts. A pale white scar lined my olive skin. A reminder of what I'd endured. I was lucky to be alive—even if other scars ran far deeper than this one.

Mama's eyes filled with tears as she looked at me like only a mother could. "My girl," she said softly. "You've been so brave."

"Mama," I rasped, my voice breaking on the word. Tears streamed down my cheeks as she held me in her arms. I nestled in, taking comfort in the steady rise and fall of her chest. I let myself sob, my back shuddering and the breath catching in my throat as my shoulders heaved. Snot filled my nostrils, but I didn't care.

She passed me a cloth wordlessly and I held it to my nose, squeezing my eyes shut as I tried to forget everything that had happened. My magic lay dormant for now, but I could still feel the urges of that darker power. I'd enjoyed it, had taken pleasure in inflicting pain, in *death*. What did that say about me?

And then there was Dante. He'd hurt me in places I'd never known possible. He'd betrayed me, after everything we'd been through. I'd made space for him in my heart that no one else had ever occupied. I'd opened myself to him, set down my walls for him and this was what came of it.

My lip wobbled again and I took a deep breath. I could analyse that later, but I would not give him my tears. He didn't deserve them.

I pulled back from Mama, searching her brown eyes. "You came for me," I whispered. "But ... how?"

She didn't need me to clarify. Her gaze softened, and she clasped my hand in her own once more. "Dante sent a missive the day you left Mistvellen, warning me of your intentions. I couldn't stand by and do nothing. Caitlin forbade Erika and I from leaving with any táltosok, but there is no world in which I'd let my daughter fall to the hands of that wicked creature," she hissed.

My stomach climbed into my throat at the memory of my mother fighting Baba Yaga. Of what could have happened if things went even worse. "Mama, everything the coven thought they knew about the banya was a lie. Baba Yaga was the one responsible for killing those girls. For killing Hanna." I swallowed, sadness forming a heavy lump in my chest.

Mama shook her head, her eyes dulled by pain. She looked exhausted. Under her eyes were shadows as dark as storm clouds and lines had settled in the tautness of her face. It wouldn't surprise me if she hadn't left my side the whole time I'd been out. "We've been naive about many things, but we know better now. The coven is in an uproar, calling for Caitlin to be renounced from the council. The witches want change."

I sat up, feeling my sorrow harden to resolve. "Then I shall give it to them. We've been living in the past for too long, Mama. It's time our coven re-joined the world and remembered who we are. We are witches and we will not bow down before the Dark Queen."

She looked at me for a long minute, her eyes glimmering with hope. "What do you plan to do?"

"Sylvie thinks she can break us, but a new age awaits. I swear, Mama, I will make sure we survive this. As lady of Mistvellen, I will have power and sway. We can call upon our sisters in Transylvania and combine the might of the covens. All of them. And, when the Dark Queen comes, we'll see where the true crown lies."

Mama's eyes shone with pride as she stared at me. "You plan to go through with the wedding," she stated simply.

I looked out the window at the buttery sunlight gilding the room, a soft smile curving my face as the beginnings of a plan formed in my mind.

Oh, yes. Dante might have broken my trust and destroyed any hope for the future, but I wasn't finished with him yet. In order to strengthen our alliances, I would have to bed my enemy. I would go through with the marriage and secure my place as lady of Mistvellen, and then the hunt for Death's crown would begin.

But once I found it, I had no plans of handing it over to the horseman himself.

Not yet ...

Language Guide

A dictionary of Hungarian terms, and explanations of Hungarian folklore/mythical creatures. Note: There are items using Hungarian language that, for the purposes of this book, are entirely fictional.*

Adrian (AD-ree-uhn) – *Kitarni's father and once a soldier in the Wolfblood Clan.*

András (AHRN-drash) – *Dante's second in command.*

Arló (AH-low) – *Kitarni's horse.*

Árnyalat (ARN-yah-laht) – *Shade/Shadow. An ancient order of protectors, tasked with protecting the old gods.* *

Banya/Baba Yana (BA-nyuh/BA-buh YA-nuh) – *Protector of the witch coven.*

Baba Yaga (BA-buh Yah-guh) – *Leader of the cultists.*

Boszorkány/Boszorkányok (BAH-sarh-kahn-yah / BAH-sarh-kahn-yah-) – *Witch/Witches.*

Bejgli (BAY-glee) – *Walnut or poppyseed sweet roll.*

Caitlin Vargo (KATE-linn Vah-go) – *Chief elder in Kitarni's village.*

Dante Sándor (DUN-tay SHAN-dorh) – *Firstborn son of Farkas Sándor and Kitarni's betrothed.*

Elátkozottak Napja (EL-ahth-cos-oh-tack NARP-yah) – *The Day of the Cursed. As punishment for the Dark Queen's treachery, Death comes once a year to claim the souls of wayward witches. If a witch has not warded her home with the required spells, he may lay claim to their souls.*

Eszter Bárány (ES-ter BARH-ray-nee) – Kitarni's sister.

Erika (Eh-ree-kuh) – Elder and magic tutor in Kitarni's village.

Farkas Sándor (FOR-kosh SHAN-dorh) – The lord of Mistvellen.

Garabonc (GURRA-bonz) – A mythical being with likeness to the táltos but born with all its teeth. The garabonc will visit homes asking for milk and eggs. If the owner lies about not having any, they will earn its wrath.

Hanna (HA-nah) – a witch from Kitarni's village.

Hadúr (HAH-duhr) – The god of war, also known as the blacksmith god.

Imre (IM-ray) – A baker in Mistvellen.

Iren (EYE-ren) – Elder and spymaster of Kitarni's village.

Isten (ISH-ten) The Golden Father, ruler of the Middle World.

Istenanya (ISH-ten-ahn-yah) Goddess of the moon, fertility and childbirth.

Jazmin (JAZZ-min) – A water faerie residing in the Sötét Erdő. Twin to Lili.

Kakaós csiga (KAH-kow-tsee-gah) – Sweet rolls in spirals of melted chocolate.

Kitarni Bárány (KEE-tah-nee BAHR-ray-nee)

Kürtős kalács (Keur-twos KOHL-ahsh – A spit cake made from sweet dough and rolled with sugar.

Laszlo (LAHZ-low) – Kitarni's dog.

Lidérc/Lidércek (LEE-dertsk/LEE-der-tsek) – A supernatural being in Hungarian folklore. There are several traditional versions of this creature, but in this tale the lidérc acts as an incubus, attaching itself to a lover and sometimes inducing nightmares or sucking blood.

Lili (LI-lee) – A water faerie residing in the Sötét Erdő. Twin to Jazmin.

Lukasz (LOO-kahsh) – Second-born son of Farkas Sándor and soldier of the Wolfblood Clan.

Napkirály (NAHP-kihr-ah-lee) – King of the Sun and rider of his beloved silver-haired horse.

Margit (MARH-git) – Seer and lady of Mistvellen. She is also Dante's cousin.

Mistvellen (MIST-vell-en) – Stronghold of the Táltosok and home to the Sándor family.

Nora Bárány (NOR-ah BAHR-ray-nee) – Kitarni's mother and elder of her village.

Palacsinta (PAHL-ah-shin-tah) – A thin pancake rolled or folded into triangles, and often filled with chocolate, fruit, nuts, cream, or custard.

Sötét Erdő (SHO-tay-et AIR-do) – dark wood. *

Sylvie Morici (SILL-vee MORE-ee-chee) – the Dark Queen.

Szaloncukor – (Tsalon-zoo-korh) A traditional Hungarian Christmas candy made from fondant and covered in chocolate.

Szélkirály –King of the Wind, charged with the winds, rain, and storms.

Szenteste (CEN-tesh-teh) – Holy Eve/Christmas Eve.

Táltos/ Táltosok (TAHL-tosh/TAHL-tosh- – A mythical being with likeness to a shaman. Their power is spiritual in nature. In this book, the traditional táltos has been adapted to have necromantic power.

Tündér/ Tündérek (TUHN-dehr/TUHN-derh-eck – Faery/Faeries.

Turul (TUH-rool) – Mythological bird of prey often depicted as an eagle. It is a national symbol of Hungary.

A SMALL FAVOUR...

Readers make the world go round—authors' worlds, that is. Without you, we wouldn't be able to do what we love! Your opinions, posts, stories, videos, shares and reviews help us find our place in the book world, and our book into new hands. If you enjoyed this book, please leave a review on your preferred websites. Sites like Goodreads and Amazon drive new eyes to our books, and ultimately, traffic to our sales pages. As always, thank you for your incredible support. That's true magic, that.

MORE BOOKS BY CHLOE HODGE

The Guardians of the Grove trilogy

-An epic YA Fantasy series-

This magical tale bleeds excitement and thrills, with darkness lingering at every twist and turn. Described as Lord of the Rings meets Throne of Glass, this sword and sorcery adventure is perfect for fans of J.R.R Tolkien, Sarah J Maas, and Holly Black.

START THIS EPIC ADVENTURE WITH VENGEANCE BLOOMS

'She peered at her hands, stained red with the lifeblood of her family.'

Orphaned and alone, Ashalea Kindaris has just one goal in life~ to avenge the death of her parents. But when darkness descends on the land, she discovers her motives are linked to a much larger quest.

To protect the world from elimination, she must find the next Guardians of the Grove~ Everosia's inner sanctum and gateway to other dimensions.

As shadows disperse and the forces of evil mount, Ashalea travels through water and wood, sewer and summit, to reach the chosen.

Will her training lead to victory, or will the weight of unravelling secrets lead to her ruin?

ACKNOWLEDGEMENTS

Where to begin? This book took me by surprise in the best possible way. When I started drafting project ideas, I knew I wanted *The Cursed and the Broken* to be dark and gritty while being magical in all the ways that counted.

This project was born out of a love for family—starting with my roots—which is why it's set in the Kingdom of Hungary. Before my grandad passed, he would often make Hungarian dishes for the family and I have fond memories of him making me palacsinta and cooking delicious meals for us all.

When we were together, he would joke to us: "I wonder what the poor people are doing?" It always made us smile, because it wasn't meant to be pretentious or insulting—we were a middle-class family with no riches to brag of and our meals were humble, but we were rich in so many other ways. We had love, a roof over our head, a warm meal in front of us. Family was always the richest gift we could ask for.

Behind the scenes, this book has had so much love poured into it and it wouldn't have been possible without the efforts of the team! A huge thank you to Aidan for your editing genius (and for bearing with the spice levels!)

To my cover designer, Franziska, thank you! I am so in love with your work and this cover is beyond perfect. You took my ideas and turned them into something incredible!

Thank you to Amy for the wonderful formatting and giving

this book the make-over it so deserves on the inside.

To Carmen, Sara, Kseniya, I'll forever be grateful for your vision and bringing my characters to life. I am obsessed with your art!

Thank you to the many wonderful businesses who have worked with me over the years—produced merch, shown support, stocked my books, extended the love, drawn fan-art and so much more. Special mentions to indie stores, No Shelf Control, Black Veil Bookshop, Literary Collectors, Off the Book Pages and Sarah's Self Checkout.

Thank you to the beta readers, ARC readers, my Instagram family, Booktok supporters, and to all the book lovers! You mean the world!

Lots of love to my patrons: Ben, Donna, Lauren, Luthienara, Jason, Victoria. Our family is small but I'm so grateful for you!

Last, endless love to my family. Jason, you're forever pushing me to reach for the stars and seize my dreams. I love you, always. Big love to my family—especially my mum. You'll always be my biggest advocate!

Thank you all so much. Much love, and hopefully see you soon for the next adventure!

ABOUT THE AUTHOR

Chloe Hodge has always had a fondness for the fantastical. Before her love of books led her to publish the Guardians of the Grove trilogy, she completed a Bachelor of Journalism and Professional Writing and worked as a journalist. She currently lives in Queensland, Australia, crafting new worlds, running editing business, Chloe's Chapters, drinking copious amounts of tea, and playing video games.

Stay in touch!
Instagram @chloeschapters
TikTok @chloehodgeauthor
www.chloehodge.com

Printed in Australia
AUHW020841240322
361329AU00005B/5